The New Girl

ALSO BY DANIEL SILVA

The Other Woman

House of Spies

The Black Widow

The English Spy

The Heist

The English Girl

The Fallen Angel

Portrait of a Spy

The Rembrandt Affair

The Defector

Moscow Rules

The Secret Servant

The Messenger

Prince of Fire

A Death in Vienna

The Confessor

The English Assassin

The Kill Artist

The Marching Season

The Mark of the Assassin

The Unlikely Spy

The New Girl

A Novel

Daniel Silva

An Imprint of HarperCollins*Publishers*

THE NEW GIRL. Copyright © 2019 by Daniel Silva. All rights reserved. Printed in the United States of America. No part of this book may be used or reproduced in any manner whatsoever without written permission except in the case of brief quotations embodied in critical articles and reviews. For information, address HarperCollins Publishers, 195 Broadway, New York, NY 10007.

HarperCollins books may be purchased for educational, business, or sales promotional use. For information, please e-mail the Special Markets Department at SPsales@harpercollins.com.

FIRST HARPERLUXE EDITION

ISBN: 978-0-06-283513-0

HarperLuxe™ is a trademark of HarperCollins Publishers.

Library of Congress Cataloging-in-Publication Data is available upon request.

19 20 21 22 23 LSC 10 9 8 7 6 5 4 3 2 1

For the fifty-four journalists
who were killed worldwide in 2018.
And, as always, for my wife, Jamie,
and my children, Nicholas and Lily.

What's done cannot be undone.
—MACBETH (1606), ACT 5, SCENE 1

Norway

Sweden

NORTH SEA

Denmark

Ireland

England

Berlin

Frinton-on-Sea

Netherlands

Ouddorp

Germany

London

Renesse

Belgium

Czech Republic

Lux.

Paris

Austria

France

Switzerland

Geneva

Lyon

Annecy

ATLANTIC OCEAN

Italy

Areatza

Carcassonne

Portugal

Spain

MEDITERRANEAN SEA

Morocco

Tunisia

Algeria

250 km

0

200 mi.

Foreword

In August 2018, I commenced work on a novel about a crusading young Arab prince who wanted to modernize his religiously intolerant country and bring sweeping change to the Middle East and the broader Islamic world. I set aside that manuscript two months later, however, when the model for that character, Mohammed bin Salman of Saudi Arabia, was implicated in the brutal murder of Jamal Khashoggi, a Saudi dissident and columnist for the *Washington Post*. Elements of *The New Girl* are quite obviously inspired by events surrounding Khashoggi's death. The rest occur only in the imaginary world inhabited by Gabriel Allon, his associates, and his enemies.

PART ONE

Abduction

1

Geneva

It was Beatrice Kenton who first questioned the identity of the new girl. She did so in the staff room, at a quarter past three, on a Friday in late November. The mood was festive and faintly rebellious, as was the case most Friday afternoons. It is a truism that no profession welcomes the end of the workweek with more anticipation than teachers—even teachers at elite institutions such as the International School of Geneva. The chatter was of plans for the weekend. Beatrice abstained, for she had none, a fact she did not wish to share with her colleagues. She was fifty-two, unmarried, and with no family to speak of other than a rich old aunt who granted her refuge each summer at her estate in Norfolk. Her weekend routine consisted of a trip to the Migros and a walk along the lakeshore for the sake of her waistline, which, like the universe, was ever expanding. First period Monday was an oasis in an otherwise Empty Quarter of solitude.

Founded by a long-dead organization of multilateralism, Geneva International catered to the children of the city's diplomatic community. The middle school, where Beatrice taught reading and composition, educated students from more than a hundred different countries. The faculty was a similarly diverse lot. The head of personnel went to great effort to promote employee bonding—cocktail parties, potluck dinners, nature outings—but in the staff room the old tribalism tended to reassert itself. Germans kept with other Germans, French with French, Spanish with Spanish. On that Friday afternoon, Miss Kenton was the only British subject present other than Cecelia Halifax from the history department. Cecelia had wild black hair and predictable politics, which she insisted on sharing with Miss Kenton at every opportunity. Cecelia also divulged to Miss Kenton details of the torrid sexual affair she was having with Kurt Schröder, the Birkenstocked math genius from Hamburg who had given up a lucrative engineering career to teach multiplication and division to eleven-year-olds.

The staff room was on the ground floor of the eighteenth-century château that served as the administration building. Its leaded windows gazed across the forecourt, where presently Geneva International's privileged young students were clambering into the backs of German-made luxury sedans with diplomatic license plates. Loquacious Cecelia Halifax had planted herself next to Beatrice. She was prattling on about a scandal in London, something involving MI6 and a Russian spy. Beatrice was scarcely listening. She was watching the new girl.

As usual, she was at the hindmost end of the daily exodus, a wispy child of twelve, already beautiful, with liquid brown eyes and hair the color of a raven's wing. Much to Beatrice's dismay, the school had no uniform, only a dress code, which several of the more freethinking students flouted with no official sanction. But not the new girl. She was covered from head to toe in expensive wool and plaid, the sort of stuff one saw at the Burberry boutique in Harrods. She carried a leather book bag rather than a nylon backpack. Her patent leather ballet slippers were glossy and bright. She was proper, the new girl, modest. But there was something else about her, thought Beatrice. She was cut from different cloth. She was regal. Yes, that was the word. *Regal . . .*

She had arrived two weeks into the autumn term— not ideal but not unheard of at an institution like Geneva International, where the parent body came and went like the waters of the Rhône. David Millar, the headmaster, had crammed her into Beatrice's third period, which was already two pupils on the heavy side. The copy of the admissions file he gave her was gossamer, even by the school's standards. It stated that the new girl's name was Jihan Tantawi, that she was of Egyptian nationality, and that her father was a businessman rather than a diplomat. Her academic record was unexceptional. She was deemed bright but in no way gifted. "A bird ready to take flight," wrote David in a sanguine margin note. Indeed, the only noteworthy aspect of the file was the paragraph reserved for the student's "special needs." It seemed privacy was of grave concern to the Tantawi family. Security, wrote David, was a high priority.

Hence the presence in the courtyard that afternoon—and every afternoon, for that matter—of Lucien Villard, the school's capable head of security. Lucien was a French import, a veteran of the Service de la Protection, the National Police unit responsible for safeguarding visiting foreign dignitaries and senior French officials. His final posting had been at the Élysée Palace, where he had served on the personal detail of the president of the Republic. David Millar used Lucien's impressive résumé as proof of the school's commitment to safety. Jihan Tantawi was not the only student with security concerns.

But no one arrived and departed Geneva International quite like the new girl. The black Mercedes limousine into which she slipped was fit for a head of state or potentate. Beatrice was no expert when it came to automobiles, but it looked to her as though the chassis was armor plated and the windows were bulletproof. Behind it was a second vehicle, a Range Rover, containing four unsmiling brutes in dark jackets.

"Who do you suppose she is?" wondered Beatrice as she watched the two vehicles turn into the street.

Cecelia Halifax was bewildered. "The Russian spy?"

"The *new* girl," drawled Beatrice. Then she added dubiously, "Jihan."

"They say her father owns half of Cairo."

"Who says that?"

"Veronica." Veronica Alvarez was a hot-tempered Spaniard from the art department and one of the least reliable sources of gossip on the faculty, second only to Cecelia herself. "She says the mother is related to the Egyptian president. His niece. Or maybe his cousin."

Beatrice watched Lucien Villard crossing the forecourt. "Do you know what I think?"

"What?"

"I think someone is lying."

And so it came to pass that Beatrice Kenton, a battle-scarred veteran of several lesser British public schools who had come to Geneva looking for romance and adventure and found neither, undertook a wholly private inquiry to determine the true identity of the new girl. She began by entering the name JIHAN TANTAWI in the little white box of her Internet browser's default search engine. Several thousand results appeared on her screen, none corresponding to the beautiful twelve-year-old girl who came through her classroom door at the beginning of each third period, never so much as a minute late.

Next Beatrice searched the various social media sites but again found no trace of her student. It seemed the new girl was the only twelve-year-old on God's green earth who did not lead a parallel life in cyberspace. Beatrice found this commendable, for she had witnessed firsthand the destructive emotional and developmental consequences of incessant texting, tweeting, and sharing of photographs. Regrettably, such behavior was not limited to children. Cecelia Halifax could scarcely go to the loo without posting an airbrushed photo of herself on Instagram.

The father, one Adnan Tantawi, was similarly anonymous in the cyber realm. Beatrice found a few references to a Tantawi Construction and a Tantawi Holdings and a Tantawi Development but nothing at all about the man himself. Jihan's admissions file listed a chic address on the route de Lausanne. Beatrice walked by it on a Saturday afternoon. It was a few doors down from the home of the famous Swiss industrialist Martin Landesmann. Like all properties on that part of Lake Geneva, it was surrounded by high walls and watched over by security cameras. Beatrice peered through the bars of the gate and glimpsed a manicured green lawn stretching toward the portico of a magnificent Italianate villa. At once, a man came pounding toward her down the drive, one of the brutes from the Range Rover, no doubt. He made no effort to conceal the fact he had a gun beneath his jacket.

"Propriété privée!" he shouted in heavily accented French.

"Excusez-moi," murmured Beatrice, and walked quickly away.

The next phase of her inquiry commenced the following Monday morning, when she embarked on three days of close observation of her mysterious new student. She noted that Jihan, when called upon in class, was sometimes slow in responding. She noted, too, that

Jihan had formed no friendships since her arrival at the school, and had made no attempt to do so. Beatrice also established, while purporting to lavish praise on a lackluster essay, that Jihan had only a passing familiarity with Egypt. She knew that Cairo was a large city and that a river ran through it, but little else. Her father, she said, was very rich. He built high-rise apartment houses and office towers. Because he was a friend of the Egyptian president, the Muslim Brotherhood didn't like him, which was why they were living in Geneva.

"Sounds perfectly reasonable to me," said Cecelia.

"It sounds," answered Beatrice, "like something someone made up. I doubt she's ever set foot in Cairo. In fact, I'm not sure she's even Egyptian."

Beatrice next focused her attention on the mother. She viewed her mainly through the tinted, bulletproof windows of the limousine, or on those rare occasions when she alighted from the car's backseat to greet Jihan in the courtyard. She was fairer complected than Jihan and lighter haired—attractive, thought Beatrice, but not quite in Jihan's league. Indeed, Beatrice was hardpressed to find any familial resemblance whatsoever. There was a conspicuous coldness in their physical relationship. Not once did she witness a kiss or warm embrace. She also detected a distinct imbalance of power. It was Jihan, not the mother, who held the upper hand.

As November turned to December, and the winter break loomed, Beatrice conspired to arrange a meeting with the aloof mother of her mysterious pupil. The pretext was Jihan's performance on an English spelling and vocabulary test—the bottom third of the class but much better than young Callahan, the son of an American foreign service officer and, purportedly, a native speaker of the language. Beatrice drafted an e-mail requesting a consultation at Mrs. Tantawi's convenience and dispatched it to the address she found in the admissions file. When several days passed with no reply, she sent it again. At which point she received a mild rebuke from David Millar, the headmaster. It seemed Mrs. Tantawi wished to have no direct contact with Jihan's teachers. Beatrice was to state her concerns in an e-mail to David, and David would address the matter with Mrs. Tantawi. Beatrice suspected he was aware of Jihan's real identity, but she knew better than to raise the subject, even obliquely. It was easier to pry secrets from a Swiss banker than Geneva International's discreet headmaster.

Which left only Lucien Villard, the school's French-born head of security. Beatrice called on him on a Friday afternoon during her free period. His office was in the basement of the château, next door to the broom closet occupied by the shifty little Russian who made the computers work. Lucien was lean and sturdy and more youthful-looking than his forty-eight years. Half the female members of the staff lusted after him, including Cecelia Halifax, who had made an unsuccessful run at Lucien before bedding her sandaled Teutonic math genius.

"I was wondering," said Beatrice, leaning with feigned nonchalance against the frame of Lucien's open door, "whether I might have a word with you about the new girl."

Lucien regarded her coolly over his desk. "Jihan? Why?"

"Because I'm worried about her."

Lucien placed a stack of papers atop the mobile phone that lay on his blotter. Beatrice couldn't be sure, but she thought it was a different model than the one he usually carried. "It's my job to worry about Jihan, Miss Kenton. Not yours."

"It's not her real name, is it?"

"Wherever did you get an idea like that?"

"I'm her teacher. Teachers see things."

"Perhaps you didn't read the note in Jihan's file regarding loose talk and gossip. I would advise you to follow those instructions. Otherwise, I will be obliged to bring this matter to the attention of Monsieur Millar."

"Forgive me, I meant no—"

Lucien held up a hand. "Don't worry, Miss Kenton. It is *entre nous*."

Two hours later, as the hatchlings of the global diplomatic elite waddled across the courtyard of the château, Beatrice was watching from the leaded window of the staff room. As usual, Jihan was among the last to leave. No, thought Beatrice, not Jihan. *The new girl . . .* She was skipping lightly across the cobbles and swinging her book bag, seemingly oblivious to the presence of Lucien Villard at her side. The woman was waiting next to the open door of the limousine. The new girl passed her with scarcely a glance and tumbled into the backseat. It was the last time Beatrice would ever see her.

2

New York

Sarah Bancroft knew she had made a dreadful mistake the instant Brady Boswell ordered a second Belvedere martini. They were dining at Casa Lever, an upscale Italian restaurant on Park Avenue decorated with a small portion of the owner's collection of Warhol prints. Brady Boswell had chosen it. The director of a modest but well-regarded museum in St. Louis, he came to New York twice each year to attend the major auctions and sample the city's gastronomic delights, usually at the expense of others. Sarah was the perfect victim. Forty-three, blond, blue eyed, brilliant, and unmarried. More important, it was common knowledge in the incestuous New York art world that she had access to a bottomless pit of money.

"Are you sure you won't join me?" asked Boswell as

he raised the fresh glass to his damp lips. He had the pallor of roasted salmon, medium well, and a meticulous gray comb-over. His bow tie was askew, as were his tortoiseshell spectacles. Behind them blinked a pair of rheumy eyes. "I really do hate to drink alone."

"It's one in the afternoon."

"You don't drink at lunch?"

Not anymore, but she was sorely tempted to renounce her vow of daytime abstinence.

"I'm going to London," blurted Boswell.

"Really? When?"

"Tomorrow evening."

Not soon enough, thought Sarah.

"You studied there, didn't you?"

"The Courtauld," said Sarah with a defensive nod. She had no desire to spend lunch reviewing her curriculum vitae. It was, like the size of her expense account, well known within the New York art world. At least a portion of it.

A graduate of Dartmouth College, Sarah Bancroft had studied art history at the famed Courtauld Institute of Art in London before earning her PhD from Harvard. Her costly education, funded exclusively by her father, an investment banker from Citigroup, won her a curator's position at the Phillips Collection in Washington, for which she was paid next to nothing. She left the Phillips under ambiguous circumstances and, like a Picasso purchased at auction by a mysterious Japanese buyer, disappeared from public view. During this period she worked for the Central Intelligence Agency and undertook a pair of dangerous undercover assignments on behalf of a legendary Israeli operative named Gabriel Allon. She was now nominally employed by the Museum of Modern Art, where she oversaw the museum's primary attraction—an astonishing $5 billion collection of Modern and Impressionist works from the estate of the late Nadia al-Bakari, daughter of the fabulously wealthy Saudi investor Zizi al-Bakari.

Which went some way to explaining why Sarah was having lunch with the likes of Brady Boswell in the first place. Sarah had recently agreed to lend several lesser works from the collection to the Los Angeles County Museum of Art. Brady Boswell wanted to be next in line. It wasn't in the cards, and Boswell knew it. His museum lacked the necessary prominence and pedigree. And so, after finally placing their lunch orders, he postponed the inevitable rejection with small talk. Sarah was relieved. She didn't like confrontation. She'd had enough of it to last a lifetime. Two, in fact.

"I heard a naughty rumor about you the other day."

"Only one?"

Boswell smiled.

"And what was the topic of this rumor?"

"That you've been doing a bit of moonlighting."

Trained in the art of deception, Sarah easily concealed her discomfort. "Really? What sort of moonlighting?"

Boswell leaned forward and lowered his voice to a confiding whisper. "That you're KBM's secret art adviser." KBM were the internationally recognized initials of Saudi Arabia's future king. "That you were the one who let him spend a half billion dollars on that questionable Leonardo."

"It's not a *questionable* Leonardo."

"So it's true!"

"Don't be ridiculous, Brady."

"A non-denial denial," he replied with justifiable suspicion.

Sarah raised her right hand as though swearing a solemn oath. "I am not now, nor have I ever been, an art adviser to one Khalid bin Mohammed."

Boswell was clearly dubious. Over antipasti he finally broached the topic of the loan. Sarah feigned dispassion before informing Boswell that under no circumstances would she be lending him a single painting from the al-Bakari Collection.

"What about a Monet or two? Or one of the Cézannes?"

"Sorry, but it's out of the question."

"A Rothko? You have so many, you wouldn't miss it."

"Brady, please."

They finished their lunch agreeably and parted on the pavements of Park Avenue. Sarah decided to walk back to the museum. Winter had finally arrived in Manhattan after one of the warmest autumns in memory. Heaven only knew what the new year might bring. The planet seemed to be lurching between extremes. Sarah, too. Secret soldier in the global war on terror one day, caretaker of one of the world's grandest art collections the next. Her life knew no middle ground.

But as Sarah turned onto East Fifty-Third Street, she realized quite suddenly she was terminally bored. She was the envy of the museum world, it was true. But the Nadia al-Bakari Collection, for all its glamour and the initial buzz of its opening, largely saw to itself. Sarah was little more than its attractive public face. Lately, she had been having too many lunches with men like Brady Boswell.

In the meantime her private life had languished. Somehow, despite a busy schedule of fund-raisers and receptions, she had failed to meet a man of appropriate age or professional accomplishment. Oh, she met many men in their early forties, but they had no interest in a long-term relationship—God, how she hated the phrase—with a woman of commensurate age. Men in their early forties wanted a nubile nymphet of twenty-three, one of those languorous creatures who paraded around Manhattan with their leggings and their yoga mats. Sarah feared she was entering the realm of a second wifedom. In her darkest moments she saw herself on the arm of a wealthy man of sixty-three who dyed his hair and received regular injections of Botox and testosterone. The children from his first marriage would cast Sarah as a home-wrecker and despise her. After prolonged fertility treatments, she and her aging husband would manage to have a single child, which Sarah, after her husband's tragic death while making his fourth attempt to scale Everest, would raise alone.

The hum of the crowds in MoMA's atrium temporarily lifted Sarah's spirits. The Nadia al-Bakari Collection was on the second floor; Sarah's office, the fourth. Her telephone log showed twelve missed calls. It was the usual fare—press inquiries, invitations to cocktail parties and gallery openings, a reporter from a scandal sheet looking for gossip.

The last message was from someone called Alistair Macmillan. It seemed Mr. Macmillan wanted a private after-hours tour of the collection. He had left no contact information. It was no matter; Sarah was one of the few people in the world who had his private number. She hesitated before dialing. They had not spoken since Istanbul.

"I was afraid you were never going to return my call." The accent was a combination of Arabia and Oxford. The tone was calm, with a trace of exhaustion.

"I was at lunch," said Sarah evenly.

"At an Italian restaurant on Park Avenue with a creature named Brady Boswell."

"How did you know?"

"Two of my men were sitting a few tables away."

Sarah hadn't noticed them. Obviously, her counter-surveillance skills had deteriorated in the eight years since she had left the CIA.

"Can you arrange it?" he asked.

"What's that?"

"A private tour of the al-Bakari Collection, of course."

"Bad idea, Khalid."

"That's the same thing my father said when I told him I wanted to give the women of my country the right to drive."

"The museum closes at five thirty."

"In that case," he said, "you should expect me at six."

3

New York

It was *Tranquillity*, reputedly the second-largest motor yacht in the world, that gave even his staunchest defenders in the West pause for thought. The future king saw it for the first time, or so the story went, from the terrace of his father's holiday villa on Majorca. Captivated by the vessel's sleek lines and distinctive neon-blue running lights, he immediately dispatched an emissary to make inquiries as to its availability. The owner, a billionaire Russian oligarch named Konstantin Dragunov, knew an opportunity when he saw one, and demanded five hundred million euros. The future king agreed, provided the Russian and his large party leave the yacht at once. They did so by the ship's helicopter, which was included in the sale price. The future king, a ruthless businessman in his own right, billed the Russian exorbitantly for the fuel.

The future king had hoped, perhaps naively, that his purchase of the yacht would remain private until such time as he could find the words to explain it to his father. But just forty-eight hours after he took possession of the vessel, a London tabloid published a remarkably accurate account of the affair, presumably with the assistance of none other than the Russian oligarch. The official media in the future king's country, which was Saudi Arabia, turned a blind eye to the story, but it set fire to social media and the underground blogosphere. Owing to a drop in the worldwide price of oil, the future king had imposed harsh austerity measures on his cosseted subjects that had sharply reduced their once-comfortable standard of living. Even in Saudi Arabia, where royal gluttony was a permanent feature of national life, the future king's avarice did not sit well.

His full name was Khalid bin Mohammed bin Abdulaziz Al Saud. Raised in an ornate palace the size of a city block, he attended a school reserved for male members of the royal family and then Oxford, where he read economics, pursued Western women, and drank a great deal of forbidden alcohol. It was his wish to remain in the West. But when his father assumed the throne, he returned to Saudi Arabia to become minister of defense, a remarkable achievement for a man who had never worn a uniform or wielded any weapon other than a falcon.

The young prince promptly launched a devastating and costly war against Iran's proxy in neighboring Yemen and imposed a blockade on upstart Qatar that plunged the Gulf region into crisis. Mainly, he plotted and schemed inside the royal court to weaken his rivals, all with the blessing of his father, the king. Aged and ill with diabetes, the king knew his reign would not be long. It was customary in the House of Saud that brother succeed brother. But the king upended that tradition by designating his son the crown prince and thus next in line to the throne. At just thirty-three, he became the de facto ruler of Saudi Arabia and leader of a family whose net worth was in excess of $1 trillion.

But the future king knew that his country's wealth was largely a mirage; that his family had squandered a mountain of money on palaces and trinkets; that in twenty years, when the transformation from fossil fuels to renewable sources of energy was complete, the oil beneath Saudi Arabia would be as worthless as the sand that covered it. Left to its own devices, the Kingdom would return to what it once was, an arid land of warring desert nomads.

To spare his country this calamitous future, he resolved to drag it out of the seventh century and into the twenty-first. With the help of an American consulting firm, he produced an economic blueprint he grandly called *The Way Forward*. It envisioned a modern Saudi economy powered by innovation, foreign investment, and entrepreneurship. No longer would its pampered citizenry be able to count on government jobs and cradle-to-grave benefits. Instead, they would actually have to work for their living and study something other than the Koran.

The crown prince understood that the workforce of this new Saudi Arabia could not be comprised of men alone. Women would be required, too, which meant the religious shackles that kept them in a state of near slavery would have to be loosened. He granted them the right to drive, long forbidden, and allowed them to attend sporting events where men were present.

But he was not content with small religious reforms. He wanted to reform the religion itself. He pledged to shut down the pipeline of money that fueled the global spread of Wahhabism, Saudi Arabia's puritanical version of Sunni Islam, and crack down on private Saudi support for jihadi terrorist groups such as al-Qaeda and ISIS. When an important columnist from the *New York Times* wrote a flattering portrait of the young prince and his ambitions, the Saudi clerical establishment, the ulema, seethed with a sacred rage.

The crown prince jailed a few of the religious hotheads and, unwisely, a few of the moderates, too. He also jailed supporters of democracy and women's rights and anyone foolish enough to criticize him. He even rounded up more than a hundred members of the royal family and Saudi Arabia's business elite and locked them away in the Ritz-Carlton Hotel. There, in rooms without doors, they were subjected to harsh interrogations, sometimes at the hands of the crown prince himself. All were eventually freed, but only after surrendering more than $100 billion. The future king claimed the money had been acquired through bribery and kickback schemes. The old way of doing business in the Kingdom, he declared, was over.

Except, of course, for the future king himself. He accumulated personal wealth at a dizzying pace and spent it lavishly. He bought whatever he wanted, and what he couldn't buy he simply took. Those who refused to bend to his will received an envelope containing a single .45-caliber round.

Which prompted, mainly in the West, a great reassessment. Was KBM truly a reformer, wondered the policy makers and the Middle East experts, or was he just another power-mad desert sheikh who was locking away his opponents and enriching himself at the expense of his people? Did he really intend to remake the Saudi economy? End the Kingdom's support for Islamic zealotry and terrorism? Or was he merely trying to impress the smart set in Georgetown and Aspen?

For reasons Sarah could not explain to friends and colleagues in the art world, she initially counted herself among the skeptics. And so she was understandably reticent when Khalid, during a visit to New York, asked to see her. Sarah eventually agreed, but only after first clearing it with the security division at Langley, which was watching over her from afar.

They met in a suite at the Four Seasons Hotel, with no bodyguards or aides present. Sarah had read the many laudatory pieces about KBM in the *Times* and had seen photographs of him wearing a traditional Saudi robe and headdress. In his tailored English suit, however, he was a far more impressive figure—eloquent, cultured, sophisticated, dripping with confidence and power. And money, of course. An unimaginable amount of money. He intended to use a small portion of it, he explained, to acquire a world-class collection of paintings. And he wanted Sarah to serve as his adviser.

"What do you intend to do with these paintings?"

"Hang them in a museum I'm going to build in Riyadh. It will be," he said grandly, "the Louvre of the Middle East."

"And who will visit this Louvre of yours?"

"The same people who visit the Louvre in Paris."

"Tourists?"

"Yes, of course."

"In Saudi Arabia?"

"Why not?"

"Because the only tourists you allow are the Muslim pilgrims who visit Mecca and Medina."

"For now," he said pointedly.

"Why me?"

"Are you not the curator of the Nadia al-Bakari Collection?"

"Nadia was a reformer."

"So am I."

"Sorry," she said. "Not interested."

A man like Khalid bin Mohammed was not used to rejection. He pursued Sarah ruthlessly—with phone calls, flowers, and lavish gifts, none of which she accepted. When she finally relented, she insisted her work would be pro bono. Though she was intrigued by the man known as KBM, her past would not allow her to accept a single riyal from the House of Saud. Furthermore, for his sake and hers, their relationship would be strictly confidential.

"What shall I call you?" she asked.

"Your Royal Highness will be fine."

"Try again."

"How about Khalid?"

"Much better."

They acquired swiftly and aggressively, at auction and through private sales—Postwar, the Impressionists, Old Masters. They did little negotiating. Sarah would name her price, and one of Khalid's courtiers would handle the payment and see to the shipping arrangements. They conducted their shopping spree as quietly as possible and with the subterfuge of spies. Still, it didn't take long for the art world to realize there was a major new player in their midst, especially after Khalid plunked down a cool half billion for Leonardo's *Salvator Mundi*. Sarah had advised against the purchase. No painting, she argued, save for perhaps the *Mona Lisa*, was worth that kind of money.

While building the collection, she spent many hours alone in Khalid's company. He spoke to her of his plans for Saudi Arabia, at times using Sarah as a sounding board. Gradually, her skepticism faded. Khalid, she thought, was an imperfect vessel. But if he were able to bring real and lasting change to Saudi Arabia, the Middle East and the broader Islamic world would never be the same.

All that changed after Omar Nawwaf.

Nawwaf was a prominent Saudi journalist and dissident who had taken refuge in Berlin. A critic of the House of Saud, he held Khalid in particularly low esteem, regarding him as a charlatan who whispered sweet nothings into the ears of gullible Westerners while enriching himself and jailing his critics. Two months earlier, Nawwaf had been brutally murdered inside the Saudi consulate in Istanbul, and his body dismembered for disposal.

Outraged, Sarah Bancroft was among those who severed ties with the once-promising young prince who went by the initials KBM. "You're just like all the rest of them," she told Khalid in a voice mail message. "And by the way, Your Royal Highness, I hope you rot in hell."

4

New York

The first announcement came a few minutes after five p.m. Polite in tone, it advised patrons that the museum would be closing soon and invited them to begin making their way toward the exit. By 5:25 all had complied, save for a distraught-looking woman who could not tear herself away from Van Gogh's *Starry Night.* Security saw her gently into the late afternoon before scouring the museum room by room to make certain it was free of any clever stay-behind art thieves.

The "all clear" went out at 5:45. By then, most of the administrative staff had departed. Therefore, none witnessed the arrival on West Fifty-Third Street of a caravan of three black SUVs with diplomatic plates. Khalid, in a business suit and dark overcoat, emerged from the second and made his way swiftly across the sidewalk to the entrance. Sarah, after a moment's hesitation, admitted him. They regarded one another in the half-light of the atrium before Khalid offered a hand in greeting. Sarah did not accept it.

"I'm surprised they let you into the country. I really shouldn't be seen with you, Khalid."

The hand hovered between them. Quietly, he said, "I am not responsible for Omar Nawwaf's death. You have to believe me."

"Once upon a time, I did believe you. So did a lot of other people in this country. Important people. Smart people. We wanted to believe you were somehow different, that you were going to change your country and the Middle East. And you made fools of us all."

Khalid withdrew his hand. "What's done cannot be undone, Sarah."

"In that case, why are you here?"

"I thought I made that clear when we spoke on the phone."

"And I thought I made it clear you were never to call me again."

"Ah, yes, I remember." From the pocket of his overcoat he drew his phone and played Sarah's last message.

And by the way, Your Royal Highness, I hope you rot in hell . . .

"Surely," said Sarah, "I wasn't the only one who left a message like that."

"You weren't." Khalid returned the phone to his pocket. "But yours hurt the most."

Sarah was intrigued. "Why?"

"Because I trusted you. And because I thought you understood how difficult it was going to be to change my country without plunging it into political and religious chaos."

"That doesn't give you the right to murder someone because he criticized you."

"It's not as simple as that."

"Isn't it?"

He offered no retort. Sarah could see that something was bothering him, something more than the humiliation he must have felt over his precipitous fall from grace.

"May I see it?" he asked.

"The collection? Is that really why you're here?"

He adopted an expression of mild offense. "Yes, of course."

She led him upstairs to the al-Bakari Wing. Nadia's portrait, painted not long after her death in the Empty Quarter of Saudi Arabia, hung outside the entrance.

"She was the real thing," said Sarah. "Not a fraud like you."

Khalid glared at her before lifting his gaze toward the portrait. Nadia was seated at one end of a long couch, shrouded in white, with a strand of pearls at her throat and her fingers bejeweled with diamonds and gold. A clock face shone moonlike over her shoulder. Orchids lay at her bare feet. The style was a deft blend of contemporary and classical. The draftsmanship and composition were flawless.

Khalid took a step closer and studied the bottom right corner of the canvas. "There's no signature."

"The artist never signs his work."

Khalid indicated the information placard next to the painting. "And there's no mention of him here, either."

"He wished to remain anonymous so as not to over-shadow his subject."

"He's famous?"

"In certain circles."

"You know him?"

"Yes, of course."

Khalid's eyes moved back to the painting. "Did she sit for him?"

"Actually, he painted her entirely from memory."

"Not even a photograph?"

Sarah shook her head.

"Remarkable. He must have admired her to paint something so beautiful. Unfortunately, I never had the pleasure of meeting her. She had quite a reputation when she was young."

"She changed a great deal after her father's death."

"Zizi al-Bakari didn't *die*. He was murdered in cold blood in the Old Port of Cannes by an Israeli assassin named Gabriel Allon." Khalid held Sarah's gaze for a moment before entering the wing's first room, one of four dedicated to Impressionism. He approached a Renoir and eyed it enviously. "These paintings belong in Riyadh."

"Nadia entrusted them permanently to MoMA and named me as the caretaker. They're staying exactly where they are."

"Perhaps you'll let me buy them."

"They're not for sale."

"Everything is for sale, Sarah." He smiled briefly. It was an effort, she could see that. He paused before the next painting, a landscape by Monet, and then surveyed the room. "Nothing by Van Gogh?"

"No."

"Rather odd, don't you think?"

"What's that?"

"For a collection like this to have so glaring a hole."

"A quality Van Gogh is hard to come by."

"That's not what my sources tell me. In fact, I have it on the highest authority that Zizi briefly owned a little-known Van Gogh called *Marguerite Gachet at Her Dressing Table*. He purchased it from a gallery in London." Khalid studied Sarah carefully. "Shall I go on?"

Sarah said nothing.

"The gallery is owned by a man named Julian Isherwood. At the time of the sale, an American woman was working there. Apparently, Zizi was quite smitten with her. He invited her to join him on his annual winter cruise in the Caribbean. His yacht was much smaller than mine. It was called—"

"*Alexandra*," said Sarah, cutting him off. Then she asked, "How long have you known?"

"That my art adviser is a CIA officer?"

"*Was*. I no longer work for the Agency. And I no longer work for you."

"What about the Israelis?" He smiled. "Do you really think I would have allowed you to come anywhere near me without first having a look into your background?"

"And yet you pursued me."

"I did indeed."

"Why?"

"Because I knew that one day you might be able to help me with more than my art collection." Khalid walked past Sarah without another word and stood before Nadia's portrait. "Do you know how to reach him?"

"Who?"

"The man who produced this painting without so much as a photograph to guide his hand." Khalid pointed toward the bottom right corner of the canvas. "The man whose name should be right there."

"You're the crown prince of Saudi Arabia. Why do you need me to contact the chief of Israeli intelligence?"

"My daughter," he answered. "Someone has taken my daughter."

5

Ashtara, Azerbaijan

Sarah Bancroft's call to Gabriel Allon went unanswered that evening, for as was often the case
he was in the field. Due to the sensitive nature of his
mission, only the prime minister and a handful of his
most trusted senior officers knew his whereabouts—a
moderate-size villa with ocher-colored walls, hard along
the shore of the Caspian Sea. Behind the villa, rectangular plots of farmland stretched toward the foothills of
the eastern Caucasus Mountains. Atop one of the hills
stood a small mosque. Five times each day the crackling
loudspeaker in the minaret summoned the faithful to
prayer. His long quarrel with the forces of radical Islam
notwithstanding, Gabriel found the sound of the muezzin's voice comforting. At that moment in time, he had

no better friend in the world than the Muslim citizens of Azerbaijan.

The nominal owner of the villa was a Baku-based real estate holding company. Its true owner, however, was Housekeeping, the division of the Israeli intelligence service that procured and managed safe properties. The arrangement had been covertly blessed by the chief of the Azerbaijani security service, with whom Gabriel had cultivated an unusually close relationship. Azerbaijan's neighbor to the south was the Islamic Republic of Iran. Indeed, the Iranian border was only five kilometers from the villa, which explained why Gabriel had not set foot beyond its walls since his arrival. Had the Iranian Revolutionary Guard Corps known of his presence, it would have doubtless mounted an attempt to assassinate or abduct him. Gabriel did not begrudge their loathing of him. Such were the rules of the game in a rough neighborhood. Besides, if presented with the chance to kill the head of the Revolutionary Guard, he would have gladly pulled the trigger himself.

The villa by the sea was not the only logistical asset Gabriel had at his disposal in Azerbaijan. His service—those who worked there referred to it as "the Office" and nothing else—also maintained a small fleet of fishing boats, cargo ships, and fast motor launches, all with proper Azerbaijani registry. The vessels shuttled regularly between Azerbaijani harbors and the Iranian coastline, where they inserted Office agents and operational teams and collected valuable Iranian assets willing to do Israel's bidding.

A year earlier, one of those assets, a man who worked deep inside Iran's secret nuclear weapons program, had been brought by boat to the Office's villa in Ashtara. There he had told Gabriel about a warehouse in a drab commercial district of Tehran. The warehouse contained thirty-two safes of Iranian manufacture. Inside were hundreds of computer disks and millions of pages of documents. The source claimed the material proved conclusively what Iran had long denied, that it had worked methodically and tirelessly to construct an implosion nuclear device and attach it to a delivery system capable of reaching Israel and beyond.

For the better part of the last year, the Office had been watching the warehouse with human surveillance artists and miniature cameras. They had learned that the first shift of security guards arrived each morning at seven. They had also learned that for several hours each night, beginning around ten o'clock, the warehouse was protected only by the locks on its doors and the surrounding fence. Gabriel and Yaakov Rossman, the chief of special operations, had agreed that the team would remain inside no later than five a.m. The source had told them which safes to open and which to ignore. Owing to the method of entry—torches that burned at 3,600 degrees Fahrenheit—there was no way to conceal the operation. Therefore, Gabriel had ordered the team not to copy the relevant material but to steal it outright. Copies were easily denied. Originals were harder to explain. Furthermore, the brazenness of seizing Iran's nuclear archives and smuggling them out of the country would humiliate the regime in front of its restive populace. Gabriel loved nothing more than embarrassing the Iranians.

But stealing the original documents increased the risk of the operation exponentially. Encrypted copies could be carried out of the country on a couple of high-capacity flash drives. The originals would be much harder to move and conceal. An Iranian asset of the Office had purchased a Volvo cargo truck. If the security guards at the warehouse kept to their normal schedule, the team would have a two-hour head start. Their route would take them from the fringes of Tehran, over the Alborz Mountains, and down to the shore of the Caspian. The exfiltration point was a beach near the town of Babolsar. The backup was a few miles to the east at Khazar Abad. All sixteen members of the team planned to leave together. Most were Farsi-speaking Iranian Jews who could easily pass as native Persians. The team leader, however, was Mikhail Abramov, a Moscow-born officer who had carried out numerous dangerous assignments for the Office, including the assassination of a top Iranian nuclear scientist in the center of Tehran. Mikhail was the operation's sore thumb. In Gabriel's experience, every operation needed at least one.

Once upon a time, Gabriel Allon would have undoubtedly been a part of such a team. Born in the Valley of Jezreel, the fertile plot of land that had produced many of Israel's finest warriors and spies, he was studying painting at the Bezalel Academy of Art and Design in Jerusalem in September 1972 when a man named Ari Shamron came to see him. A few days earlier a terrorist group called Black September, a front for the Palestine Liberation Organization, had murdered eleven Israeli athletes and coaches at the Olympic Games in Munich. Prime Minister Golda Meir had ordered Shamron and the Office to "send forth the boys" to hunt down and assassinate the men responsible. Shamron wanted Gabriel, a fluent speaker of Berlin-accented German who could pose convincingly as an artist, to be his instrument of vengeance. Gabriel, with the defiance of youth, had told Shamron to find someone else. And Shamron, not for the last time, had bent Gabriel to his will.

The operation was code-named Wrath of God.

For three years Gabriel and a small team of operatives stalked their prey across Western Europe and the Middle East, killing at night and in broad daylight, living in fear that at any moment they might be arrested by local authorities and charged as murderers. In all, twelve members of Black September died at their hands. Gabriel personally killed six of the terrorists with a .22-caliber Beretta pistol. Whenever possible, he shot his victims eleven times, one bullet for each murdered Jew. When finally he returned to Israel, his temples were gray from stress and exhaustion. Shamron called them smudges of ash on the prince of fire.

It had been Gabriel's intention to resume his career as an artist, but each time he stood before a canvas, he saw only the faces of the men he had killed. And so he traveled to Venice as an expatriate Italian named Mario Delvecchio to study the craft of restoration. When his apprenticeship was complete, he returned to the Office, and to the waiting arms of Ari Shamron. Posing as a gifted if taciturn European-based art restorer, he eliminated some of Israel's most dangerous enemies and carried off some of the most celebrated operations in Office history. Tonight's would rank among his finest. But only if it succeeded. *And if it failed?* Sixteen highly trained Office agents would be arrested, tortured, and in all likelihood publicly executed. Gabriel would have no choice but to resign, an ignoble end to a career against which all others would be measured. It was even possible he might take down the prime minister with him.

For now, there was nothing Gabriel could do but wait and worry himself half to death. The team had entered the Islamic Republic the previous evening and made their way to a network of safe houses in Tehran. At 10:15 p.m. Tehran time, Gabriel received a message from the Operations Desk at King Saul Boulevard over the secure link, informing him that the last shift of security guards had left the warehouse. Gabriel ordered the team to enter, and at 10:31 p.m. they were in. That left them six hours and twenty-nine minutes to torch their way into the targeted safes and seize the nuclear archives. It was a minute less than Gabriel had hoped they would have, a small setback. In his experience, every second counted.

Gabriel was blessed with a natural patience, a trait that had served him well as both a restorer and an intelligence operative. But that night on the shore of the Caspian Sea, all forbearance abandoned him. He paced the half-furnished rooms of the villa, he muttered to himself, he ranted nonsense at his two long-suffering bodyguards. Mainly, he thought about all the reasons why sixteen of his finest officers would never make it out of Iran alive. He was certain of only one thing: if confronted by Iranian forces, the team would not surrender quietly. Gabriel had granted Mikhail, a former Sayeret Matkal commando, wide latitude to fight his way out of the country if necessary. If the Iranians intervened, a good many of them would die.

Finally, at 4:45 a.m. Tehran time, a message flashed over the secure link. The team had left the warehouse with the files and computer disks and was making their escape. The next message arrived at 5:39 a.m., as the team was headed into the Alborz Mountains. It stated that one of the security guards had arrived at the warehouse early. Thirty minutes later Gabriel learned that the NAJA, Iran's national police force, had ordered a nationwide alert and was blocking roads around the country.

He slipped from the villa and in the half-light of dawn walked down to the shore of the lake. In the low hills at his back, the muezzin summoned the faithful. *Prayer is better than sleep . . .* At that moment in time, Gabriel couldn't agree more.

6

Tel Aviv

When Sarah Bancroft received no reply to her phone call or subsequent text messages, she concluded she had no choice but to leave New York and fly to Israel. Khalid saw to her travel arrangements. Consequently, she made the journey privately and in considerable luxury, with the only inconvenience being a brief refueling stop in Ireland. Forbidden to use any of her old CIA identities, she cleared passport control at Ben Gurion Airport under her real name—a name that was well known to the intelligence and security services of the State of Israel—and rode in a chauffeured car to the Tel Aviv Hilton. Khalid had booked the largest suite in the hotel.

Upstairs, Sarah dispatched another text message to Gabriel's private mobile, this one stating that she had come to Tel Aviv on her own initiative to discuss a matter of some urgency. The message, like all the others, went unanswered. It was not like Gabriel to ignore her. It was possible he had changed his number or had been forced to relinquish his private device. It was also possible he was simply too busy to see her. He was, after all, the director-general of Israel's secret intelligence service, which meant he was one of the most powerful and influential figures in the country.

Sarah, however, would always think of Gabriel Allon as the cold, unapproachable man she encountered for the first time in a graceful redbrick town house on N Street in Georgetown. He had pried into every padlocked room of her past before asking whether she would be willing to go to work for Jihad Incorporated, which was how he referred to Zizi al-Bakari, the financier and facilitator of Islamic terror. Sarah had been fortunate to survive the operation that followed and spent several months recuperating at a CIA safe house in the horse country of Northern Virginia. But when Gabriel needed one final piece of an operation against a Russian oligarch named Ivan Kharkov, Sarah leapt at the chance to work with him again.

At some point she also managed to fall quite in love with him. And when she discovered he was unavailable, she began an ill-advised affair with an Office field operative named Mikhail Abramov. The relationship was doomed from the beginning; they were both technically forbidden to date officers from other services. Even Sarah, when she analyzed the situation honestly, admitted the affair was a transparent attempt to punish Gabriel for rejecting her. Predictably, it ended badly. Sarah had seen Mikhail only once since then, at a party celebrating Gabriel's promotion to director-general. He had had a pretty French Jewish doctor on his arm. Sarah had coolly offered him her hand rather than her cheek.

When another hour passed with no response from Gabriel, Sarah went downstairs to walk along the Promenade. The weather was fine and soft, and a few fat white clouds were scudding like dirigibles across the blue Levantine sky. She walked north, past trendy beachfront cafés, among the spandexed and the suntanned. With her blond hair and Anglo-Saxon features, she looked only mildly out of place. The vibe was secular and Southern Californian, Santa Monica on the shores of the Mediterranean. It was hard to imagine that the chaos and civil war of Syria lay just over the border. Or that less than ten miles to the east, atop a bony spine of hills, were some of the most restive Palestinian villages of the West Bank. Or that the Gaza Strip, a ribbon of human misery and resentment, was less than an hour's drive to the south. In hip Tel Aviv, thought Sarah, Israelis might be forgiven for believing the dream of Zionism had been achieved without cost.

She turned inland and wandered the streets, seemingly without purpose or destination. In truth, she was engaging in a surveillance-detection run using techniques taught to her by both the Agency and the Office. On Dizengoff Street, while leaving a pharmacy with a bottle of shampoo she did not need, she concluded she was being followed. There was nothing specific, no confirmed sighting, just a nagging sense that someone was watching her.

She walked through the cool shadows of the chinaberry trees. The pavements were crowded with midmorning shoppers. *Dizengoff Street . . .* The name was familiar. Something awful had happened on Dizengoff Street, Sarah was certain of it. And then she remembered. Dizengoff Street had been the target of a Hamas suicide bombing in October 1994 that killed twenty-two people.

Sarah knew someone who had been wounded, an Office terrorism analyst named Dina Sarid. She had once described the attack to Sarah. The bomb had contained more than forty pounds of military-grade TNT and nails soaked in rat poison. It exploded at nine a.m., aboard the Number 5 bus. The force of the blast hurled human limbs into the nearby cafés. For a long time afterward, blood dripped from the leaves of the china-berry trees.

It rained blood that morning on Dizengoff Street, Sarah . . .

But where exactly had it happened? The bus had just picked up several passengers in Dizengoff Square and was heading north. Sarah checked her current position on her iPhone. Then she crossed to the opposite side of the street and continued south, until she came upon a small gray memorial at the base of a chinaberry tree. The tree was much shorter than the others on the street, and younger.

Sarah approached the memorial and scrutinized the names of the victims. They were written in Hebrew.

"Can you read it?"

Startled, Sarah turned and saw a man standing on the pavement in a pool of dappled light. He was tall and long-limbed, with fair hair and pale, bloodless skin. Dark glasses concealed his eyes.

"No," answered Sarah at length. "I can't."

"You don't speak Hebrew?" The man's English contained the unmistakable trace of a Russian accent.

"I studied it briefly, but I stopped."

"Why?"

"It's a long story."

The man crouched before the memorial. "Here are

the names you're looking for. Sarid, Sarid, Sarid." He looked up at Sarah. "Dina's mother and two of her sisters."

He stood and raised his dark glasses, revealing his eyes. They were blue-gray and translucent—like glacial ice, thought Sarah. She had always loved Mikhail's eyes.

"How long have you been following me?"

"Since you left your hotel."

"Why?"

"To see if anyone *else* was following you."

"Countersurveillance."

"We have a different word for it."

"Yes," said Sarah. "I remember."

At once, a black SUV drew to the curb. A young man in a khaki vest climbed out of the passenger seat and opened the rear door.

"Get in," said Mikhail.

"Where are we going?"

Mikhail said nothing. Sarah climbed into the backseat and watched a Number 5 bus slide past her blacked-out window. It didn't matter where they were going, she thought. It was going to be a very long ride.

7

Tel Aviv–Netanya

"Couldn't Gabriel have found someone else to bring me in?"

"I volunteered."

"Why?"

"I wanted to avoid another awkward scene."

Sarah gazed out her window. They were driving through the heart of Israel's version of Silicon Valley. Shiny new office buildings lined both sides of the flawless highway. In the space of a few years, Israel had traded its socialist past for a dynamic economy driven by the technology sector. Much of that innovation went directly to the military and the security services, giving Israel a decided edge over its Middle East adversaries. Even Sarah's former colleagues at the CIA's Counterterrorism Center used to marvel at the high-tech prowess of the Office and Intelligence Unit 8200, Israel's electronic eavesdropping and cyberwarfare service.

"So the nasty rumor is true, after all."

"What nasty rumor is that?"

"The one about you and that pretty French woman getting married. Forgive me, but her name slips my mind."

"Natalie."

"Nice," said Sarah.

"She is."

"Still practicing medicine?"

"Not exactly."

"What does she do now?"

With his silence, Mikhail confirmed Sarah's suspicion that the pretty French doctor was employed by the Office. Sarah's memory of Natalie, while clouded by jealousy, was of a darkly exotic-looking woman who could easily pass for an Arab.

"I suppose there are fewer complications that way. It's much easier when husband and wife are employed by the same service."

"That isn't the only reason we—"

"Let's not do this, Mikhail. I haven't thought about it in a long time."

"How long?"

"At least a week."

They slid beneath Highway 5, the secure road linking the Coastal Plain with Ariel, the Jewish settlement block deep inside the West Bank. The junction was known as the Glilot Interchange. Beyond it was a shopping center with a multiplex movie theater. There was also another new office complex, partially concealed by thick trees. Sarah supposed it was the headquarters of yet another Israeli tech titan.

She looked at Mikhail's left hand. "Did you misplace it already?"

"What's that?"

"Your wedding band."

Mikhail seemed surprised by its absence. "I took it off before I went into the field. We got back late last night."

"Where were you?"

Mikhail looked at her blankly.

"Come now, darling. We have a past, you and I."

"The past is the past, Sarah. You're an outsider now. Besides, you'll know soon enough."

"At least tell me where it was."

"You wouldn't believe me."

"Wherever it was, it must have been awful. You look like hell."

"The ending was messy."

"Anyone get hurt?"

"Only the bad guys."

"How many?"

"Lots."

"But the operation was a success?"

"One for the books," said Mikhail.

The high-tech office blocks had given way to the affluent northern Tel Aviv suburb of Herzliya. Mikhail was reading something on his mobile phone. He looked bored, his default expression.

"Do give her my best," said Sarah archly.

Mikhail returned the phone to his jacket pocket.

"Tell me something, Mikhail. Why did you really volunteer to bring me in?"

"I wanted a word with you in private."

"Why?"

"So I could apologize for the way it turned out between us."

"Turned out?"

"For the way I treated you in the end. I behaved badly. If you could find it in your heart to—"

"Was Gabriel the one who told you to end it?"

Mikhail seemed genuinely surprised. "Wherever did you get an idea like that?"

"I always wondered, that's all."

"Gabriel told me to go to America and spend the rest of my life with you."

"Why didn't you take his advice?"

"Because this is my home." Mikhail gazed at the patchwork quilt of farmland beyond his window. "Israel and the Office. There was no way I could live in America, even if you were there."

"I could have come here."

"It's not such an easy life."

"Better than the alternative." She immediately regretted her words. "But the past is the past—isn't that what you said?"

He nodded slowly.

"Did you ever have any second thoughts?"

"About leaving you?"

"Yes, you idiot."

"Of course."

"And are you happy now?"

"Very."

She was surprised at how badly his answer wounded her.

"Perhaps we should change the subject," suggested Mikhail.

"Yes, let's. What shall we talk about?"

"The reason you're here."

"Sorry, but I can't discuss it with anyone but Gabriel. Besides," said Sarah playfully, "I have a feeling you'll know soon enough."

They had reached the southern fringes of Netanya. The tall white apartment houses lining the beach reminded Sarah of Cannes. Mikhail spoke a few words in Hebrew to the driver. A moment later they stopped at the edge of a broad esplanade.

Mikhail pointed toward a dilapidated hotel. "That's where the Passover Massacre happened back in 2002. Thirty dead, a hundred and forty wounded."

"Is there any place in this country that *hasn't* been bombed?"

"I told you, life isn't so easy here." Mikhail nodded toward the esplanade. "Take a walk. We'll do the rest."

Sarah climbed out of the car and started across the square. *The past is the past* . . . For a moment, she almost believed it was true.

8

Netanya

At the center of the esplanade was a blue reflecting pool, around which several young Orthodox boys, *payess* flying, played a noisy game of tag. They were speaking not in Hebrew but in French. So were their wigged mothers and the two black-shirted hipsters who eyed Sarah approvingly from a table at a brasserie called Chez Claude. Indeed, were it not for the worn-out khaki-colored buildings and the blinding Middle Eastern sunlight, Sarah might have imagined she was crossing a square in the twentieth arrondissement of Paris.

Suddenly, she realized someone was calling her name, with the emphasis on the second syllable rather than the first. Turning, she spotted a petite dark-haired woman waving to her from across the square. The woman approached with a slight limp.

Sarid, Sarid, Sarid . . .

Dina kissed Sarah on both cheeks. "Welcome to the Israeli Riviera."

"Is everyone here French?"

"Not everyone, but more are coming every day." Dina pointed toward the far end of the square. "There's a little place called La Brioche right over there. I recommend the *pain au chocolat*. They're the best in Israel. Order enough for two."

Sarah walked to the café. She made a few moments of small talk in fluent French with the woman behind the counter before ordering an assortment of pastries and two coffees, a café crème and an espresso.

"Sit anywhere you like. Someone will bring your order."

Sarah went outside. Several tables stood along the edge of the square. At one sat Mikhail. He caught Sarah's eye and nodded toward the man of late middle age sitting alone. He wore a dark gray suit and white dress shirt. His face was long and narrow at the chin, with wide cheekbones and a slender nose that looked as though it had been carved from wood. His dark hair was cropped short and shot with gray at the temples. His eyes were an unnatural shade of green.

Rising, he extended his hand, formally, as though meeting Sarah for the first time. She held it a moment too long. "I'm surprised to see you in a place like this."

"I go out in public all the time. Besides," he added with a glance toward Mikhail, "I have him."

"The man who broke my heart." She sat down. "Is he the only one?"

Gabriel shook his head.

"How many?"

His green eyes searched the square. "Eight, I believe."

"A small battalion. Who have you managed to offend this time?"

"I imagine the Iranians are a bit miffed at me. So is my old friend in the Kremlin."

"I read something in the newspapers about you and the Russians a couple of months ago."

"Did you?"

"Your name came up during that spy scandal in Washington. They said you were aboard the private plane that took Rebecca Manning from Dulles Airport to London."

Rebecca Manning was the former MI6 Head of Station in Washington. She now reported for work each morning at Moscow Center, headquarters of the SVR, Russia's Foreign Intelligence Service.

"There was also a suggestion," Sarah went on, "that you were the one who killed those three Russian agents they found on the C&O Canal in Maryland."

A waiter appeared with their order. He placed the espresso in front of Gabriel with inordinate care.

"What's it like to be the most famous man in Israel?" asked Sarah.

"It has its drawbacks."

"Surely, it isn't all bad. Who knows? If you play your cards right, you might even be prime minister one day." She tugged at the sleeve of his suit jacket. "I must say, you look the part. But I think I like the old Gabriel Allon better."

"Which Gabriel Allon was that?"

"The one who wore blue jeans and a leather jacket."

"We all have to change."

"I know. But sometimes I wish I could turn back the clock."

"Where would you go?"

She thought about it for a moment. "The night we had dinner together in that little place in Copenhagen. We sat outside in the freezing cold. I told you a deep, dark secret I should have kept to myself."

"I don't remember it."

Sarah plucked a *pain au chocolat* from the basket. "Aren't you going to have one?"

Gabriel held up a hand.

"Maybe you haven't changed, after all. In all the years I've known you, I don't think I've ever seen you eat a bite of food during the daytime."

"I make up for it after the sun goes down."

"You haven't gained an ounce since I saw you last. I wish I could say the same."

"You look wonderful, Sarah."

"For a woman of forty-three?" She added a packet of artificial sweetener to her coffee. "I was beginning to think you'd changed your number."

"I was out of pocket when you called."

"I *called* several times. I also left you about a dozen text messages."

"I had to take certain precautions before responding."

"With me? Whatever for?"

Gabriel offered a careful smile. "Because of your relationship with a certain high-profile member of the Saudi royal family."

"Khalid?"

"I didn't realize you two were on a first-name basis."

"I insisted on it."

Gabriel was silent.

"You obviously disapprove."

"Only with some of your recent acquisitions. One in particular."

"The Leonardo?"

"If you say so."

"You're dubious about the attribution?"

"I could have painted a better Leonardo than that one." He looked at her seriously. "You should have come to me when he approached you about working for him."

"And what would you have told me?"

"That his interest in you was no accident. That he was well aware of your ties to the CIA." Gabriel paused. "And to me."

"You would have been right."

"I usually am."

Sarah picked at her pastry. "What do you think of him?"

"As you might imagine, Crown Prince Khalid bin Mohammed is of particular interest to the Office."

"I'm not asking the Office, I'm asking you."

"The CIA and the Office were far less impressed with Khalid than the White House and my prime minister. Our concerns were confirmed when Omar Nawwaf was killed."

"Did Khalid order his murder?"

"Men in Khalid's position don't have to give a direct order."

"'Will no one rid me of this meddlesome priest?'"

Gabriel nodded thoughtfully in agreement. "A perfect example of a tyrant making his wishes abundantly clear. Henry spoke the words, and a few weeks later Becket was dead."

"Should Khalid be removed from the line of succession?"

"If he is, it's likely someone worse will take his place. Someone who will undo the modest social and religious reforms he's put in place."

"And if you learned of a threat to Khalid? What would you do?"

"We hear things all the time. Much of it from the mouth of the crown prince himself."

"What does that mean?"

"It means your client is the target of aggressive collection by the Office and Unit 8200. Not long ago, we managed to hack into the supposedly secure phone he carries around. We've been listening to his calls and reading his texts and e-mails ever since. The Unit also managed to activate the phone's camera and microphone, so we've been able to listen to many of his face-to-face conversations as well." Gabriel smiled. "Don't look so surprised, Sarah. As a former CIA officer, you should have realized that once you went to work for a man like Khalid bin Mohammed, you could expect no zone of privacy."

"How much do you know?"

"We know that six days ago, the crown prince placed a number of urgent calls to the French National Police concerning an incident that took place in the Haute-Savoie, not far from the Swiss border. We know that later that same night, the crown prince was driven under police escort to Paris, where he met with a number of senior French officials, including the interior minister and the president. He remained in Paris for seventy-two hours before traveling to New York. There he had a single appointment."

Gabriel removed a BlackBerry from the breast pocket of his jacket and tapped the screen twice. A few seconds later Sarah heard the sound of two people conversing. One was the future king of Saudi Arabia. The other was the director of the Nadia al-Bakari Collection at the Museum of Modern Art in New York.

"Do you know how to reach him?"

"Who?"

"The man who produced this painting without so much as a photograph to guide his hand. The man whose name should be right there."

Gabriel tapped PAUSE. "I had breakfast with my prime minister this morning and told him in no uncertain terms that I want nothing to do with this."

"And what did your prime minister say?"

"He asked me to reconsider." Gabriel returned the BlackBerry to his pocket. "Send a message to your friend, Sarah. Choose your words carefully to protect my identity."

Sarah removed her iPhone from her handbag and typed the message. A moment later the device pinged.

"Well?"

"Khalid wants to see us tonight."

"Where?"

Sarah posed the question. When the response arrived, she handed the phone to Gabriel.

He stared gloomily at the screen. "I was afraid he was going to say that."

9

Nejd, Saudi Arabia

The plane that delivered Sarah Bancroft to Israel was a Gulfstream G550, a ninety-six-foot aircraft with a cruising speed of 561 miles per hour. Gabriel replaced the flight crew with two retired IAF combat pilots, and the cabin crew with four Office bodyguards. They departed Ben Gurion Airport shortly after seven p.m. and streaked down the Gulf of Aqaba with the transponder switched off. To their right, ablaze in the fiery orange light of the setting sun, was the Sinai Peninsula, a virtual safe haven for several violent Islamic militias, including a branch of ISIS. To their left was Saudi Arabia.

They crossed the Saudi coastline at Sharma and headed eastward over the Hejaz Mountains to the Nejd.

It was there, in the early eighteenth century, that an obscure desert preacher named Muhammad Abdul Wahhab came to believe that Islam had strayed dangerously from the ways of the Prophet and the *al salaf al salih*, the earliest generations of Muslims. During his travels throughout Arabia, he was horrified to see Muslims smoking, drinking wine, and dancing to music while dressed in opulent clothing. Worse still was their veneration of trees and rocks and caves linked to holy men, a practice Wahhab condemned as polytheism, or *shirk*.

Determined to return Islam to its roots, Wahhab and his zealous band of followers, the *muwahhidoon*, launched a violent campaign to cleanse the Nejd of anything not sanctioned by the Koran. He found an important ally in a Nejdi tribe called the Al Saud. The pact they formed in 1744 became the basis of the modern Saudi state. The Al Saud held earthly power, but matters of faith they left in the hands of the doctrinal descendants of Muhammad Abdul Wahhab—men who despised the West, Christianity, Jews, and Shiite Muslims, whom they regarded as apostates and heretics. Osama bin Laden and al-Qaeda shared their view. So, too, did the Taliban and the holy warriors of ISIS and every other Sunni jihadist terrorist group. The toppled skyscrapers in Manhattan, the bombs in Western European train stations, the beheadings and the shattered markets in Baghdad: all of it could be traced back to the covenant reached more than two and a half centuries ago in the Nejd.

The city of Ha'il was the region's capital. It had several palaces, a museum, shopping malls, public gardens, and a Royal Saudi Air Force base, where the Gulfstream landed shortly after eight. The pilot taxied toward a quartet of black Range Rovers waiting at the edge of the tarmac. Surrounding the vehicles were uniformed security men, all armed with automatic weapons.

"Maybe this wasn't such a good idea after all," murmured Gabriel.

"Khalid assured me you would be safe," replied Sarah.

"Did he? And what if one those nice Saudi security guards is loyal to another faction of the royal family? Or better yet, what if he's a secret member of al-Qaeda?"

Sarah's phone pinged with an incoming message.

"Who's it from?"

"Who do you think?"

"Is he in one of those Range Rovers?"

"No."

"So who are *they*?"

"Our ride, apparently. Khalid says one of them is an old friend of yours."

"I don't have any Saudi friends," said Gabriel. "Not anymore."

"Maybe I should go first."

"An unveiled American blonde? It might send the wrong message."

The Gulfstream's forward cabin door had a built-in airstair. Gabriel lowered it and, trailed by the four bodyguards, descended to the tarmac. A few seconds later the door of one of the Range Rovers opened and a single figure emerged. Dressed in a plain olive-drab uniform, he was tall and angular, with small dark eyes and an aquiline nose that gave him the appearance of a bird of prey. Gabriel recognized him. The man worked for the Mabahith, the secret police division of the Saudi Interior Ministry. Gabriel had once spent a month at the Mabahith's central interrogation facility in Riyadh. The man with the bird-of-prey face had handled the questioning. He was not a friend, but nor was he an enemy.

"Welcome to Saudi Arabia, Director Allon. Or should I say welcome back? You're looking much better than when I saw you last." He grasped Gabriel's hand tightly. "I trust your wound healed well?"

"It only hurts when I laugh."

"I see you haven't lost your sense of humor."

"A man in my position needs one."

"Mine, too. Business is quite brisk, as you might imagine." The Saudi glanced at Gabriel's bodyguards. "Are they armed?"

"Heavily."

"Please instruct them to return to the aircraft. Don't worry, Director Allon. My men will take very good care of you."

"That's what I'm afraid of."

The bodyguards reluctantly complied with Gabriel's order. A moment later Sarah appeared in the cabin door, her blond hair moving in the desert wind.

The Saudi frowned. "I don't suppose she has a veil."

"She left it in New York."

"Not to worry. We brought one, just in case."

The highway was smooth as glass and black as an old vinyl record album. Gabriel had only the vaguest idea of its direction; the throwaway phone he had slipped into his pocket before leaving Tel Aviv read NO SERVICE. After leaving the air base, they had passed through miles of wheat fields—Ha'il was the breadbasket of Saudi Arabia. Now the land was harsh and unforgiving, like the brand of Islam practiced by Wahhab and his intolerant followers. Surely, thought Gabriel, it was no accident. The cruelty of the desert had influenced the faith.

From his vantage point in the Range Rover's rear passenger-side seat he could see the speedometer. They were traveling in excess of one hundred miles per hour. The driver was from the Mabahith, as was the man seated next to him. One Range Rover was in front of them, the other two were trailing. It had been a long time since Gabriel had seen another car or truck. He supposed the road had been closed.

"I can't breathe. I actually think I'm beginning to lose consciousness."

Gabriel looked across the backseat toward the black lump that was Sarah Bancroft. She was cloaked in the heavy black abaya that the senior Mabahith man had tossed over her a few seconds after her feet touched Saudi soil.

"The last time I wore one of these things was the night the Zizi operation fell apart. Do you remember, Gabriel?"

"Like it was yesterday."

"I don't know how Saudi women wear these things when it's a hundred and twenty degrees in the shade."

She was fanning herself. "Khalid once showed me a photograph from the sixties of unveiled Saudi women walking around Riyadh in skirts."

"It was like that all over the Arab world. Everything changed after 1979."

"That's exactly what Khalid says."

"Is that right?"

"The Soviets invaded Afghanistan, and Khomeini seized power in Iran. And then there was Mecca. A group of Saudi militants stormed the Grand Mosque and demanded the Al Saud give up power. They had to bring in a team of French commandos to end the siege."

"Yes, I remember."

"The Al Saud felt threatened," said Sarah, "so they trimmed their sails accordingly. They promoted the spread of Wahhabism to counter the influence of the Shiite Iranians and allowed hard-liners at home to enforce religious edicts strictly."

"That's a rather charitable view, don't you think?"

"Khalid is the first to admit mistakes were made."

"How magnanimous of him."

The Range Rovers turned onto an unpaved track and followed it into the desert. Eventually, they came to a checkpoint, through which they passed without slowing. The camp appeared a moment later, several large tents standing at the foot of a towering rock formation.

Sarah unconsciously straightened her abaya as the Range Rover drew to a stop. "How do I look?"

"Never better."

"Do try to keep that Israeli sarcasm of yours in check. Khalid doesn't appreciate irony."

"Most Saudis don't."

"And whatever you do, don't argue with him. He doesn't like to be challenged."

"You're forgetting one thing, Sarah."

"What's that?"

"He's the one who needs my help, not the other way around."

Sarah sighed. "Maybe you're right. Maybe this wasn't such a good idea after all."

10

Nejd, Saudi Arabia

In press interviews in the West, Prince Khalid bin Mohammed spoke often of his reverence for the desert. He loved nothing more, he said, than to slip anonymously from his palace in Riyadh and venture alone into the Arabian wilderness. There he would establish a crude camp and engage in several days of falconry, fasting, and prayer. He would also contemplate the future of the Kingdom that bore his family's name. It was during one such sojourn, in the Sarawat Mountains, that he conceived *The Way Forward*, his ambitious plan to remake the Saudi economy for the post-petroleum age. He claimed to have hit upon the idea of granting women the right to drive while camping in the Empty Quarter. Alone amid the ever-shifting dunes, he was reminded that nothing is permanent, that even in a land like Saudi Arabia change is inevitable.

The truth about KBM's desert adventures was far different. The tent into which Gabriel and Sarah were shown bore little resemblance to the camel-hair shelters in which Khalid's Bedouin ancestors had dwelled. It was more like a temporary pavilion. Rich carpets covered the floor, crystal chandeliers burned brightly overhead. The news of the day played out on several large televisions—CNN International, the BBC, CNBC, and, of course, Al Jazeera, the Qatar-based network that Khalid was doing his best to destroy.

Gabriel had anticipated a private meeting with His Royal Highness, but the tent was occupied by KBM's traveling court—the retinue of aides, functionaries, factotums, groupies, and general hangers-on who accompanied the future king everywhere he went. All wore the same clothing, a white *thobe* and a red-checkered *ghutra* held in place by a black *agal*. There were also several officers in uniform, a reminder that the young, untested prince was waging war on the other side of the Sarawat Mountains in Yemen.

Of the crown prince, however, there was no sign. One of the factotums deposited Gabriel and Sarah in a waiting area. It was furnished with overstuffed couches and chairs, like the lobby of a luxury hotel. Gabriel declined an offer of tea and sweets, but Sarah attempted to eat a honey-drenched Arab pastry while still wearing the abaya.

"How do they do it?"

"They don't. They eat with other women."

"I'm the only one—have you noticed? There isn't another woman in this tent."

"I'm too busy worrying about which one is planning to kill me." Gabriel glanced at his wristwatch. "Where the hell is he?"

"Welcome to KBM time. It's an hour and twenty minutes later than the rest of the world."

"I don't like to be kept waiting."

"He's testing you."

"He shouldn't."

"What are you going to do? Leave?"

Gabriel ran his palm over the silken fabric of the couch. "It's not so crude, is it?"

"You didn't really believe all that?"

"Of course not. I'm just wondering why he bothered to say it at all."

"Why does it matter?"

"Because men who tell one lie usually tell others."

A sudden commotion erupted among the white-robed courtiers as Crown Prince Khalid bin Mohammed entered the tent. He was dressed traditionally in a *thobe* and *ghutra*, but unlike the other men he also wore a *bisht*, a brown ceremonial cloak trimmed in gold. He was holding it closed with his left hand. With his right he was pressing a mobile phone to his ear. The same phone, Gabriel assumed, that Unit 8200 had compromised. He could only wonder who else might be listening—the Americans and their partners in the Five Eyes, perhaps even the Russians or the Iranians.

Khalid terminated the call and stared at Gabriel as though astonished to see Israel's avenging angel in the land of the Prophet. After a moment he crossed the richly carpeted floor, warily. So did four heavily armed bodyguards. Even when surrounded by his closest aides, thought Gabriel, KBM feared for his life.

"Director Allon." The Saudi did not offer his hand, which was still clutching the phone. "It was good of you to come on such short notice."

Gabriel nodded once but said nothing.

Khalid looked at Sarah. "Are you under there somewhere, Miss Bancroft?"

The black mound moved in the affirmative.

"Please remove your abaya."

Sarah lifted the veil from her face and draped it over her head like a scarf, leaving a portion of her hair visible.

"Much better." It was obvious that Khalid's body-guards did not agree. They quickly averted their eyes and fixed them coldly on Gabriel. "You must forgive my security men, Director Allon. They're not accustomed to seeing Israelis on Saudi soil, especially one with a reputation like yours."

"And what's that?"

Khalid's smile was brief and insincere. "I hope your flight was pleasant."

"Quite."

"And the drive wasn't too arduous?"

"Not at all."

"Something to eat or drink? You must be famished."

"Actually, I would prefer to—"

"So would I, Director Allon. But I am bound by the traditions of the desert to show hospitality toward a visitor to my camp. Even if the visitor was once my enemy."

"Sometimes," said Gabriel, "the only person you can trust is your enemy."

"Can I trust you?"

"I'm not sure you have much of a choice." Gabriel glanced at the bodyguards. "Tell them to take a walk, they're making me nervous. And give them that phone of yours. You never know who might be listening."

"My experts tell me it's totally secure."

"Humor me, Khalid."

The crown prince handed the phone to one of the bodyguards, and all four withdrew. "I assume Sarah told you why I wanted to see you."

"She didn't have to."

"You knew?"

Gabriel nodded. "Has there been any contact from the kidnappers?"

"I'm afraid so."

"How much are they asking for?"

"If only it were that simple. The House of Saud is worth somewhere in the neighborhood of a trillion and a half dollars. Money is not the issue."

"If they don't want money, what do they want?"

"Something I can't possibly give them. Which is why I need you to find her."

11

Nejd, Saudi Arabia

The ransom note was seven lines in length and rendered in English. It was accurately spelled and properly punctuated, with none of the awkward wording associated with translation software. It stated that His Royal Highness Prince Khalid bin Mohammed had ten days to abdicate and thus relinquish his claim to the throne of Saudi Arabia. Otherwise, his daughter, Princess Reema, would be put to death. The note did not specify the manner of her execution, or whether it would be in accordance with Islamic law. In fact, there were no religious references at all, and none of the rhetorical flourishes common in communications from terrorist groups. On the whole, thought Gabriel, the tone was rather businesslike.

"When did you receive it?"

"Three days after Reema was taken. Long enough for the damage to be done. Unlike my father and his brothers, I have only one wife. Unfortunately, she cannot have another child. Reema is all we have."

"Did you show it to the French?"

"No. I called you."

They had left the encampment and were walking in the bed of a wadi, with Sarah between them and the bodyguards following. The stars were incandescent, the moon shone like a torch. Khalid was fussing with his *bisht*, a habit of Saudi men. In his native dress he looked at home in the emptiness of the desert. Gabriel's Western suit and oxford shoes gave him the appearance of the interloper.

"How was the note delivered?"

"By courier."

"Where?"

Khalid hesitated. "To our consulate in Istanbul."

Gabriel's eyes were on the rocky earth. He looked up sharply. "Istanbul?"

Khalid nodded.

"It sounds to me as though the kidnappers were trying to send you a message."

"What sort of message?"

"Maybe they're trying to punish you for killing Omar Nawwaf and chopping his body into pieces that could fit inside carry-on luggage."

"It's rather ironic, don't you think? The great Gabriel Allon moralizing about a little wet work."

"We engage in targeted killing operations against known terrorists and other threats to our national security, many of them funded and supported by elements from your country. But we don't kill people who write nasty things about our prime minister. If that were the case, we'd be doing nothing else."

"Omar Nawwaf is none of your concern."

"Neither is your daughter. But you've asked me to find her, and I need to know whether there might be a link between her disappearance and Nawwaf's murder."

Khalid appeared to consider the question carefully. "I doubt it. The Saudi dissident community doesn't have the capability to carry out something like this."

"Your intelligence services must have a suspect."

"The Iranians are at the top of their list."

The default Saudi position, thought Gabriel. Blame everything on the Shiite heretics of Iran. Still, he did not dismiss the theory out of hand. The Iranians viewed Khalid as a primary threat to their regional ambitions, second only to Gabriel himself.

"Who else?" he asked.

"The Qataris. They loathe me."

"With good reason."

"And the jihadis," said Khalid. "The hard-liners inside the Saudi religious community are furious at me for the things I've said about radical Islam and the Muslim Brotherhood. They also don't like the fact I've allowed women to drive and attend sporting events. The threat level against me inside the Kingdom is very high."

"I doubt that ransom note was written by a jihadist."

"For now, those are our only suspects."

"The Iranians, the Qataris, and the ulema? Come now, Khalid. You can do better than that. What about all the relatives you pushed aside to become crown prince? Or the one hundred prominent Saudis and members of the royal family you locked away in the Ritz-Carlton? Please remind me how much you managed to extort from them before letting them leave. The figure slips my mind."

"It was one hundred billion dollars."

"And how much of it ended up in your pocket?"

"The money was placed in the treasury."

"Which is your pocket by another name."

"L'état, c'est moi," said Khalid. *I am the state.*

"But some of the men you fleeced are still very rich. Rich enough to hire a team of professional operatives to kidnap your daughter. They knew they could never get to you, not when you're surrounded day and night by an army of bodyguards. But Reema was another story." Greeted by silence, Gabriel asked, "Have I left anyone out?"

"My father's second wife. She opposed changing the line of succession. I placed her under house arrest."

"Every Jewish boy's dream." The air was suddenly very cold. Gabriel turned up the collar of his suit jacket. "Why did you send Reema to school in Switzerland? Why not England, where you were educated?"

"The United Kingdom was my first choice, I must admit, but the director-general of MI5 couldn't guarantee Reema's security. The Swiss were much more accommodating. The headmaster at the school agreed to protect Reema's identity, and the Swiss security service kept an eye on her from afar."

"That was very generous of them."

"Generosity had nothing to do with it. I paid the government a great deal of money to cover the additional costs of Reema's security. They're good hoteliers, the Swiss, and discreet. In my experience, it comes naturally to them."

"And what about the French? Did they know Reema was spending weekends at that ridiculous château of yours in the Haute-Savoie?" Gabriel lifted his gaze briefly to the stars. "I can't remember how much you spent on that place. Almost as much as you paid for that Leonardo."

Khalid ignored the remark. "I might have mentioned it to the president, but I made no request of the French government for security. Once Reema's motorcade crossed the border, my bodyguards were responsible for her protection."

"That was a mistake on your part."

"In retrospect," agreed Khalid. "The people who kidnapped my daughter were quite professional. The question is, for whom were they working?"

"You've managed to make a lot of enemies in a short period of time."

"We have that in common, you and I."

"My enemies are in Moscow and Tehran. Yours are much closer. Which is why I want nothing to do with this. Show the demand note to the French, give them everything you have. They're good," said Gabriel. "I should know. Thanks to Saudi ideology and Saudi money, I've been forced to work closely with them on a number of counterterrorism operations."

Khalid smiled. "Feel better?"

"I'm getting there."

"I can't change the past, only the future. We can do it together, you and I. We can make history. But only if you can find my daughter."

Gabriel slowed to a stop and contemplated the tall robed figure standing before him in the starlight. "Who are you, Khalid? Are you the real thing, or was Omar Nawwaf right about you? Are you just another power-mad sheikh who happens to have a good public-relations strategist?"

"I'm as close to the real thing as Saudi Arabia will allow at this time. And if I am forced to renounce my claim to the throne, there will be dire consequences for Israel and the West."

"That much I believe. As for the rest of it . . ." Gabriel left the thought unfinished. "You're to say nothing to anyone about my involvement. And that includes the Americans."

With his expression, Khalid made it clear he did not appreciate diktats from commoners. Exhaling heavily, he made a subtle change to the arrangement of his *ghutra*. "You surprise me."

"How so?"

"You've agreed to help me. And yet you've asked for nothing in return."

"One day I will," said Gabriel. "And you will give me what I want."

"You sound very sure of yourself."

"That's because I am."

12

Jerusalem

Gabriel's motorcade was waiting on the tarmac at Ben Gurion Airport when the Gulfstream touched down a few minutes after midnight. Sarah accompanied him to Jerusalem. He dropped her at the entrance of the King David Hotel.

"The room is one of ours," he explained. "Don't worry, we switched off the cameras and the microphones."

"Somehow I doubt that." She smiled. "What are your plans?"

"Against all better judgment, I'm going to undertake a rapid search for the daughter of His Royal Highness Prince Khalid bin Mohammed."

"Where do you intend to start?"

"Since she was kidnapped in France, I thought it might be a good idea to start there."

Sarah frowned.

"Forgive me, it's been a long day."

"I speak French very well, you know."

"So do I."

"And I attended the International School of Geneva when my father was working in Switzerland."

"I remember, Sarah. But you're going home to New York."

"I'd rather go to France with you."

"That's not possible."

"Why not?"

"Because you traded the secret world for the overt world a long time ago."

"But the secret world is so much more interesting." She checked the time. "My God, it's late. When are you leaving for Paris?"

"The ten o'clock El Al to Charles de Gaulle. These days, I seem to have a standing reservation on it. I'll pick you up at eight and take you back to the airport."

"Actually, I think I'll hang around Jerusalem for a day or two."

"You're not thinking about doing something foolish, are you?"

"Like what?"

"Making contact with Mikhail."

"I wouldn't dream of it. Besides, Mikhail made it abundantly clear he's very happy with what's-her-name."

"Natalie."

"Oh, yes, I keep forgetting." She kissed Gabriel's cheek. "Sorry to drag you into all of this. Don't hesitate to call if there's anything more I can do."

She climbed out of the SUV without another word and disappeared through the entrance of the hotel. Gabriel dialed the Operations Desk at King Saul Boulevard and informed the duty officer of his intention to travel to Paris later that morning.

"Anything else, boss?"

"Activate Room 435 at the King David. Audio only."

Gabriel killed the connection and leaned his head wearily against the window. She was right about one thing, he thought. The secret world was much more interesting.

It was a five-minute drive from the King David Hotel to Narkiss Street, the quiet, leafy lane in the historic Jerusalem neighborhood of Nachlaot where Gabriel Allon, despite the objections of his security department and many of his neighbors, continued to make his home. There were checkpoints at either end of the street, and a guard stood watch outside the old limestone apartment building at Number 16. As Gabriel alighted from the back of his SUV, the air smelled of eucalyptus and, faintly, of Turkish tobacco. There was little mystery as to the source. Ari Shamron's flashy new armored limousine was parked along the curb in the space reserved for Gabriel's motorcade.

"He arrived around midnight," the guard explained. "He said you were expecting him."

"And you believed him?"

"What was I supposed to do? He's the Memuneh."

Gabriel shook his head slowly. He was two years into his term as director-general, and yet even the members of his security detail still referred to Shamron as "the one in charge."

He headed up the garden walk, entered the foyer, and climbed the brightly lit stairs to the third floor. Chiara, in black leggings and a matching black pullover, was waiting in the open door of the apartment. She appraised Gabriel coolly for a moment before finally throwing her arms around his neck.

"I should go to Saudi Arabia more often."

"When were you planning to tell me?"

"Right about now." He followed Chiara inside. Scattered across the coffee table in the sitting room were cups and glasses and half-consumed plates of food, evidence of a tense late-night vigil. The television, tuned to CNN International, played silently. "Did I make the evening news?"

Chiara glared at him but said nothing.

"How did you find out?"

"How do you think?" She glanced toward the terrace, where Shamron was no doubt listening to every word they were saying. "He was even more worried than I was."

"Really? I find that hard to believe."

"He ordered Air Defense Command to track your plane. The tower at Ben Gurion alerted us when you landed. We expected you sooner, but apparently you made a slight detour on the way home." Chiara gathered the dishes from the coffee table. She always tidied up when she was annoyed. "I'm sure you enjoyed seeing Sarah again. She was always fond of you."

"That was a long time ago."

"Not *that* long ago."

"You know I never had any feelings for her."

"It would have been completely understandable if you had. She's very beautiful."

"Not as beautiful as you, Chiara. Not even close."

It was true. Chiara's was a timeless beauty. In her face Gabriel saw traces of Arabia and North Africa and Spain and all the other lands through which her ancestors had passed before finding themselves behind the locked gates of Venice's ancient ghetto. Her hair was dark and riotous and streaked with highlights of auburn and chestnut. Her eyes were wide and brown and flecked with gold. No, he thought, no woman would ever come between them. Gabriel only feared that one day Chiara would come to the realization she was far too young and beautiful to be married to a wreck like him.

He went onto the terrace. There were two wrought-iron chairs and a small table, upon which was the plate Shamron had commandeered for his ashtray. Six cigarette butts lay side by side, like spent cartridges. Shamron was in the process of igniting a seventh with his old Zippo lighter when Gabriel plucked the cigarette from his lips.

Shamron frowned. "One more won't kill me."

"It might."

"Do you know how many of those I've smoked in my life?"

"All the stars in the sky and the sand on the seashore."

"You shouldn't borrow from Genesis when discussing a vice like smoking. It's bad karma."

"Jews don't believe in karma."

"Wherever did you get an idea like that?"

Shamron extracted another cigarette from his packet

with a tremulous liver-spotted hand. He was dressed, as usual, in a pair of pressed khaki trousers, a white oxford cloth shirt, and a leather bomber jacket with an unrepaired tear in the left shoulder. He had damaged the garment the night a Palestinian master terrorist named Tariq al-Hourani planted a bomb beneath Gabriel's car in Vienna. Daniel, Gabriel's young son, was killed in the explosion. Leah, his first wife, suffered catastrophic burns. She lived now in a psychiatric hospital atop Mount Herzl, trapped in a prison of memory and a body ravaged by fire. And Gabriel lived here on Narkiss Street, with his beautiful Italian-born wife and two young children. From them, he hid his unending grief. But not from Shamron. Death had joined them in the beginning. And death remained the foundation of their bond.

Gabriel sat down. "Who told you?"

"About your flying visit to Saudi Arabia?" Shamron's smile was mischievous. "I believe it was Uzi."

Uzi Navot was the previous director-general and, like Gabriel, one of Shamron's acolytes. In a break with Office tradition, he had agreed to remain at King Saul Boulevard, thus allowing Gabriel to function as an operational chief.

"How much were you able to beat out of him?"

"No coercion was necessary. Uzi was deeply concerned about your decision to return to the country where you spent nearly a month in captivity. Needless to say," said Shamron, "I shared his opinion."

"You traveled secretly to Arab countries when you were the chief."

"Jordan, yes. Morocco, of course. I even went to Egypt after Sadat made his visit to Jerusalem. But I never set foot in Saudi Arabia."

"I wasn't in danger."

"With all due respect, Gabriel, I doubt that was the case. You should have conducted the meeting on neutral ground, in an environment controlled by the Office. He has a tempestuous streak, the crown prince. You're lucky you didn't end up like that journalist he killed in Istanbul."

"I've always found journalists to be much more useful alive than dead."

Shamron smiled. "Did you read the piece they wrote about Khalid in the *New York Times*? They said the Arab Spring had finally come to Saudi Arabia. They said an untested boy was going to transform a country founded on a shotgun marriage between Wahhabism and a desert tribe from the Nejd." Shamron shook his head. "I didn't believe the story then, and I surely don't believe it now. Khalid bin Mohammed is interested in two things. The first is power. The second is money. For the Al Saud, they are one and the same. Without power, there is no money. And without money, there is no power."

"But he fears the Iranians as much as we do. For that reason alone, he can prove quite useful."

"Which is why you agreed to find his daughter." Shamron gave Gabriel a sidelong glance. "That *is* why he wanted to see you, isn't it?"

Gabriel handed Shamron the demand note, which he read by the flickering light of the Zippo. "It looks as though you've gotten yourself into the middle of a royal family feud."

"That's exactly what it looks like."

"It's not without risk."

"Nothing worth doing is."

"I agree." Shamron closed the lighter with a snap of his thick wrist. "Even if you fail to find her, your efforts will pay dividends in the royal court of Riyadh. And if you succeed . . ." Shamron shrugged. "The crown prince will be forever in your debt. For all intents and purposes, he will be an asset of the Office."

"So you approve?"

"I would have done exactly the same thing." Shamron returned the note to Gabriel. "But why did Khalid offer you this opportunity to compromise him? Why turn to the Office? Why didn't he ask his good friend in the White House for help?"

"Perhaps he thinks I might prove more effective."

"Or more ruthless."

"That, too."

"You should consider one possibility," said Shamron after a moment.

"What's that?"

"That Khalid knows full well who kidnapped his daughter, and he's using you to do his dirty work."

"He's proven himself more than willing to do his own."

"Which is why you should make no more trips to Saudi Arabia." Shamron looked at Gabriel seriously for a moment. "I was in Langley that night—do you remember? I watched the entire thing through the camera of that Predator drone. I saw them leading you and Nadia into the desert to be executed. I pleaded with the Americans to drop a Hellfire missile on you to spare you the pain of the knife. I've had many terrible nights in my life, but that might have been the worst. If she hadn't stepped in front of that bullet . . ." Shamron looked at his big stainless-steel wristwatch. "You should get some sleep."

"It's too late now," said Gabriel. "Stay with me, Abba. I'll sleep on the way to Paris."

"I didn't think you could sleep on airplanes."

"I can't."

Shamron watched the wind moving in the eucalyptus trees. "I never could, either."

13

Princess Reema bint Khalid Abdulaziz Al Saud endured the many indignities of her captivity with as much grace as possible, but the bucket was the last straw.

It was pale blue and plastic, the sort of thing an Al Saud never touched. They had placed it in Reema's cell after she had misbehaved during a visit to the toilet. According to a typewritten note taped to the side, Reema was to use it until further notice. Only when her conduct returned to normal would her bathroom privileges be restored. Reema refused to relieve herself in such a shameful manner and did so on the floor of her cell instead. At which point her captors, again in writing, threatened to withhold food and water. "Fine!" Reema shouted at the masked figure who delivered the note. She would rather starve to death than eat another wretched meal that tasted as though it had been cooked in its own can. The food was not fit for pigs, let alone the daughter of the future king of Saudi Arabia.

The cell was small—smaller, perhaps, than any room in which Reema had ever set foot. Her cot consumed most of the space. The walls were white and smooth and cold, and in the ceiling a light burned always. Reema had no concept of time, even day or night. She slept when she was tired, which was often, and dreamed of her old life. She had taken it all for granted, the unimaginable wealth and luxury, and now it was gone.

They did not chain her to the floor the way they did in the American movies her father used to allow her to watch. Nor did they gag her or bind her hands and feet or force her to wear a hood—only for a few hours, during the long drive after she was taken. Once she was safely in the cell, *they* were the ones to cover their faces. There were four in all. Reema could tell them apart by their size and shape and the color of their eyes. Three were men, one was a woman. None were Arabs.

Reema did her best to hide her fear but made no attempt to conceal the fact she was bored out of her mind. She asked for a television to watch her favorite programs. Her captors, in writing, refused. She asked for a computer to play games, or an iPod and headphones to listen to music, but again her request was denied. Finally, she asked for a pen and a pad. Her plan was to record her experiences in a story, something she might show to Miss Kenton after she was released. The woman appeared to consider Reema's appeal carefully, but when her next meal arrived, there was a terse note of rejection. Reema ate the dreadful food nonetheless, for she was too famished to carry on with her hunger strike. Afterward, they allowed her to use the toilet, and when she returned to the cell the bucket was gone. It seemed all was right in Reema's tiny world.

She thought of Miss Kenton often. Reema had fooled them all—Miss Halifax, Herr Schröder, the mad Spanish woman who tried to teach Reema to paint like Picasso—but not Miss Kenton. She had been standing in the window of the staff room on the afternoon Reema left the school for the last time. The attack had happened in France, on the road between Annecy and her father's château. Reema remembered a van parked along the side of the road, a man changing a tire. A car had smashed into theirs, an explosion had blown open the doors. Salma, the bodyguard who pretended to be Reema's mother, had been shot. So had the driver and all the other bodyguards in the Range Rover. Reema they forced into the back of the van. They covered her head with a hood and gave her a shot to make her sleep, and when she woke she was in the small white room. The smallest room she had ever seen in her life.

But why had they abducted her? In the movies, the kidnappers always wanted money. Reema's father had all the money in the world. It meant nothing to him. He would pay the kidnappers what they wanted, and Reema would be released. And then her father would send out men to find the kidnappers and kill them all. Or perhaps her father might kill one or two himself. To Reema he was very kind, but she had heard about the things he did to people who opposed him. He would show no mercy to the people who kidnapped his only child.

And so Princess Reema bint Khalid Abdulaziz Al Saud endured the many indignities of her captivity with as much grace as possible, secure in the knowledge she would soon be released. She ate their dreadful food without complaint and behaved herself when they took her down the darkened corridor to the toilet. After one visit she returned to her cell to find a pen and a notebook lying at the foot of her cot. *You're dead*, she wrote on the first page. *Dead, dead, dead . . .*

14

Jerusalem–Paris

Though Princess Reema did not know it, her father had already retained the services of a dangerous and sometimes violent man to find her. He passed the remainder of that night in the company of an old friend for whom sleep was no longer possible. And at dawn, after kissing his sleeping wife and children, he traveled by motorcade to Ben Gurion Airport, where yet another flight awaited him. His name did not appear on the passenger manifest. As usual, he was the last to board. A seat had been reserved for him in first class. The seat next to it, as was customary, was empty.

A flight attendant offered him a preflight beverage. He requested tea. Then he asked for the passenger in 22B to be invited to take the seat next to him. Ordinarily, the flight attendant would have explained that passengers from economy class were not allowed in the aircraft's forward cabin, but she offered no objection. The flight attendant knew who the man was. Everyone in Israel did.

The flight attendant headed aft, and when she returned, she was accompanied by a woman of forty-three with blond hair and blue eyes. A murmur arose in the first-class cabin as the woman lowered herself into the seat next to the man who had boarded the plane last.

"Did you really think my security department would allow me to get on a plane without first reviewing every name on the manifest?"

"No," replied Sarah Bancroft. "But it was worth a try."

"You deceived me. You asked me about my travel plans, and I foolishly told you the truth."

"I was trained by the best."

"How much of it do you remember?"

"All of it."

Gabriel smiled sadly. "I was afraid you were going to say that."

It was a few minutes after four o'clock when the flight landed in Paris. Gabriel and Sarah cleared passport control separately—Gabriel falsely, Sarah under her real name—and reunited in the busy arrivals hall of Terminal 2A. There they were met by a courier from Paris Station, who handed Gabriel the key to a car. It was waiting on the second level of the short-term car park.

"A Passat?" Sarah dropped into the passenger seat. "Couldn't they have given us something a little more exciting?"

"I don't want exciting. I want reliability and anonymity. It's also rather fast."

"When was the last time you drove a car?"

"Earlier this year, when I was in Washington working on the Rebecca Manning case."

"Did you kill anyone?"

"Not with the car." Gabriel opened the glove box. Inside was a Beretta 9mm pistol with a walnut grip.

"Your favorite," remarked Sarah.

"Transport thinks of everything."

"What about bodyguards?"

"They make it hard to operate effectively."

"Is it safe for you to be in Paris without a security detail?"

"That's what the Beretta is for."

Gabriel reversed out of the space and followed the ramp to the lower level. He paid the attendant in cash and did his best to shield his face from the security camera.

"You're not fooling anyone. The French are going to figure out that you're in the country."

"It's not the French I'm worried about."

Gabriel followed the A1 through the gathering dusk to the northern fringes of Paris. Night had fallen by the time they arrived. The rue la Fayette bore them westward across the city, and the Pont de Bir-Hakeim carried them over the Seine to the fifteenth arrondissement. Gabriel turned onto the rue Nélaton and stopped at a formidable security gate manned by heavily armed officers of the National Police. Behind the gate stood a charmless modern office block. A small sign warned that the building belonged to the Interior Ministry and was under constant video surveillance.

"It reminds me of the Green Zone in Baghdad."

"These days," said Gabriel, "the Green Zone is safer than Paris."

"Where are we?"

"The headquarters of the Alpha Group. It's an elite counter- terrorism unit of the DGSI." The *direction générale de la sécurité intérieure*, or DGSI, was France's internal security service. "The French created the Alpha Group not long after you left the Agency. It used to be hidden inside a beautiful old building on the rue de Grenelle."

"The one that was destroyed by that ISIS car bomb?"

"The bomb was in a van. And I was inside the building when it exploded."

"Of course you were."

"So was Paul Rousseau, Alpha Group's chief. I introduced you to him at my swearing-in party."

"He looked more like a professor than a French spy."

"He was once, actually. He's one of France's foremost scholars of Proust."

"What's the Alpha Group's role?"

"Human penetration of jihadist networks. But Rousseau has access to everything."

A uniformed officer approached the car. Gabriel gave him two pseudonymous names, one male, the other female, both French and both inspired by the novels of Dumas, a particularly Rousseauian touch. The Frenchman was waiting in his new lair on the top floor. Unlike the other offices in the building, Rousseau's was somber and wood-paneled and filled with books and files. Like Gabriel, he preferred them to digital dossiers. He was dressed in a crumpled tweed jacket and a pair of gray flannel trousers. His ever-present pipe belched smoke as he shook Gabriel's hand.

"Welcome to our new Bastille." Rousseau offered his hand to Sarah. "So good to see you again, Madame Bancroft. When we met in Israel, you told me you were a museum curator from New York. I didn't believe it then, and I surely don't believe it now."

"It's true, actually."

"But obviously there's more to the story. Where Monsieur Allon is concerned, there usually is." Rousseau released Sarah's hand and contemplated Gabriel over his reading glasses. "You were rather vague on the phone this morning. I assume this isn't a social call."

"I heard you recently had a bit of unpleasantness in the Haute-Savoie." Gabriel paused, then added, "A few miles west of Annecy."

Rousseau raised an eyebrow. "What else have you heard?"

"That your government chose to cover up the incident at the request of the victim's father, who happens to own the largest château in the region. He also happens to be—"

"The future king of Saudi Arabia." Rousseau lowered his voice. "Please tell me you didn't have anything to do—"

"Don't be ridiculous, Paul."

The Frenchman nibbled thoughtfully at the stem of his pipe. "The unpleasantness, as you call it, was quickly designated a criminal act rather than an act of terrorism. Therefore, it fell outside the purview of the Alpha Group. It is none of our affair."

"But you must have been at the table during the first hours of the crisis."

"Of course."

"You also have access to all the information and intelligence gathered by the National Police and the DGSI."

Rousseau pondered Gabriel at length. "Why is the abduction of the crown prince's daughter of interest to the State of Israel?"

"Our interest is humanitarian in nature."

"A refreshing change of pace. On whose behalf have you come?"

"The future king of Saudi Arabia."

"My goodness," said Rousseau. "How the world has changed."

15

Paris

It soon became apparent that Paul Rousseau did not approve of his government's decision to conceal the abduction of Princess Reema. It had been made easier, he said, by the remote location—the intersection of two rural roads, the D14 and the D38, west of Annecy. As it happened, the first person on the scene was a retired gendarme who lived in a nearby village. The next to arrive were the crown prince himself and his usual retinue of bodyguards. They surrounded the two vehicles of the princess's motorcade, along with a third vehicle that had been abandoned by the kidnappers. To subsequent passersby it looked like a serious traffic accident involving wealthy men from the Middle East.

"Hardly an unusual occurrence in France," said Rousseau.

The retired gendarme was sworn to secrecy, he continued, as were the officers who took part in a rapid nationwide search for the princess. Rousseau offered the assistance of the Alpha Group but was informed by his chief and his minister that his services were not required.

"Why not?"

"Because His Royal Highness told my minister that his daughter's abduction was not the work of terrorists."

"How could he have known that so quickly?"

"You'd have to ask him. But the logical explanation is—"

"He already knew who was behind it."

They were gathered around a stack of files piled on Rousseau's conference table. He opened one and removed a single photograph, which he placed before Gabriel and Sarah. A Range Rover riddled with bullet holes, a smashed Mercedes Maybach, a crumbled Citroën estate car. The corpses of the dead Saudi bodyguards had been removed. Their blood, however, was spattered over the interior of the Range Rover and the Maybach. There was a lot of blood, thought Gabriel, especially in the backseat of the limousine. He wondered whether some of it had been shed by the princess.

"There was at least one other vehicle involved, a

Ford Transit van." Rousseau pointed toward the grassy verge along the D14. "It was parked right here. Maybe the driver was looking under the hood or pretending to change a tire when the motorcade approached. Or maybe he didn't bother."

"How do you know it was a Ford Transit?"

"In a minute." Rousseau pointed toward the smashed front end of the Citroën. "There were no witnesses, but the tire marks and the collision damage paint an accurate picture of what happened. The motorcade was heading west on the D14 toward the crown prince's château. The Citroën was headed north on the D38. Obviously, it didn't stop at the intersection. Based on the tire marks, the driver of the Maybach swerved to avoid the collision, but the Citroën struck the driver's side of the limousine with enough force to damage the armor plating and force it off the road. The driver of the Range Rover slammed on his brakes and came to a stop behind the Maybach. In all likelihood, the four bodyguards were killed instantly. The ballistics and forensic analysis indicate the gunshots came from the direction of both the Citroën and the Ford Transit."

"How did they get the girl out of an armor-plated car with bulletproof windows?"

Rousseau removed a second photograph from the file. It showed the passenger side of the Maybach. The armor-plated doors had been blown open—rather expertly, thought Gabriel. The Office could not have done it any better.

"I assume your forensics experts analyzed the blood inside the Maybach."

"It came from two people, the male driver and the female bodyguard. Like the four bodyguards from the Range Rover, they were killed by nine-millimeter rounds. The markings on the shell casings are consistent with an HK MP5 or one of its variants."

Rousseau produced another photograph. A Ford Transit, light gray. The photograph had been taken at night. The flash of the camera had illuminated a small patch of dry, rocky earth. It was not, thought Gabriel, the soil of the north of France.

"Where did they find it?"

"On a deserted road outside the village of Vielle-Aure. It's—"

"In the Pyrenees a few miles from the Spanish border."

"Sometimes I forget how well you know our country." Rousseau pointed at one of the van's tires. "It was a perfect match for the tracks found at the scene of the kidnapping."

Gabriel studied the photograph of the van. "I assume it was stolen."

"Of course. So was the Citroën."

"Was there any blood in the storage compartment?"

Rousseau shook his head.

"What about DNA?"

"A great deal."

"Any of it belong to Princess Reema?"

"We asked for a sample and were told in no uncertain terms we couldn't have one."

"By Khalid?"

Rousseau shook his head. "We've had no direct contact with the crown prince since he left France. All communication now flows through a certain Monsieur al-Madani of the Saudi Embassy in Paris."

Sarah looked up suddenly. "Rafiq al-Madani?"

"You know him?"

Sarah made no reply.

"It is my assumption, Miss Bancroft, that you are either a current or former officer of the Central Intelligence Agency. Needless to say, your secrets are safe within these walls."

"Rafiq al-Madani served at the Saudi Embassy in Washington for several years as the representative of the Ministry of Islamic Affairs. It's one of the official conduits the House of Saud uses to spread Wahhabism around the globe."

Rousseau smiled charitably. "Yes, I know."

"The FBI didn't care much for al-Madani," said Sarah. "And neither did the Counterterrorism Center at Langley. We didn't like the company he'd kept before coming to Washington. And the FBI didn't like some of the projects he was funding in America. The State Department quietly asked Riyadh to find work for him elsewhere. And much to our surprise, the Saudis agreed to our request."

"Unfortunately," said Rousseau, "they sent him to Paris. From the moment he arrived, he's been funneling Saudi money and support to some of the most radical mosques in France. In our opinion, Rafiq al-Madani is a hard-liner and a true believer. He is also quite close to His Royal Highness. He is a frequent visitor to the prince's château, and last summer he spent several days aboard his new yacht."

"I take it al-Madani is a target of DGSI surveillance," said Gabriel.

"Intermittent."

"Do you suppose he knew Khalid's daughter was going to school across the border in Geneva?"

Rousseau shrugged. "It's hard to say. The crown prince told almost no one, and security at the school was very tight. It was handled by a man named Lucien Villard. He's French, not Swiss. He used to work for the Service de la Protection."

"Why was a veteran of an elite unit like the SDLP running security at a private school in Geneva?"

"Villard didn't leave the service on the best of terms. There were rumors he was having an affair with the president's wife. When the president found out about it, he had him fired. Apparently, Villard took the girl's abduction quite hard. He resigned his post a few days later."

"Where is he now?"

"Still in Geneva, I suppose. I can get you an address if you—"

"Don't bother." Gabriel contemplated the three photographs arrayed on the table.

"What are you thinking?" asked Rousseau.

"I'm wondering how many operatives it took to pull off something like this."

"And?"

"Eight to ten for the kidnapping itself, not to mention the support agents. And yet somehow the DGSI, which is confronting the worst terrorism threat in the Western world, missed them all."

Rousseau removed a fourth photo from his file. "No, my friend. Not all of them."

16

Paris

Brasserie Saint-Maurice was located in the heart of medieval Annecy, on the ground floor of a teetering old building that was a riot of mismatched windows, shutters, and balustrades. Several square tables stood along the pavement beneath the shelter of three modern retractable awnings. At one, a man was drinking coffee and contemplating a mobile device. His hair was fair and straight and neatly arranged. So was his face. He wore a woolen peacoat, a stylishly knotted silk scarf, and a pair of wraparound sunglasses. The time code in the bottom right corner of the photo read 16:07:46. The date was the thirteenth of December, the day of Princess Reema's abduction.

"As you can see from the resolution," said Rousseau, "the image has been magnified. Here's the original."

Rousseau slid another photograph across the conference table. The perspective was wide enough so that the street was visible. Several cars lined the curb. Gabriel's eye was drawn instantly toward a Citroën estate car.

"Our national traffic surveillance system isn't as Orwellian as yours or Britain's, but the threat of terrorism has compelled us to improve our capabilities substantially. It didn't take long to find the car. Or the man who was driving it."

"How much do you know about him?"

"He rented a holiday villa outside Annecy two weeks before the abduction. He paid for a one-month stay entirely in cash, which the estate agent and the owner of the villa were more than happy to accept."

"I don't suppose he had a passport."

"A British one, actually. The estate agent made a photocopy."

Rousseau slid a sheet of paper across the tabletop. It was a photocopy of a photocopy, but the resolution was clear. The name on the passport was Ronald Burke. It claimed he had been born in Manchester in 1969. The photograph bore a vague resemblance to the man who had been sitting at Brasserie Saint-Maurice a few hours before Princess Reema had been kidnapped.

"Have you asked the British whether it's genuine?"

"And what should we tell the British? That he is a suspect in a kidnapping that *didn't* happen?"

Gabriel studied the man's face. His skin was taut and unlined, and the unnatural shape of his eyes suggested a recent visit to a cosmetic surgeon. The irises stared blankly into the camera lens. His lips were unsmiling. "What was his accent like?"

"He spoke British-accented French to the estate agent."

"Do you have any record of him entering the country?"

"No."

"Were there any sightings of him after the abduction?"

Rousseau shook his head. "He seems to have vanished into thin air. Just like Princess Reema."

Gabriel pointed to the wide shot of the man sitting at Brasserie Saint-Maurice. "I assume this is a still image from a video recording."

Rousseau opened a laptop and tapped a few keys with the air of a man who was still not comfortable with the conveniences of modern technology. Then he turned the computer so Gabriel and Sarah could see the screen and tapped the PLAY button. The man was looking at something on his phone. So was the woman who was drinking white wine at the next table. She was professionally dressed, with dark hair that fell about an attractive face. She, too, was wearing sunglasses, despite the fact the café was in heavy shadow. The lenses were large and rectangular. They were the kind of glasses, thought Gabriel, that famous actresses wore when they wanted to avoid being recognized.

At 16:09:22 the woman raised the phone to her ear. Whether she had initiated the call or received it, Gabriel could not discern. But a few seconds later, at 16:09:48, he noticed the man was talking on his phone, too.

Gabriel tapped PAUSE. "Quite a coincidence, don't you think?"

"Keep watching."

Gabriel pressed PLAY and watched the two people at Brasserie Saint-Maurice complete their phone calls, the woman first, the man twenty-seven seconds later, at 16:11:34. He left the café at 16:13:22 and climbed into the Citroën estate car. The woman departed three minutes later on foot.

"You can pause it now."

Gabriel did.

"We were never able to determine with certainty that the two people at Brasserie Saint-Maurice were conducting a cellular call or Internet-based conversation at eleven minutes past four o'clock on the Friday afternoon in question. If I had to guess—"

"The phones were a ruse. They were talking directly to one another in the café."

"Simple, but effective."

"Where did she go next?"

Rousseau dealt another photo across the tabletop. A professionally dressed woman climbing into the passenger seat of a Ford Transit, light gray. The woman's gloved hand was on the door latch.

"Where was it taken?"

"The avenue de Cran. It runs through a working-class area on the western edge of the city."

"Did you get a look at the driver?"

Another photo came sliding across the conference table. It depicted a blunt object of a man wearing a woolen watch cap and, of course, sunglasses. Gabriel supposed there were several other operatives in the compartment behind him, all armed with HK MP5 submachine pistols. He returned the photo to Rousseau, who was engaged in the ritualistic preparation of his pipe.

"Perhaps now might be a good time for you to explain your involvement in this affair."

"His Royal Highness has requested my help."

"The government of France is more than capable

of recovering Princess Reema without the assistance of Israel's secret intelligence service."

"His Royal Highness disagrees."

"Does he?" Rousseau struck a match and touched it to the bowl of his pipe. "Has he received any communication from the kidnappers?"

Gabriel handed over the demand letter. Rousseau read it through a haze of smoke. "One wonders why Khalid didn't tell us about this. I can only assume he doesn't want us poking our noses into an internal struggle for control of the House of Saud. But why on earth would he trust you instead?"

"I've been asking myself the same thing."

"And if you're unable to find her by the deadline?"

"His Royal Highness will have a difficult decision to make."

Rousseau frowned. "I'm surprised a man like you would offer your services to a man like him."

"You disapprove of the crown prince?"

"I think it's safe to assume he spends more time in my country than yours. As a senior officer of the DGSI, I've had a chance to observe him up close. I never believed the fairy tales about how he was going to change Saudi Arabia and the Middle East. Nor was I surprised when he ordered the murder of a journalist who dared to criticize him."

"If France was so appalled by the murder of Omar Nawwaf, why did you allow Khalid into the country every weekend to spend time with his daughter?"

"Because His Royal Highness is a one-man economic stimulus program. And because, like it or not, he is going to be the ruler of Saudi Arabia for a long time." Quietly, Rousseau added, "If you can find his daughter."

Gabriel made no reply.

The room filled with smoke as Rousseau considered his options. "For the record," he said finally, "the government of France will not tolerate your involvement in the search for Prince Khalid's daughter. That said, your participation might prove useful to the Alpha Group. Provided, of course, we establish certain ground rules."

"Such as?"

"You will share information with me, as I have shared it with you."

"Agreed."

"You will not bug, blackmail, or brutalize any citizen of the Republic."

"Unless he deserves it."

"And you will undertake no attempt to rescue Princess Reema on French soil. If you discover her whereabouts, you will tell me, and our tactical police units will free her."

"Inshallah," muttered Gabriel.

"So we have a deal?"

"It seems we do. I will find Princess Reema, and you will receive all the credit."

Rousseau smiled. "By my calculation, you now have approximately five days before the deadline. How do you intend to proceed?"

Gabriel pointed to the photograph of the man sitting at Brasserie Saint-Maurice. "I'm going to find him. And then I'm going to ask him where he's hiding the princess."

"As your clandestine partner, I'd like to offer one piece of advice." Rousseau pointed toward the photograph of the woman climbing into the van. "Ask her instead."

17

Paris–Annecy

The Israeli Embassy was located on the opposite bank of the Seine, on the rue Rabelais. Gabriel and Sarah remained there for nearly an hour—Gabriel in the station's secure communications vault, Sarah in the ambassador's antechamber. Leaving, they purchased sandwiches and coffee from a carryout around the corner, then made their way through the southern districts of Paris to the A6, the Autoroute du Soleil. The evening rush was long over, and the road before Gabriel was nearly empty of traffic. He pressed the accelerator of the Passat to the floor and felt a small rebellious thrill as the engine responded with a roar.

"You've proven your point about the damn car. Now please slow down." Sarah unwrapped one of the sandwiches and ate ravenously. "Why does everything taste better in France?"

"It doesn't, actually. That sandwich will taste exactly the same when we cross the Swiss border."

"Is that where we're going?"

"Eventually."

"Where's our first stop?"

"I thought we should have a look at the crime scene."

Sarah took another bite of the sandwich. "Are you sure you won't have one?"

"Maybe later."

"The sun has set, Gabriel. You're allowed to eat."

She switched on her overhead reading lamp and opened the dossier that Paul Rousseau had slipped into Gabriel's attaché case as they were leaving Alpha Group headquarters. It contained a surveillance photo of Khalid and Rafiq al-Madani aboard *Tranquillity*. Gabriel gave it a sidelong glance before returning his gaze to the road.

"When was it taken?"

Sarah turned over the photo and read the DGSI caption on the back. "The twenty-second of August on the Baie de Cannes." She scrutinized the image carefully. "I know that expression on Khalid's face. It's the one he adopts when someone is telling him something he doesn't want to hear. I saw it for the first time when I told him I didn't want to be his art adviser."

"And the second?"

"When I said he would be a fool to spend a half billion dollars on a suspect Leonardo."

"Have you ever been aboard the yacht?"

Sarah shook her head. "Too many bad memories. Every time Khalid invited me, I always made up some excuse to turn him down." She looked at the photograph again. "What do you suppose they're talking about?"

"Maybe they're discussing the best way to get rid of a meddlesome journalist named Omar Nawwaf."

Sarah returned the photograph to the file. "I thought Khalid was going to cut off the flow of money to the radicals."

"So did I."

"So why is he hanging out with a Wahhabi true believer like al-Madani?"

"Good question."

"If I were you, I'd put him under surveillance."

"What do you think I was doing downstairs at the embassy?"

"I wouldn't know, I wasn't invited." Sarah drew another photograph from Rousseau's dossier. A man and a woman sitting at separate tables at Brasserie Saint-

Maurice in Annecy, each holding a mobile phone. "And what do you suppose *they* were talking about?"

"It can't be good."

"They're obviously not Saudi."

"Obviously."

Sarah studied the passport photo. "He doesn't look British to me."

"What do British people look like?"

Sarah unwrapped another sandwich. "Eat something. You'll be less surly."

Gabriel took a first bite.

"Well?"

"It might be the finest sandwich I've ever eaten."

"I told you," said Sarah. "Everything tastes better in France."

It was a few minutes after midnight when they arrived in Annecy. They left the Passat outside Brasserie Saint-Maurice and checked into a small hotel near the cathedral. Gabriel was awakened shortly after four a.m. by a quarrel in the street beneath his window. Unable to sleep again, he went downstairs to the breakfast room and over several cups of coffee read the newspapers from Paris and Geneva. They were filled with accounts of the latest outrage from Washington, but there was no mention of a missing princess from Saudi Arabia.

Sarah appeared a few minutes after nine. Together they walked for an hour along the moss-green canals of the old town to determine whether they were being followed. While crossing the Pont des Amours, they agreed they were not.

They returned to the hotel long enough to collect their luggage, then walked to Brasserie Saint-Maurice. Sarah drank a café crème while Gabriel, in the manner of a stranded motorist, searched the Passat for explosives or a tracking device. Finding no evidence to suggest the car had been tampered with, he tossed their bags into the backseat and summoned Sarah with a nod. They left Annecy by way of the avenue de Cran, passing the spot where the woman had entered the Transit van, and made their way to the D14.

It bore them westward through a string of Alpine towns and villages that lay along the banks of the Fier River. Beyond the hamlet of La Croix the road climbed sharply into a coppice of trees before emerging once more into a Van Gogh landscape of groomed farmland. At the intersection of the D38, Gabriel eased onto the grassy verge and switched off the engine. The silence was complete. A single villa occupied a hilltop about a kilometer away. Otherwise, there was not a building or residence in sight.

Gabriel opened his door and placed a foot on the

ground. Instantly, he felt shattered auto glass beneath his shoe. It was everywhere, the glass, at all four corners of the imperfect intersection. The French police, in their haste, hadn't given the scene a proper cleaning. There was even a bit of blood still on the asphalt, like an oil stain, and a long set of tire marks. Gabriel reckoned they were the ones left by the Range Rover. He saw it all clearly—the collision, the gunshots, the controlled explosion, a child being ripped from the back of a luxury automobile. With his right hand he was counting the seconds. Twenty-five, thirty at most.

He climbed into the car next to Sarah. His finger hovered over the start button.

"What are you thinking?"

"I don't think Ronald Burke looks British, either." Gabriel started the engine. "Have you ever been to Khalid's château?"

"Once."

"Do you remember the way?"

Sarah pointed to the west.

Even before they reached the main gate, the property made its presence known. There was, for a start, the wall. Many kilometers in length, it was fashioned of local stone and topped by outward-leaning rows of barbed wire. It reminded Gabriel of the fence that ran along Grosvenor Place in London, separating the grounds of Buckingham Palace from the rabble of neighboring Belgravia. The gate itself was a monstrosity of iron bars and gold-dipped lamps, behind which a perfect gravel drive stretched toward a garish private Versailles.

Gabriel pondered it in silence. Finally, he asked, "Why am I trying to help a man who would waste four hundred million euros on a house like that?"

"What's the answer?"

Before Gabriel could respond, his BlackBerry shivered. He frowned at the screen.

"What is it?" asked Sarah.

"Rafiq al-Madani just entered the Interior Ministry in Paris."

18

Geneva

During his brief stay in the Office station in Paris, Gabriel had done more than place Rafiq al-Madani under surveillance. He had also ordered Unit 8200 to find the address of Lucien Villard, the former chief of security at the International School of Geneva. The cyberthieves of the Unit obtained it in a matter of minutes from the personnel section of the school's computer network, which they entered as though passing through an open door. Villard lived in a busy quarter of Parisian-style apartment buildings. His street was a watcher's paradise of shops and cafés. There was even a modest hotel, where Gabriel and Sarah arrived at midday. Gabriel asked to see a guest named Lange and was directed to a room on the third floor. They arrived to find a DO NOT DISTURB sign hanging from the latch and Mikhail Abramov standing in the breach of the half-open door.

He looked at Sarah and smiled. "Something wrong?"

"I was just—"

"Expecting to see someone else?"

"Hoping, actually." Sarah looked at Gabriel. "You might have mentioned he was going to be here."

"Mikhail is a professional, and so are you. I'm sure you two can set aside your differences and play nicely together."

"Like Israel and the Palestinians?"

"Anything's possible."

Gabriel slipped past them and entered the room. The lights were doused, the shades were tightly drawn. The only sources of illumination were the open laptop computer on the writing desk and Mikhail's secure Office BlackBerry.

He drew a thin file from the outside pocket of his overnight bag. "We ran those photographs of the man and woman from Annecy through all the databases last night."

"And?"

"Nothing. Same for the passport."

Gabriel went to the window and peered around the edge of the blinds. "Which building is Villard's?"

"Number twenty-one." Mikhail handed Gabriel a Zeiss monocular. "Third floor, right side of the building."

Gabriel scanned the two street-facing windows of Lucien Villard's flat. He saw a sparsely furnished bachelor's sitting room but no sign of Villard himself. "Are you sure he's there?"

Mikhail raised the volume on the laptop. A few seconds later Gabriel heard the opening phrase of Coltrane's "I Want to Talk About You."

"What's the source of the audio?"

"His mobile phone. The Unit got the number from the school's internal directory. By the time I'd landed this morning, the phone was hot and we were reading his e-mails and texts."

"Anything interesting?"

"He's leaving for Marrakesh tomorrow afternoon."

Gabriel aimed the monocular at Mikhail. "Is he really?"

"He's booked on Lufthansa with a brief stopover in Munich. First class all the way."

Gabriel lowered the glass. "When is he coming back?"

"The ticket is open ended. He hasn't booked the return yet."

"Now that he's no longer working, I suppose he has a lot of time on his hands."

"And Morocco is lovely this time of year."

"I remember," said Gabriel distantly. "Was the Unit able to see his file?"

"They grabbed a copy on their way out the door."

"Was there any mention of the fact he was run out of the SDLP for having an affair with the wife of the French president?"

"He seems to have neglected to mention it when he interviewed for the job."

"Any black marks?"

Mikhail shook his head.

"How much were they paying him?"

"Enough to rent a flat in a chic Geneva neighborhood, but not enough for the little things."

"Like a long trip to Morocco?"

"Don't forget the first-class air travel."

"I haven't." Lucien Villard's music filled the silence. "What about his private life?"

"He was married once a hundred years ago."

"Kids?"

"A daughter. They exchange the odd e-mail."

"Nice."

"I'd reserve judgment until you read the e-mails."

Gabriel raised the monocular to his eye again and trained it on Villard's apartment. "Is there a woman over there?"

"If there is, she isn't awake yet. But he's having drinks with someone named Isabelle Jeanneret at five o'clock."

"Who is she?"

"For now, she's an e-mail address. The Unit is working on it."

"Where are they meeting?"

"Café Remor on the Place du Cirque."

"Who chose the venue?"

"She did." A silence fell between them. Then Mikhail asked, "You think he knows something?"

"We wouldn't be here otherwise."

"How do you intend to play it?"

"I'd like to have a word with him in private."

"A friendly word?"

"That depends entirely on Lucien."

"When are we going to make our move?"

"After he's finished having drinks with Madame Jeanneret at Café Remor. You and Sarah will be sitting at the next table." Gabriel smiled. "Just like old times."

The Coltrane piece ended, and the next began.

"What's that one called?" asked Sarah.

" 'You Say You Care.' "

Sarah shook her head slowly. "Couldn't you have found someone else to send to Geneva?"

"He volunteered."

They saw Villard for the first time at half past one, standing in the window of his sitting room, stripped to the waist, his compromised mobile phone to his ear. He was speaking in French to a woman whom the device identified only as Monique. They were obviously well acquainted. Indeed, for some ten minutes, the woman explained in excruciating detail all the things she would do to Villard's body if only he would agree to see her that evening. Villard, citing a scheduling conflict, declined. He made no mention of the fact he was having drinks with someone named Isabelle Jeanneret at five o'clock. Nor did he make reference to his pending trip to Marrakesh. Gabriel found much to admire in the performance. Lucien Villard, he surmised, was a man who lied often and well.

The woman ended the call abruptly, and Villard disappeared from their view. They glimpsed him occasionally when he passed within range of the phone's camera, but mainly they listened to drawers opening and closing—a sound that Gabriel, a veteran of many surveillance operations, associated with the packing of a suitcase. There were two, actually, a duffel bag and a rolling rectangular behemoth the size of a steamer trunk. Villard left them both in the entrance hall before heading downstairs.

When they saw him next he was stepping into the busy street, dressed in a mid-length leather coat, dark jeans, and suede chukka boots. He paused on the pavement briefly, his eyes moved left and right—perhaps out of habit, thought Gabriel, or perhaps because he feared someone might be watching. A cigarette found its way to his lips, a lighter flared, an exhalation of smoke was carried away by a cold winter's wind. Then he shoved his hands deep into his pockets and set off toward the center of Geneva.

Gabriel remained in the hotel room while Mikhail and Sarah followed Villard on foot. The phone allowed Unit 8200 to track his every move from afar. Mikhail and Sarah served merely as human eyes on the target. They kept to a safe distance, sometimes posing as a couple, sometimes working alone. Consequently, only Sarah observed Villard entering a small private bank off the rue du Rhône. The compromised phone allowed Gabriel to monitor the transaction Villard conducted inside—the transfer of a rather large sum of money to a bank in Marrakesh. Villard then requested access to his safe-deposit box. Because the phone was in his pocket at the time, the camera was effectively blinded. But the sequence of sounds—the squeak of a hinge, the rustle of paper, the zipping of a leather jacket—led Gabriel to conclude that items had been removed from the box rather than added.

Mikhail was drinking coffee in the Starbucks across the street from the bank when Villard finally emerged. The Frenchman checked the time on his wristwatch— it was half past four exactly—and struck out along the rue du Rhône. He followed it to the river and then wound his way through the narrow, quiet streets of the Old Town to the Place de la Synagogue, where Gabriel was sitting behind the wheel of the Passat.

Café Remor was a hundred meters farther along the boulevard Georges-Favon. There were several unoc-cupied tables on the Place du Cirque, and several more beneath the shelter of the awning. Villard sat down outside along the square. Mikhail joined Sarah under the awning. A gas heater burned the evening chill from the air.

Sarah raised a glass of red wine to her lips. "How did I do?"

"Not bad," said Mikhail. "Not bad at all."

For ten minutes no one appeared. Villard smoked two cigarettes, lighting the second with the first, and cast several glances toward his mobile phone, which was lying on the tabletop. Finally, at five fifteen, he signaled a passing waiter and ordered. A single bottle of Kronenbourg arrived a moment later.

"Looks like she stood him up," said Mikhail. "If I were him, I'd call Monique before it's too late."

But Sarah wasn't listening; she was watching a man walking toward the café along the boulevard. In dress and aspect, he looked to be a Swiss banker or businessman, late forties or early fifties, on his way home after a prosperous day at the office. His costly overcoat was tan, and the leather attaché case he carried in his left hand was the color of oxblood. He placed it on the pavement next to Lucien Villard before sitting down at an adjacent table.

Quietly, Mikhail asked, "Think it's a coincidence he chose to sit next to our boy when there are several other tables available?"

"No," answered Sarah. "It isn't."

"His face looks familiar."

"It should."

"Where have I seen it before?"

"At Brasserie Saint-Maurice in Annecy."

Mikhail stared at Sarah, perplexed.

"It's the face you ran through the databases at King Saul Boulevard last night."

Mikhail drew his BlackBerry and dialed. "You'll never guess who just walked into Café Remor."

"I know," said Gabriel. "I'm right across the street."

19

Geneva

The space where Gabriel was parked in the Place du Cirque was by no means legal. Neither was the 9mm Beretta pistol with a walnut grip that lay on the passenger seat beneath a copy of that morning's *Le Temps.* Gabriel had placed the gun there after spotting the man in the tan overcoat walking along the boulevard. His dress was more businesslike, his hair was arranged in a different manner, he was wearing dark-rimmed eyeglasses. Nevertheless, there was no mistaking him for anyone else. Having spent a lifetime repairing Old Master canvases, Gabriel had developed a near-perfect ability to spot familiar faces, even faces that had been heavily disguised. The man now seated next to Lucien Villard had been at Brasserie

Saint-Maurice in Annecy the day of Princess Reema's abduction.

Gabriel considered attempting to take the man into custody but rejected the idea at once. The man was a professional and no doubt heavily armed. His surrender would not be amicable. It was likely bullets would fly in a busy square in the heart of Geneva.

It was a risk Gabriel was not prepared to take. The code of the Office forbade the use of deadly force in crowded urban settings unless the officer in question was in danger of losing his life or his liberty, especially to a hostile power. Such was not the case now. Gabriel and Mikhail could follow the man after he left Café Remor and take him into their possession at a time and place of their choosing. They would then encourage the man to reveal Princess Reema's whereabouts, either through persuasion or force. Or perhaps, if fortune was in their favor, he might lead them directly to the princess. Better to wait, Gabriel reckoned, than to act rashly and risk losing the opportunity to save the child's life.

From his vantage point, he could see the man in the tan overcoat had yet to order. His pose was identical to the one he had adopted at Brasserie Saint-Maurice— legs casually crossed, right elbow on the table, left hand resting on his thigh, within easy reach of his gun. The attaché case he had carried into the café was standing upright on the pavement between his table and Villard's. It was an odd place to leave it. Unless, thought Gabriel, he had no intention of taking it with him when he departed.

But why was the man in the tan overcoat sitting in a café next to the former director of security at the International School of Geneva? Villard's compromised phone lay on the tabletop before him. Unit 8200 had routed the feed securely to Gabriel's BlackBerry. The audio quality was crystalline—Gabriel could hear the clinking of cutlery and glass in the café and the chatter of pedestrians as they passed along the pavement—but there was a transmission delay of several seconds. It was like watching an old movie where sound and picture were not in sync. The two central characters in this film had yet to speak. It was possible, thought Gabriel, they never would.

Just then, there was a knock at his window, two firm raps of a policeman's knuckle, followed by a curt wave of a gloved hand. Gabriel raised his own hand in a gesture of apology and eased away from the curb, into the swiftly flowing evening traffic. He made a series of rapid turns—right into the avenue du Mail, left on the rue Harry-Marc, left again on the boulevard Georges-Favon—and returned to the Place du Cirque.

A red traffic light gave him an excuse to loiter. Several pedestrians flowed through the crosswalk directly in front of him. One was a prosperous-looking man in a tan overcoat. A few paces behind him was Mikhail Abramov. Sarah was still at Café Remor. Her eyes were fixed on Lucien Villard, who was reaching toward the briefcase standing upright on the pavement.

He noticed him for the first time, the long-limbed man with pale skin and colorless eyes, sitting next to the attractive blonde at Café Remor. And now here he was again, the same man, following him through the darkness along the rue de la Corraterie. A car was following him, too—the same car that had been parked illegally in the Place du Cirque. He had seen nothing of the driver other than a smudge of gray at the temples.

But how had they found him? He was confident he had not been followed to Café Remor. Therefore, the logical explanation was that it was Villard, not him, who was under surveillance. It was no matter; Villard knew next to nothing. And in a very few minutes, he would no longer be a threat.

He removed his phone from his coat pocket and dialed a preloaded number. The conversation was brief, coded. When it was over he killed the connection and paused in a shop window. Glancing to his left, he saw the man with pale skin—and farther along the street, the car.

He waited for a tram to pass, crossed to the opposite side of the street, and went into a small movie house. The feature had just begun. He purchased a ticket and entered the darkened, half-empty theater. On the left side of the screen was the emergency exit. The alarm chirped loudly as he leaned on the panic latch and went once more into the night.

He found himself in a courtyard surrounded by a high wall. He scaled it effortlessly, dropped onto a cobbled street, and followed it through a passageway into the Old Town. A Piaggio motor scooter was parked outside an antiquarian bookshop, a leathered, helmeted figure perched atop the saddle. He climbed onto the back and wrapped his arms around a slender waist.

The fire alarm was still howling when Mikhail barged through the entrance of the cinema. He did not bother with the ruse of a ticket, and it took him two attempts to scale the wall of the rear courtyard. The street onto which he toppled was empty of traffic and pedestrians. Rising, he sprinted pell-mell along the cobbles until he reached a quaint square in the heart of the Old Town. There he saw the man in the tan overcoat climbing onto the back of a motorbike. Mikhail briefly considered drawing his weapon and taking the shot. Instead, he jogged back to the rue de la Corraterie, where Gabriel was waiting.

"Where is he?"

Mikhail explained about the motorbike.

"Did you see the driver?"

"She was wearing a helmet."

"It was a woman? Are you sure?"

Mikhail nodded. "Where's Villard?"

"He's leaving Café Remor now."

"Followed by an unarmed museum curator with limited training in street surveillance techniques."

Gabriel put his foot to the floor and swung a U-turn in front of an approaching streetcar.

"You're going the wrong way on a one-way street."

"If I go the right way, it will take us ten minutes to get back to the Place du Cirque."

Mikhail drummed his fingers nervously on the center console. "What do you suppose is in the briefcase?"

"I hope it's money."

"I hope so, too."

Sarah's first mistake was that she failed to pay the check in advance, a cardinal sin of the watcher's trade. By the time she managed to catch the waiter's indifferent eye, Lucien Villard had left the Place du Cirque and was a long way up the boulevard Georges-Favon. Fearful of losing him in the evening crowds, Sarah hastened too quickly after her quarry, which was how she made her second.

It happened at the intersection of the rue du Stand. Villard was about to cross the street, but when the light changed to red, he stopped abruptly and removed a packet of cigarettes. The breeze was from the Rhône, which was directly before him. Turning, he spotted Sarah gazing into the window of a wineshop, about thirty meters away. He stared at her unabashedly for a long moment, the cigarette between his lips, the lighter in his right hand, the briefcase in his left. The briefcase that had been given to him by the man in the tan overcoat.

All at once Villard flicked the cigarette to the pavement and took two violent steps toward Sarah. It was then she saw the flash of brilliant white light and felt a hurricane-force gust of superheated air rush over her. It lifted her from her feet and hurled her to the pavement. She lay very still, unable to move or breathe, wondering whether she was alive or already dead. She was aware only of shattered glass and human limbs and viscera. And blood. It was all around her, the blood. Some of it, she feared, was her own. And some of it was dripping on her from the bare limbs of the tree under which she had come to rest.

At last, she heard someone calling her name, with the emphasis on the second syllable rather than the first. She saw a woman limping slowly across a sun-drowned esplanade by the sea, her face shrouded in a black veil. Then the woman was gone, and a man took her place. His eyes were blue-gray, like glacial ice, and he was shouting at the top of his voice.

"Sarah! Sarah! Can you hear me, Sarah?"

PART TWO

Abdication

20

Geneva—Lyon

The bomb had been small, just five kilograms of military-grade high explosive, but of expert construction. It had been contained not in a car or truck but a briefcase. The man who was holding it when it detonated was reduced largely to a collection of organs and extremities, including a hand that landed on the windshield of a car traveling along the boulevard Georges-Favon. A billfold was found inside the remnants of a leather coat, which was wrapped around the remnants of a human torso. All belonged to one Lucien Villard, a veteran of the French Service de la Protection who until recently had held the position of chief of security at the International School of Geneva. Two other people, a man of twenty-eight and a woman of thirty-three, were killed in the explosion. Both had been standing directly next to Villard as he waited to cross the rue du Stand. Both were Swiss citizens and residents of the canton of Geneva.

The briefcase was harder to identify, for there was almost nothing left of it. The Swiss Federal Police would obtain closed-circuit video showing Lucien Villard taking possession of the bag at Café Remor. It had been discarded there by a bespectacled man in a tan overcoat. As the man left the café on foot, he was followed by a tallish man with fair skin and hair, and by a second man driving a Passat sedan. The man in the tan overcoat had conducted a brief phone conversation before entering, and then quickly leaving, a movie house on the rue de la Corraterie. Onyx, Switzerland's capable signals intelligence system, would eventually produce an intercept of the call. The recipient was a female, and they had communicated tersely in French. Linguistics analysts would determine that neither came by the language naturally.

As for Lucien Villard, he departed Café Remor with the briefcase at 5:17 p.m., followed by a woman who had been at the café with the tallish man. She was standing a half block from Villard on the boulevard Georges-Favon when the bomb detonated. For several minutes she lay on the pavement, unmoving, as though she were among the dead rather than the living. Then the tallish man appeared and placed her hurriedly into the backseat of the Passat sedan.

The car was of French registry, and it was to France, within minutes of leaving the scene of the explosion, that it returned. Shortly before nine p.m., it entered a parking garage in central Lyon, with much of its rear registration plate smeared by mud. Gabriel concealed the key beneath the left rear wheel well while Mikhail helped Sarah from the backseat. Her steps were unsteady as they crossed the street to the Gare de la Part Dieu.

The night's last train to Paris was boarding. Mikhail quickly purchased three tickets in cash, and together they made their way to the platform. The carriage they entered was nearly empty. Mikhail sat alone in a rear-facing seat at the front; Gabriel and Sarah, on the train's starboard side. Her face was ashen, her hair was damp. Mikhail had washed the blood from it with a couple of liters of Vittel before dressing her in clean clothing. Fortunately, the blood was not Sarah's. It was the blood of Lucien Villard.

She examined her reflection in the window. "Not a mark. How do you explain that?"

"The bomb was designed to limit collateral casualties."

"Did you see the explosion?"

Gabriel shook his head. "We only heard it."

"I saw it. At least I think I did. All I remember is the look on Lucien Villard's face as he was being ripped to pieces. It was like he was . . ."

"A suicide bomber?"

Sarah nodded slowly. "Have you ever seen one before?"

"A suicide bomber? I've lost count."

Sarah winced suddenly. "I feel like I've been run over by a truck. I think I might have broken a rib or two."

"We'll have a doctor take a look at you before your flight."

"What flight?"

"The flight that's going to take you from Paris back to New York."

"I'm not going anywhere."

Gabriel didn't bother to respond. The face in the glass was contorted with pain.

"The evening didn't go exactly as planned," said Sarah. "Lucien Villard got blown to bits. And one of Reema's kidnappers slipped through our fingers."

"I'm afraid that sums it up rather nicely."

"He walked straight into our arms, and we let him get away."

"Mikhail and I were the ones who lost him, not you."

"Maybe we should have taken him at the café."

"Or maybe we should have put a bullet in him while he was walking along that quiet street near the movie house. A bullet tends to make even the hardest of men talkative."

"I remember that, too." Sarah watched an ugly banlieue slide past her window. "I guess we know how the kidnappers learned that Khalid's daughter was enrolled at that school."

"I doubt they needed Villard to tell them that."

"So what did he do for them?"

"That," said Gabriel, "would require speculation on my part."

"It's a long way to Paris. Speculate away."

"Close observation of the target," said Gabriel after a moment.

"Go on."

"They couldn't do it themselves because they knew the Swiss services were watching her. So they hired someone to do the job for them. Someone who was supposed to be looking after her safety."

"Did he know who he was working for?"

"I doubt it."

"Then why kill him?"

"I suppose they wanted to eliminate anyone who could implicate them. Or it's possible Lucien might have done something foolish."

"Like what?"

"Maybe he threatened them. Or maybe he asked for more money."

"He must have thought there was money in the briefcase. Why else would he have taken it?" Sarah looked at Mikhail, who was watching them from the front of the carriage. "You should have seen his face when he thought I might be dead."

"I did see it."

"I know he's in love with what's-her-name, but he still cares about me." She leaned her head against Gabriel's shoulder. "What are we going to do now?"

"You're going home, Sarah."

"I am home," she said, and closed her eyes.

21

Later that same evening, as a train bearing the chief of Israeli intelligence approached the Gare de Lyon in Paris, three hooded figures roused Princess Reema bint Khalid Abdulaziz Al Saud from a tormented sleep. They were clearly agitated, which surprised her. Since the incident involving the notepad, Reema's interactions with her captors had been formal and silent but without undue rancor. All three of the hooded figures were men. In fact, it had been some time since she had seen the woman. Reema could not say for certain how long it had been. She measured the passage of the hours and days not with a clock or calendar but by the rhythm of her meals and her supervised visits to the toilet.

One of the men was holding a hairbrush and a small paddle-shaped mirror. He also had a note. He wanted

Reema to improve her appearance—for what reason, he did not say. The first glimpse of the creature in the looking glass shocked her. She scarcely recognized the pale, gaunt face. Her raven hair was a tangled, filthy mess.

The man withdrew while Reema, holding the mirror before her, forced the brush through the thicket of her hair. He returned a moment later with a copy of a London newspaper and a bright red instant camera. It looked like a toy, not something a ruthless criminal might wield. He handed Reema the newspaper—it was that morning's edition of the *Telegraph*—and with crude hand gestures instructed her to hold it beneath her chin. For her photograph she adopted a *juhaymin*, the traditional "angry face" of the Arabian Bedouin. With her eyes, however, she pleaded with her father to end her suffering.

The camera flashed and a few seconds later ejected the photograph. Then the man took a second photo, which he preferred to the first. He kept both as he and the other two men prepared to take their leave.

"May I have it?"

The eyes behind the mask gazed at her quizzically.

"The one you're not going to send to my father to prove I'm still alive."

The eyes appeared to weigh her request carefully.

Then the unwanted photo came spinning through the air, curving gently before landing on the cot next to Reema. The door closed, the deadbolts snapped. The light in the ceiling burned on.

Reema picked up the snapshot. It was, she thought, quite good. She looked older than twelve, slightly drunk or drugged, a little sexy, like the models in *Vogue* and *Glamour*. She doubted her father would see it the same way.

She stretched her body on her cot, supine, and stared into the eyes of the girl in the photograph. "You're dead," she whispered. "Dead, dead, dead."

22

Paris—London

The safe flat was located in a small apartment building at the edge of the Bois de Boulogne. Mikhail
and Sarah each claimed a bedroom, leaving the dav-
enport in the sitting room—the bed of nails, as it was
known inside the Office—to Gabriel. Consequently,
like Princess Reema, he did not sleep well that night.

He rose early, dressed, and went into the cold, nick-
eled light of morning. A two-man security team from
the embassy waited curbside in a Renault sedan with
diplomatic plates. They drove along quiet streets to the
Gare du Nord, where Gabriel boarded an eight fifteen
Eurostar bound for London. His seat was in business
class. Surrounded by merchants and financiers, he read
the morning papers. They were filled with misleading
accounts of the mysterious bombing in Geneva involv-

ing the former head of security from an elite private school for the children of diplomats.

As the train approached the Channel Tunnel, Gabriel dispatched an encrypted text message, informing the recipient of his imminent arrival in the British capital. The reply was a long time in coming and inhospitable in tone. It contained no greeting or salutation, only an address. Gabriel assumed it was the address of a safe house. Or perhaps not. The British didn't have any safe houses, he thought. At least none Moscow Center didn't know about.

It was half past nine when the train drew into London's St. Pancras International. Gabriel expected to be met on arrival, but as he crossed the gleaming ticket hall he saw no evidence of a British reception committee. He should have immediately called London Station and requested a driver and escort. Instead, he spent the next two hours wandering the streets of the West End, searching for evidence he was being followed. It was a violation of Office protocol but in Gabriel's case not without precedent. The last time he ventured into public alone he had encountered Rebecca Manning, MI6's traitorous Washington Head of Station, and a heavily armed Russian extraction team. The Russians had not survived. Rebecca Manning, for better or worse, had lived.

The Russian Embassy in London, with its generously staffed SVR *rezidentura*, occupied a valuable plot of land near Kensington Palace. Gabriel walked past it along Bayswater Road and made his way to Notting Hill. St. Luke's Mews lay at the northern fringe of the fashionable neighborhood, near the Westway. Number 7, like all the other cottages along the street, was a converted garage. The exterior was a gray scale— light gray for the brickwork, dark gray for the trim and the door. The knocker was a large silver ring. Gabriel banged it twice. And when he received no answer, he banged it again.

At length, the door opened and Nigel Whitcombe admitted him. Whitcombe had recently turned forty, but he still looked like an adolescent who had been stretched and molded into manhood. Gabriel had known him since he was a probationer at MI5. Now he was the personal aide-de-camp and primary runner of off-the-record errands for the director-general of the Secret Intelligence Service, or MI6.

"I'm well," said Gabriel pointedly after Whitcombe had closed the door. "How are you, Nigel?"

"Davies," he answered. "We don't use real names in safe flats, only work names."

"And who am I today?"

"Mudd," said Whitcombe.

"Catchy."

"You should have heard the one we rejected."

"I can only imagine." Gabriel looked around the interior of the tiny house. It was recently renovated and freshly painted, but largely unfurnished.

"We took possession of it only last week," explained Whitcombe. "You're the first guest."

"I'm honored."

"Trust me, that wasn't our intention. We're in the process of liquidating our entire inventory of safe houses. And not just in London. Worldwide."

"But I wasn't the one who betrayed them to the Russians. Rebecca Manning did that."

A moment passed. Then Whitcombe said, "We go back a long way, Mr. Mudd."

"If you call me that again—"

"All the way back to the Kharkov operation. And you know I have nothing but the utmost respect for you."

"But?"

"It would have been better if you'd let her defect."

"Nothing would have changed, Nigel. There still would have been a scandal, and you still would have been forced to dump all your safe houses."

"It's not just the safe properties. It's everything. Our networks, our station heads, our ciphers and encryption. For all intents and purposes, we are no longer in the business of espionage."

"That's what happens when the Russians plant a mole at the highest level of an intelligence service. But at least you get new safe houses," said Gabriel. "This is much better than that dump in Stockwell."

"That's gone, too. We're selling and acquiring properties so quickly we've actually had an impact on the London real estate market."

"I have a lovely flat in Bayswater I'm looking to unload."

"That place overlooking the park? Everyone in the business knows it's an Office safe flat." Whitcombe smiled for the first time. "Forgive me, the last few months have been a nightmare. Rebecca must be enjoying the show from her new office in Moscow Center."

"How's 'C' holding up?"

"I'll let him answer that."

Through the front window Gabriel glimpsed Graham Seymour hauling himself from the backseat of a Jaguar limousine. He seemed out of place in the trendy little mews, like a wealthy older man calling on his young bohemian mistress. Seymour always had that air about him. With his camera-ready features and plentiful pewter-colored locks, he looked like one of those male models one saw in advertisements for costly trinkets like fountain pens and Swiss watches. Entering the cottage, he surveyed the sitting room as though he were trying to hide his enthusiasm from an estate agent.

"How much did we pay for this place?" he asked Whitcombe.

"Almost two million, chief."

"I remember the days when a bedsit in Chiswick would do. Have the housekeepers stocked the pantry?"

"I'm afraid not."

"There's a Tesco around the corner. Tea and milk and a tin of biscuits. And take your time, Nigel." The front door opened and closed. Seymour removed his Crombie overcoat and tossed it over the back of a chair. It looked as though it had come from Ikea. "I suppose there wasn't much left over for decoration. Not with a two-million-pound price tag."

"It's better not to cram too much furniture into small places like these."

"I wouldn't know." Seymour lived in a grand Georgian house in Eaton Square with a wife named Helen who cooked enthusiastically but quite badly. The money came from Helen's family. Seymour's father had been a legendary MI6 officer who had plied his trade mainly in the Middle East. "I hear you've been a busy boy."

"Have I?"

Seymour smiled without parting his lips. "GCHQ

picked up an unusual burst of radio and telephone traffic in Tehran a few nights ago." GCHQ, the Government Communications Headquarters, was Britain's signals intelligence service. "Frankly, it sounded as though the place was going up in flames."

"What was it?"

"Someone broke into a warehouse and stole a couple of tons of files and computer disks. Apparently, these documents represent the entire archives of Iran's nuclear weapons program."

"Imagine that."

Another smile, longer than the last. "As your partner in numerous operations against the Iranian nuclear program, including one code-named Masterpiece, we would like to see those documents."

"I'm sure you would."

"*Before* you show them to the Americans."

"How do you know we haven't already shared them with Langley?"

"Because you haven't had enough time to analyze a treasure trove like that. And if you'd given any of the material to the Americans, they would have given it to me."

"I wouldn't be so sure about that. The Americans have the same concerns about your service as we do. And with good reason. After all, Rebecca spent the final months of her MI6 career stealing every American secret she could lay her hands on."

Seymour's expression darkened, as though a shadow had fallen across his face. "Rebecca is gone."

"No, she isn't, Graham. She's working in the United Kingdom Department at Moscow Center. And you're dead in the water because you're not sure whether she has another agent inside MI6."

"Which is why I need a nice, juicy secret to prove I'm still in the game."

"Then perhaps you should go out and steal one."

"We're too busy tearing ourselves to pieces to commit an act of honest-to-goodness espionage. We're totally paralyzed."

"Just like you were after—"

"Yes," said Seymour, cutting Gabriel off. "The parallels between then and now are striking. It took years for us to get back on our feet after Philby brought us down. I'm determined not to let that happen again."

"And you'd like my help."

Seymour said nothing.

"How can I be sure the Iranian documents won't end up on Rebecca's desk at Moscow Center?"

"They won't," intoned Seymour gravely.

"And if I give them to you? What do I get in return?"

"A truce in our internecine conflict and a gradual return to business as usual."

"How about something more tangible?"

"All right," said Seymour. "If you give me those documents, I'll help you find KBM's daughter before he's forced to abdicate."

"How did you find out?"

Seymour shrugged. "Sources and methods."

"Do the Americans know?"

"I spoke to Morris Payne last night on another matter." Payne was the CIA director. "He knows Khalid's daughter has been kidnapped, but he seems unaware of your involvement." Seymour added suddenly, "He's in town, you know."

"Morris?"

"Khalid. He flew into London yesterday afternoon." Seymour regarded Gabriel carefully. "I'm surprised, given the closeness of your newfound relationship, he didn't tell you he was coming."

"He didn't mention it."

"And you're not tracking that mobile phone of his?"

"It went dark. We assume he got a new one."

"GCHQ concur."

"What brought him to town?"

"He had dinner last night with his beloved uncle Abdullah. He's the current king's younger brother."

"Half brother," said Gabriel. "There's a big difference."

"Which is why Abdullah spends most of his time here in London. In fact, we're practically neighbors. Abdullah initially opposed Khalid's rise, but he fell in line after Khalid threatened to bankrupt him and put him under house arrest. He's now one of KBM's closest advisers." Seymour frowned. "One can only imagine the sort of things they talk about. Despite his fancy London address, Abdullah isn't terribly fond of the West."

"Or Israel," added Gabriel.

"Quite. But he's an influential figure inside the House of Saud, and Khalid needs his support."

"Is he an MI6 asset?"

"Abdullah? Wherever would you get an idea like that?" Seymour sat down. "I'm afraid you've got yourself mixed up in a real game of thrones. If you had any sense, you'd walk away and let the Al Saud fight it out amongst themselves."

"The Middle East is too dangerous a place to allow instability in Saudi Arabia."

"We agree. Which is why we've been willing to overlook KBM's obvious shortcomings, including his murder of Omar Nawwaf."

"Why did he do it?"

"One hears rumors," said Seymour vaguely.

"What sort of rumors?"

"That Nawwaf knew something he wasn't supposed to."

"Like what?"

"Why don't you ask your friend? He's staying at the Dorchester under an assumed name." Seymour shook his head reproachfully. "I must say, if my child had been kidnapped, the last place I'd be is a luxury suite at the Dorchester Hotel. I'd be looking for the people who took her."

"That's why he came to me." Gabriel removed a photograph from his attaché case. It showed a man sitting in a French café.

"Who is he?"

"I was hoping you might be able to tell me." Gabriel handed Seymour the photocopy of the passport. "He's rather good. He dropped Mikhail in about five seconds flat in Geneva last night."

Seymour looked up. "Geneva?"

"Could he be one of yours, Graham? A former MI6 officer who's selling his services on the open market?"

"I'll check it out, but I doubt it. In fact, he doesn't look British to me." Seymour scrutinized the image. "You think he's a professional?"

"Definitely."

Seymour returned the photograph and the copy of the passport. "Perhaps you should show those to someone who's familiar with the dark side of the trade."

"Know anyone like that?"

"I might."

"Mind if I pay him a visit?"

"Why not? He has a lot of free time on his hands at the moment." Seymour looked around the half-furnished room. "We all do."

23

Kensington, London

There are some men who walk a straight path to redemption and others, like Christopher Keller, who take the long road. He lived in a luxury maisonette in Queen's Gate Terrace in Kensington. Its many rooms were largely empty of furnishings or decoration, evidence that his affair with Olivia Watson, a former fashion model who owned a successful modern art gallery in St. James's, had ended. Olivia's past was almost as complicated as Keller's. Gabriel was the one common denominator.

"You didn't do something foolish, did you?"

"Let me count the ways." Keller smiled in spite of himself. He had bright blue eyes, sun-bleached hair, and a thick chin with a notch in the center. His mouth seemed permanently fixed in an ironic smile.

"What happened?"

"Olivia happened."

"Meaning?"

"In case you haven't noticed, she's become quite the star of the London art world. Lots of glamorous photos in the papers. Lots of speculation about her mysterious love life. It got to the point where I couldn't go out in public with her anymore."

"Which understandably caused tension in your relationship."

"Olivia isn't exactly the stay-at-home type."

"Neither are you, Christopher."

A veteran of the elite Special Air Service, Keller had served under deep cover in Northern Ireland and fought in the first Gulf War. He had also performed services for a certain notable Corsican crime figure that might loosely be described as murder for hire. But all that was behind him. Thanks to Gabriel, Christopher Keller was a respectable officer of Her Majesty's Secret Intelligence Service. He was restored.

He filled the electric teakettle with bottled water and flipped the power switch. The kitchen was on the ground floor of the old Georgian house. It looked like something from a design magazine. The granite counters were vast and tastefully lit, the gas stove was a Vulcan, the refrigerator was a stainless-steel Sub-Zero, and the island where Gabriel sat atop a tall stool had a sink and wine cooler. Through the windows he glimpsed the lower legs of pedestrians rushing along the pavement through the rain. It was only half past three but nearly dark. Gabriel had endured many English winters— he had once lived in a cottage by the sea in far West Cornwall—but rainy December afternoons in London always depressed him.

Keller opened a cabinet and reached for a box of Twinings—with his left arm, noted Gabriel, not his right.

"How is it?"

Keller placed a hand on his right clavicle. "That bullet did more damage than I thought. It's taken a long time to heal."

"That's what happens when we get old."

"You obviously speak from experience. Frankly, it's all rather embarrassing. It seems I'm the only officer in MI6 history to have been shot by a colleague."

"Rebecca wasn't a colleague, she was a full colonel in the SVR. She told me she never thought of herself as an MI6 officer. She was a straight agent of penetration."

"Just like her father." Keller took down the box of tea and closed the cabinet without a sound. "I was beginning to think I was never going to see you again, not after the way things ended in Washington. Needless to say, I was pleasantly surprised when Graham gave me permission to renew our friendship."

"How much did he tell you?"

"Only that you've got yourself mixed up with Prince Chop Chop."

"He's a valuable asset in a troubled region."

"Spoken like a true espiocrat. Once upon a time, you wouldn't have soiled your hands with someone like him."

"Did Graham tell you there was a child involved?"

Keller nodded. "He said you had a photo you wanted me to take a look at."

Gabriel laid it on the countertop. A man sitting in a café, a woman at the next table.

"Where was it taken?"

Gabriel answered.

"Annecy? I remember it fondly."

"Do you recognize him?"

"Can't say I do."

"How about this one?"

Gabriel handed Keller the passport photo. "We Englishmen come in all shapes and sizes, but I doubt he's one of us."

Just then, Gabriel's BlackBerry pulsed with an incoming message.

"Judging from the expression on your face," said Keller, "it isn't good news."

"The kidnappers just gave Khalid until midnight tomorrow to abdicate."

The BlackBerry shivered with another text. This time, Gabriel smiled.

"What is it?"

"A way out."

"What does that mean?"

"I'll explain on the way."

"Where are we going?"

Gabriel rose abruptly. "The Dorchester Hotel."

24

Mayfair, London

Gabriel reflexively gripped the leather armrest of Keller's flashy Bentley Continental as they shot past Harrods in a blur. They plunged into the underpass beneath Hyde Park Corner and emerged a moment later in Piccadilly. Keller navigated the labyrinthine streets of Mayfair with the adroitness of a London cabbie and stopped with a lurch outside the Dorchester's entrance. It was lit up like a Christmas tree.

"Wait here," said Keller.

"Where else would I go?"

"Are you armed?"

"Only with a quick wit and abundant charm."

Keller dug an old Walther PPK from the pocket of his overcoat and gave it to Gabriel.

"Thank you, Mr. Bond."

"It's easy to conceal and packs quite a punch."

"A brick through a plate-glass window." Gabriel slipped the gun into the waistband of his trousers at the small of his back. "He's registered under the name al-Jubeir."

"Who am I?"

"Mr. Allenby."

"Like the bridge?"

"Yes, Christopher, like the bridge."

"What happens if he refuses to come without a security detail?"

"Tell him it's the only way to get his daughter back. That should get his attention."

Keller went into the hotel. A couple of well-fed Saudi toughs were eating pistachios in the lobby, but there were no reporters present. Somehow the British press were unaware of the fact that the most reviled man in the world was staying in London's grandest hotel.

The two Saudis eyed Keller warily as he walked over to reception. The face of the pretty woman behind the counter brightened automatically, like a lamp switched on by a motion detector.

"I'm here to see Mr. al-Jubeir. He's expecting me."

"Name, please?"

Keller told her.

The woman lifted a phone to her ear and purred

something agreeable down the line. Then she replaced the receiver and gestured toward the elevator foyer. "One of Mr. al-Jubeir's aides will escort you up to his suite."

Keller walked over to the elevators, watched by the two Saudi goons. Five minutes elapsed before the aide materialized, a sleepy-eyed little man in an immaculate suit and tie.

"I was expecting Allon."

"And I was expecting the crown prince."

"His Royal Highness doesn't meet with underlings."

"If I were you, *habibi*, I'd take me upstairs. Otherwise, I'm going to walk out of here, and you'll have to explain to Prince Bone Saw that you let me get away."

The little Saudi allowed a few seconds to pass before pressing the call button. Khalid was staying in the Terrace Penthouse. He was pacing before the tall windows overlooking Hyde Park, a phone to his ear, as Keller and the little Saudi factotum entered. One of the security men ordered Keller to raise his arms so he could be searched for a weapon. Keller, in rapid Arabic, told the guard to perform an unspeakable sexual act on a camel.

Khalid stopped pacing and lowered the phone. "Who is this man?"

The little aide, to the best of his ability, explained.

"Where is Allon?"

This time it was Keller who answered. The chief of Israeli intelligence, he said, was waiting downstairs in an automobile. He neglected to mention the Walther pistol.

"It's urgent I speak to him at once," said Khalid. "Please ask him to come upstairs."

"I'm afraid that's not possible."

"Why not?"

"Because this is probably the least secure room in all of London."

Khalid spoke a few words in rapid Arabic to the factotum.

"No," said Keller in the same language. "No limousine or bodyguards. You're coming with me. Alone."

"I can't possibly leave here without a security detail."

"You don't need one. Now get your coat, Khalid. We haven't got all night."

"Your Royal Highness," said the crown prince imperiously.

"That's rather a mouthful, isn't it?" Keller smiled. "Why don't you just call me Ned instead."

Khalid never traveled in the West without a fedora and a pair of false dark-rimmed eyeglasses. The crude disguise rendered him almost unrecognizable. Indeed, even the two Saudi toughs in the lobby scarcely looked up from their pistachios as their future king strode across the gleaming marble floor with Keller at his side. Gabriel had moved to the backseat of the Bentley. Keller dropped behind the wheel while Khalid lowered himself into the front passenger seat. A moment later they were racing along Park Lane through the rush-hour traffic.

Khalid glanced over his shoulder at Gabriel. "Does he always drive like this?"

"Only when a life is at stake."

"Where are you taking me?"

"The last place on earth you should be."

Khalid looked approvingly around the interior of the Bentley. "At least you hired a decent car for the ride."

"You like it?"

"Yes, very much."

"Good," said Gabriel. "I can't tell you how happy that makes me."

Keller spent the next half hour tearing around the West End of London—through Knightsbridge and Belgravia and Chelsea and Earl's Court—until Gabriel was certain no one was following them. Only then did he instruct Keller to make his way to Kensington Palace Gardens. A diplomatic enclave, the street was blocked to normal traffic. Keller's Bentley flowed through the checkpoint without scrutiny and turned into the fore-court of a redbrick Victorian building, above which flew the blue-and-white flag of the State of Israel.

Khalid stared out the window in disbelief. "You can't be serious."

With his silence, Gabriel made it clear he was.

"Do you know what will happen if I so much as set foot in there?"

"You'll be murdered by a fifteen-member hit team and chopped into little pieces."

Khalid stared at Gabriel with a look of genuine alarm.

"Just kidding, Khalid. Now get out of the car."

25

Kensington, London

Khalid's simple disguise did not fool the embassy security staff or the ambassador, who happened to be leaving for a diplomatic reception as Israel's legendary spy chief came bursting into the chancellery with the de facto ruler of Saudi Arabia at his side. "I'll explain later," said Gabriel quietly in Hebrew, and the ambassador was heard to mutter, "You're damn right you will."

Downstairs, Gabriel placed Khalid's new mobile phone in a signal-blocking box known as a beehive before opening the station's vaultlike door. Moshe Cohen, the new chief, was waiting on the other side. His eyes settled first on his director-general, then, in astonishment, on the crown prince of Saudi Arabia.

"What in God's name is—"

"His phone is in the beehive," interjected Gabriel in terse Hebrew.

Cohen did not require additional instructions. "How long can you give us?"

"Five minutes."

"Ten would be better."

Khalid did not understand the exchange but was visibly impressed by its tenor. He trailed Gabriel along the station's central corridor to another secure door. The room behind it was small, about eight feet by ten. There were two telephones, a computer, and a wall-mounted video screen. The air was several degrees colder than in the rest of the station. Khalid kept his overcoat on.

"A safe-speech room?"

"We have another name for it."

"What's that?"

Gabriel hesitated. "The Holy of Holies."

It was clear that Khalid, despite his Oxford education, did not understand the reference.

"The Holy of Holies was the inner sanctuary of the Temple of Jerusalem. It was a perfect cube, twenty cubits by twenty cubits by twenty cubits. It contained the Ark of the Covenant, and inside the Ark were the original Ten Commandments that God gave Moses on Sinai."

"Stone tablets?" asked Khalid incredulously.

"God didn't print them on an HP LaserJet."

"And you believe this nonsense?"

"I'm willing to debate the authenticity of the tablets," said Gabriel. "But not the rest of it."

"The so-called Temple of Solomon never existed. It is a lie used by Zionists to justify the Jewish conquest of Arab Palestine."

"The Temple was described in great detail in the Torah long before the advent of Zionism."

"That doesn't change the fact that it is untrue." Khalid was clearly enjoying the debate. "I remember a few years ago when your government claimed to have found the pillars of the so-called Temple."

"I remember it, too," said Gabriel.

"They were placed in the Israel Museum, were they not?" Khalid shook his head disdainfully. "That exhibit is a piece of crude propaganda designed to justify your existence on Muslim lands."

"My wife designed that exhibit."

"Did she?"

"And I was the one who discovered the pillars."

This time, Khalid offered no objection.

"The Waqf had hidden them in a chamber one hundred and sixty-seven feet beneath the surface of the Temple Mount." The Waqf was the Islamic religious authority that administered the Dome of the Rock and the al-Aqsa Mosque. "They assumed no one would ever find them. They were mistaken."

"Another lie," said Khalid.

"Come to Israel," suggested Gabriel. "I'll take you to the chamber."

"Me? Visit Israel?"

"Why not?"

"Can you imagine the reaction?"

"Yes, I can."

"I must admit, it would be a great privilege to pray in the Noble Sanctuary." The Noble Sanctuary was how Muslims referred to the Temple Mount.

"We can do that, too."

Khalid sat down along one side of the small conference table and glanced around the interior of the room. "How fortunate we were both in London at the same time."

"Yes," agreed Gabriel. "I'm searching desperately for your daughter, and you're having dinner with Uncle Abdullah and staying in the most expensive suite at the Dorchester."

"How did you know I saw my uncle?"

Ignoring the question, Gabriel held out a hand and asked to see the demand letter. Khalid placed it on the table. It was a photocopy. The original, he said, had been delivered to the Saudi Embassy in Paris. The typeface and margins were identical to those of the first letter. So was the flat, matter-of-fact wording. Khalid had until midnight the following evening to abdicate. If he refused, he would never see his daughter again.

"Was there any proof of life?"

Khalid handed over a copy of the photograph. The child was holding the previous day's edition of the *Telegraph* and staring directly into the lens of the camera. She had her father's eyes. She looked exhausted and unkempt, but not at all frightened.

Gabriel returned the photograph. "No father should ever have to see a picture like that."

"Perhaps I deserve it."

"Perhaps you do." Gabriel laid a photograph of his own on the table. A man sitting in a café in Annecy. "Do you recognize him?"

"No."

"What about this man?" Gabriel laid a second photo on the table. It was the DGSI surveillance shot of Rafiq al-Madani sitting next to Khalid aboard *Tranquillity*.

"Where did you get this?"

"The *Tatler*." Gabriel withdrew the photo. "Is he a friend of yours?"

"I don't have friends. I have subjects, houseguests, and family."

"Into which category does al-Madani fall?"

"He is a temporary ally."

"I thought you were going to shut down the flow of money to the jihadis and the Salafists."

Khalid's smile was condescending. "You don't know much about Arabs, do you?" He rubbed his thumb against his fingertips. "Shwaya, shwaya. Slowly, slowly. Little by little."

"Which means you're still funding the extremists with the help of your friend Rafiq al-Madani."

"Which means I have to move carefully and with the support of someone like Rafiq. Someone who has the trust of important clerics. Someone who can provide me with the necessary cover. Otherwise, the House of Saud will crumble, and Arabia will be ruled by the sons of al-Qaeda and ISIS. Is that what you want?"

"You're playing the same old double game."

"I am holding a tiger by the ears. And if I let go, it will devour me."

"It already has." Gabriel called up a message on his BlackBerry. It was the message he had received while sitting in Christopher Keller's kitchen. "It was al-Madani who told you about the second demand letter. He did so at three twelve p.m. London time."

"I see you're monitoring my phone."

"Not yours, al-Madani's. And five minutes after he

called you, he sent an encrypted message to someone else. Because we were seeing his keystrokes, we had no problem reading it."

"What does it say?"

"Enough to make it clear he knows where your daughter is."

"May I see the message?"

Gabriel handed over his phone.

The Saudi swore softly in Arabic. "I'm going to kill him."

"Perhaps you should find out where your daughter is first."

"That's your job."

"My role in this affair is officially over. I'm not going to get myself into the middle of a Saudi family fight."

"You know what they say about family, don't you?"

"What's that?"

"It's the other F-word."

Gabriel smiled in spite of himself.

Khalid returned the BlackBerry. "Perhaps we can come to some sort of business arrangement."

"Save your money, Khalid."

"Will you at least help me?"

"You'd like *me* to interrogate one of your government officials?"

"Of course not. I'll question him myself. It shouldn't take long." Khalid lowered his voice. "After all, I have something of a reputation."

"That's putting it mildly."

"Where shall we interrogate him?" asked Khalid.

"It has to be somewhere isolated. Somewhere the police won't find us." Gabriel paused. "Somewhere the neighbors won't hear a bit of noise."

"I have just the place."

"Can you get him there without making him suspicious?"

Khalid smiled. "All I need is my phone."

26

Haute-Savoie, France

Khalid had a Gulfstream waiting at London City
Airport. They stopped at Paris–Le Bourget long
enough to collect Mikhail and Sarah and then flew on to
Annecy, where a caravan of black Range Rovers waited
on the darkened tarmac. It was a drive of twenty minutes to Khalid's private Versailles. The household staff,
a mixture of French and Saudi nationals, stood like a
choir in the soaring entrance hall. Khalid greeted them
curtly before escorting Gabriel and the others into the
château's main public room—the great hall, as he referred to it. It was long and rectangular, like a basilica,
and hung with a portion of Khalid's collection, including
Salvator Mundi, his dubious Leonardo. Gabriel studied
the panel carefully, a hand to his chin, his head tilted

slightly to one side. Then he crouched and examined the brushstrokes in raked lighting.

"Well?" asked Sarah.

"How could you let him buy this thing?"

"Is it a Leonardo?"

"Maybe a small portion of it, a long time ago. But it isn't a Leonardo anymore."

Khalid joined them. "Magnificent, is it not?"

"I don't know what was dumber," answered Gabriel. "Killing Omar Nawwaf or wasting a half billion dollars on an overrestored workshop devotional piece."

"Workshop? Miss Bancroft assured me it was an authentic Leonardo."

"Miss Bancroft studied art history at the Courtauld and Harvard. I'm confident she did no such thing." Gabriel watched despairingly as one of the servants entered the hall bearing a tray of drinks. "This isn't a party, Khalid."

"That doesn't mean we shouldn't have refreshment after our journey."

"How many staff are there?"

"Twenty-two, I believe."

"How do you possibly manage?"

The irony bounced harmlessly off Khalid. "The senior staff are Saudis," he explained, "but most of my employees are French."

"Most?"

"The gardeners are Moroccans and West Africans." His tone was derogatory. "The Saudis live in a separate house at the northern end of the property. The others live in Annecy or nearby villages."

"Give them all the night off. The drivers, too."

"But—"

"And switch off the security cameras," interjected Gabriel. "The way you did in Istanbul."

"I'm not sure I know how."

"Flip the little switch from on to off. That should do the trick."

Khalid had instructed Rafiq al-Madani to come to the château alone. Al-Madani, however, had promptly disobeyed his future king by requesting a car and driver from the embassy motor pool. They left the eighth arrondissement of Paris at six p.m. and, followed by a team of Office watchers, headed for the A6. Based on their conversation, which Gabriel and Khalid monitored via the compromised phone, it was clear the two men were well acquainted. It was also clear that both were armed.

When they reached the town of Mâcon, Gabriel commandeered one of Khalid's Range Rovers and drove with Sarah into the countryside. The night was cold and clear. He parked on a rise overlooking the intersection of the D14 and the D38, doused the headlamps, and switched off the engine.

"What do we do if a gendarme happens upon us?"

"Office doctrine dictates we pretend to be lovers."

Sarah smiled. "My wildest dream come true."

Gabriel's BlackBerry lay on the console between them. It was emitting the audio feed from al-Madani's phone. At present, it was limited to the drone of a German-made engine and a rhythmic rattling that sounded like the clicking of chess pieces.

"What is that?"

"Prayer beads."

"He sounds worried."

"Wouldn't you be if Khalid sent for you in the middle of the night?"

"He did it all the time."

"And you never suspected he wasn't the great reformer he was made out to be?"

"The Khalid I knew wouldn't have countenanced the murder of Omar Nawwaf. I suppose having all that power changed him. It was thrust upon him too quickly, and it brought out the hamartia in his character. The fatal flaw," added Sarah.

"I know what it means, Dr. Bancroft. Thanks to the

THE NEW GIRL · 195

Office, I never finished my formal education, but I'm not an idiot."

"You're the smartest person I've ever met."

"If I'm so smart, why am I sitting by the side of a French road in the middle of the night?"

"Trying to prevent our tragic hero from destroying himself."

"Maybe I should let it happen."

"You're a restorer, Gabriel. You fix things." From the BlackBerry came the clicking of the prayer beads. "Khalid always told me something like this would happen. He knew they would try to destroy him. He said it would be someone close to him. Someone from inside his family."

"It's not a family, it's a business. And the spoils go to those in power."

"Is that what this is about? Money?"

"We'll find out soon enough."

Al-Madani's phone pinged with an incoming text message. The clicking of the beads fell silent.

"Who do you suppose it's from?"

A moment later Gabriel's phone vibrated. The message was from the operations desk at Unit 8200. "It was Khalid. He was wondering when Rafiq might arrive."

They listened to al-Madani type out a response and

send it to Khalid with a *bloop*. Then al-Madani typed and transmitted a second message. A transcript arrived on Gabriel's phone a few seconds later, along with the number to which it had been sent.

"He just told the kidnappers he's about to meet with Khalid. He promised to send an update as soon as it's over."

"There he is."

Sarah pointed toward a single car, a Mercedes S-Class sedan, moving across the landscape. It passed through the intersection where Khalid's child had been taken— *click-click, click-click, click-click*—and disappeared from view. Gabriel allowed thirty seconds to elapse and then started the Range Rover's engine.

The rattle of the prayer beads grew more insistent as the Mercedes made the final run toward Khalid's château. Rafiq al-Madani murmured an Arabic expression of surprise that the gold-crowned iron gate was open. He was surprised, too, to find none other than Khalid himself waiting outside in the cold of the motor court.

There followed the opening and closing of a well-made car door and the usual Islamic greetings of peace. Next came the sound of footfalls, first on gravel, then marble. Al-Madani remarked about the lack of light in the entrance hall. Khalid explained, somewhat genially, that his four-hundred-million-euro palace had faulty wiring.

The remark elicited from al-Madani a staccato laugh. It would be his last. There was a struggle, very brief, followed by the sound of several blows connecting with a cheekbone and jaw. Later, Gabriel would chastise Keller and Mikhail for using excessive force to neutralize their subject. Both took exception to his characterization. It was Khalid who had administered the terrible beating, they said, not they.

By the time Gabriel turned into the motor court, the compromised phone had been switched off and was no longer emitting a signal. Mikhail was inflicting permanent damage to the right arm of the driver, who had foolishly refused a polite request to hand over his weapon. Inside the château, Keller was duct-taping a semiconscious Rafiq al-Madani to a chair in the great hall. His Royal Highness Prince Khalid bin Mohammed Abdulaziz Al Saud was twirling a set of prayer beads around the first two fingers of his left hand. And in his right hand was a gun.

27

Haute-Savoie, France

I t took Rafiq al-Madani another moment or two to fully appreciate the severity of his circumstances. Slowly, his chin rose from his chest and his eyes cast uncertainly around the enormous room. They settled first on his future regent, who was still fiddling with the prayer beads, and then on Gabriel. They were soft and brown, al-Madani's eyes, like the eyes of a deer. With his elongated face and unruly dark hair, he bore an unfortunate resemblance to Osama bin Laden.

Another moment passed before al-Madani recognized the face of Israel's intelligence chief. The soft brown eyes widened. The Saudi was frightened, observed Gabriel, but not surprised.

Al-Madani looked contemptuously at Khalid and addressed him in Saudi Arabic. "I see you brought along your friend the Jew to do your dirty work. And you wonder why you have so many enemies at home."

Khalid lashed out with the butt of the pistol. Al-Madani glared at Sarah as blood flowed from a gash above his left eye. "Cover your face in my presence, you American bitch!"

Khalid raised the weapon in anger.

"No!" shouted Sarah. "Not again."

When Khalid lowered the gun, al-Madani managed to smile through his pain. "Taking orders from a woman? Soon you'll be dressing like one, too."

Khalid struck him again. Sarah winced at the sound of bone cracking.

"Where is she?" demanded Khalid.

"Who?" asked al-Madani through a mouthful of blood.

"My daughter."

"How should I know?"

"Because you're in contact with the kidnappers." Khalid seized al-Madani's phone from Keller. "Shall I show you the text messages?"

Al-Madani said nothing.

Khalid quickly pressed his advantage. "Why did

you harm my daughter, Rafiq? Why didn't you just kill me instead?"

"I tried, but it couldn't be done. You were too well protected."

The sudden confession surprised even Khalid. "I treated you well, did I not?"

"You treated me like a servant. You used me as a means of keeping the ulema in line while you gave women the right to drive and befriended the Americans and the Jews."

"We have to change, Rafiq."

"Islam is the answer!"

"Islam is the problem, *habibi*."

"You are an apostate," seethed al-Madani.

There was no greater insult in Islam. Khalid endured the charge with admirable restraint. "Who put you up to this, Rafiq?"

"I acted alone."

"You're not smart enough to plan something like this."

Al-Madani managed a contemptuous smile. "Reema might think otherwise."

The blow was sudden and vicious. "Her name is *Princess* Reema." Khalid's face was contorted with rage. "And you, Rafiq, are not fit to lick the bottom of her shoes."

"She is the daughter of an apostate. And if you don't abdicate by midnight tomorrow, she will die."

Khalid held the gun before al-Madani's eyes.

"What are you going to do? Kill me?"

"Yes."

"And if I *do* tell you? What then?" Al-Madani answered his own question. "I'm already dead."

Khalid ground the end of the barrel into the center of al-Madani's forehead.

"Kill me, Your Royal Highness. It's the only thing you're good at."

Khalid laid his finger on the trigger.

"Don't do it," said Gabriel calmly.

Khalid glanced over his shoulder and saw Gabriel studying the screen of his BlackBerry.

"We located the position of the phone at the other end of those text messages."

"Where is it?"

"A house in the Basque Country of Spain."

Rafiq al-Madani spat a mouthful of blood and mucus in Gabriel's direction. "Jew!"

Gabriel returned the BlackBerry to his pocket. "On second thought," he said, "go ahead and kill him."

After breaking the driver's arm and dislocating his shoulder, Mikhail had forced him into the boot of the

Mercedes S-Class sedan. Now, with Keller's help, he added Rafiq al-Madani. Khalid looked on in approval, the gun in his hand.

He turned to Gabriel. "What shall we do with them?"

"I suppose we could take them to Spain."

"It's a long way to ride in the boot of a car. Perhaps we should leave them in some deserted wood here in the Haute-Savoie."

"It will be a long, cold night."

"The colder the better." Khalid approached the back of the car and stared down at the two men squeezed into the confined space. "Perhaps there's something we can do to make them a bit more comfortable."

"Like what?"

Khalid raised the pistol and emptied the magazine into his two subjects. Then he looked over his shoulder at Gabriel and smiled, unaware of the blood spattered on his face. "You didn't think I was going to kill them in the house, did you? That place cost me a fortune."

Gabriel gazed down at the two bullet-torn bodies. "What are we going to do with them now?"

"Don't worry." Khalid slammed the lid. "I'll take care of it."

28

Auvergne–Rhône–Alpes

"For the record, I was only joking when I said you should kill him."

"Were you? Sometimes it's hard to tell."

They were racing westward along the A89 Autoroute, the chief of the Israeli secret intelligence service and the future king of Saudi Arabia. Gabriel was at the wheel, Khalid was slouched wearily in the passenger seat. Between them, drawing power from the adapter, was Rafiq al-Madani's iPhone. A few minutes earlier, imitating al-Madani's cryptic style, Khalid had sent an update to the kidnappers. The gist of the message was that His Royal Highness was desperate to secure the release of his daughter and was preparing to abdicate. As yet, there had been no reply.

Khalid checked the phone again, then slammed it onto the console.

"Careful, Prince Hothead. Phones break."

"What do you think it means?"

"It means you probably shouldn't have killed Rafiq before we were certain your daughter was really at that address in Spain."

"You were the one who said she was there."

"What I said," replied Gabriel, "was that we located the phone. I would have preferred to test the proposition against a living, breathing witness."

"He all but confirmed it."

"He had a gun pointed at his head at the time."

"I believe he was telling us the truth about the safe house. But the rest was a lie."

"You don't think he organized it by himself?"

"Al-Madani is a small cog. Others are involved in the plot against me."

"Perhaps we should interrogate him again and find out who they are." Gabriel glanced into the rearview mirror. Mikhail, Keller, and Sarah were a couple of hundred meters behind them. "What are you going to do about the bodies?"

"Rest assured, the bodies will disappear."

"Make your gun disappear, too."

"It wasn't mine, it was Rafiq's."

"But it's got your fingerprints all over it." After a silence, Gabriel said, "You shouldn't have killed them, Khalid. I'm now implicated in their murders. Sarah, too."

"No one will ever know."

"But *you* know. And you can hold it over me whenever it suits you."

"It wasn't my intention to compromise you."

"Given your track record for rash behavior, I'm inclined to believe you."

Khalid glanced at the phone again. "Was it my imagination, or was Rafiq not surprised by your presence at my home?"

"You noticed that, too?"

"Someone clearly told him you were involved in the search for Reema."

"A couple hundred members of your royal court saw me in Saudi Arabia the other night."

"I'm afraid I never go anywhere alone."

"You're alone now, Khalid."

"With you, of all people." His smile was brief. "I must say, my art adviser didn't seem shocked by the sight of a little blood."

"She doesn't faze easily, not after what Zizi al-Bakari did to her."

"What happened, exactly?"

Gabriel decided there was no harm in telling him; it was a long time ago. "When Zizi figured out that Sarah was a CIA agent on loan to the Office, he handed her over to an al-Qaeda cell to be interrogated and executed."

"But you were able to save her."

"And in the process," said Gabriel, "I prevented a Saudi-financed plot to assassinate the pope."

"You've lived quite a life."

"And yet what do I have to show for it? I don't have a palace in the Haute-Savoie."

"Or the second-largest superyacht in the world," Khalid pointed out.

"Or a Leonardo."

"It seems I don't have a Leonardo, either."

"Why do you need all of it?" asked Gabriel.

"It makes me happy."

"Does it really?"

"Not all of us are as lucky as you. You are a man of extraordinary gifts. You don't need toys to make you happy."

"One or two would be nice."

"What do you want? I'll give you anything."

"I want to see you holding your daughter in your arms again."

"Can't you drive any faster?" asked Khalid impatiently.

"No, I can't."

"Then let me drive."

"Not without training wheels."

Khalid gazed at the darkened countryside. "Do you think she'll be there?"

"Yes," said Gabriel with more certainty than he intended.

"And if she's not?"

Gabriel was silent.

"Do you know what my uncle Abdullah told me? He said a daughter can be replaced, but not a king."

The drone of the engine filled the silence. After a moment, Gabriel noticed that Khalid was working a set of prayer beads with the fingers of his left hand. "Are those al-Madani's?"

"I left mine at the Dorchester."

"Surely, there's an Islamic prohibition against using the prayer beads of a man you just murdered."

"No," said Khalid. "Not that I'm aware of."

The courier was waiting at the edge of a moonlit field in the commune of Saint-Sulpice. The nylon sports bag he delivered to Gabriel contained two Uzi Pro compact submachine pistols, a pair of .45-caliber Jerichos, and a Beretta 9mm. Gabriel gave the Uzis and the Jerichos to Mikhail and Keller and kept the Beretta for himself.

"Nothing for me?" asked Khalid when they were moving again.

"You're not going anywhere near that house."

By the time they reached Bordeaux, Gabriel could see a fiery sun rising in his rearview mirror. They headed south along the Bay of Biscay and crossed the Spanish border without a check of their passports. The weather was capricious, golden sunlight one minute, black skies and windblown rain the next.

"Have you spent much time in Spain?" asked Khalid.

"I had occasion to visit Seville recently."

"It was a Muslim city once."

"At the rate things are going, it will be a Muslim city again."

"There were Jews in Seville, too."

"And we all know how that ended."

"One of history's great acts of injustice," said Khalid. "And five centuries later, you did the same thing to the Palestinians."

"Would you like to discuss how many people the Al Saud killed and displaced while establishing control over the Arabian Peninsula?"

"We were not a colonial entity."

"Neither were we."

They were approaching San Sebastián, the resort city the Basques referred to as Donostia. Bilbao was the next major city, but before they reached it Gabriel turned south, into the Basque interior. In a village called Olarra he stopped by the side of the highway long enough for Sarah to join them. She crawled into the backseat, her hair in disarray, her eyes heavy with fatigue. Mikhail and Keller turned onto a side road and vanished from their view.

"I should be with your men," said Khalid.

"You'd only get in their way." Gabriel glanced at Sarah. "Do you still think the secret world is more interesting?"

"Is there coffee in the secret world?"

Villaro, the town the Basques called Areatza, was a few miles farther to the south. It was not a popular tourist destination, but there were several small hotels in the town center and a café on the plaza. Gabriel, in decent Spanish, ordered.

"Is there a language you *don't* speak?" asked Khalid when the waitress was gone.

"Russian."

Through the window of the café Khalid watched the shifting light in the plaza and the little tornadic gusts chasing newsprint around the arcades. "I've never seen a day like this before. So beautiful and so foul at the same time."

Gabriel and Sarah exchanged a glance as three young women, their hair blown by the wind, came in out of the cold. Their leggings were torn, their noses were pierced, they had tattoos on their hands and many bangles and bracelets on their wrists that clattered and clanged as they collapsed into three chairs at a table near the bar. They were known to the waitress, who remarked on their lack of sobriety. They were at the end of their day, thought Gabriel, not the beginning.

"Look at them," said Khalid contemptuously. "They look like witches. I suppose this is what we have to look forward to in Saudi Arabia."

"You should be so lucky."

Al-Madani's iPhone, muted, lay at the center of the table, next to Gabriel's BlackBerry. Khalid was rubbing a thumb over the prayer beads.

"Maybe you should put those things away," said Gabriel.

"They're comforting."

"They make you look like a Saudi prince who's wondering whether he's ever going to see his daughter again."

Khalid slipped the beads into his pocket as their breakfast arrived. "Those girls are looking at me."

"They probably think you're attractive."

"Do they know who I am?"

"Not a chance."

Khalid picked up al-Madani's iPhone. "I don't understand why they never responded."

Just then, Gabriel's BlackBerry flared with an incoming message.

"What does it say?"

"They located the house."

"When are they going in?"

Gabriel returned the BlackBerry to the tabletop as a sudden rain hammered on the paving stones of the plaza.

"Now."

29

Areatza, Spain

Mikhail had studied an ordinary commercial satellite image of the house during the long night of driving. Viewed from overhead, it was a perfect square with a red tile roof—one level or two, he could not tell—set in the middle of a clearing and reached by a long private track. Viewed through the lens of the monocular from the shelter of the wood, it was a modest but well-maintained two-story dwelling with recently painted blue shutters, all of which were tightly closed. There were no vehicles in the drive and no smell of coffee or cooking on the cold, thin air of morning. A large Belgian shepherd, a particularly ill-tempered breed, thrashed at the end of its long tether like a fish on a hook. It was barking inconsolably, a deep sonorous bark that seemed to make the trees vibrate.

"Can you imagine living next door to that?" asked Keller.

"Some people have no manners."

"Why do you suppose it's so upset?"

"Maybe it heard through the grapevine that Gabriel was in town. You know how dogs feel about him."

"He doesn't get on well with canines?"

Mikhail shook his head gravely. "Gasoline and a match." The dog barked without pause. "Why hasn't anyone come out of the house to see what all the fuss is about?"

"Maybe the damn thing barks all the time."

"Or maybe it's the wrong house."

"We're about to find out."

Keller jerked the slide on the Uzi Pro and went silently into the clearing, the gun in his outstretched hand, Mikhail a few paces behind. The dog was now fully alert to their presence and so enraged that Keller feared it might snap the wire lead.

It was about ten meters, the lead, which gave the dog dominion over the front door. Keller went to the back of the house. Here, too, the shutters were tightly closed, and a blind was drawn over the paned-glass window in the rear door.

Keller applied a few ounces of pressure to the latch. It was locked. Gabriel could have opened it in ten seconds flat, but neither Keller nor Mikhail possessed his uncanny skill with a simple lock pick. Besides, an elbow through the glass was much faster.

The act itself produced less sound than he had feared—the initial crunch of glass followed by the tinkle of the shards falling to a tile floor. Keller reached through the empty pane, turned the latch, and with Mikhail at his back burst into the house.

The text message hit Gabriel's BlackBerry two minutes later. He thrust a few banknotes into the palm of the waitress and hurried into the plaza with Sarah and Khalid. The Range Rover was around a corner. Khalid maintained his composure until they were inside and the doors were closed. Gabriel tried to talk him out of going to the house, but it was no use; Khalid insisted on seeing the place where they had held his daughter. Gabriel couldn't blame him. If he were in Khalid's position, he would want to see it, too.

They could hear the mad barking of the dog as they came into the clearing. Keller was standing in the drive. He led them through the back door, over the broken glass, and down a flight of stairs to the cellar. A professional-grade padlock lay on the floor outside a metal door, next to a plastic bucket, pale blue. Khalid gagged at the odor as he entered the cell.

It was a small room with bare white walls, scarcely large enough for the cot. Atop the soiled bedding was an instant photograph and a notebook. The photograph was a different version of the one the kidnappers had sent to the Saudi Embassy in Paris. The notebook was filled with the looping handwriting of a twelve-year-old girl. It was all the same, page after page.

You're dead . . . Dead, dead, dead . . .

30

Paris–Jerusalem

The aides and bodyguards Khalid had abandoned at the Dorchester were waiting in the VIP lounge at Paris–Le Bourget. They reclaimed their crown prince as though receiving stolen contraband and hustled him aboard his private plane. An Israeli Embassy car took Gabriel and the others to nearby Charles de Gaulle. Inside the terminal they went their separate ways. Keller returned to London, Sarah to New York. Gabriel and Mikhail had to wait two hours for an El Al flight to Tel Aviv. Having nothing better to do, Gabriel informed CIA director Morris Payne that the American president's favorite leader in the Arab world was about to abdicate in order to save his daughter's life. Payne pressed Gabriel for the source of his information. Gabriel, as usual, played hard to get.

It was early evening when he and Mikhail arrived at Ben Gurion. They headed straight for King Saul Boulevard, where Gabriel spent an hour in Uzi Navot's office, clearing away the operational and administrative debris that had accumulated during his absence. In his fashionable striped dress shirt and trendy rimless eyewear, Navot looked as though he had just stepped from the boardroom of a Fortune 500 company. At Gabriel's request, he had turned down a high-paying job at a defense contractor in California to remain at the Office as deputy director. Navot's demanding wife, Bella, had never forgiven Gabriel. Or her husband, for that matter.

"The analysts are making good progress on the Tehran documents," explained Navot. "There's no evidence of an active program, but we've got them cold on their previous work, both warheads and delivery systems."

"How soon can we go public?"

"What's the rush?"

"In a few hours' time, the mullahs are going to be celebrating Khalid's demise. A regional change of subject might help."

"It won't change the fact your boy is going down."

"He was never my boy, Uzi. He was the prime minister's."

"He wants to see you."

"I can't face it. I'll call him from the car."

Gabriel placed the call as his motorcade was making the ascent up the Bab al-Wad, into the Judean Mountains. The prime minister took the news about as well as Morris Payne. Khalid was the linchpin of a regional strategy to isolate Iran, normalize relations with the Sunni Arab regimes, and reach a peace deal with the Palestinians on terms favorable to Israel. Gabriel supported the overall goals of the strategy, but he had warned the prime minister repeatedly that the crown prince was an erratic and unstable actor who would prove to be his own worst enemy.

"It seems you got your wish," said the prime minister in his baritone voice.

"With all due respect, that is a mischaracterization of my position."

"Can we intervene?"

"Believe me, I tried."

"When will it happen?"

"Before midnight Riyadh time."

"Will he go through with it?"

"I can't imagine he won't. Not after what I saw today."

It was a few minutes after nine o'clock when Gabriel's motorcade rumbled into Narkiss Street. Usually, the

THE NEW GIRL • 219

children were asleep by that hour, but much to Gabriel's
surprise they flung themselves into his arms as he came
through the door. Raphael, a future painter, displayed
his latest work. Irene read a story she had composed
with the help of her mother. The notebook in which it
was written was identical to the one they had found in
Princess Reema's crude cell in the Basque Country of
Spain.

You're dead . . . Dead, dead, dead . . .

Gabriel volunteered to put the children to bed, an
operation that proved no more successful than his attempt to find Khalid's daughter. When he emerged
from their room, he found Chiara removing an orange
casserole dish from the oven. He recognized the savor.
It was osso buco, one of his favorites. They ate at the
small café-style table in the kitchen, a bottle of Galilean
Shiraz and Gabriel's BlackBerry between them. The
television played silently on the counter. Chiara was
puzzled by her husband's choice of a channel.

"Since when do you watch Al Jazeera?"

"They have excellent sources inside Saudi Arabia."

"What's happening?"

"An earthquake."

Except for a couple of vaguely worded text messages, Gabriel had had no contact with Chiara since the
morning he departed for Paris. Now he told her ev-

erything that had transpired. He did so in Italian, the language of their marriage. Chiara listened intently. She loved nothing more than to hear about Gabriel's exploits in the field. His stories gave her a connection, however tenuous, to the life she had given up to become a mother.

"It must have been quite a surprise."

"What's that?"

"Finding Sarah on your flight to Paris." She glanced at the television. There were scenes of the latest eruption of violence along the border of the Gaza Strip. Israel, it seemed, was entirely to blame. "They don't seem to know that anything unusual is going on."

"They will soon."

"How will it unfold?"

"The crown prince will tell his father the king that he has no choice but to abdicate. His father, who has twenty-eight other children by four different wives, will undoubtedly take issue with his son's decision."

"Who will succeed King Mohammed now?"

"That depends on who was behind the plot to force Khalid from power." Gabriel checked the time. It was 9:42 in Jerusalem, 10:42 in Riyadh. "He's cutting it rather close."

"Maybe he's having second thoughts."

"Once he steps down, he loses everything. He probably won't be able to remain in Saudi Arabia. He'll be just another prince in exile."

"I'd love to be a fly on the wall in the royal court right now."

"Would you really?" Gabriel picked up his Black-Berry and dialed the Operations Desk at King Saul Boulevard. A few minutes later the BlackBerry began to emit the sound of an old man shouting in Arabic.

"What is he saying?"

"A child can be replaced, but not a king."

It was half past eleven in Riyadh when Al Arabiya, the state-run Saudi news channel, interrupted its usual late-evening fare with an urgent announcement from the palace. The newscaster appeared stricken as he read it. His Royal Highness Prince Khalid bin Mohammed Abdulaziz Al Saud had abdicated, thus relinquishing his claim to the throne. The Allegiance Council, a body of senior princes that determines who among them will rule next, planned to convene soon to appoint a replacement. For the moment, however, Saudi Arabia's terminally ill and mentally incompetent absolute mon-arch had no chosen successor.

Al Jazeera, which delivered the news to the wider world, could scarcely contain its glee. Nor could the Iranians, the Muslim Brotherhood, the Palestinians,

Hezbollah, ISIS, or the widow of Omar Nawwaf. The White House instantly released a statement declaring its determination to work closely with Khalid's successor. Downing Street murmured something similar a few minutes later, as did the Élysée Palace. The government of Israel, for its part, said nothing at all.

But why had Khalid surrendered the throne for which he had fought so ruthlessly? The media could only speculate. The Middle East experts were unanimous in the opinion that Khalid had not abdicated voluntarily. The only question was whether the pressure had been applied from within the House of Saud or without. Few reporters or commentators made any attempt to hide their joy over his fall, especially those early supporters who had cheered his rise to power. "Good riddance," declared the important columnist from the *New York Times* who had prematurely crowned Khalid the savior of the Arab world.

Among the many mysteries that night were Khalid's exact whereabouts. Had anyone bothered to ask the chief of Israeli intelligence, he could have told them definitively that Khalid flew to Paris immediately after his contentious meeting with his father and, absent his usual entourage, slipped anonymously into the Hôtel de Crillon. At five the following afternoon, he received a phone call. The voice at the other end, digitized and perversely affable in tone, issued a set of instructions, then the call went dead. Frantic, Khalid rang Sarah Bancroft in New York. And Sarah, at Khalid's request, called Gabriel at King Saul Boulevard. Needlessly, as it turned out, for he was monitoring events in the Op Center and had overheard everything. The kidnappers wanted more than Khalid's abduction. They wanted him.

31

Tel Aviv–Paris

Actually, it was a bit more complicated than that. What the kidnappers wanted was for Gabriel to handle the final negotiations and logistics of Princess Reema's release. They characterized their demand not as a threat but as a humanitarian gesture, one that would guarantee the safe return of the hostage, always the most perilous element of a kidnapping. They preferred to deal with a professional, they said, rather than a desperate and sometimes volatile father. Gabriel, however, was under no illusion as to why the kidnappers wanted him at the other end of the phone. The men behind the plot, whoever they were, whatever their motive, intended to kill him at the first opportunity. And Khalid, too.

Not surprisingly, the demand did not meet with a

favorable reception inside the walls of King Saul Boulevard. Uzi Navot said it was out of the question, a sentiment shared by the rest of Gabriel's senior staff—including Yaakov Rossman, who threatened to handcuff Gabriel to his desk. Even Eli Lavon, the chief of the watchers and Gabriel's closest friend, thought it a fool's errand. Besides, Lavon added, now that Khalid had abdicated, he was no longer worth the effort, and certainly not worth the risk.

Gabriel did not bother to consult with the prime minister. Instead, he called his wife. The conversation was brief, two or three minutes, no more. Afterward, he and Mikhail slipped quietly out of King Saul Boulevard and headed for Ben Gurion. There were no more flights to Paris that night. It was no matter; Khalid had sent a plane for them.

It was shortly after one a.m. when they arrived at the Crillon. Christopher Keller was in the lounge bar, flirting with the pretty hostess in his Corsican-accented French.

"Have you been upstairs yet?" asked Gabriel.

"Why do you think I'm down here? He was driving me crazy."

"How's he holding up?"

"Sixes and sevens."

Khalid was staying in a grand apartment on the

fourth floor. It was a shock to see him perform so ordinary a task as opening a door. He closed it again quickly and engaged the locks. The coffee table in the main sitting room was littered with the tins and wrappers of complimentary snacks from his personal bar. Somewhere his phone was playing an annoying electronic melody.

"The damn thing won't stop ringing." He raised a hand in anger toward the enormous television. "They're laughing at me! They're saying I was forced to abdicate because of Omar Nawwaf."

"You can set the record straight later," said Gabriel.

"What good will it do?" The phone was ringing again. Khalid dispatched the call to voice mail. "Another so-called friend."

"Who was it?"

"The president of Brazil. And before him it was the head of a Hollywood talent agency, wondering whether I still planned to invest in his company." He paused. "Everyone except the people who took my daughter."

"If I had to guess, you'll be hearing from them any minute."

"How can you be sure?"

"Because undoubtedly they know I've arrived."

"They're watching the hotel?"

Gabriel nodded.

"When they call back, I'll offer them a hundred million dollars. That should be enough to convince them to live up to their end of the original bargain."

Gabriel smiled briefly. "If only it were that simple."

"Surely," said Khalid after a moment, "you have no wish to die for a man like me."

"I don't," conceded Gabriel. "I'm here for your daughter."

"Can you get her back?"

"I'll do what I can."

"I understand," replied Khalid. "You're the director of the secret intelligence service of the State of Israel. And I'm the man who just gave away a throne, which means I'm no longer of any use to you."

"I have two young children."

"How lucky you are. I have only one."

A leaden silence fell over the room. It was broken by the cloying melody of Khalid's phone. He snatched it up, then declined the call.

"Who was it?" asked Gabriel.

"The White House." Khalid rolled his eyes. "Again."

"Don't you think you should take his call?"

He waved his hand dismissively and fixed his gaze on the television. KBM meeting with the British prime minister at Downing Street. KBM before the fall.

"I should never have listened to him," he said to no one in particular.

"Listened to whom?" asked Gabriel, but Khalid didn't answer. The phone was ringing again. "Who is it now?"

"You wouldn't believe me if I told you."

Gabriel accepted the phone and saw the given name of the Russian president.

"Answer it," said Khalid. "I'm sure he'd love to hear from you."

Gabriel allowed the phone to ring for several more seconds. Then, with profound satisfaction, he tapped DECLINE.

For the remainder of that long night, the clock moved with the slowness of shifting tectonic plates. Khalid's mood, however, careened wildly between rage at those who had betrayed him and fear for his daughter's life. Each time his phone rang, he would seize it as though it were a live grenade and stare hopefully at the screen, only to toss it carelessly onto the coffee table when it turned out to be just another former friend or associate calling to wallow in schadenfreude. "I know, I know," he would say to Gabriel. "Phones break, Prince Hothead."

Mikhail and Keller managed to get a few hours of sleep, but Gabriel remained at Khalid's side. He had never believed in the fairy tale of KBM the great Arabian reformer, and yet when confronted with the terrible choice of losing his throne or his child, Khalid had acted like a human being rather than the spoiled, unimaginably rich tyrant whose lust for power and possessions had known no bounds. Whether he knew it or not, thought Gabriel, there was hope for Khalid yet.

Finally, a dirty gray dawn crept into the magnificent sitting room. An hour or so later, while standing in one of the windows overlooking the Place de la Concorde, Gabriel witnessed a most remarkable spectacle. From the Musée du Louvre to the Arc de Triomphe, police fought running battles with thousands of protesters, all clad in the yellow vests of street sweepers. Before long, the entire first arrondissement was hung with a dense cloud of tear gas. Gabriel switched the television to France 2 and was informed that the "Yellow Vests" were enraged at the French president over a recent increase in the price of fuel.

"This is what democracy looks like," sneered Khalid. "The barbarians are at the gates."

Perhaps he had been mistaken, thought Gabriel. Perhaps Khalid was a lost cause after all.

And there they stood, the spymaster and the fallen monarch, watching as the great experiment known broadly as Western civilization crumbled beneath their feet. Khalid was so entranced that for once he didn't hear the ringing of his phone. Gabriel walked over to the coffee table and saw the device shivering amid the rubbish of the long night of waiting. He looked at the screen. The caller was not identified and there was no number.

He tapped ACCEPT and raised the device to his ear. "It's about time," he said in English, making no effort to conceal his Israeli accent. "Now listen very carefully."

32

Paris

When dealing with kidnappers, be they criminals or terrorists, it is customary for the negotiator to hear out their demands. But that presumes the negotiator has something to offer in return for the captive's freedom—money, for example, or a jailed comrade in arms. Gabriel, however, had nothing of value with which to barter, leaving him no choice but to immediately go on offense. He informed the kidnappers that Princess Reema would be free by day's end. If she were harmed in any way—or if any attempt were made on Gabriel's life or the life of the former Saudi crown prince—Israeli intelligence would hunt down every last member of the conspiracy and kill them. The best course of action, he concluded, would be to wrap things up as quickly as possible, with no melodrama or last-minute snags.

232 • DANIEL SILVA

Then he severed the connection and handed the phone to Khalid.

"Are you mad?"

"I wouldn't be here if I wasn't."

"Do you realize what you've just done?"

"I've given us a very slim chance of getting your daughter back without getting us killed in the process."

"Did they give you any instructions?"

"I didn't give them a chance."

"Why not?"

"I thought Arabs were supposed to be good negotiators."

Khalid's eyes widened with rage. "They'll never call back now!"

"Of course they will."

"How can you be so sure?"

Gabriel walked calmly to the window and watched the riot below. "Because I wasn't bluffing. And they know it."

Much to Gabriel's relief, he had to endure a wait of only twenty minutes before being proven at least partially correct. The instructions were delivered by a recorded text-to-speech message, in the manner of a spam call. The voice was female, cheerful, and vaguely erotic. It said that Gabriel and the former crown prince were to board the noon TGV from Paris to Marseilles. Additional instructions would be conveyed while they were in transit. They were not to involve the French police. Nor were they to travel with a security detail. Any deviation from the instructions would result in the child's death. "You are being watched," the voice warned before the connection went dead.

The terms were hardly equitable, but under the circumstances they were the best Gabriel could expect. Besides, he had no intention of honoring them, and neither for that matter did the kidnappers.

Khalid arranged for a hotel limousine. As they crawled eastward across Paris, they were jeered, cursed, and spat upon by the yellow-vested protesters. Tear gas stung their eyes as they hurried through the entrance of the Gare de Lyon. Mikhail and Keller were standing like strangers beneath the departure board, each looking in a different direction.

Khalid gazed upward toward the glass atrium in wonder. "Wasn't there a terrorist attack in this station a few years ago?"

"Keep moving," said Gabriel. "Otherwise, we're going to miss our train."

"There's the memorial," said Khalid suddenly, pointing toward a black slab of polished granite.

The departure board clattered with an update. The

train for Marseilles was boarding. Gabriel led Khalid to an automated ticket kiosk and instructed him to purchase two first-class seats. Khalid stared at the contraption, mystified.

"I'm not sure I would know—"

"Never mind." Gabriel slid a credit card into the reader. His fingers moved deftly over the touchscreen, and the machine ejected two tickets and a receipt.

"What now?" asked Khalid.

"We get on the train."

Gabriel guided Khalid to the appropriate platform and into a first-class carriage. Mikhail was seated at one end, Keller at the other. Both were facing the center, which was where Gabriel directed Khalid. The carriage was about one-third full. None of the other passengers appeared to realize that the man who had just relinquished his claim to the throne of Saudi Arabia was sitting among them.

"You know," he said quietly into Gabriel's ear, "I can't remember the last time I took a train journey. Do you travel by rail often?"

"No," said Gabriel as the TGV jerked forward. "Never."

For the first three hours of the trip south, Khalid's silenced phone vibrated almost without cease, but the kidnappers waited until the train reached Avignon before issuing their next set of instructions. Once again there was no name or number, only the automated female voice. She told Gabriel to hire a car at the Gare de Marseilles–Saint-Charles and drive to the ancient citadel town of Carcassonne. There was a pizzeria on the avenue du Général Leclerc called Plein Sud. They would drop the girl somewhere nearby. "And don't bring the two bodyguards," the voice warned flirtatiously. "Otherwise, the girl dies."

Gabriel rang King Saul Boulevard and ordered two Hertz cars, one for Mikhail and Keller, the other for Khalid and himself. They were both Renault hatchbacks. Mikhail and Keller departed first and headed north toward Aix-en-Provence. Gabriel headed westward along the coast, into the blinding late-afternoon sun.

Khalid trailed a forefinger through the dust on the dashboard. "At least they could have given us a clean car."

"I should have told them it was for you. I'm sure they would have found something nicer."

"Why did you send your men toward Aix?"

"To see whether the kidnappers will be stupid enough to follow them."

"And if they do?"

"They're likely to get a rather rude surprise. And

our chances of getting out of this in one piece will increase dramatically."

Khalid was admiring the sea. "Beautiful, isn't it?"

"I'm sure it looks better from the deck of the world's largest yacht."

"*Second* largest," Khalid corrected him.

"We all have to economize."

"I suppose I'll be spending much more time aboard it. Riyadh is no longer safe for me. And when my father dies—"

"The new crown prince will treat you the same way you treated your predecessor and everyone else who posed a threat to you."

"That's the way it works in my family. We give the word *dysfunction* a whole new meaning." Khalid smiled in spite of himself. "I plan to devote the rest of my life to Reema. She loves *Tranquillity*. Perhaps we'll take a trip around the world together."

"She's going to need a great deal of medical and psychiatric care to recover from what she's been through."

"You sound as though you speak from experience."

"Read my file."

"I have," said Khalid. "It contained a reference to something that happened in Vienna. There was a bombing. They say—"

"'This might come as a surprise to you, but it's not something I wish to discuss."

"So it's true? Your wife and child were killed in front of you?"

"No," said Gabriel. "My wife survived."

The sun was blazing on the horizon—like a car, thought Gabriel, burning brightly in an otherwise quiet square in Vienna. He was relieved when Khalid abruptly changed the topic.

"I've never been to Carcassonne."

"It was a Cathar stronghold in the Middle Ages."

"Cathar?"

"They believed, among other things, that there were two gods, the God of the New Testament and the God of the Old. One was good, the other was evil."

"Which was which?"

"What do you think?"

"The God of the Jews was the evil one."

"Yes."

"What happened to them?" asked Khalid.

"Despite incredible odds, they founded a modern state in their ancient homeland."

"I was talking about the Cathars."

"They were wiped out in the Albigensian Crusade. The most famous massacre took place in the village of

Montségur. Two hundred Cathar Perfects were hurled onto a great pyre. The place where it happened became known as the field of the burned."

"It seems Christians can be violent, too."

"It was the thirteenth century, Khalid."

Gabriel's BlackBerry vibrated with an incoming call. It was Mikhail with an update. Gabriel listened, then ordered him to proceed to Carcassonne.

"Were they followed?" asked Khalid.

"No," said Gabriel. "No such luck."

The sun was slipping below the horizon. Soon it would be gone. For that, if nothing else, he was grateful.

33

Mazamet, France

In the forty-eight hours since Princess Reema's hasty evacuation from the safe house in the Basque Country of Spain, she had been kept in a state of near-constant motion. Her memories of the odyssey were fragmentary, for they were fogged by regular injections of sedative. She recalled a warehouse stacked with wooden crates, and a filthy shed that smelled of goat, and a tiny kitchen where she had overheard a quarrel in the next room between two of her captors. It was the first time she had heard them speak. The language shocked her.

Not long after the dispute was resolved, they gave her another injection of the drug. She awoke, as usual, with a blinding headache and a mouth as dry as the Arabian Desert. The rags in which they had kept her for some two weeks had been removed, and she was dressed in the outfit she had been wearing on the afternoon of her abduction. She was even wearing her favorite Burberry coat. It seemed heavier than normal, though Reema couldn't be certain. She was weakened by inactivity, and the drugs made her feel as though her limbs were made of iron.

The final injection contained a smaller dose of the sedative. Reema seemed to be hovering close to consciousness. She was certain she was riding in the trunk of a moving car, for she could hear the rushing of the tires beneath her. She could also hear two voices from the passenger compartment. They were speaking the same language, the language that had shocked her. She recognized only two words.

Gabriel Allon . . .

The rocking of the car and the close smell of the dirty trunk were turning her stomach. Reema seemed to be having trouble drawing air into her lungs. Perhaps it was the drugs they had given her. No, she thought, it was the coat. It was pressing down on her.

Her hands were unbound. She loosened the toggles and pulled at the lapels, but it was no use, it wouldn't open. She closed her eyes, and for the first time in many days she wept.

The coat was sewn shut.

The avenue du Général Leclerc was located beyond the double walls of Carcassonne's ancient citadel and possessed none of the old quarter's beauty or charm. Plein Sud occupied a pie-shaped building on the south side of the street, the last in a short parade of shops and enterprises that catered to the working-class residents of the neighborhood. The interior was clean and neat and brightly lit. There was a large man with southern features who worked the pizza ovens, and a mournful-looking woman who saw to the paella. Four tables stood in a small seating area. The walls were hung with African art, and a large sliding glass door overlooked the street. It was a sniper's shooting gallery, thought Gabriel.

He and Khalid sat down at the only available table. The occupants of the other three looked like the people they had seen rioting in the streets of Paris that morning. They were citizens of the other France, the France one didn't read about in guidebooks. They were the put-upon and the left-behind, the ones without glittering degrees from elite institutions of learning. Globalization and automation had eroded their value in the workforce. The service economy was their only option. Their counterparts in Britain and America had already had their say at the ballot box. France, reckoned Gabriel, would be next.

A message hit his BlackBerry. He read it, then returned the device to his pocket. Khalid's phone was between them on the tabletop, darkened, silenced.

"Well?" he asked.

"My men."

"Where are they?"

With a movement of his eyes, Gabriel indicated they were parked nearby.

"What about the kidnappers?"

"They're not in here."

"Do they know we've arrived?"

"Absolutely."

"How do you know?"

"Check your phone."

Khalid looked down. He had an incoming call. No name. No number.

Gabriel tapped ACCEPT and lifted the device to his ear. The voice that addressed him was female and vaguely erotic. It was not, however, a recording.

The voice was real.

34

Carcassonne, France

"You couldn't resist, could you?"

"I suppose not. After all, how often does one get to speak to a man like you?"

"And what kind of man is that?"

"A war criminal. A murderer of those who struggle for dignity and self-determination."

Her English was flawless. The accent was German but there was a trace of something else. Something farther to the east, thought Gabriel. "Are you a freedom fighter?" he asked.

"I am a professional, Allon. Like you."

"Really? And what kind of work do you do when you're not kidnapping and torturing children?"

"The child," she replied, "has been well cared for."

"I saw the room in Areatza where you kept her. It wasn't fit for a dog, let alone a twelve-year-old girl."

"A girl who has spent her entire life surrounded by unimaginable luxury. At least now she has some sense of how the vast majority of the people in the world live."

"Where is she?"

"Close."

"In that case, leave her in front of the restaurant. I won't make any attempt to follow you."

She laughed, low and throaty. Gabriel raised the volume on the phone to full and pressed it tightly to his ear. She was in a moving car, he was certain of it.

"Are you ready for the next set of instructions?" she asked.

"They'd better be the last."

"There's a village north of Carcassonne called Saissac. Follow the D629 to the border of the next *département*. After a kilometer you'll see a break in the fence on the right side of the road. Follow the track into the field exactly one hundred meters and then switch off your headlamps. Any deviation on your part," said the woman, "will result in the girl's death."

"If you harm a hair on her head, I'm going to put a bullet in yours."

"Like this?"

At once, the café's sliding glass door shattered, and

a superheated round split the air between Gabriel and Khalid and embedded in the wall.

"You have thirty minutes," said the woman calmly. "Otherwise, the next one is for her."

Gabriel and Khalid followed the other panicked patrons of Plein Sud into the busy avenue. The Renault was parked outside the neighboring shop. Gabriel dropped behind the wheel, started the engine, and raced along the walls of the ancient citadel. Khalid charted their course on his mobile phone. In truth, Gabriel didn't need the help—the route to Saissac was clearly marked with signposts—but it gave Khalid something to do other than shout at Gabriel to drive faster.

It was a drive of nearly forty kilometers to Saissac alone. Gabriel covered the distance in about twenty minutes. They flashed through the town's old center in a blur. In his peripheral vision he glimpsed a rampart overlooking a lowland, the ruins of a battlement, and a single café. The newer quarter of the town was to the northwest. There was an outpost of the gendarmerie and a traffic circle where for an instant Gabriel feared the Renault might overturn.

Beyond the circle, the town dwindled. For a mile or so the countryside was groomed and cultivated, but gradually it turned wild. The road narrowed, spanned a riverbed over a stone bridge, and narrowed again. Gabriel glanced at the dashboard clock. By his calculation they were already three or four minutes late. Then he checked the rearview mirror and saw a set of headlights. Somehow the lights were drawing nearer. He found his BlackBerry and dialed.

It was Keller who answered.

"Back off," said Gabriel.

"Not a chance."

"Tell Mikhail to pull over now."

Gabriel overheard Keller reluctantly relay the instructions and watched a few seconds later as the car moved onto the verge. Then he severed the connection and returned the phone to his pocket. Khalid's was suddenly ablaze with light. No name. No number.

"Put her on speaker."

Khalid tapped the screen.

"You're late," said the woman.

"I think we're almost there."

"You are. And so are your men."

"I told them to pull over. They won't come any closer."

"They'd better not."

A sign appeared: DÉPARTEMENT DU TARN.

"I'm crossing the border," said Gabriel.

"Keep going."

They were in a tunnel of trees. When they emerged, Gabriel saw a line of sagging wire fencing along the right side of the road. The field beyond it was in darkness. Heavy cloud had rendered the night moonless.

"Slow down," commanded the woman. "The break in the fence is just ahead."

Gabriel eased off the throttle and turned through the breach. The track was unpaved, deeply rutted, and wet with a recent rain. Gabriel bumped along for what he thought was a hundred meters and braked.

"Keep going," said the woman.

Gabriel crept forward, the car rocking like a boat rising and falling on swells.

"That's far enough."

Gabriel stopped.

"Switch off the engine and the headlamps."

Gabriel hesitated.

"Now," said the woman. "Or the next bullet comes through the windscreen."

Gabriel killed the engine and the lights. The darkness was absolute. So was the silence at the other end of the cellular connection. The woman, he thought, had muted her phone.

"How long do you think she'll make us wait?" asked Khalid.

"*She* can hear you," said the woman.

"And I can hear *you*," said Khalid coldly.

"Was that a threat?"

Before Khalid could answer, the Renault's rear window exploded. Gabriel drew a Beretta from the small of his back and chambered the first round.

"I know you're rather good with a gun, Mr. Allon, but I wouldn't try anything. Besides, it's almost over now."

"Where is she?"

"Turn on your headlamps," said the woman, and the connection went dead.

35

Département du Tarn, France

She was standing on the track about fifty meters in front of the car, atop a slight rise in the land. Silver duct tape covered her mouth and bound her hands. They had dressed her in a tartan skirt, dark tights, and a schoolgirl's toggle coat. It looked as though they had buttoned the coat out of proper sequence, but that wasn't the case. It wasn't buttoned at all.

All at once Khalid threw open his door and, shouting Reema's name, sprinted up the muddy path. Gabriel followed a few paces behind him, bent slightly at the waist, the Beretta in his outstretched hands. He pivoted left and right, looking for what, he did not know. Reema and the land behind her were awash in light, but otherwise the darkness in the field was com-

plete. Gabriel could see nothing, only a father careen-
ing toward a child whose eyes were filled with terror.

Something wasn't right. Why wasn't she relieved by
the sound of her father's voice? And where was the next
gunshot? The promised bullet through Gabriel's head?
And then he understood why Reema's coat did not fit
her properly. There was no sniper, not any longer. The
child was the weapon.

"Don't go near her!" shouted Gabriel, but Khalid
plunged forward along the slippery path. It was then
Gabriel saw a glimmer of light in the trees bordering
the field.

A mobile phone . . .

It was a long way off, a hundred meters at least. Gabriel leveled the Beretta toward the light and pulled
the trigger until the magazine was empty. Then he
dropped the gun and hurled himself toward Khalid.

The Saudi was a much younger man, but he was
no athlete and Gabriel had the advantage of a kind of
madness. He closed the space between them with a few
wild strides and dragged Khalid to the damp earth as
the bomb beneath Reema's toggle coat exploded.

A flash of searing light illuminated the field in all
directions, and rushing metal filled the air above Gabriel's head like outgoing artillery. When he looked

up again, Reema was gone. What remained of her was strewn along both sides of the pathway.

Gabriel tried to pin Khalid to the ground, but the Saudi wrenched himself free and clambered to his feet. He was covered in Reema's blood, they both were. Gabriel turned away and covered his ears as the first terrible scream of agony poured from Khalid's lungs.

A car was racing up the road. Gabriel found the Beretta, ejected the spent cartridge, and inserted a new one. Then he turned slowly and saw Khalid desperately collecting his daughter's limbs. "Call an ambulance," he was saying. "Please, we must get her to a hospital."

Gabriel dropped to his knees and was violently sick. Then he raised his face to the moonless sky and prayed for a sudden rain to wash the blood of the child from his face. "You're dead!" he shouted at the top of his voice. "Dead, dead, dead!"

PART THREE

Absolution

36

Southwest France–Jerusalem

Mikhail Abramov and Christopher Keller had heard the frenzied burst of gunfire—ten shots, all discharged by the same weapon—followed a few seconds later by an explosion. It was relatively small, judging by the sound of it, but the flash of the detonation was enough to illuminate the sky above the remote corner of the Département du Tarn. The tableau they encountered upon their arrival in the field was like something from Dante's *Inferno*. Both men were combat veterans who had carried out numerous extrajudicial killings, and yet both were sickened by what they saw. Gabriel was on his knees in the mud, drenched in blood, raging against the heavens. Khalid was holding something that looked like a small arm, and screaming about an ambulance. Mikhail and Keller would never speak of it again. Not to one another, and certainly not to the French.

After regaining a small measure of composure, Gabriel had called Paul Rousseau in Paris—and Rousseau had called his chief, who called his minister, who called the palace. Within minutes, the first units of the gendarmerie were streaking up the D629, and the entire field was soon ablaze with crime-scene lights. On the direct orders of the French president, no attempt was made to question the victim's overwrought father or the devastated chief of Israeli intelligence.

The forensic teams meticulously gathered up the remains of the victim; the explosives experts, the fragments of the bomb that killed her. All the evidence was flown to Paris that night by police helicopter. So, too, were Gabriel, Khalid, Mikhail, and Keller. By dawn, Khalid and his daughter's remains were airborne once more, this time bound for Saudi Arabia. For Gabriel and his accomplices, however, the French had other plans.

He was an ally—indeed, he had all but single-handedly destroyed ISIS's terror network in France— and they treated him accordingly. The inquisition, such as it was, took place later that same day, in a gilded, chandeliered room in the Interior Ministry. Present were the minister himself, the chiefs of the various police and intelligence services, and several note takers, cupbearers, and assorted fonctionnaires. Mikhail and Keller were spared direct questioning, and the French pledged there would be no electronic recording. Gabriel assumed the French were lying.

The minister began the proceedings by demanding to know how the chief of Israeli intelligence had become involved in the search for the princess in the first place. Gabriel replied, truthfully, that he undertaken the assignment at the behest of the child's father.

"But Saudi Arabia is your adversary, is it not?"

"I was hoping to change that."

"Did you receive assistance from anyone inside the French security and intelligence establishment?"

"I did not."

The minister wordlessly presented Gabriel with a photograph. A Passat sedan entering Alpha Group headquarters on the rue Nélaton. The visit, explained Gabriel, had been a courtesy call only.

"And the woman in the passenger seat?" wondered the minister.

"She's a colleague."

"According to the Swiss Federal Police, that same car was in Geneva the following evening when Lucien Villard was killed by a briefcase bomb. I assume you were there, too?"

"I was."

"Did Israeli intelligence kill Lucien Villard?"

"Don't be ridiculous."

The minister thrust a photograph beneath Gabriel's nose. A man sitting in a café in Annecy. "Did he?"

Gabriel nodded.

"Were you able to identify him?"

"No."

Another photograph. "What about her?"

"I believe I spoke to her last night."

"She handled the negotiations?"

"There were none."

"There was no exchange of money?"

"The demand was abdication."

"And the ten shots you fired?"

"I saw the light of a mobile phone. I assumed he was using it to detonate the bomb."

"He?"

Gabriel inclined his head toward the man in the photograph. "If I had hit him—"

"You might have saved the child."

Gabriel said nothing.

"It was a mistake not to involve us. We could have brought her in safely."

"They said they would kill her."

"Yes," said the minister. "And now she is dead."

And on it went, deep into the afternoon, until the lights of Paris glowed beyond the ministry's windows. It was a folly, and both sides knew it. The French intended to sweep the entire messy episode under the rug. When at last the questions stopped and the note takers laid down their pens, there were handshakes all around. They were of the graveside variety, fleeting, consoling. A ministry car took Gabriel, Mikhail, and Keller to Charles de Gaulle. Keller boarded a plane bound for London; Gabriel and Mikhail, for Tel Aviv. During the four-hour flight they did not speak of what had transpired in the field in the Département du Tarn. They never would.

There was a small item the next day in one of the southern papers, something about a set of remains being found in a remote field, an adolescent, almost certainly a female. It made Le Figaro, and a short story was read on one of the evening newscasts, but the French cover-up was so thorough—and the French media was so distracted by the "Yellow Vests"—it was soon forgotten. At times, even Gabriel wondered whether he had dreamed it. He had only to listen to the recordings of his conversations with the woman to be reminded that a child had been blown to pieces before his eyes.

If he was grieving, he gave no sign of it, at least not

within the walls of King Saul Boulevard. Khalid's abdication had thrown Saudi Arabia—and by extension the entire region—into political turmoil. To make matters worse, the American president declared his intention to withdraw all U.S. forces from Syria, effectively ceding control of the country to the Iranians and their ally, Russia. Within hours of the announcement, which he made via Twitter, a Hezbollah missile fired from Syrian territory crossed into Israeli airspace and was intercepted over Hadera. Gabriel supplied the prime minister with the location of a secret Iranian command bunker south of Damascus. Several officers of the Iranian Revolutionary Guard Corps were killed in the retaliatory strike, drawing Israel and the Islamic Republic ever closer to war.

But it was Saudi Arabia that occupied the lion's share of Gabriel's time during those endless days after his return from France. His accurate prediction that Khalid was about to abdicate had suddenly made him flavor of the week at Langley, which was grasping at straws trying to figure out what was happening inside the royal court of its closest ally in the Arab world. Was Khalid in Riyadh? Was he even alive? Gabriel was able to offer the Americans precious little intelligence, for his own attempts to reach Khalid had proved fruitless, and the Saudi's compromised phone was no longer emitting a signal. Nor was Gabriel able to provide the Americans—or his prime minister, for that matter—reliable intelligence as to Khalid's likely successor. Consequently, when Gabriel was awakened at three in the morning with the news that it was Prince Abdullah, the king's London-based half brother, he was as surprised as everyone else.

The Office knew the basics of Abdullah's undistinguished career, and in the days following his elevation, Collections and Research rapidly filled in the missing pieces. He was anti-Israel, anti-West, and harbored an abiding resentment of America, which he blamed for much of the Middle East's violence and political chaos. He had two wives in Riyadh whom he rarely saw and a stable of high-priced prostitutes, boys and girls, who tended to his sexual needs at his mansion in Belgravia. A devout Wahhabi Muslim, he was a heavy drinker who had thrice received treatment at an exclusive facility outside Zurich. In business he had been aggressive but unwise. Despite a generous monthly stipend, money was constantly an issue.

There was speculation in the media that Abdullah was merely a caretaker crown prince who would remain in the post only until a suitable candidate from the next generation could be chosen. Abdullah, however, quickly consolidated his hold on power by purging the royal court and the Saudi security services of his nephew's influence. He also scrapped *The Way Forward*, Khalid's ambitious plan to transform the Saudi economy, and made it clear there would be no more talk of reforming the faith. Wahhabism, he proclaimed, was the Kingdom's official religion and would be practiced in its purest and sternest form. Women were summarily stripped of the right to drive or attend sporting events—and the Mutaween, the dreaded Saudi religious police, were once again given license to enforce the rules of Islamic purity, with arrests and physical brutality if necessary. Those who objected were jailed or publicly flogged. The fleeting Riyadh Spring was over.

Which prompted, mainly in the West, another great reassessment. Had the Americans and their European allies been too hard on KBM for his misdeeds? Had they foolishly backed the House of Saud into a corner, leaving them no choice but to revert to their tried-and-true method of survival? Had they let a golden opportunity to fundamentally change the Middle East slip through their fingers? In the secure rooms and salons of Washington and London, they quarreled among themselves over who had lost Saudi Arabia. In Tel Aviv, however, Gabriel approached the question altogether differently. Saudi Arabia, he concluded, had not been lost, it had been taken from them. But by whom?

Though Gabriel managed to conceal his grief from his troops, Chiara saw through him as though he were made of glass. It wasn't difficult; he relived it each night in the sweat-drenched tumult that passed for his sleep. Several times she was awakened by his shouting. His words were always the same. "You're dead," he would cry out. "Dead, dead, dead!"

He had given her a highly abridged version of the story after his return from France. He and Khalid had been led by the kidnappers to a remote field, the child had died. Chiara had resisted the temptation to press him for more details. She knew that one day he would tell her everything.

It was clawing at him, that much was obvious. What he needed, she thought, was a painting, a few square meters of damaged canvas that he could make right again. But he had no painting, he had only a country to protect, and he was haunted by the prospect of war in the north. Hezbollah and the Iranians had stockpiled more than one hundred and fifty thousand missiles and rockets in Syria and Lebanon. The largest could reach Tel Aviv and beyond. In the event of a conflict, the entire Galilee and much of the Coastal Plain would be within range. Thousands might die.

"Which is why the American presence in Syria is

264 · DANIEL SILVA

so important. They're a tripwire. Once they're gone, there will be only one check on Hezbollah and Iranian aggression."

"The Russians," said Chiara.

It was after midnight. Gabriel was propped upright in bed, a stack of Office files on his lap, a halogen reading lamp burning brightly over his shoulder. The television was muted so as not to wake the children. Earlier that evening Hezbollah had fired four rockets into Israel. Three had been destroyed by the Iron Dome missile defense system, but one had landed outside Ramat David, the town in the Valley of Jezreel where Gabriel had lived as a child. The IAF was preparing a massive retaliatory strike based on intelligence supplied by the Office.

"A preview of coming attractions," he said softly.

"How do we stop it?"

"Short of all-out war?" Gabriel closed the file he had been reading. "With a strategy to drive the Russians, the Iranians, and Hezbollah out of Syria."

"And how do we do that?"

"By creating a decent central government in Damascus led by the Sunni majority instead of a brutal dictatorial regime led by a tiny Alawite minority."

"And I thought it was going to be something difficult." Chiara slipped into bed next to him. "The Arabs

THE NEW GIRL · 265

have proven beyond a shadow of a doubt they're not ready to govern themselves."

"I'm not talking about Jeffersonian democracy. I'm talking about an enlightened despot."

"Like Khalid?" asked Chiara skeptically.

"That depends which Khalid we're talking about."

"How many are there?"

"Two," said Gabriel. "The first was handed absolute power before he was ready."

"And the second?"

"He was the man who watched his child die an unimaginable death."

There was a silence. Then Chiara asked, "What happened in that field in France?"

"I saved Khalid's life," said Gabriel. "And I'm not sure he'll ever forgive me for it."

Chiara gazed at the television. The new de facto ruler of Saudi Arabia was meeting with senior clerics, including an imam who regularly denounced Jews as the descendants of apes and pigs. "What are you going to do?" she asked.

"I'm going to find out who stole Saudi Arabia."

"And then?"

Gabriel switched off the lamp. "Steal it back."

37

Tel Aviv

It was at this point, in late February, as Israel was lashed by a series of winter storms, that there commenced a great search the Office would later refer to as "Where in the World Is Khalid?" That he was even among the living was a matter of considerable internal debate. Eli Lavon was convinced that Khalid was a few feet beneath the surface of the Nejd, probably in several pieces. To support his case, he pointed to the fact that Khalid's mobile phone was off the air. Even more alarming was a report, never corroborated, that Khalid had been taken into custody not long after the Allegiance Council appointed Abdullah crown prince. Khalid, surmised Lavon, was never supposed to leave France alive in the first place. Returning to Saudi Arabia with the remains of his daughter had given the plotters the perfect opportunity to make certain he would never pose a threat in the future.

Gabriel did not dismiss Lavon's theory out of hand, for in the hours after Reema's murder he had warned Khalid he would be a fool to return to Riyadh. Quietly, he reached out to his old nemesis from the Saudi secret police to see whether he had news of Khalid's fate, but there was no response. The old nemesis, said Eli Lavon, had probably been caught up in the post-Khalid purge and cast out. Or perhaps, Lavon added darkly, the old nemesis was the one who had plunged the dagger into Khalid's back.

Gabriel and the Office were not the only ones looking for Khalid. So were the Americans and much of the world's media. The former crown prince was sighted variously on the Pacific coast of Mexico, on the enchanted Caribbean island of Saint Barthélemy, and in a gulfside villa in Dubai. None of the reports proved remotely accurate. Nor was the report in *Le Monde* that Khalid was living in splendid exile at his lavish château in the Haute-Savoie. Paul Rousseau confirmed that the French had not been able to find him, either.

"We have one or two questions we'd like to ask him about Rafiq al-Madani. He's missing, too."

"He's probably back in Riyadh."

268 • DANIEL SILVA

"If he is, he didn't get his passport stamped on the way out of France. You haven't seen him, have you?"

Gabriel replied, with some truth, that he did not know al-Madani's whereabouts. Khalid's remained a mystery, too. And when another week passed with no sign of him, Gabriel feared the worst. In the end, it was Sarah Bancroft who found him. More to the point, it was Khalid who found her. He was very much alive and hiding out aboard *Tranquillity* with a skeleton crew and a couple of trusted bodyguards. He was wondering whether Gabriel might have a few minutes to talk.

"He's anchored off Sharm el-Sheikh in the Red Sea," said Sarah. "He'll send the helicopter to pick you up."

"That's very generous of him, but I have a better idea."

"What's that?"

Gabriel explained.

"You can't be serious."

"He promised to give me anything I wanted. This is what I want."

38

Eilat, Israel

As director-general of the Office, Gabriel possessed the broad authority to undertake sensitive operations without first obtaining approval from the prime minister. His mandate, however, did not grant him license to invite the deposed leader of a formally hostile Arab nation to visit the State of Israel, even unofficially. It was one thing to slip Khalid into the London embassy in the heat of battle, quite another to grant him access to the world's most contested piece of real estate. The prime minister, after an hour of tense debate, approved of the visit, provided it remained secret. Gabriel, who had all but given the Saudi prince up for dead, was comfortable with the terms. The last thing they needed to worry about, he said, was a selfie popping up on social media. Khalid's old Twitter and Instagram accounts were dormant, and the House of Saud had erased his memory from existence. Khalid was an unperson.

His Airbus H175 VIP helicopter plopped down in a cloud of dust at the edge of the Gulf of Aqaba at eight o'clock the following morning. A crewman opened the cabin door, and Khalid, in chinos and an Italian blazer, stepped hesitantly onto Israeli soil for the first time. Only Gabriel and his small security detail were on hand to witness the occasion. Smiling, Gabriel extended his hand, but Khalid drew him into a crushing embrace instead. For better or worse, and for all the wrong reasons, they were now the closest of friends.

Khalid surveyed the harsh khaki-colored landscape. "I had hoped to come here one day under different circumstances."

"Perhaps," said Gabriel, "I can arrange that, too."

They headed north into the Negev Desert in Gabriel's armored SUV. Khalid seemed surprised to see other traffic on the road.

"It's better," explained Gabriel, "if we hide in plain sight."

"What if someone recognizes me?"

"Israel is the last place in the world anyone would expect to see you."

"That's because it's the last place in the world I

should be. But then again, I suppose I have nowhere else to go."

Khalid was clearly uncomfortable with his reduced circumstances and diminished global status. As they plunged deeper into the desert beneath a cloudless sky, he spoke of what had transpired when he returned to Saudi Arabia after Reema's murder. He buried her in the Wahhabi tradition, he said, in an unmarked grave in the desert. Then he quickly set about trying to reclaim his place in the line of succession. As he had feared, it was not possible. The Allegiance Council had already settled on Abdullah, Khalid's mentor and confessor, as the new crown prince. Khalid dutifully pledged his loyalty to his uncle, but Abdullah, fearing Khalid's influence, summarily stripped him of all his powerful government posts. When Khalid objected, he was arrested and taken to a room at the Ritz-Carlton Hotel, where he was forced to surrender much of his net worth. Fearing for his life, he gathered up his remaining liquid assets and took refuge aboard *Tranquillity*. Asma, his wife, had refused to go into exile with him.

"She blames you for Reema's death?"

Khalid nodded slowly. "Rather ironic, don't you think? I championed the rights of women in Saudi Arabia, and as my reward I have been forsaken by my wife."

"And by your uncle, too."

"So much for his advice not to abdicate," agreed Khalid. "It seems Abdullah was plotting against me from the beginning. The Allegiance Council gave no serious consideration to any other candidate. The cake, as they say, was already in the oven. Once I was out of the way, the throne was Abdullah's for the taking. Not even my father could stop it."

"How is he?"

"My father? He has moments of lucidity, but for the most part he exists in a fog of dementia. Abdullah has complete control of the machinery of the Kingdom, and you've seen the results. Rest assured, he's not finished. Those senators and congressmen in Washington who were baying for my blood will rue the day they ever criticized me."

It was approaching ten o'clock when the mercury-colored surface of the Dead Sea appeared on the horizon. At Ein Gedi, Gabriel asked Khalid whether he wanted to have a swim, but Khalid, with a wave of his hand, declined. He had once bathed on the Jordanian side of the Dead Sea and had not enjoyed the experience.

They flashed through a checkpoint without slowing and entered the West Bank. At Jericho was the turnoff for Jerusalem. They continued north instead. Khalid's expression darkened as they passed through a chain of Israeli settlements along the Jordan River.

"How do you expect them to build a state if you've taken all the land?"

"We haven't taken *all* the land," responded Gabriel. "But I can assure you we're never leaving the Jordan Valley."

"There can't be two states if there are Jews on both sides of the border."

"I'm afraid that train has left the station."

"What train?"

"The two-state solution. It's dead and buried. We have to think outside the box."

"What's the alternative?"

"First we have peace. After that," said Gabriel, "anything is possible."

They passed through another checkpoint into Israel proper and sped through flat, fertile farmland to the southern end of the Sea of Galilee. There they turned to the east and scaled the Golan Heights. In the Druze town of Majdal Shams they peered through a razor-wire fence into southern Syria. The Syrian military and their Russian and Iranian allies had wiped out the last of the rebel forces. The regime was once again in control of the territory along Israel's border.

They stopped for lunch in Rosh Pina, one of the oldest Zionist settlements in Israel, before starting across the Upper Galilee. Gabriel pointed out the footprints of abandoned Arab villages. He even walked with Khalid among the ruins of al-Sumayriyya, the Arab village in the Western Galilee whose residents had fled to Lebanon in 1948. The shimmering new skyline of Tel Aviv they viewed from Highway 6, and Jerusalem, God's fractured city upon a hill, they approached from the west. After crossing the invisible border into East Jerusalem, they made their way along the Ottoman walls of the Old City to Lions' Gate. The small square that lay beyond it was empty of pedestrians. There were only Israeli police officers and soldiers present.

"Where are we?" asked Khalid, his voice tense.

Gabriel opened his door and climbed out. "Come with me," he said. "I'll show you."

The small square inside Lions' Gate was not the only section of the Muslim Quarter that Gabriel had arranged to be closed to the public that evening. So was the broad, sacred esplanade to the south known to Jews as the Temple Mount and to Muslims as the Haram al-Sharif, the Noble Sanctuary. Gabriel and Khalid entered the compound through the Bab al-Huttah, the Gate of Absolution. The golden Dome of the Rock glowed softly in the cold light of early evening. The mighty al-Aqsa Mosque was in silhouette.

"You did this for me?"

Gabriel nodded.

"How?"

"I am a man," said Gabriel, "of some influence."

A few representatives of the Waqf were huddled on the eastern side of the esplanade. "Who do they think I am?" asked Khalid.

"An Arab notable from one of the emirates."

"Not Qatar, I hope."

They entered the Dome of the Rock and together gazed solemnly at the Foundation Stone. It was the summit of Mount Moriah, the spot where Muslims believe Muhammad ascended into heaven and where Jews believe Abraham would have sacrificed his young son were it not for the intercession of an archangel called Gabriel. Afterward, Khalid prayed in the al-Aqsa Mosque while the angel's namesake, alone in the esplanade, contemplated the risen moon over the Mount of Olives.

Night had fallen by the time Khalid came out of the mosque. "Where is the chamber where you found the pillars of the so-called Temple of Solomon?"

Gabriel pointed downward, into the depths of the plateau.

"And the Wailing Wall?"

Gabriel inclined his head toward the west.

"Can you take me to the chamber?" asked Khalid.

"Perhaps another time."

"What about the wall?"

They were standing only a few meters from the top of the Western Wall, but they drove there in Gabriel's SUV. The giant Herodian ashlars were ablaze with light, as was the broad plaza that lay at their base. Gabriel had made no attempt to close it for Khalid's visit. It was crowded with worshippers and tourists.

"The men and women pray separately," the Saudi observed archly.

"Much to the dismay of more liberal Jews."

"Perhaps we can change that."

"Shwaya, shwaya," said Gabriel.

Khalid removed a small slip of paper from the breast pocket of his jacket. "It's a prayer for Reema. I'd like to leave it in the wall."

Gabriel placed a *kippah* atop Khalid's dark hair and watched as he approached the wall. He slipped the note between two of the ashlars and bowed his head in silent prayer, and when he returned his eyes were wet with tears. Gabriel's SUV was parked outside Dung Gate. They crossed to the western side of the city and made their way to the old neighborhood known as Nachlaot. At the entrance of Narkiss Street was a security checkpoint. They passed through without slowing and parked outside the limestone apartment house at Number 16.

"Where are we now?" asked Khalid.

"Home," said Gabriel.

39

Jerusalem

Chiara had opened a bottle of Domaine du Castel, a Bordeaux-style wine from the Judean Hills. Khalid readily accepted a glass. Now that he had been deposed, he said, he no longer had any excuse to maintain the appearance of strict Wahhabi piety. He seemed surprised a man as powerful as Gabriel Allon lived in so modest a dwelling. But then again, almost any home would seem humble to a prince who had been raised in a palace the size of a city block.

His gaze traveled expertly over the paintings hanging on the walls of the sitting room. "Yours?"

"Some," answered Gabriel.

"And the others?"

"My mother and grandfather. And one or two by my first wife."

Chiara had prepared enough food for Khalid and the entourage that used to accompany him everywhere he went. It was arrayed on the buffet in the dining room. Khalid sat at the head of the table, with Gabriel and Chiara on one side and Raphael and Irene on the other. Gabriel introduced Khalid to the children as "Mr. Abdulaziz," but he insisted they refer to him only by his given name. They were clearly intrigued by his presence in the Allon home. Gabriel rarely entertained outsiders at Narkiss Street, and the children, despite living in close proximity to East Jerusalem, seldom saw Arabs, let alone dined with them.

Nevertheless, it took only a few minutes for the children to fall under Khalid's spell. With his black hair, sharp features, and warm brown eyes, he looked like the Hollywood version of an Arab prince. One could easily picture Khalid, in the robes and headdress of the desert, riding into battle at the side of T. E. Lawrence. Even without the money and expensive toys, his charm and charisma were irresistible.

They spoke only of safe topics—paintings, books, his journey through a portion of Israel and the West Bank, anything but Reema's death and Khalid's fall from grace. He was telling the children tales of falconry when sirens wailed over Nachlaot. Gabriel rang King Saul Boulevard and learned there was yet another incoming missile from Syria, this one heading in the general direction of Jerusalem.

"What if it hits the Haram al-Sharif?" asked Khaled.

"Your trip to Israel will get a lot more interesting."

For several minutes they sat waiting for the thud of impact until finally the sirens went silent. Gabriel rang King Saul Boulevard a second time and learned the missile had been intercepted. Its wreckage had fallen harmlessly to earth in a field outside the West Bank settlement of Ofra.

By nine o'clock the children began to squirm and slump. Chiara shepherded them off to bed while Gabriel and Khalid finished the last of the wine on the terrace. Khalid sat in Shamron's usual chair. The smell of eucalyptus was intoxicating.

"Is this part of hiding in plain sight?"

"I'm afraid my address is the worst-kept secret in Israel."

"And your first wife? Where is she?"

Gabriel gazed toward the west. The hospital, he explained, was located in the old Arab village of Deir Yassin, where Jewish fighters from the Irgun and Lehi paramilitary groups massacred more than a hundred Palestinians on the night of April 9, 1948.

"How terribly poignant she should live in a place like that."

"Such is life," replied Gabriel, "in the twice-promised land."

Khalid smiled sadly. "Did you see it happen?"

"What's that?"

"The bomb that killed your child and wounded your wife?"

Gabriel nodded slowly.

"You spared me such a memory. I suppose I should be grateful." Khalid drank some of the wine. "Do you remember the things you said to the kidnappers when you were negotiating Reema's return?"

"I have the recordings."

"And what about the words you were shouting after the bomb went off?"

Gabriel said nothing.

"I must admit," said Khalid, "I have thought of nothing else since that night."

"You know what they say about vengeance?"

"What's that?"

" 'If you live to seek revenge, dig a grave for two.' "

"That's a very old Arab proverb."

"It's Jewish, actually."

"Don't be silly," said Khalid with a flash of his old arrogance. "Have you made any attempt to find them?"

"We've made inquiries," answered Gabriel vaguely.

"Have any borne fruit?"

Gabriel shook his head.

"Neither have mine."

"Perhaps we should pool our resources."

"I agree," said Khalid. "Where should we begin?"

"Omar Nawwaf."

"What about him?"

"Why did you give the order for him to be killed?"

Khalid hesitated, then said, "I was advised to."

"By whom?"

"My dear uncle Abdullah," said Khalid. "The next king of Saudi Arabia."

40

Jerusalem

But it was the Americans, began Khalid, only half in jest, who were ultimately to blame. After the attacks of 9/11, they demanded the royal family crack down on al-Qaeda and stem the flow of money and Wahhabi ideology that had given rise to it. The Kingdom's links to the worst attack on the American homeland in history were undeniable. Fifteen of the nineteen hijackers were Saudi citizens, and Osama bin Laden, al-Qaeda's founder and guiding light, was the scion of a notable Saudi family that had grown fabulously wealthy through its close financial ties to the House of Saud.

"There are many reasons why nine-eleven happened," said Khalid, "but we Saudis must accept responsibility for our role. The attack left an indelible stain on our country and on my family, and something like it must never happen again."

To effectively combat al-Qaeda, the Kingdom sorely needed cybersurveillance technology so it could monitor the Internet-based communications of suspected terrorists and their fellow travelers, especially after the global jihadist movement morphed and shapeshifted with the advent of social media. To that end, it established the vaguely named Royal Data Center and filled it with sophisticated cybertools purchased from the tech-savvy Emiratis and a private Italian firm. The center even acquired mobile phone-hacking software from an Israeli company called ONS Systems. Gabriel was aware of the transaction. He had vehemently opposed it, as had the chief of Unit 8200, but both were overruled by the prime minister.

The Royal Data Center allowed the regime to monitor not only potential terrorists but ordinary political opponents as well. For that reason, Khalid seized control of it when he became crown prince. He used it to spy on the mobile devices of his enemies and track their activity in cyberspace. The center also gave Khalid the power to monitor and manipulate the social network. He was not ashamed to admit that, like the American president, he was obsessed by his standing in the parallel universe of Twitter and Facebook. It was not merely vanity that drove his preoccupation. He feared he might be toppled by an Internet-inspired "hashtag" uprising like the one that had brought down Mubarak of Egypt. Qatar, his blood rival in the Gulf, was working against him online. So were a number of commentators and journalists who had acquired large cyberfollowings of young, restless Arabs desperate for political change. One such commentator was a Saudi named Omar Nawwaf.

Nawwaf was the editor in chief of the *Arab News*, Saudi Arabia's most prominent English-language daily. A veteran Middle East correspondent, he had managed to maintain good relations with both the House of Saud, to whom he owed his survival as a journalist, and al-Qaeda and the Muslim Brotherhood. As a result, the royal court regularly used him as an emissary to the forces of political Islam. Religiously secular himself, Nawwaf had long championed loosening the Wahhabi-inspired restrictions on women in Saudi society, and initially he greeted the rise of a young reform-minded KBM with editorial enthusiasm. His support dissolved as Khalid ruthlessly suppressed political opposition and enriched himself at the public trough.

It did not take Khalid and his courtiers long to realize they had "an Omar Nawwaf problem." At first, they tried to defuse the situation with charm and engagement. But when Nawwaf's criticism intensified, he was warned to cease and desist, or suffer dire consequences. Faced with a choice between silence or exile, Nawwaf chose exile. He took refuge in Berlin and found work at *Der Spiegel*, Germany's most important newsmagazine. Now free of Saudi Arabia's machinery of repression, he unleashed a torrent of biting commentary targeted at its headstrong crown prince, painting him as a fraud and a grifter who had no intention of delivering real political reform to the calcifying Kingdom. Khalid waged war on Nawwaf from within the Royal Data Center, but it was no use. On Twitter alone, Nawwaf had some ten million followers, many more than Khalid. The meddlesome exiled journalist was winning the battle of ideas on social media.

"And then," said Khalid, "there was a most intriguing development. Omar Nawwaf, my great detractor, requested an interview."

"And you declined?"

"I didn't give it a moment's thought."

"What happened?"

Nawwaf made a second request. Then a third. And when none met with a response, he used his contacts inside the House of Saud to send a message to Khalid directly.

"It seemed the interview request was a ruse from

the beginning. Omar claimed he had uncovered information regarding a threat against me. He insisted on telling me about this threat in person. Obviously, given everything he had written and said about me, I was skeptical. So were my security men. They were convinced he wanted to kill me."

"With what? A pen and a notebook?"

"When Bin Laden killed Ahmad Shah Massoud of the Northern Alliance two days before nine-eleven, the assassins posed as television journalists."

"Go on," said Gabriel.

"I know you think I'm impulsive and reckless, but I gave the matter thorough consideration. In the end, I decided to see him. I sent a message through the Saudi Embassy in Berlin inviting Omar to return to the Kingdom, but he refused. He said he would only meet in a neutral location, somewhere he would feel safe. My security men were more convinced than ever that Omar intended to kill me."

"And you?"

"I wasn't so sure. Frankly, if I were in Omar's position, I wouldn't return to the Kingdom, either."

"But you wanted to hear what he had to say?"

"His sources," said Khalid, "are impeccable. Omar had the entire region wired."

"So what did you do?"

"I sought advice from someone I thought I could trust."

"Uncle Abdullah?"

Khalid nodded. "The next king of Saudi Arabia."

Abdullah bin Abdulaziz Al Saud was not a member of the Sudairi Seven, the internal royal bloodline of the Founder's sons that had produced three Saudi monarchs, including Khalid's father. Therefore, he had assumed he would never be a king. He had lived his life accordingly, with one foot in Saudi Arabia and another in the West. Nevertheless, he remained an important figure inside the House of Saud, respected for his intellect and political acumen. Khalid found his uncle to be a source of sage counsel, precisely because he opposed many of Khalid's reforms, including those involving women, for whom Abdullah had but one use.

"And when you told your uncle about Omar Nawwaf?"

"He was alarmed."

"What did he suggest?"

Khalid drew a forefinger across his throat.

"Rather drastic, don't you think?"

"Not by our standards."

"But you were supposed to be different, Khalid. You

were supposed to be the one who was going to change the Middle East and the Islamic world."

"I can't change the world if I'm dead, can I?"

"What about the blowback?"

"Abdullah promised there wouldn't be any."

"How wise of him," said Gabriel dryly. "But why would he say such a thing?"

"Because my hands would be clean."

"Abdullah said he would take care of it?"

Khalid nodded.

"How did he get Nawwaf to come to the consulate in Istanbul?"

"How do you think?"

"Nawwaf was told you were going to be there."

"Very good."

"And the nonsense you put out after he was dead? The happy talk about a rendition operation that went sideways?"

"Omar Nawwaf," said Khalid gravely, "was never going to leave that consulate alive."

"Rather sloppy, don't you think?"

"Abdullah wanted a noisy kill to scare off other potential assassins."

"It was noisy, all right. And now your uncle is next in line to the throne."

"And I'm sitting here with you in al-Quds." Khalid listened to the stirring of the ancient city. "It does look as though Abdullah baited me into a reckless act in order to damage my international standing and weaken me at home."

"Yes, it does."

"But what if we're looking at this the wrong way?"

"What would be the right way?"

"What if Omar Nawwaf really wanted to warn me about a grave threat?" Khalid checked his wristwatch. "My God, look at the time."

"It's early by our standards."

Khalid placed a hand on Gabriel's shoulder. "I can't thank you enough for inviting me here."

"It will be our little secret."

Khalid smiled. "I considered bringing you a gift, but I knew you wouldn't accept it, so I'm afraid this will have to do." He held up a flash drive. "Beautiful, isn't it?"

"What's on it?"

"Some of the financial records I acquired during the affair at the Ritz-Carlton. My uncle Abdullah was a terrible businessman, but a couple of years ago he became a billionaire almost overnight." He pressed the flash drive into Gabriel's palm. "Perhaps you can figure out exactly how he did it."

41

New York–Berlin

On the evening of Khalid's unlikely visit to Jerusalem, Sarah Bancroft was on a date with the man of her nightmares. His name was David Price, and they had been thrust together by a mutual friend at an auction at Christie's. David was fifty-seven and did something with money, a virile-looking creature with sleek black hair, gleaming white teeth, and a deep tan he had acquired while on holiday in the Caribbean with his ex-wife and their two college-age children. He took her to a new play the *Times* had declared important and, afterward, to Joe Allen, where he was well known to the bartenders and the waitstaff. Later, at the entrance of her apartment building on East Sixty-Seventh Street, Sarah avoided his lips as though she were sidestepping a puddle. Upstairs, she rang her mother, something she rarely did, and lamented the state of her love life. Her mother, who knew little of Sarah's secret past, suggested she take up yoga, which she swore had done wonders for her.

In fairness, it was not entirely David Price's fault the evening had not gone well. Sarah had been preoccupied by Khalid's sudden request to once again place him in touch with Gabriel. It was the first contact she had had with either man since returning to New York. She had learned of Khalid's abdication by watching CNN and had assumed that Reema had been returned safely. Gabriel, however, had told her the truth. Sarah knew that such an act would not go unpunished. The people responsible would be hunted down, there would be an operation of retribution. All the more reason why her mind had wandered during the play—she could scarcely recall a line the actors spoke—and over dinner at Joe Allen. She wanted to be back in the field with Gabriel and Mikhail and the mysterious Englishman named Christopher Keller, not making small talk over liver and onions with a divorced hedgie from Connecticut.

And so Sarah was not at all displeased when three days later she woke to find in her in-box a boarding pass for that evening's Lufthansa flight to Berlin. She informed her staff of her travel plans, inaccurately, and saw herself to Newark Airport. It seemed her seatmate, an investment banker from Morgan Stanley, had vowed to drink the aircraft dry. Sarah picked at her dinner and then slept until a snow-dusted German field appeared beneath her window. A courier from the Office's Berlin Station approached her in the arrivals hall and directed her to a waiting BMW sedan. Mikhail was behind the wheel.

"At least it's not another damn Passat," she said as she slid into the passenger seat.

Mikhail followed the airport exit ramp to the autobahn and headed into Charlottenburg. Sarah knew the neighborhood well. While still at the CIA, she had spent six months in Berlin working with the German BfV against an al-Qaeda cell plotting another 9/11 from an apartment on Kantstrasse. Mikhail had secretly visited Sarah several times during her assignment.

"It's good to be back," said Sarah provocatively. "I've always enjoyed Berlin."

"Especially in late winter." The guardrails were spattered with dirty snow, and at half past eight in the morning the sky was still dark. "I suppose we should consider ourselves lucky she isn't living in Oslo."

"Who?"

Mikhail didn't answer.

"Were you there when Reema was killed?"

"Close enough," answered Mikhail. "Keller, too."

"Is he in Berlin?"

"Keller?" Mikhail shot her a sidelong glance. "Why do you ask?"

"Just curious, that's all."

"Christopher is otherwise engaged at the moment. It's just the three of us again."

"Where's Gabriel?"

"The safe flat."

Mikhail turned onto Bundesstrasse and followed it to the Tiergarten. There was a demonstration at the Brandenburg Gate, a couple of hundred people, mainly in their twenties, wearing jeans and Scandinavian-style woolen sweaters. They looked like Green Party stalwarts or peace protesters. Their signs, however, betrayed their true political convictions.

"They're from a group called Generation Identity," explained Mikhail. "They look quite harmless, but they espouse the same ideology as the skinheads and the rest of the neo-Nazis."

He made a right turn into Ebertstrasse and lapsed into silence as they passed Berlin's stark Holocaust memorial, with its twenty-seven hundred slabs of gray concrete arranged on a plot of land the size of a city block. Sarah had taken Mikhail to the memorial during one of his secret visits to Berlin. It had ruined the weekend.

At Potsdamer Platz, once a Cold War wasteland, now a glass-and-steel monument to German economic might, Mikhail headed eastward into the district of Mitte. He made a series of consecutive right turns, a time-tested countersurveillance maneuver, before abruptly pulling to the curb on Kronenstrasse and switching off the engine.

"How much do you know about Gabriel's family?" he asked.

"The basics, I suppose."

"He's a German Jew, our Gabriel. Even though he was born in Israel, he learned to speak German before Hebrew. That's why he has such a pronounced Berlin accent. He picked it up from his mother." Mikhail pointed toward a modern apartment block with windows that shone like polished onyx. "When she was a child, she lived in a building that stood right there. In the autumn of 1942, she was shipped to Auschwitz in a cattle car along with the rest of her family. She was the only one to survive."

A tear spilled onto Sarah's cheek. "Is there a reason you wanted me to see this?"

"Because the safe flat is right there." Mikhail pointed

toward the building opposite. "Gabriel took out a long-term lease when he became chief."

"Does he come often?"

"To Berlin?" Mikhail shook his head. "He hates the place."

"So why are we here?"

"Hanifa," answered Mikhail as he opened the car door. "We're here because of Hanifa."

42

Berlin

It was 8:15 p.m. when Hanifa Khoury, a veteran field producer for the German state broadcaster ZDF, stepped onto the damp pavements of Unter den Linden. A cold wind blew through the leafless trees that gave the famous boulevard its name. Shivering, Hanifa wrapped a black-and-white checkered keffiyeh tightly around her neck. Unlike most Germans, she did not wear the garment for reasons of fashion or anti-Israeli politics; Hanifa was of Palestinian lineage. Her eyes scanned the street in both directions. Having worked as a journalist throughout the Middle East, she was adept at spotting surveillance, especially when carried out by fellow Arabs. She saw nothing suspicious. In fact, it had been several weeks since she had noticed anyone watching her. Perhaps, she thought, they had finally decided to leave her alone.

She followed Unter den Linden to Friedrichstrasse and turned left. Near the old Checkpoint Charlie was the café-bar where she used to meet Omar after work. An attractive woman, blond, early forties, was sitting at their usual table, the one in the back corner with an unobstructed view of the front door. She was reading a volume of poetry by Mahmoud Darwish, the bard of the Palestinian national movement. As Hanifa approached, the woman lifted her eyes from the page, smiled, and looked down again.

Hanifa stopped suddenly. "Are you enjoying it?"

The woman was slow in responding. "I'm sorry," she said in English. "I don't speak German."

The accent was unmistakably American. Hanifa considered feigning incomprehension and finding a table as far away from the attractive blond woman as possible—or perhaps, she thought, in another café altogether. The only people Hanifa despised more than Americans were Israelis, though at times, depending on the whims of American policy in the Middle East, it was a close contest.

"The book," she said, this time in English. "I asked whether you were enjoying it."

"Can one truly enjoy such painful verse?"

The remark surprised Hanifa, pleasantly. "I met him not long before he died."

"Darwish? Really?"

"I produced one of the last interviews he ever gave."

"You're a journalist?"

Hanifa nodded. "ZDF. And you?"

"At the moment I'm on an extended holiday."

"Lucky you."

"Hardly."

"You're an American?"

"I'm afraid so." The woman contemplated the black-and-white keffiyeh around Hanifa's neck. "I hope that's not a problem."

"Why would it be?"

"We're not terribly popular right now." The woman placed the book upon the table so Hanifa could see the open page. "Are you familiar with this one?"

"Of course. It's very famous." Hanifa recited the poem's opening words from memory. " 'Here on the slopes of hills, facing the dusk and the cannon of time . . .' " She smiled. "It sounds much better in the original Arabic."

"You're from Palestine?"

"My parents were from the Upper Galilee. They

were expelled to Syria in 1948 and eventually came here." Hanifa lowered her voice and asked archly, "I hope that's not a problem."

The woman smiled.

Hanifa glanced at the empty chair. "Are you waiting for someone?"

"As a general proposition, yes. But not at the moment."

"May I join you?"

"Please."

Hanifa sat down and introduced herself.

"What a beautiful name," said the woman. Then she extended her hand. "I'm Sarah Bancroft."

For the next ninety minutes, alone in the safe flat on Kronenstrasse, Gabriel suffered through a discourse on the subject of Israel and the Jews, delivered by one Hanifa Khoury, journalist, exile, widow of the martyr Omar Nawwaf. She left no wound unopened: the Holocaust, the flight and expulsion of the Palestinian people, the horror of Sabra and Shatila, the Oslo peace process, which she declared a dangerous folly. On that much, at least, she and Gabriel were in complete agreement.

The source of the audio was the phone that Sarah had laid on the table immediately after sitting down at the café. Its camera was aimed toward the ceiling. Gabriel occasionally glimpsed Hanifa's hands as she described her plan to bring peace to Palestine. She declared the idea of two states, one for Jews, the other for Arabs, a dead letter. The only just solution, she said, was a single binational state, with a full and irrevocable "right of return" for all five million registered Palestinian refugees.

"But wouldn't that mean an end to the Jewish state?" asked Sarah.

"Yes, of course. But that's the point."

Hanifa then treated Gabriel to a reading of poetry by Mahmoud Darwish, the voice of Palestinian suffering and Israeli oppression, before finally asking her newfound American acquaintance why she had decided to take an extended holiday in Berlin, of all places. Sarah recited the story that Gabriel had composed that afternoon. It concerned the disastrous dissolution of a childless marriage. Humiliated and brokenhearted, Sarah had decided to spend a few months in a city where no one knew her. A friend had offered his Berlin pied-à-terre. It was around the corner from the café, she explained, on Kronenstrasse.

"And what about you?" asked Sarah. "Are you married?"

"Only to my work."

"Your name is familiar."

"It's quite common, actually."

"Your face is familiar, too. It's almost as if we've met before."

"I get that a lot."

By then, it was half past nine. Hanifa announced she was famished. She suggested they order something to eat, but Sarah insisted they have dinner at her apartment instead. The cupboard was bare, but they could grab a couple of bottles at Planet Wein and some crunchy shrimp rolls from Sapa Sushi.

"I prefer Izumi," said Hanifa.

"Izumi it is."

Sarah paid for the two bottles of chilled Austrian Grüner Veltliner; Hanifa, for the sushi. A few minutes later, Gabriel glimpsed them walking side by side along Kronenstrasse. He closed his laptop computer, doused the lights, and sat down on the couch. "Don't scream," he said softly. "Whatever you do, Hanifa, please don't scream."

43

Berlin

Hanifa Khoury did not scream, but she dropped the bag of takeaway sushi and emitted a sharp gasp that the neighbors might well have heard had Mikhail not closed the door behind her. Startled by the sound, she glared at him for a moment before turning her gaze once more to Gabriel. A range of expressions passed like the shadow of a cloud over her face. The last was an unmistakable look of recognition.

"My God, it's—"

"Yes," said Gabriel, cutting her off. "It's me."

She reached for the door, but Mikhail was leaning against it in the manner of a man waiting for a bus. Then she dug a phone from her handbag and tried to dial a number.

"I wouldn't bother," said Gabriel. "The service is terrible in this building."

"Or maybe you're blocking it so I can't call for help."

"You're perfectly safe, Hanifa. In fact, you're much safer now than you've been in some time."

Gabriel glanced at Mikhail, who plucked the phone from Hanifa's grasp. Next he took her handbag and searched its contents.

"What's he looking for?"

"A suicide vest, an AK-47 . . ." Gabriel shrugged. "The usual."

Mikhail kept the phone but returned the handbag. Hanifa looked at Sarah. "Is she Israeli, too?"

"What else would she be?"

"She speaks English like an American."

"The diaspora gives us a decided advantage when recruiting officers."

"The Jews are not the only people who were scattered to the four winds."

"No," agreed Gabriel. "The Palestinians have suffered, too. But they have never been the target of an organized campaign of physical annihilation like the Shoah. That is why we must have a state of our own. We cannot count on Germans or Poles or Hungarians or Latvians to protect us. That is history's lesson."

Gabriel spoke these words not in English but in German. Hanifa replied in the same language. "Is that why you've kidnapped me? To once again throw the Holocaust in my face to justify turning me into an exile?"

"We haven't kidnapped you."

"The Bundespolizei might see it differently."

"They might," replied Gabriel. "But I have a very good relationship with the chief of the BfV, mainly because I provide him with a great deal of intelligence about threats to German security. Oh, I suppose you could cause me a bit of embarrassment, but you would be missing out on an important opportunity."

"What kind of opportunity?"

"To change the course of events in the Middle East."

She regarded him inquiringly. Her eyes were almost black and prominently lidded. It was like being contemplated by Klimt's Adele Bloch-Bauer. "How?" she asked at last.

"By giving me the story Omar was working on before he was killed." Receiving no answer, Gabriel said, "Omar wasn't murdered in that consulate because of the things he was writing on social media. He was killed because he tried to warn Khalid about a plot against him."

"Says who?"

"Khalid."

Hanifa's eyes narrowed. "As usual," she said bitterly, "Khalid is mistaken."

"How so?"

"Omar wasn't the one who tried to warn him about the plot."

"Who was it?"

Hanifa hesitated, then said, "It was me."

44

Berlin

The sushi lay scattered over the floor of the entrance hall, so Mikhail went downstairs to the local Persian takeaway and picked up several orders of grilled meat and rice. They ate at the flat's small rectangular table, which was set against a window overlooking Kronenstrasse. Gabriel sat with his back to the street, with Hanifa Khoury, his new recruit, at his left hand. Throughout the meal, she scarcely looked in Sarah's direction. It was obvious she had not forgiven her for using a volume of Mahmoud Darwish, Palestine's literary treasure, as bait to ensnare her. It was obvious, too, that she did not believe Sarah to be a citizen of the state she wished to inundate beneath a sea of returning Palestinian exiles.

All Hanifa Khoury had to do to prove her point was

to ask Sarah to speak a few words in Hebrew. Instead, she used the occasion to berate the legendary chief of Israeli intelligence for the crimes he and his people had committed against hers. Gabriel suffered through the tirade largely in silence. He had learned long ago that most debates over the Arab-Israeli conflict quickly took on the quality of a cat chasing its own tail. Besides, he did not want to lose Hanifa as a temporary ally. The Jews had prevailed in the contest for Palestine, the Arabs had lost. They had been outsmarted and outfought at every turn. They had been ill served by their leaders. Hanifa was entitled to her pain and anger, though her lecture might have been more tolerable had it not been delivered in German in the city where Hitler and the Nazis had conceived and executed their plan to rid Europe of the Jews. There was nothing to be done about the setting. The great roulette wheel of providence had placed Gabriel Allon and Hanifa Khoury, both children of Palestine, in Berlin that night.

Over coffee and baklava, Hanifa attempted to draw out Gabriel on some of his exploits. And when he gently fended her off, she trained her rhetorical fire on the Americans and their disastrous intervention in Iraq. She had entered Baghdad behind the advancing Coalition forces and had chronicled Iraq's rapid descent into insurgency and sectarian civil war. In the autumn of

2003, during the bloody Ramadan Offensive, she met a tall, handsome Saudi journalist in the bar of the Palestine Hotel, where she had taken up residence. The Saudi, while not well known to most Western reporters, was one of the most influential and best-sourced journalists in the Arab world.

"His name," she said, "was Omar Nawwaf."

They were both single and, truth be told, both a little frightened. The Palestine Hotel was located outside the American Green Zone and was a frequent target of the insurgents. Indeed, on that very night, it came under sustained mortar fire. Hanifa took shelter in Omar's room. She returned the next night, which was peaceful, and the night after that as well. They soon fell desperately in love, though they quarreled often about the American presence in Iraq.

"Omar believed Saddam was a menace and a monster who needed to be removed, even if it had to be done with American troops. He also accepted the proposition that the establishment of a democracy in the heart of the Arab world would inevitably spread freedom to the rest of the region. I thought the Iraq adventure would end in disaster. I was right, of course." She smiled sadly. "Omar didn't like that. He was a secular, Western-looking Saudi, but he was still a Saudi, if you know what I mean."

"He didn't like being proven wrong by a woman?"

"And a Palestinian woman at that."

For a brief moment, however, it appeared Omar had been right after all. Beginning in early 2011, the popular uprising known as the Arab Spring swept the region. Oppressive regimes crumbled in Tunisia, Egypt, Yemen, and Libya, and a full-fledged civil war erupted in Syria. The old ancestral monarchies fared better, but in Saudi Arabia there were violent clashes. Dozens of demonstrators were shot or executed. Hundreds were jailed, including many women.

"During the Arab Spring," said Hanifa, "Omar was no longer a mere correspondent. He was the editor in chief of the *Arab News*. Privately, he hoped His Majesty would meet the same fate as Mubarak or even Gadhafi. But he knew that if he pushed too hard, the Al Saud would shut down the paper and throw him into jail. He had no choice but to editorially support the regime. He even signed his name to a column criticizing the protesters as foreign-inspired hooligans. After that, he fell into a deep depression. Omar never forgave himself for sitting out the Arab Spring."

Hanifa tried to convince Omar to leave Saudi Arabia and settle with her in Germany, where he would be free to write whatever he wanted without fear of arrest. And in early 2016, as the Saudi economy stag-nated under the pressure of falling oil prices, he finally agreed. He changed his mind a few weeks later, how-ever, after meeting a rising young Saudi prince named Khalid bin Mohammed.

"It was not long after Khalid's father ascended to the throne. Khalid was already the minister of defense, deputy prime minister, and chairman of the economic planning council, but he was not yet the crown prince and the heir apparent. He invited Omar to his palace one afternoon for an off-the-record briefing. Omar arrived, as instructed, at four o'clock. It was well past midnight when he left."

There was no recording of the session—Khalid wouldn't permit it—and no contemporaneous notes, only the memo Omar hastily composed after returning to his office. He e-mailed a copy to Hanifa for safekeep-ing. She was shocked when she read it. Khalid pre-dicted that in twenty years, the price of oil would fall to zero. If Saudi Arabia was to have any future, it had to change, and quickly. He wanted to modernize and di-versify the economy. He wanted to loosen the Wahhabi shackles on women and draw them into the workforce. He wanted to break the covenant between the Al Saud and the bearded Ikhwan from the Nejd. He wanted

Saudi Arabia to be a *normal* country, with movie theaters, music, nightclubs, and cafés where people of both sexes could mingle without fear of the Mutaween.

"He even talked about allowing hotels and restaurants to serve alcohol so Saudis wouldn't have to make the drive across the causeway to Bahrain every time they wanted a drink. It was radical stuff."

"Omar was impressed?"

"No," said Hanifa. "Omar wasn't impressed. Omar was in love."

There soon appeared in the pages of the *Arab News* many flattering articles about the dynamic young son of the Saudi monarch who went by the initials KBM. But Omar turned on Khalid not long after he became crown prince, when he ordered a roundup of scores of dissidents and pro-democracy activists, including several of Omar's closest friends. The *Arab News* was editorially silent on the arrests, but Omar unleashed a barrage of criticism on social media, including a blistering Twitter post that compared KBM to the ruler of Russia. The chief of KBM's court sent Omar a message instructing him to refrain from any further criticism of His Royal Highness. Omar responded by ridiculing KBM for purchasing more than a billion dollars' worth of homes, yachts, and paintings while ordinary Saudis suffered under his economic austerity measures.

"After that," said Hanifa, "it was game on."

But in a country like Saudi Arabia, there was only one possible outcome for a contest between the royal family and a dissident journalist. The Royal Data Center monitored Omar's phones and intercepted his e-mails and text messages. The center even tried to disable his social media feeds. And when that failed, they attacked them with thousands of fake postings from bots and trolls. But the last straw was the bullet, a single .45-caliber round, delivered to Omar's office at the *Arab News*. He left Saudi Arabia that night and never returned.

He moved into Hanifa's apartment, married her in a quiet ceremony, and found work at *Der Spiegel*. As his social media posts grew ever more critical of KBM, his number of online followers increased dramatically. Saudi agents brazenly trailed him through the streets of Berlin. His phone was besieged by threatening e-mails and texts.

"The message was unmistakable. It didn't matter that Omar had left the Kingdom, they could still get to him. He became convinced he was going to be kidnapped or killed."

Nevertheless, he decided to risk a trip to Cairo to write a story about life in Egypt under the new pharaoh, whom Omar despised almost as much as Khalid. And in the lobby of the Hotel Sofitel, he happened upon

314 • DANIEL SILVA

a minor Saudi prince whom Khalid had fleeced in the Ritz-Carlton Hotel. The minor prince, like Omar, was now living in exile. They agreed to have dinner that night at a restaurant in Zamalek, an affluent quarter of Cairo located on Gezira Island. It was late summer, August, and the night was stifling. Even so, the minor prince insisted on dining al fresco. When they were seated, he instructed Omar to switch off his phone and remove the SIM card. Then he told Omar about a rumor he had heard concerning a plot to remove Khalid from the line of succession.

"Omar expressed skepticism over the plot's chances for success. KBM had been the target of numerous assassination and coup attempts, and all had failed because he controlled the security services and the Royal Data Center. But the prince insisted this plot was different."

"Why?"

"A foreign power was involved."

"Which one?"

"The prince didn't know. But he told Omar the plot involved Khalid's daughter. The conspirators were planning to kidnap her in order to force Khalid to abdicate."

"You're sure it was August?"

"I can show you the text messages Omar sent from Cairo."

"Did they contain any reference to the plot against Khalid?"

"Of course not. Omar knew the Royal Data Center was monitoring his communications. He waited until he was back in Berlin before telling me. We spoke in the Tiergarten, no phones. I'm afraid Omar didn't care much for my reaction."

"You wanted Omar to tell Khalid about the plot."

"I said he was obliged to."

"Because Khalid's daughter might be killed?"

She nodded. "And because, despite all his faults and failings, Khalid was better than the alternative."

"I take it Omar disagreed."

"He said it would be journalistically unethical for him to tell Khalid what he'd learned."

"What did he do?"

"He went back to the Middle East to try to turn a rumor into an actual news story."

"And you?"

"I pretended to be Omar."

"How?"

She created a Yahoo account with an address that was a play on Omar's name: omwaf5179@yahoo.com.

Then she sent a series of e-mails to the Saudi Ministry of Media requesting an interview with His Royal
Highness Prince Khalid bin Mohammed. There was no
reply—not unusual where the Saudis were concerned—
so she dispatched a warning to an address she found
in Omar's contacts. It was someone close to KBM, a
senior man in his royal court.

"You told him about the plot?"

"Not in any detail."

"Did you mention Reema?"

"No."

A few days later Hanifa received an e-mail from the
Saudi Embassy in Berlin. Khalid wanted Omar to return to Riyadh so they could meet. Hanifa's response
made it clear Omar would never set foot in the Kingdom again. A week passed. Then she received a final
e-mail from the address of the senior man in Khalid's
court. He wanted Omar to come to the consulate in Istanbul the following Tuesday at one fifteen in the afternoon. Khalid would be waiting.

45

Berlin

When Omar returned to Berlin, Hanifa told him what she had done in his name. Once again, they spoke in the Tiergarten, no phones, but this time it was obvious they were being followed. Omar was furious with her, though he hid his anger from the watching Saudi agents. His reporting trip to the Middle East had borne fruit. He had confirmed everything he had been told by his source in Cairo, including the involvement of a foreign power in the plot against Khalid. Omar now faced a difficult choice. If he wrote what he knew in the pages of *Der Spiegel*, Khalid would use the information to crush the coup and consolidate his grip on power. But if Omar allowed the conspiracy to unfold as planned, an innocent child might be harmed, or even killed.

"And the invitation to come to Istanbul?" asked Gabriel.

"Omar thought it was a trap."

"So why did he agree to go?"

"Because I convinced him." Hanifa was silent for a moment. "I'm to blame for Omar's death. He would have never walked into that consulate were it not for me."

"How did you change his mind?"

"By telling him he was going to be a father."

"You're pregnant?"

"I *was* pregnant. I'm not anymore."

Their conversation in the Tiergarten occurred on the Friday. Hanifa sent an e-mail to the address of Khalid's aide and informed him that Omar would arrive at the consulate the following Tuesday, as requested, at 1:15 p.m. He spent Saturday and Sunday turning his recordings and notes into a coherent story for *Der Spiegel*, and on Monday he and Hanifa flew to Istanbul and checked into the InterContinental Hotel. That evening, as they strolled along the Bosporus, they were followed by both Saudi and Turkish surveillance teams.

"On Tuesday morning, Omar was so nervous I was afraid he might have a heart attack. I managed to calm him down. 'If they're going to kill you,' I said, 'the last place on earth they would do it is inside one of their consulates.' We left the hotel at twelve thirty. The traffic was so terrible we barely made it on time. At the security barricades, Omar gave me his phone. Then he kissed me and went inside."

It was 1:14 p.m. Shortly after three, Hanifa rang the consulate's main number and asked if Omar was there. The man who answered said Omar had never arrived for his appointment. And when Hanifa called back an hour later, a different man said Omar had already left. At four fifteen she saw several men walk out of the building with large pieces of luggage. His Royal Highness Prince Khalid bin Mohammed was not one of them.

When Hanifa finally returned to the InterContinental, the room had been ransacked and Omar's laptop was missing. She rang ZDF headquarters and filed an urgent report about a journalist from *Der Spiegel* who had disappeared after entering the Saudi consulate in Istanbul. Within forty-eight hours, much of the world was asking the same question: Where was Omar Nawwaf?

Ten days later, after finally being allowed to enter the consulate, the Turkish police declared that Omar had been murdered while he was inside and that his body had been gruesomely dismembered and disposed of. Almost overnight, KBM, the great Arab reformer, beloved by the financial and intellectual elites of the West, became an untouchable.

Hanifa remained in Istanbul until late October, monitoring the Turkish investigation. When she finally returned to Berlin she found that her apartment, like her room at the InterContinental, had been torn to pieces. All of Omar's papers had been stolen, including the notes he had taken during his last reporting trip to the Middle East. Heartbroken, Hanifa consoled herself with the knowledge she was carrying Omar's child. But in early November she suffered a miscarriage.

Her first assignment after returning to work took her, of all places, to Geneva. Posing as the wife of a security-conscious Jordanian diplomat, she visited the International School, where she observed the afternoon exodus of the student body. One child, a girl of twelve, departed the school in an armored Mercedes limousine. The headmaster intimated the girl was the daughter of a wealthy Egyptian construction magnate. Hanifa, however, knew the truth. She was Reema bint Khalid Abdulaziz Al Saud, the child of the devil.

"And you never tried to warn the devil his child was in danger?"

"After what he'd done to Omar?" She shook her head. "Besides, I didn't think I needed to."

"Why not?"

"Khalid had Omar's computer and his notes."

Unless, thought Gabriel, it wasn't the Saudis who had taken them. "And when you heard Khalid had abdicated?"

She wept with joy and posted a taunting message on her Twitter feed. A few days later she returned to Geneva to watch the afternoon departure of students from the International School. The child of the devil was nowhere to be seen.

"And yet you remained silent."

Her dark eyes flashed. "If Khalid had killed your—"

"He'd be dead already." After a silence, Gabriel said, "But Khalid isn't solely to blame for Omar's death."

"Don't you dare try to absolve him."

"It's true he authorized it, but it wasn't his idea. In fact, he wanted to meet with Omar to hear what he had to say."

"Why didn't he?"

"He was told Omar intended to kill him."

She was incredulous. "Omar never hurt anyone in his life. Who would say such a thing?"

"Abdullah," said Gabriel. "The next king of Saudi Arabia."

Hanifa's eyes widened. "Abdullah engineered Omar's murder so Khalid wouldn't learn of the plot against him—is that what you're saying?"

"Yes."

"It all fits together very nicely, doesn't it?"

"Your version of the story matches Khalid's perfectly. There's one part, though, that makes no sense at all."

"What's that?"

"There's no way a pair of veteran Middle East reporters like you and Omar didn't make a copy of the story."

"Actually, Mr. Allon, I never said we didn't."

They had made several, in fact. Hanifa had e-mailed encrypted copies of the story to her work account at ZDF and to a personal Gmail account. Fearful of the hackers at the Royal Data Center, she had also loaded the file onto three flash drives. One was carefully hidden in her apartment, and another was locked in her desk at ZDF's Berlin bureau, which was protected by round-the-clock security.

"And the third?" asked Gabriel.

Hanifa produced a flash drive from a zippered compartment of her handbag and laid it on the table. Gabriel opened his laptop and inserted the device into one of the USB ports. An unnamed folder appeared on the screen. When he clicked it, a dialogue box requested a user name.

"Yarmouk," said Hanifa. "It's the refugee camp—"

"I know what it is." Gabriel entered the seven characters, and a single icon appeared.

"Omar," said Hanifa as tears washed over her cheeks. "The password is Omar."

46

Gulf of Aqaba

It was a few minutes after four in the afternoon when El Al Flight 2372 from Berlin landed at Ben Gurion Airport. Gabriel, Mikhail, and Sarah squeezed into the backseat of an Office SUV waiting on the tarmac. Yossi Gavish, the bookish head of Research, was in the passenger seat. As the SUV lurched forward, he handed Gabriel a file. It was a forensic analysis of Crown Prince Abdullah's checkered business career, based in part on the material supplied by Khalid during his visit to Gabriel's home.

"We've got it cold, boss. All the money came from you-know-who."

The SUV stopped next to a private Airbus H175 VIP helicopter that stood, rotors drooping, at the northern end of the airport. Khalid's pilot was behind the controls. Yossi handed a Jericho .45 pistol to Mikhail and a Beretta 9mm to Gabriel.

"The IAF will shadow you as far as they can. Once you get into Egyptian airspace, you're on your own."

Gabriel left his Office BlackBerry and laptop in the SUV and followed Mikhail and Sarah into the Airbus's luxuriously appointed cabin. They flew southward along the coast, over the towns of Ashdod and Ashkelon, then turned inland to avoid the airspace of the Gaza Strip. Fires burned in fields of grain on the Israeli side of the armistice line.

"Hamas starts them with incendiary kites and balloons," Mikhail explained to Sarah.

"It's not such an easy life."

He pointed toward the chaotic skyline of Gaza City. "But it's better than theirs."

Gabriel read Yossi's file twice as the Negev passed beneath them. The sky outside his window darkened slowly, and by the time they reached the southern end of the Gulf of Aqaba the sea was black. *Tranquillity* lay at anchor off Tiran Island, aglow with its distinctive neon-blue running lights. A shore craft hovered protectively off the massive superyacht's port side, another off its starboard.

The Airbus alighted on *Tranquillity*'s forward helipad—there were two—and the pilot shut down the engine. Mikhail exited the cabin and was confronted by a pair of Saudi security men in nylon jackets bearing *Tranquillity*'s insignia. One of the men held out a hand, palm up.

"I have a better idea," said Mikhail. "Why don't you shove—"

"It's all right," Khalid called down from somewhere in the upper reaches of the ship. "Send them up right away."

Gabriel and Sarah joined Mikhail on the foredeck. The two guards scrutinized them, Sarah especially, but made no offer to escort them to Khalid's quarters. Unchaperoned, they wandered *Tranquillity* at their leisure, through the piano lounge and the discotheque, the conference room and the movie cinema, the billiards room, the steam room, the snow room, the ballroom, the fitness center, the archery center, the rock-climbing room, the children's playroom, and the undersea observation center, where the many species of Red Sea aquatic life darted and frolicked for their private amusement on the other side of the thick glass.

They found Khalid on Deck 4, on the terrace outside the owner's suite. He was wearing a zippered North Face fleece, faded jeans, and a pair of elegant Italian suede moccasins. The wind was making waves on the surface of a small swimming pool and fanning the

flames of the inferno that crackled and spat in the out-
door fireplace. It was the last of his wood, he explained.
Otherwise, he was well provisioned with food, fuel, and
fresh water. "I can remain at sea for a year or more if
necessary." He rubbed his hands vigorously together.
"It's cold tonight. Perhaps we should go inside."

He led them into the suite. It was larger than Gabriel's apartment in Jerusalem. "It must be nice," he said
as he surveyed his opulent surroundings. "I don't know
how I ever managed without a private discotheque or a
snow room."

"They mean nothing to me."

"That's because you're the son of a king." Gabriel
displayed the file Yossi had given him at Ben Gurion.
"But you might feel differently if you were merely the
king's half brother."

"I take it you reviewed the documents I gave you in
Jerusalem."

"We used them only as a starting point."

"And where did they lead you?"

"Here," said Gabriel. "To *Tranquillity*."

The primary system by which the Kingdom of Saudi
Arabia funnels the country's immense oil wealth to
members of the royal family is the official monthly stipend. Not all Saudi royals, however, are created equal.

A lowly member of the House of Saud might collect a cash payment of a few thousand dollars, but those with direct blood ties to Ibn Saud receive far more. A grandchild of the Founder typically receives about $27,000 a month; a great-grandchild, about $8,000. Additional payments are available for the construction of a palace, for a marriage, or for the birth of a child. In Saudi Arabia, at least for members of the royal family, there is a financial incentive to procreate.

The largest stipends are reserved for those privileged few at the top of the food chain—the sons of the Founder. He had forty-five in all, including Abdullah bin Abdulaziz. Before his elevation to crown prince, he received a monthly payment of $250,000, or $3 million per year. It was more than enough money to live comfortably, but not lavishly, especially in the Al Saud playgrounds of London and the Côte d'Azur. To supplement his wages, Abdullah siphoned money directly from the state budget or received bribes and kickbacks from Western companies wishing to do business in the Kingdom. A British aerospace firm paid him $20 million in "consulting fees." He used a portion of the money, explained Gabriel, to purchase a grand house at 71 Eaton Square in Belgravia.

"I believe you dined there recently, did you not?"

Receiving no reply, Gabriel continued with his briefing. Abdullah, he said, was quite good at the *other* family business—the business of graft and theft—but in 2016 he got himself into serious financial trouble with a string of bad investments and questionable expenditures. He begged His Majesty King Mohammed for a few extra riyals to cover his living expenses. And when His Majesty refused to bail him out, he prevailed upon his next-door neighbor, the owner of 70 Eaton Square, for a loan. The man's name was Konstantin Dragunov, better known as Konnie Drag to his friends.

"You remember Konstantin, don't you, Khalid? Konstantin is the Russian billionaire who sold you this ridiculous boat." Gabriel made a show of thought. "Remind me how much you paid for it."

"Five hundred million euros."

"In cash, right? Konstantin insisted the money be wired into one of his accounts at Gazprombank in Moscow before he would agree to leave the boat. A few days later he lent your uncle a hundred million pounds." Gabriel paused. "I suppose that's what it means to recirculate petrodollars."

Khalid was silent.

"He's an interesting fellow, our Konstantin. He's a second-generation oligarch, not one of the original robber barons who looted the assets of the old Soviet Union after the fall. Unlike many of the oligarchs, Konstantin is diversified. He's also quite close to the Kremlin. In Russian business circles it is assumed that most of Konstantin's money actually belongs to the Tsar."

"That's the way it works for people like us."

"Us?"

"The Tsar and me. We operate through cutouts and fronts. I'm not the nominal owner of this boat, as you call it, and I don't own the château in France, either." He glanced at Sarah. "Or the Leonardo."

"And when people like you are no longer in power?"

"The money and the toys have a way of disappearing. Abdullah has already taken billions from me. *And* the Leonardo," he added.

"Somehow you'll survive." Gabriel admired Khalid's view of the Egyptian coast. "But back to your uncle. Needless to say, Abdullah never repaid the hundred million pounds Konstantin Dragunov lent him. That's because it wasn't a loan. And it was only the beginning. While you were engaging in court intrigue in Riyadh, Abdullah was doing lucrative business deals in Moscow. He earned more than three billion dollars in the last two years, all through his association with Konstantin Dragunov, which is another way of saying the president of Russia."

"Why was he so interested in Abdullah?"

"I suppose he wanted an ally inside the House of Saud. Someone who was respected for his political acumen. Someone who hated the Americans as much as he did. Someone who could serve as a trusted adviser to a young and untested future king. Someone who might be able to convince the future king to tilt Moscow's way and thus expand the Kremlin's regional influence." Gabriel turned and looked at Khalid. "Someone who might offer to rid the future king of a meddlesome priest. Or a dissident journalist who was trying to warn the future king about a plot to force him to abdicate."

"Are you saying Abdullah conspired with the Russians to seize the throne of Saudi Arabia?"

"I'm not saying it, Omar Nawwaf is." Gabriel drew Hanifa Khoury's flash drive from his pocket. "I don't suppose there's a computer on this boat, is there?"

"Yacht," said Khalid. "Come with me."

There was an iMac in the suite's private study, but Khalid had the good sense not to allow the chief of the Office to impale it with a flash drive. Instead, he led Gabriel down to *Tranquillity*'s hotel-style business center. It contained a half dozen workstations with Internet-connected computers, printers, and multiline phones tied into the ship's satellite communications system.

Khalid sat down at one of the terminals and inserted the flash drive. A dialogue box queried him for a user name.

"Yarmouk," said Gabriel.

"The camp?"

"Her parents ended up there in 1948."

"Yes, I know. We have a file on her, too." Khalid entered the name of the refugee camp, and an icon appeared.

"Omar," said Gabriel. "The password is Omar."

47

Gulf of Aqaba

The story was twelve thousand words in length and rendered in the free-flowing fashion of a reporter at large. Its opening scene described a chance encounter with an exiled Saudi prince in the lobby of a Cairo hotel. Over dinner that evening, the prince told the reporter a remarkable tale about a plot against his country's future king, whom he described unflatteringly as "the most interesting man in the world," a reference to a character in a Mexican beer commercial.

What followed was an account of the reporter's rapid quest to corroborate what he had been told. He traveled far and wide to confer with his many regional sources—including to Dubai, where he spent an anxious forty-eight hours within easy reach of Riyadh's secret services. It was there, in a suite at Burj Al Arab, that a prized source wove the disparate threads he had gathered into a coherent narrative. KBM, he said, had worn out his welcome inside the House of Saud. The White House and the Israelis were in love with him, but he had dispensed with the Al Saud tradition of ruling by consensus and was running roughshod over his kin. A palace coup, or something like it, was inevitable. The Allegiance Council was coalescing around Abdullah, mainly because Abdullah was desperately lobbying for the job.

"And, oh, by the way," the source was quoted as saying, "did I mention Moscow Center is pulling the strings? Abdullah is totally in the Tsar's pocket. If he manages to seize the throne, he's going to tilt so far toward the Kremlin he's likely to fall flat on his face."

From Dubai, the reporter returned to Berlin, where he discovered that his wife, a journalist herself, had been communicating secretly with a member of the crown prince's court. After much soul-searching, chronicled in the article's final passage, he had decided to travel to Turkey to meet with the man who had driven him into exile. The encounter was to take place at the Saudi consulate in Istanbul, at one fifteen in the afternoon.

"So it was Hanifa, not Omar, who was trying to reach me?"

"Yes," answered Gabriel. "And it was Hanifa who convinced Omar to walk into that consulate. She blames herself for his death. Almost as much as she blames you."

"She danced on my grave after I abdicated."

"She had a right."

"She should have told me Reema was in danger."

"She tried."

Khalid had grown weary of reading the long article on a computer screen and was sitting at the table in the adjacent conference room with a printout. Several pages lay on the carpet at his feet, where he had tossed them in anger.

"If she hates me so much, why did she agree to give you Omar's magnum opus?" He snatched up one of the pages and, scowling, reread it. "I can't believe he dared to write these things about me. He called me a spoiled child."

"You are a spoiled child. But what about the rest of it?"

"You mean the part about the Tsar being behind the plot to overthrow me?"

"Yes, that part."

Khalid plucked another page from the floor. "According to Omar's sources, it began after my last visit to Washington, when I agreed to spend a hundred billion dollars on American weaponry instead of buying the arms from Russia."

"Sounds plausible."

"It *sounds* plausible, but it isn't accurate." There was a silence. Then Khalid said quietly, "In fact, if I had to guess, the Tsar probably made up his mind to get rid of me much sooner than that."

"Why?"

"Because he had a plan for the Middle East," replied Khalid. "And I wanted no part of it."

They returned to the owner's suite. Outside on the windblown terrace, Khalid fed Omar Nawwaf's story into the flame, one page at a time. When at last he spoke, it was of Moscow. He made his first trip there, he reminded Gabriel needlessly, a year before he became crown prince. He had just released his economic plan, and the Western press was hanging on his every word. He could get the CEO of any company in the world on the phone in a matter of minutes. Hollywood was head over heels. Silicon Valley, too.

"They were days of wine and roses. Salad days." Mockingly, he added, "I was the most interesting man in the world."

The agenda for the Moscow visit, he explained, was

purely economic. It was part of Khalid's effort to secure the technology and investment he needed to transform the Saudi economy into something other than the
world's gas station. In addition, he and his Russian
hosts planned to discuss means of shoring up the price
of oil, which was bumping along at about forty-five dollars a barrel, an unsustainable level for the Saudi and
Russian economies. Khalid spent the first day meeting
with Russian bankers, and the second with the CEOs
of Russian technology companies, who left him deeply
unimpressed. His meeting with the Tsar was scheduled
for ten a.m. on the third day, a Friday, but it didn't
begin until one in the afternoon.

"He makes *me* seem punctual."

"And the meeting?"

"It was dreadful. He slumped in his chair with his
legs spread wide and his crotch on full display. Aides
interrupted us constantly, and he excused himself three
times to take phone calls. It was a power play, of course.
Head games. He was putting me in my place. I was the
son of an Arab king. To the Tsar, I was nothing."

So Khalid was surprised when, at the conclusion of
the frozen encounter, the Tsar invited him to spend
the weekend at his palace on the Black Sea. Among its
many luxurious appointments was a gold-plated indoor
swimming pool. Khalid was installed in his own wing,

but his aides were scattered among several guesthouses. There was no evidence of the Tsar's wife or children. It was just the two of them.

"I will admit," said Khalid, "I did not feel altogether safe being alone with him."

They spent Saturday morning relaxing by the pool— it was high summer of 2016—and in the afternoon they went for a sail. That evening they dined in a cavernous cream-and-gold chamber. Afterward, they walked to a tiny dacha atop a cliff overlooking the sea.

"And that," said Khalid, "was when he told me."

"Told you what?"

"The master plan. The blueprint."

"For what?"

Khalid thought about it for a moment. "The future."

"And what does this future look like?"

"Where would you like me to begin?"

"Since it's the summer of 2016," said Gabriel, "why don't we begin with America."

The Tsar, said Khalid, had high hopes for the American presidential election that fall. He was also confident Washington's days as the hegemon in the Middle East were nearing an end. The Americans had blundered into Iraq and paid a high price in blood and treasure. They were eager to put the entire region, with its intractable problems, in their rearview mirror. In contrast, the Tsar had prevailed in the fight for Syria. He had ridden to the rescue of an old friend and in the process sent a signal to the rest of the region that Moscow, not Washington, could be counted on in times of trouble.

"He wanted you to jettison the Americans and become a Russian ally?"

"You're thinking too small," answered Khalid. "The Tsar wanted to form a partnership. He said the West was dying, in part because he was doing his best to sow social division and political chaos wherever he could. He said the future lay in Eurasia, with its massive supplies of energy and water and people. Russia, China, India, Turkey, Iran . . ."

"And Saudi Arabia?"

Khalid nodded. "We were going to rule the world together. And the best part was that he would never lecture me about democracy or human rights."

"How could you refuse an offer like that?"

"Quite easily. I wanted American technology and expertise to power my economy, not Russian." He was suddenly animated, like the KBM of old. "Tell me something, what was the last Russian product you purchased? What do they export other than vodka and oil and gas?"

"Wood."

"Really? Perhaps we should begin exporting sand. That would solve all our problems."

"Did you tell the Tsar how you felt?"

"Yes, of course."

"How did he take it?"

"He gave me that dead-fish stare and told me I had made a mistake."

"You and your father went to Moscow a few months later. You announced a deal to increase the price of oil. You also purchased a Russian air defense system."

"We were hedging our bets, that's all."

"What about that ridiculous handshake in Buenos Aires? You and the Tsar looked as though you'd just scored the winning goal in the World Cup."

"And do you know what he whispered into my ear after we sat down? He asked whether I'd had a chance to reconsider his offer."

"What was your answer?"

"To be honest, I don't remember. Whatever it was, it was obviously wrong. Reema was kidnapped two weeks later." Khalid surveyed the mammoth vessel that was not really his. He was rubbing his hands together again, as though trying to remove a stain. "I suppose this means I'll never be able to avenge her death."

"Why would you say that?"

"The Tsar is the most powerful man in the world,

never forget that. And that woman who led us to that field in France is almost certainly a Russian intelligence officer."

"The man who detonated the bomb, too. But what's your point?"

"They're back in Moscow. You'll never find them."

"You'd be surprised. Besides," said Gabriel, "vengeance comes in all shapes and sizes."

"Is that another Jewish proverb?"

Gabriel smiled. "Close enough."

48

Notting Hill, London

At half past five on a sodden London afternoon, Gabriel Allon, director-general of the Israeli secret intelligence service, swung the heavy steel knocker against the door of the safe house in St. Luke's Mews in Notting Hill and was admitted by a boyish-looking man of forty who insisted on referring to him as "Mr. Mudd." In the cramped sitting room he found Graham Seymour staring despondently at the television. Prime Minister Jonathan Lancaster's plan to withdraw the United Kingdom from the European Union in accordance with the wishes of the British electorate had just gone down to a humiliating defeat in the House of Commons.

"It's the worst drubbing for any British leader in

modern times." Seymour's eyes were still fastened to the screen. "Jonathan will no doubt have to face a vote of no confidence."

"Will he survive?"

"Probably. But there's no guarantee, not after this. If his government falls, there's a good chance Labour will win the next election. Which means you will have to contend with the most anti-Israel prime minister in British history."

Seymour went to the drinks trolley, a new addition to the safe house, and thrust a handful of ice into a cut-glass tumbler. He waved a bottle of Beefeater in Gabriel's direction. Gabriel held up a hand.

"Nigel put a bottle of Sancerre in the fridge."

"It's a bit early in the day for me, Graham."

Seymour frowned at his wristwatch. "It's gone five o'clock, for heaven's sake." He poured a generous measure of gin over the ice and topped it with a dash of tonic and a wedge of lime. "Cheers."

"What are we drinking to?"

"The demise of a once-great nation. The end of Western civilization as we know it." Seymour gazed at the television and slowly shook his head. "The bloody Russians must be loving this."

"So must Rebecca."

Seymour nodded slowly. "I see that woman in my sleep. God forgive me for saying this, but sometimes I wish you'd let her drown that morning in the Potomac."

"*Let* her drown? I was the one holding her head beneath the water, remember?"

"It must have been awful." Seymour studied Gabriel carefully for a moment. "Almost as awful as what happened in France. Even Christopher seemed shell-shocked when he got home. I gather you're lucky to be alive."

"So is Khalid."

"We haven't heard a peep from him since he abdicated."

"He's aboard his yacht off Sharm el-Sheikh."

"Poor lamb." On the floor of the Commons, Jonathan Lancaster had risen to his feet to acknowledge the magnitude of the defeat he had just suffered, only to be heckled mercilessly by the back benches of the opposition. Seymour aimed the remote at the screen and pressed MUTE. "If only it were that easy." Drink in hand, he reclaimed his seat. "It's not all gloom and doom, though. Thanks to you, I had a rather pleasant meeting with my minister this morning."

"Really?"

"I showed him those Iranian nuclear documents

you gave me. And then he promptly closed the file and changed the subject to Abdullah."

"What about Abdullah?"

"How far does he intend to go to placate the religious hard-liners? Is he going to play the same old double game when it comes to the jihadists and terrorists? Is he going to be a force for regional stability or regional chaos? Mainly, my minister wanted to know whether Abdullah, given his close ties to London, might be inclined to tilt our way rather than toward the Americans."

"By that, you mean you'd like to sell Abdullah as many advanced fighter aircraft as he's willing to buy, regardless of what it means for the security of my country."

"More or less. We're thinking about beating the Americans to the punch by inviting Abdullah to come to London for an official visit."

"I think a visit to London is a wonderful idea. But I'm afraid you've missed your chance to win over Abdullah."

"Why?"

"Because he's already spoken for."

"Bloody Americans," murmured Seymour.

"We should be so lucky."

"What are you talking about?"

Gabriel picked up the remote and raised the volume on the television to full.

Over the cacophony of British parliamentary democracy, Gabriel told Graham Seymour everything that had transpired since the night of Reema's murder in France. Khalid, he said, had given Gabriel financial records concerning the sudden wealth of his uncle Abdullah. Office analysts had used the documents to establish a clear link between Abdullah and one Konstantin Dragunov, a Russian oligarch and personal friend of the Tsar. In addition, Gabriel had obtained an unpublished article written by Omar Nawwaf, purporting that Russian intelligence was involved in a plot to remove Khalid and install Abdullah as the new crown prince. It was Abdullah who had advised Khalid to have the journalist killed—and Abdullah, from his mansion in Belgravia, who had seen to the messy details. Through a cut-out, he lured Omar Nawwaf to the Saudi consulate in Istanbul with a promise that Khalid would be waiting inside. That evening, while Nawwaf's dismembered body was being disposed of, Russian agents entered the journalist's room at the InterContinental Hotel, and his apartment in Berlin, and took his computers, portable storage devices, and written notes.

"Says who?"

"Hanifa Khoury."

"Nawwaf's wife?"

"Widow," said Gabriel.

"How does she know they were Russian agents?"

"She doesn't. In fact, she assumes they were Saudi."

"Why *wouldn't* they have been Saudi?"

"If Saudi agents had raided the hotel room and the apartment, Omar's story would have ended up in Khalid's hands. He never knew about it until I showed it to him."

Seymour returned to the trolley and freshened his drink. "So what you're telling me is that KBM's defense in the murder of Omar Nawwaf is that Uncle Abdullah made him do it?"

Gabriel ignored Seymour's sarcasm. "Do you know what the Middle East will look like if Russia, Iran, and the Chinese displace the Americans in the Persian Gulf?"

"It would be a disaster. Which is why no Saudi ruler in his right mind would ever break the bond between Riyadh and Washington."

"Unless the Saudi ruler was beholden to the Kremlin." Gabriel wandered over to the French doors overlooking the tiny garden. "Did you never notice Abdullah was keeping company with one of the Tsar's closest friends?"

"We noticed, but frankly we didn't much care. Abdullah was a nobody."

"He's not a nobody anymore, Graham. He's next in line to the throne."

"Yes," said Seymour. "And when His Majesty dies, which is likely to happen soon, he will be king."

Gabriel turned. "Not if I have anything to say about it."

Seymour gave a half smile. "Do you *really* think you can choose the next ruler of Saudi Arabia?"

"Not necessarily. But I have no intention of allowing a Russian puppet to reach the throne."

"How do you intend to prevent it?"

"I suppose I could just kill him."

"You can't kill the future king of Saudi Arabia."

"Why not?"

"Because it would be immoral and against international law."

"In that case," said Gabriel, "I suppose we'll have to find someone to kill him for us."

49

Vauxhall Cross, London

One week later, as much of Westminster was engaged in a furious debate over how best to commit national suicide, Her Majesty's Government somehow managed to extend an invitation to His Royal Highness Prince Abdullah to make an official visit to London. Five days passed without a response, long enough to send a chill wind of doubt blowing through the halls of the Foreign Office, and through the secret rooms of Vauxhall Cross and King Saul Boulevard as well. When the Saudi response finally arrived—it was delivered by court messenger to the British Embassy in Riyadh—official London was much relieved. A date was set for early April. BAE Systems and the other British defense contractors were thrilled, their counterparts in America less so. The rented television experts saw the

Anglo-Saudi summit as a rebuke of the current American administration's policy in the Middle East. Washington had placed all its chips on an untested young prince with a hair-trigger temper and a lust for shiny objects. Now the young prince was gone, and Britain, faded and divided though it was, had brilliantly seized the diplomatic initiative. "All is not lost," declared the *Independent*. "Perhaps there is hope for us yet."

Charles Bennett, however, did not share the media's enthusiasm over Abdullah's pending visit, mainly because he had not been told a summit was in the works or even that Downing Street and the FO were considering one. It was a breach of normal protocols. If anyone in official London needed advance warning of a royal visit, it was MI6's controller for Middle East stations. It was Bennett's job to supply much of the intelligence the prime minister would review before sitting down with Abdullah. What kind of man was he? What were his core beliefs? Was he a Wahhabi hard-liner or was he merely playing to the base? Was he going to be a reliable partner in the fight against terrorism? What were his plans in Yemen and vis-à-vis the Qataris? Could he be trusted? Could he be manipulated?

Bennett would now have to scramble to prepare the necessary assessments and estimates. His personal opinion was that it was far too early to invite Abdullah to Downing Street. The dust had yet to settle after Khalid's messy abdication, and Abdullah was rolling back Khalid's reforms. Better to wait, Bennett would have advised, until the situation had stabilized. He knew full well why Jonathan Lancaster was so keen to meet with Abdullah. The PM needed a foreign policy success. And then, of course, there was commerce to consider. BAE and its ilk wanted a crack at Abdullah before the Americans got their hooks into him.

Bennett looked up from his personal iPhone as the 7:12 from Stoke Newington rattled into Liverpool Street Station. As usual, he left the carriage last and followed a long and indirect route to the street. Outside in Bishopsgate it was not yet properly light. He walked to the river and crossed London Bridge to Southwark.

From Borough Market it was a brisk walk of about twenty minutes to the office. Bennett liked to vary his route. Today he went via St. George's Circus and the Albert Embankment. He was below six feet and thin as a marathoner, a balding man of fifty-two with hollowed-out cheeks and deeply set eyes. His suit and overcoat were hardly Savile Row, but owing to his slender frame they fit him well. His school tie was carefully knotted, his oxfords shone with fresh polish. The trained eye might have noticed a telltale watchfulness in his gaze, but otherwise there was nothing about his dress or aspect to suggest he was bound for the hideous secret citadel that loomed over the foot of Vauxhall Bridge.

Bennett had never cared for it. He much preferred dreary old Century House, the anonymous twenty-story concrete office block where he had arrived as a new recruit in the dying days of the Cold War. Like all the other probationers in his intake, he had not applied to work for the Secret Intelligence Service. One did not ask to join Britain's most exclusive club, one was invited. And only if one came from the right sort of family, had the right sort of connections, and had earned a decent degree from either Oxford or Cambridge. In Bennett's case it was Cambridge, where he had studied the history and languages of the Middle East. By the time he arrived at MI6, he spoke Arabic and Persian fluently. After completing the rigorous IONEC training course at Fort Monckton, MI6's school for fledgling spies, he was shipped off to Cairo to recruit and run agents.

He went to Amman next and then to Damascus and Beirut before landing the job as Head of Station in Baghdad. Faulty or misleading reports from several of Bennett's Iraqi assets found their way into the infamous September Dossier, which was used by the Blair government to justify Britain's involvement in the American-led war to remove Saddam Hussein from power. Bennett, however, suffered no damage to his career. He went to Riyadh, again as Head of Station, and in 2012 was promoted to controller for the Middle East, one of the most important jobs in the service.

Bennett entered Vauxhall Cross overtly from the Albert Embankment and endured a thorough search and identity check before being allowed beyond the lobby. It was all part of the post–Rebecca Manning security overhaul. Suspicion hung over the building like the Black Death. Officers scarcely spoke to one another or shook hands for fear of catching the dreaded disease. There was no meaningful product coming in and virtually nothing going out to the customers on the other side of the river that they couldn't read in the *Economist*. Bennett's career had intersected with Rebecca's only briefly, but like many of his colleagues he had been dragged before the inquisitors for a thorough roasting. After many hours of questioning he had been given a clean bill of health, or so he had been informed. Bennett trusted no one inside MI6, least of all the bloodhounds in the vetting department.

Once free of the lobby he card-swiped, key-punched, and retina-scanned his way to his office. Entering, he closed the door behind him, engaged his privacy light, and hung his overcoat on the hook. His computer hard drive, per service regulations, was locked in his safe. He inserted it and was working his way through the overnight telegram traffic when a call on his internal phone interrupted him. The ID screen indicated it was Nigel Whitcombe on the line. Whitcombe was "C's" head butler and chief executioner. He had come to Vauxhall Cross from MI5. For that reason alone, Bennett loathed him.

He brought the phone to his ear. "Yes?"

" 'C' would like a word."

"When?"

The line went dead. Rising, Bennett straightened his jacket and self-consciously ran a hand through his hair. *Christ! We're not going on a date.* He went to the elevators and boarded the first upward-bound carriage. Whitcombe was waiting when the doors opened, a slight smirk on his face.

"Morning, Bennett."

"Nigel."

Together they entered Graham Seymour's executive suite, with its mahogany desk used by all the chiefs who had come before him, its towering windows overlooking the river Thames, and its stately old grandfather clock constructed by none other than Sir Mansfield Smith-Cumming, the first "C" of the British Secret Intelligence Service. Seymour was scribbling a note in the margin of a document with a Parker fountain pen. The ink was green, the color reserved for him.

Bennett heard a rustle and, turning, saw Whitcombe slipping from the room. Seymour looked up as though surprised by Bennett's presence, and returned the Parker pen to its holder. Stretching his frame to its full height, he stepped from behind the desk with his hand before him like a bayonet.

"Hullo, Charles. So good of you to come. I think it's about time we got you up to speed on a special operation we've been running for some time. I'm sorry we had to keep you in the dark until now, but there it is."

That evening Bennett drank a single whisky in MI6's private lounge and departed Vauxhall Cross in time to make the 7:30 out of Liverpool Street. The carriage he entered was crowded. Indeed, only a single seat was unoccupied. It was next to a small man in a duffel coat and black beret—a Pole or a Slav, reckoned Bennett—who looked as though he might at any moment pluck a volume of *Das Kapital* from his worn leather satchel. Bennett had never seen him before on the 7:30, a train he took often.

They passed the thirteen-minute ride to Stoke Newington in silence. Bennett left the carriage first and climbed the steps from the platform to the glass box that served as the station's ticket hall. It was located on a tiny triangular esplanade in Stamford Hill, next to a financial establishment that catered to the neighborhood's immigrant community, and a café called Kookies. A couple in their early forties, both blond, were drinking smoothies at one of the maroon picnic tables.

The little beret-wearing man emerged from the station a few seconds after Bennett and made straight for the Kingdom Hall in Willow Cottages. Bennett in turn set out past the parade of shops along Stamford Hill— the Princess Curtains and Bedding Palace, the Perfect Shirt, Stokey Karaoke, the New China House as opposed to the old, King's Chicken, of which Bennett was rather fond. Unlike many of his colleagues he did not come from a family of means. The smart neighborhoods like Notting Hill and Hampstead were far too expensive for a man who existed only on a service salary. Besides, he liked the fact that Stoke Newington had retained the feel of a village. Sometimes even Bennett found it hard to believe the bustle of Charing Cross was only five miles to the south.

The shops and restaurants in Church Street were of a higher caliber. Bennett, seemingly on a whim, entered the flower shop and purchased a bouquet of hyacinths for his wife, Hester. He carried the flowers in his right hand along the southern side of the street, to the corner of Albion Road. Warm light spilled from the windows of the Rose & Crown, illuminating a couple of nicotine addicts sitting at the single table on the pavement. One of the men Bennett recognized.

He turned into Albion Road and followed it past the redbrick Hawksley Court council flats. A woman pushing a pram approached from the opposite direction. Otherwise, the pavements were deserted. Bennett heard the echo of his own footsteps. The rich scent of the hyacinths was irritating his sinuses. Why did it have to be hyacinths? Why not primrose or tulips?

He thought about his summons to the top floor of Vauxhall Cross that morning and the operation that "C" had finally decided to brief him on. Upon learning that Prince Abdullah, the next king of Saudi Arabia, was a long-term asset of MI6, Bennett had struck a pose of righteous indignation. *Graham, how could you possibly keep me in the dark about a vital program for so long? It's unconscionable.* Still, he had to admire the audacity of it. Perhaps the old service was not quite dead after all.

Beyond the council flats, Albion Road turned suddenly prosperous. The house where Bennett lived was a handsome white structure, three stories, with a walled front garden. He hung his coat in the entrance hall and went into the sitting room. Hester was stretched out on the couch with the new rebus and a large glass of white wine. Something tedious was seeping from the Bose. Bennett, wincing, switched it off.

"I was listening to that." Hester looked up from the book and frowned. "Flowers again? Third time this month."

"I didn't realize you were keeping track."

"What have I done to deserve flowers?"

"Can't I bring you flowers, darling?"

"As long as you're not doing something foolish."

Hester's eyes returned to the page. Bennett dropped the flowers on the coffee table and went into the kitchen in search of dinner.

50

Harrow, London

It was not true that Charles Bennett had never ridden an evening train to Stoke Newington with the man in the beret. In fact, they had shared the same carriage on the 7:30 on two previous occasions. The little man had also taken several inbound trains with Bennett, including that very morning. He had been wearing the clerical suit and collar of a Roman Catholic priest. In Bishopsgate a beggar had asked for his blessing, which he had conferred with two sweeping movements of his right hand, the first vertical, the second horizontal.

Charles Bennett was to be forgiven for not noticing him. The man was Eli Lavon, the finest surveillance artist the Office had ever produced, a natural predator who could follow a highly trained intelligence officer or hardened terrorist down any street in the world without attracting a flicker of interest. Ari Shamron had once said of Lavon that he could disappear while shaking your hand. It was an exaggeration, but only slight.

Though he was a division chief, Lavon, like his director-general, preferred to lead his troops into battle. Besides, Charles Bennett was a special case. He was an officer of a sometimes-friendly service, a service that had been penetrated at the highest level by Russian intelligence. Bennett had survived a top-up with the vetters, but a shadow of suspicion hung over him, mainly because two important assets in Syria had recently been lost. There was broad agreement among the vetters that Rebecca Manning was likely to blame. But there was a camp that included none other than "C" himself that was not ready to close Bennett's file. Indeed, there were some in this camp who thought Bennett should be hung upside-down in the Tower until he confessed to being a poisonous Russian spy. If nothing else, they wanted to strip Bennett of his controllerate and put him out to pasture where he could do no more harm. They were overruled, however, by none other than "C" himself. "C" had declared that Bennett would remain in place until such time as the situation was no longer tenable. Or, preferably, until "C" was presented with an opportunity to undo some of the damage done to his service. In a safe house in Notting Hill, an old friend had given him that opportunity. Thus the meeting that morning during which Bennett was brought into the inner ring regarding the operational status of a certain Saudi royal who was about to ascend to the throne. Bennett was now the sole keeper of a most important, if false, secret.

Bennett also knew the tactics, and perhaps some of the identities, of his service's surveillance artists. For that reason, "C" had entrusted physical observation of him to the Office. On that evening there were twelve Israeli watchers in all, including Eli Lavon. After his brief appearance at the Kingdom Hall, where he had been welcomed with open arms, Lavon had followed Bennett along Stamford Hill to Church Street. There he had witnessed the purchase of a bunch of hyacinths from the Evergreen & Outrageous flower shop. He took note of the fact that Bennett, upon leaving the shop, had switched the flowers from his left hand to his right, so that when he rounded the corner into Albion Road they would be clearly visible to anyone sitting outside the Rose & Crown. The two men present that evening paid no attention to Lavon, but one appeared to watch Bennett carefully as he passed. Lavon, with a whisper into the miniature mic concealed at his wrist, ordered six members of his team to follow the man when he left the pub.

Lavon had continued straight along Church Street to the old town hall before reversing course and making his way back to Stamford Hill. Mikhail and Sarah Bancroft had left Kookies café and were waiting in a Ford Fiesta in the car park of a Morrisons supermarket. Lavon dropped into the backseat and soundlessly closed the door.

"Well?" asked Mikhail.

Lavon didn't answer; he was listening to the chatter of his watchers in his ear. They were in the game, he thought. They were definitely in the game.

The house overlooked the Grims Dyke Golf Club in the Hatch End section of Harrow. A sprawling Tudor pile of many wings and gables, it was surrounded by thick trees and reached by a long private drive. With a single text message to Khalid, Gabriel made a gift of the house to Her Majesty's Secret Intelligence Service, which was sorely in need of safe properties. There were eight bedrooms and a large double great room that served as the operation's nerve center. Israeli and British officers worked side by side at two long trestle tables. Large flat-screen panels displayed live CCTV images. Secure radios crackled with updates from the field in Hebrew and British-accented English.

At Gabriel's insistence there was no smoking in the op center or any other room of the house, only in the gardens. He also ruled that there would be no catering or food deliveries. They shopped for themselves at the Tesco Superstore down the road in Pinner Green and ate communally whenever possible. In the process, they became well known to each other, which was the peril of any joint operation—the exposure of personnel and tradecraft. Gabriel paid an especially high price in watchers and other field assets, most of whom would never be able to work covertly in Britain again.

But some of Gabriel's personnel were known to the British from previous joint endeavors, including Sarah, Mikhail, and Eli Lavon. It was half past eight when they returned to the house at Hatch End. Entering, they joined Gabriel, Graham Seymour, and Christopher Keller before one of the video screens. On it was the output of a CCTV camera located outside the Arsenal Tube station in Gillespie Road. The man from the Rose & Crown was now standing at the kiosk next to the station's entrance. Had he walked there directly from the pub, he might have made the journey in fifteen minutes at most. Instead, he had taken a circuitous route full of switchbacks and wrong turns that had forced five of Eli Lavon's most experienced watchers to abandon the chase.

One, however, managed to follow the man into the station and board the same inbound Piccadilly Line train. The man rode it to Hyde Park Corner. Emerging, he entered Mayfair and once again engaged in a series of textbook countersurveillance measures that compelled Lavon's final watcher to fall away. It was no matter; the cameras of London's Orwellian CCTV system never blinked.

They followed him through the streets of Mayfair to Marble Arch and then westward along Bayswater Road, where he passed beneath the darkened windows of the Office safe flat known affectionately as Gabriel's London pied-à-terre. A moment later he crossed the road illegally, ducked into Hyde Park, and vanished from view. Graham Seymour ordered the technicians to engage the cameras along Kensington Palace Gardens, and at 9:18:43 p.m. they observed the man entering the Russian Embassy. The technicians ran his photo through the database. Facial recognition flagged him as one Dmitri Mentov.

"A nobody in the consular section," said Graham Seymour.

"There are no *nobodies* at the Russian Embassy,"

replied Gabriel. "He's an SVR hood. And he just made contact with your controller for Middle East stations."

At the two long trestle tables, the news that yet another senior MI6 officer might be working for the Russians was greeted only with the tapping of keyboards and the crackle of secure radios. They were in the game. They were most definitely in the game.

51

Epping Forest, Essex

When Charles Bennett stepped from his residence in Albion Road at half past nine on Saturday morning, he was wearing a dark blue waterproof anorak and quick-dry pants. Over one shoulder was a nylon rucksack, and in his right hand he held a carbon walking stick. A devoted hiker, Bennett had traipsed across much of the British Isles. Weekends he typically had to make do with one of the many excellent trails near Greater London. Hester, who considered gardening exercise, never accompanied him. Bennett didn't mind; he preferred to be alone. In that respect, at least, he and Hester were entirely compatible.

Bennett's destination that morning was the Oak Trail in Epping Forest, the ancient woodland that stretched from Wanstead in East London to Essex in the north.

The footpath wandered for six and a half miles through the uppermost reaches of the forest near the village of Theydon Bois. Bennett drove there in Hester's Swedish sedan. He parked at the Tube station and in violation of service rules left his MI6 BlackBerry in the glove box. Then, stick in hand, rucksack on his back, he struck out along Coppice Row.

He passed a couple of shops and restaurants, the village hall, and the parish church. A thin fog hung over Theydon Plain like the smoke of a distant battle, then the forest swallowed him. The trail was wide and smooth and covered with fallen leaves. Ahead, a woman of about forty emerged from the gloom and, smiling, bade him a pleasant morning. She reminded him of Magda.

Magda . . .

He had met her at the Rose & Crown one night when he stopped for a beer rather than rush home to Hester's cold embrace. She was a recent immigrant from Poland, or so she said. She was a beautiful woman, newly divorced, with luminous white skin and a wide mouth that smiled easily. She claimed she was meeting a friend—"a girlfriend, not a man"—and that the friend was running late. Bennett was suspicious. Nevertheless, he had a second drink with her. And when the "friend" sent a text saying she had to cancel, he agreed to walk Magda home. She took him into Clissold Park and pushed him up against a tree near the old church. Before Bennett knew it, his fly was open and her mouth was upon him.

He knew what would come next. Indeed, he supposed he had known it from the moment he laid eyes on her. It happened a week later. A car drew alongside him in Stamford Hill, a hand beckoned from an open rear window. It was Yevgeny's hand. He was holding a photograph. "Why don't you let me give you a lift? It's a filthy night to be out walking."

Bennett came upon a rubbish bin. The chalk mark at the base was clearly visible. He left the trail and picked his way through the dense trees and undergrowth. Yevgeny was leaning against the trunk of a silver birch, an unlit cigarette dangling impossibly from his lips. He seemed genuinely pleased to see Bennett. Yevgeny was a cruel bastard, as most SVR officers were, but he could be pleasant when it suited his purposes. Bennett possessed the same set of skills. They were two sides of the same coin. Bennett, in a moment of weakness, had allowed Yevgeny to get the upper hand. But perhaps one day it would be Yevgeny who would be forced to reveal his country's secrets because of a personal misdeed. That was the way the game was played. All it took was a single slip.

"You were careful?" the Russian asked.

Bennett nodded. "You?"

"The oafs from A4 tried to follow me, but I lost them in Highgate." A4 were the surveillance artists of MI5, the British security and counterintelligence service. "You know, Charles, they really need to raise their game a bit. It's got to the point where it's not even sporting."

"You have more intelligence officers in London now than you did during the height of the Cold War. A4 are overwhelmed."

"There's safety in numbers." Yevgeny lit his cigarette. "That said, we shouldn't stay long. What have you got?"

"An operation your superiors in Moscow Center might find interesting."

"What sort?"

"A long-term recruitment of a highly placed asset."

"Russian?"

"House of Saud," answered Bennett. "The source has been working on our behalf for several years. He briefs us regularly on internal family matters and political developments inside the Kingdom."

"You're the Middle East controller, Charles. Why am I hearing about this only now?"

"The source was recruited and run by London Station. I was told about him only this week."

"By whom?"

" 'C' himself."

"Why did Graham decide to bring you into the picture?"

"Because the highly placed asset is coming to London in a few weeks for an official visit."

"What are you talking about?"

"Crown Prince Abdullah, the next king of Saudi Arabia, is an asset of MI6. We own him, Yevgeny. He's ours."

52

Moscow

The dream came to Rebecca, as it always did, in the last hours before dawn. She was submerged in shallow water near the bank of a tree-lined American river. A face hovered over her, blurry, indistinct, contorted with rage. Gradually, as she began to lose consciousness, the face receded into darkness, and her father appeared. He was calling to her from the door of his dacha. *Rebecca, my d-d-darling, there's something we need to discuss . . .*

She sat bolt upright in bed, gasping for air. Through her uncurtained bedroom window she could see a red star over the Kremlin. Even now, nine months after her arrival in Moscow, the view surprised her. A part of her still expected to awaken each morning in the little cottage on Warren Street in Northwest Washington where she had lived during her final posting for MI6. Were it not for the man from her dream—the man who had nearly drowned her in the Potomac River—she would be there still. She might even be the director of MI6.

The sky over the Kremlin was black, but when Rebecca checked the time on her SVR-issue phone she saw it was nearly seven a.m. The forecast for Moscow called for light snow and a high temperature of twelve degrees below zero, a warming trend. She threw aside the bedding and, shivering, pulled on her robe and padded into the kitchen.

It was bright and modern and filled with shiny German-made appliances. The SVR had done well by her—a large apartment near the Kremlin walls, a dacha in the country, a car and driver. They had even granted her a security detail. Rebecca was under no illusion as to why she had been given a perquisite usually reserved for only the highest-ranking officers of the Russian intelligence service. She had been born and bred to be a spy for the motherland and had worked for Russia throughout a long and successful career at MI6, and yet they did not quite trust her. At Moscow Center, where she reported for work each day, they derisively referred to her as *novaya devushka*: the new girl.

She pushed the BREW button on the automatic; and when it noisily coughed and spat the last of the coffee into the carafe, she drank it in a bowl with frothy steamed milk, the way she had when she was a child growing up in Paris. Her name had been Bettencourt then—Rebecca Bettencourt, the illegitimate daughter of Charlotte Bettencourt, a French communist and journalist who in the early 1960s had lived in Beirut, where she'd had a brief affair with a married freelance correspondent for the *Observer* and the *Economist*. Manning was the name Rebecca took when her mother, at the direction of the KGB, married a homosexual from the British upper classes so that her daughter might gain British citizenship and admission to Oxford or, preferably, Cambridge. Publicly, Manning was still the surname by which Rebecca was infamously known. Inside Moscow Center, however, she was called by her father's name, which was Philby.

She aimed the remote at the television, and a few seconds later the BBC appeared on the screen. For professional reasons, her viewing habits had remained decidedly British. Rebecca worked in the United Kingdom Department of Directorate PR. It was vital she kept abreast of the news from London. These days it was almost universally bad. Brexit, which was clandestinely supported by the Kremlin, was a national calamity. Britain would soon be a shell of its former self, unable to put up any meaningful resistance to Russia's spreading influence and growing military power. Rebecca had inflicted terrible damage on Britain from within the Secret Intelligence Service. Now it was her job to finish off her old country from behind a desk at Moscow Center.

While skimming the headlines from London on her phone, Rebecca smoked the day's first L&B. Her intake of cigarettes had risen sharply since her arrival in Russia. The London *rezidentura* bought them by the carton from a shop in Bayswater and sent them in the pouch to Moscow Center. Her intake of Johnnie Walker Black Label, which she purchased at a steep discount from the SVR commissary, had increased as well. It was only the winter weather, she assured herself. The melancholia would pass once summer arrived.

In her room Rebecca removed a dark pantsuit and a white blouse from the closet and laid them out on her unmade bed. Like the L&B cigarettes, the clothing came from London. Unwittingly, she had fallen into her father's old habits. He never fully adjusted to life in Moscow. He listened to the news from home on the BBC World Service, followed the cricket scores religiously in the *Times*, spread English marmalade on his toast and English mustard on his sausages, and drank Johnnie Walker Red Label, nearly always to the point of unconsciousness. As a child, Rebecca had witnessed his titanic drinking during her clandestine visits to Russia. She had loved him nonetheless and loved him still. It was his face she saw when she examined her appearance in the bathroom mirror. The face of a traitor. The face of a spy.

Dressed, Rebecca bundled herself in a woolen overcoat and scarf and rode the elevator to the lobby. Her chauffeured Mercedes sedan waited in Sadovnicheskaya Street. She was surprised to find Leonid Ryzhkov, her immediate superior at Moscow Center, in the backseat.

She ducked inside and closed the door. "Is there a problem?"

"That depends."

The driver made a hard U-turn and accelerated rapidly. Moscow Center was in the opposite direction.

"Where are we going?" asked Rebecca.

"The boss would like a word."

"The director?"

"No," answered Ryzhkov. "*The* boss."

53

The Kremlin

The red star atop the Borovitskaya Tower, the business entrance of the Kremlin, was scarcely visible through the falling snow. The driver parked in a courtyard outside the Grand Presidential Palace, and Rebecca and Leonid Ryzhkov hurried inside. The president was waiting upstairs behind the golden doors of his ornate office. Rising, he emerged from behind the desk with that peculiar walk of his, the right arm straight at his side, the left swinging mechanically. His blue suit fit him to perfection, and a few strands of gray-blond hair were combed neatly over his otherwise bald pate. His face, puffy and smooth and tanned from his annual ski trip to Courchevel, scarcely looked human. His eyes were pulled tight, giving him a vaguely Central Asian appearance.

Rebecca had expected a warm reception—she had not seen the president since the Kremlin news conference announcing her arrival in Moscow—but he gave her only a businesslike handshake before gesturing indifferently toward the seating area. Stewards entered, tea was poured. Then, without preamble, the president handed Rebecca a copy of an SVR cable. It had been transmitted to Moscow Center overnight by Yevgeny Teplov of the London *rezidentura*. The topic was a clandestine meeting Teplov had conducted with an agent code-named Chamberlain. His real name was Charles Bennett. Rebecca, while still working inside MI6, had targeted Bennett for sexual compromise and recruitment.

Her Russian had improved markedly since settling in Moscow. Even so, she read the cable slowly. When she looked up, the president was studying her without expression. It was like being contemplated by a cadaver.

"When were you planning to tell us?" he asked at last.

"Tell you what?"

"That Crown Prince Abdullah is a long-term asset of British intelligence."

A lifetime of lies and deception allowed Rebecca to conceal her unease at being interrogated by the most powerful man in the world. "While I was at MI6," she said deliberately, "I was unaware of any relationship between Vauxhall Cross and Prince Abdullah."

"You were one step away from becoming director-general of MI6. How could you not have known?"

"It's called the Secret Intelligence Service for a reason. I had no need to know." Rebecca returned the cable. "Besides, it shouldn't come as a shock that MI6 might have ties to a Saudi prince who spent most of his time in London."

"Unless the Saudi prince is supposed to be working for me."

"Abdullah?" Rebecca's tone was incredulous. Her brief was strictly limited to the United Kingdom. Even so, she had followed Khalid's spectacular fall from grace with more than a passing interest. She never imagined that Moscow Center might have had a hand in it. Or the president.

As usual, he was slouched in his chair. His chin was lowered, his eyes had a slight upward cast. Somehow he managed to convey both boredom and menace simultaneously. Rebecca supposed he practiced the expression in the mirror.

"I assume," she said after a moment, "that Khalid's abdication wasn't voluntary."

"No." The president gave a half smile. Then the life

drained once more from his features. "We encouraged him to relinquish his claim to the throne."

"How?"

The president shot a glance at Ryzhkov, who briefed Rebecca on the operation that had led to Khalid's removal from the line of succession. It was monstrous, there was no other word for it. But then Rebecca always knew the Russians didn't play by the same rules as MI6.

"We went to a great deal of trouble to make Abdullah the next king of Saudi Arabia," Ryzhkov was saying. "But now it seems we've been deceived." He waved the cable from London, dramatically, like a barrister in a courtroom. "Or maybe this is the deception. Perhaps MI6 is up to its old tricks. Perhaps they merely want us to *think* Abdullah is working for them."

"Why would they do that?"

It was the president who answered. "To discredit him, of course. To make us wary of him."

"Graham's a glorified policeman. He's not capable of something so clever."

"He caught you, didn't he?"

"It was Allon who found me out, not Graham."

"Ah, yes." Anger flashed briefly across the president's face. "I'm afraid he's involved in this, too."

"Allon?"

The president nodded. "After we kidnapped the child, Abdullah told us that his nephew had turned to Allon for help."

"You would have been wise to kill *him* instead of Khalid's daughter."

"We tried. Unfortunately, things didn't quite go as planned."

Rebecca took the cable from Ryzhkov and reread it. "It sounds to me as though Abdullah has been selling his wares on both sides of the street. He took your money and support when he needed it. But now that the keys to the Kingdom are within his grasp . . ."

"He's decided to be his own man?"

"Or London's," said Rebecca.

"And if he really is a British asset? What do I do about it? Do I let him take several billion dollars from me with no repercussions? Do I let the British laugh at me behind my back? Do I give Allon the same privilege?"

"Of course not."

He held up a hand. "Well, then?"

"You have no choice but to remove Abdullah from the line of succession."

"How?"

"In a way that does as much damage to British credibility and prestige as possible."

The president's smile appeared almost genuine. "I'm relieved to hear you say that."

"Why?"

"Because if you had suggested leaving Abdullah in place, I would have doubted your loyalty to the motherland." He was still smiling. "Congratulations, Rebecca. The job is yours."

"What job?"

"Getting rid of Abdullah, of course."

"Me?"

"Who better to run a major operation in London?"

"It's not the sort of thing I do."

"Are you not the director of the United Kingdom Department of the SVR?"

"Deputy director."

"Yes, of course." The president glanced at Leonid Ryzhkov. "My mistake."

54

Moscow–Washington–London

It was the assumption of the SVR's counterintelligence directorate that MI6 did not know Colonel Rebecca Philby's Moscow address. In point of fact, that was not the case. MI6 learned the location of her apartment quite by chance when one of its Moscow-based officers spotted her walking along the Arbat with a pair of bodyguards and a formidable-looking woman of advanced years. The officer followed them to Kuntsevo Cemetery, where they placed flowers on the grave of history's greatest traitor, then to the entrance of a smart new apartment building on Sadovnicheskaya Street.

At the direction of Vauxhall Cross, Moscow Station took great care with its discovery. No attempt was made to place Rebecca under full-time surveillance—it wasn't possible in a city like Moscow, where MI6 personnel were under near-constant watch themselves—and an ill-conceived scheme to purchase a flat in her building was quickly shelved. Instead, they watched her only occasionally and only from afar. They were able to confirm that she lived on the building's ninth floor and that she reported for work each morning at SVR headquarters in Yasenevo. They never saw her run a personal errand, dine in a restaurant, or attend a performance at the Bolshoi. There was no evidence of a man in her life, or, for that matter, a woman. In general, she seemed quite miserable, which pleased them no end.

But in early March, for reasons Moscow Station could not possibly fathom, Rebecca vanished from view. When five days passed with no sign of her, the Moscow Head informed Vauxhall Cross—and Vauxhall Cross duly sent word to the sprawling Tudor house of many wings and gables in Hatch End in Harrow. There they cautiously interpreted Rebecca's sudden disappearance as evidence that Moscow Center was feeding on the bread they had cast upon the water.

There was other evidence as well, such as an alarming spike in coded signal traffic emanating from the roof of the Russian Embassy in Kensington Palace Gardens; and a second meeting in the Epping Forest between Charles Bennett and his SVR controller, Yevgeny Teplov; and the arrival in London, in mid-March, of one Konstantin Dragunov, personal friend and business associate of both the present ruler of Russia and the future king of Saudi Arabia. Taken in isolation, the developments were proof of nothing. But when viewed through the prism of the Anglo-Israeli team at Hatch End, they appeared to be the first stirrings of a great Russian undertaking.

It was Gabriel who had once again prodded the sleeping bear, but he monitored the Russian response not from Hatch End but from his desk at King Saul Boulevard, based on his firmly held operational conviction that a watched pot never boils. In late March he paid another clandestine visit to Khalid's superyacht in the Gulf of Aqaba, if only to hear the latest gossip from Riyadh. Unbeknownst to the outside world, Khalid's father had taken a turn for the worse—another stroke, perhaps a heart attack. He was attached to several machines at the Saudi National Guard Hospital. The vultures were circling, dividing up the spoils, fighting over the scraps. Khalid had requested permission to return to Riyadh to be at his father's side. Abdullah had refused.

"If you have a card up your sleeve," said Khalid, "I suggest you play it now. Otherwise, Saudi Arabia will soon be controlled by Comrade Abdullah and his puppet master in the Kremlin."

A sudden storm grounded *Tranquillity*'s helicopter and forced Gabriel to spend that night at sea in one of the ship's luxurious guest suites. When he returned to King Saul Boulevard the next morning he found a report waiting on his desk. It was the analysis of the stolen Iranian nuclear archives. The documents proved conclusively that Iran had been working on a nuclear weapon when it was telling the global community the precise opposite. But there was no firm evidence they were violating the terms of the nuclear accord they had negotiated with the previous American administration.

Gabriel briefed the prime minister that afternoon in his office in Jerusalem. And a week later he flew to Washington to bring the Americans into the picture. Much to his surprise, the meeting took place in the White House Situation Room, with the president in attendance. He had made no secret of his intention to withdraw the United States from the Iran nuclear deal and was disappointed that Gabriel had not brought him incontrovertible proof—"a smoking mullah"—that the Iranians were secretly building a bomb.

Later that day Gabriel traveled to Langley, where he gave a more detailed briefing to the officers of the Persia House, the CIA's Iran operations unit. Afterward, he dined alone with Morris Payne in a wood-paneled room on the seventh floor. Spring had finally arrived in Northern Virginia after an inhospitable winter, and the trees along the Potomac were in new leaf. Over wilted greens and cartilaginous beef, they swapped secrets and naughty rumors, including some about the men they served. Like many of his predecessors at the Agency, Payne had no background in intelligence. Before coming to Langley, he had been a soldier, a businessman, and a deeply conservative member of Congress from one of the Dakotas. He was big and bluff and blunt, with a face like an Easter Island statue. Gabriel found him a refreshing change from the previous CIA director, who had routinely referred to Jerusalem as al-Quds.

"What do you think of Abdullah?" Payne asked abruptly over coffee.

"Not much."

"Fucking British."

"What have they done now?"

"Invited him to London before we could get him to Washington."

Gabriel shrugged indifferently. "The House of Saud can't survive without you. Abdullah will promise to buy a few British toys and then he'll come running."

"We're not so sure about that."

"Meaning?"

"We hear MI6 might have their hooks in him."

Gabriel suppressed a smile. "Abdullah? A British asset? Come on, Morris."

Payne nodded gravely. "We were wondering whether you might be interested in facilitating a change in the Saudi line of succession."

"What kind of change?"

"The kind that eventually places KBM's ass on the throne."

"Khalid is damaged goods."

"Khalid is the best we can hope for, and you know it. He loves us, and for some reason he's reasonably fond of you."

"What do we do about Abdullah?"

"He would have to be moved aside."

"Moved aside?"

Payne stared at Gabriel blankly.

"Morris, really."

After dinner Gabriel was driven in a CIA motorcade to the Madison Hotel in downtown Washington. Exhausted, he fell into a dreamless sleep but was awakened at 3:19 a.m. by an urgent message on his BlackBerry. At dawn he went to the Israeli Embassy and remained there until early afternoon, when he left for Dulles

Airport. He had told his American hosts he was planning to return to Tel Aviv. Instead, at half past five, he boarded a British Airways flight to London.

Brexit had produced at least one positive impact on the British economy. Owing to a double-digit drop in the value of the pound, more than ten million foreign tourists were pouring into the United Kingdom each month. MI5 routinely screened the new arrivals for unwanted elements such as terrorists, criminals, and known Russian intelligence operatives. At Gabriel's suggestion, the Anglo-Israeli team at Hatch End were duplicating MI5's efforts. As a result, they knew that British Airways Flight 216 from Dulles landed at Heathrow the next morning at 6:29 and that Gabriel cleared passport control at 7:12. They even found several minutes of video of his passage through the endless non-EU immigration queue. It was playing on a loop on one of the large-screen video monitors when he entered the makeshift op center.

Sarah Bancroft, in jeans and a fleece pullover, directed his attention to the adjacent video screen. On it was a still image of a lean, well-built man in a peacoat walking across a car park at night. A bag hung from his right shoulder. An American-style baseball cap obscured most of his face.

"Recognize him?" she asked.

"No."

Mikhail Abramov aimed a remote at the screen and pressed PLAY. "How about now?"

The man approached a Toyota hatchback, tossed the bag into the backseat, and dropped behind the wheel. The lights burst on automatically when the engine started, a small mistake in tradecraft. The man quickly switched them off and reversed out of the space. A few seconds later the car disappeared from the camera's view.

Mikhail hit PAUSE. "Nothing?"

Gabriel shook his head.

"Watch it again. But this time pay careful attention to the way he walks. You've seen it before."

Mikhail played the video a second time. Gabriel focused only on the man's athletic gait. Mikhail was right, he had seen it before. The man had walked past the front of Gabriel's car in Geneva, a few minutes after leaving his briefcase behind at Café Remor. Mikhail had been walking a few paces behind him.

"I wish I could take credit for spotting him," he said, "but it was Sarah."

"Where was the video taken?"

"The car park at the Holyhead ferry terminal."

"When?"

"Two nights ago."

Gabriel frowned. "Two nights?"

"We did the best we could, boss."

"How did he get to Dublin?"

"On a flight from Budapest."

"Do we know how the car got there?"

"Dmitri Mentov."

"The nobody from the consular section of the Russian Embassy?"

"I can show you the video if you like."

"I'll use my imagination. Where's our boy now?"

Mikhail tapped the remote and a new piece of video appeared on the screen. A man climbing out of a Toyota hatchback outside a seaside hotel.

"Where's Graham?"

"Vauxhall Cross."

"Doing what?"

"Waiting for you."

PART FOUR

Assassination

55

Frinton-on-Sea, Essex

In the late nineteenth century there was nothing but a church, a few farms, and a cluster of cottages. Then a man called Richard Powell Cooper laid out a golf course along the sea, and there arose a resort town with stately homes lining broad avenues and several luxury hotels along the Esplanade. Connaught Avenue, the town's main thoroughfare, became known as the Bond Street of East Anglia. The Prince of Wales was a frequent visitor, and Winston Churchill once rented a house for the summer. When the Germans dropped their last bomb on Britain in 1944, it landed on Frinton-on-Sea.

Though the town was no longer a fashionable resort, Frintonians had clung, with varying degrees of success, to the genteel ways of the past. Older, wealthier, and deeply conservative, they did not hold with immigrants, the European Union, or the policies of the Labour Party. Much to their dismay, Frinton's first pub, the Lock & Barrel, had recently opened its doors on Connaught Avenue. It was still a violation of the town's by-laws, however, to sell ice cream on the beach or to take a picnic lunch on the grassy Greensward atop the cliffs. If one wanted to spread a blanket and eat out of doors, one could drive down the road to neighboring Clacton, a place where few Frintonians ever set foot.

Between the Greensward and the sea was a prom-enade lined with pastel-colored beach huts. Because it was early April and the afternoon was chill and wind-blown, Nikolai Azarov had the walkway to himself. He carried a rucksack on his back and wore a pair of Zeiss binoculars around his neck. Had a passerby wished him a pleasant afternoon or asked for directions, he would have assumed that Nikolai was exactly what he ap-peared to be—a well-educated Englishman of the mid-dle classes, probably from London or one of the Home Counties, almost certainly a graduate of Oxbridge or one of the better redbrick universities. A more discern-ing eye might have noticed a vaguely Slavic cast to his features. But no one would have assumed he was Rus-sian, or that he was an assassin and special operative employed by Moscow Center.

It was not the career Nikolai had chosen for himself. Indeed, as a young man growing up in post-Soviet Moscow, he had dreamed of working as an actor, preferably in the West. Unfortunately, the prestigious school where he learned to speak his flawless British-accented English was the Moscow Institute for Foreign Languages, a favorite hunting ground for the SVR. Upon graduation, Nikolai entered the SVR's academy, where his instructors determined he had a natural flair for certain darker aspects of the trade, including the construction of explosive devices. At the conclusion of his training, he was assigned to the SVR directorate responsible for "active measures." They included the assassination of Russian citizens who dared to oppose the Kremlin, or intelligence officers who were spying for Russia's enemies. Nikolai had personally killed more than a dozen of his countrymen living in the West—with poison, with chemical or radiological weapons, or with a gun or a bomb—all on the direct orders of the Russian president himself.

The next town to the north of Frinton was Walton-on-the-Naze. Nikolai stopped for a coffee at the pier before making his way to the marshlands of the Hamford Water nature reserve. At the tip of the headland, he paused for a moment and, binoculars to his eyes, gazed across the North Sea toward the Netherlands. Then he headed south along the banks of Walton Channel. It led him to the river Twizzle, where he found a marina filled with many fine sailing vessels and motor yachts. Nikolai planned to leave Britain the same way he had entered it, by car ferry. But in his experience, it was always best to have an ace in the hole. Operations did not always go as planned. Like Geneva, he thought suddenly. Or France.

You're dead! Dead, dead, dead . . .

Two women, holidaymakers, pensioners, were coming up the footpath, trailed by a rust-colored spaniel. Nikolai bade them a pleasant afternoon, and they chirped a greeting in return before continuing north to the headland. Despite their age, he scrutinized them carefully as they moved off. And for an instant he even considered how best to kill them both. He had been trained to assume that every encounter—especially one that occurred in a remote location, such as a marshland in Essex—was potentially hostile. Unlike ordinary SVR operatives, Nikolai possessed the authority to kill first and worry about the consequences later. So, too, did Anna.

He checked the time. It was nearly two o'clock. He crossed the headland to Naze Tower and then retraced his steps along the seafront to Frinton. The sun had finally burned a hole in the clouds by the time he arrived at the Bedford House. One of the last surviving hotels from the town's golden age, it stood at the far southern end of the Esplanade, a Victorian mausoleum with pennants flying from its turrets. The woman had chosen it, the woman known in the West as Rebecca Manning and at Moscow Center as Rebecca Philby. The Bedford's management was under the impression that Nikolai was Philip Lane, a writer of television crime dramas who had come to Essex in search of inspiration.

Entering the hotel, he made his way to the atrium-like Terrace Café for afternoon tea. Phoebe, the tight-skirted waitress, showed him to a table overlooking the Esplanade. Nikolai, playing the role of Philip Lane, spread a Moleskine notebook before him. Then, absently, he took up his SVR-issue mobile phone.

Concealed within its applications was a protocol that allowed him to communicate securely with Moscow Center. Even so, the wording of the message he typed was so vague as to be incomprehensible to an adversarial signals intelligence service like Britain's GCHQ. It stated that he had just completed a long surveillance-detection run and had seen no evidence he was being followed. In his opinion, it was safe to insert the next member of the team. Upon arrival, she was to make her way to Frinton to collect the weapon of assassination, which Nikolai had smuggled into the country. And upon completion of her assignment, Nikolai would see that she made it out of Britain safely. For this operation, at least, he was little more than a glorified delivery boy and driver. Still, he was looking forward to seeing her again. She was always better when they were in the field.

Phoebe placed a pot of Earl Grey tea on the table, along with a plate of dainty sandwiches. "Are you working?"

"Always," drawled Nikolai.

"What kind of story is it?"

"I haven't decided."

"Does someone die?"

"Several people, actually."

Just then, an open-top Jaguar F-Type, bright red, drew up at the hotel's entrance. The driver was a good-looking man of perhaps fifty, blond, with deeply tanned skin. His passenger, a black-haired woman, was recording their arrival on a smartphone, her arm outstretched. They seemed to be dressed for a special occasion.

"The Edgertons," explained Phoebe.

"Sorry?"

"Tom and Mary Edgerton. They're newlyweds. Apparently, it was all very spur of the moment." A bellman heaved two suitcases from the car's boot while the woman snapped photographs of the sea. "Lovely, isn't she?"

"Quite," agreed Nikolai.

"I think she might be an American."

"We won't hold that against her."

Nikolai watched the couple enter the lobby, where the manager presented them each with a complimentary glass of champagne. The woman, while surveying the hotel's staid interior, inadvertently caught Nikolai's eye and smiled. The man took her proprietarily by the arm and led her to the lift.

"She's definitely American," said Phoebe.

"Indeed," agreed Nikolai. "And her husband is the jealous type."

The bridal suite was on the third floor. Keller swiped the key card, pushed open the door, and stood aside for Sarah to enter. Their bags lay on luggage stands at the foot of the bed. Keller hung the DO NOT DISTURB sign from the latch and, closing the door, engaged the safety bar.

"Is he the man you saw at Café Remor in Geneva?"

Sarah nodded once.

Keller sent a brief message on his BlackBerry to the team at Hatch End. Then he reached inside his suit jacket and removed his Walther PPK from his shoulder holster. "Ever use one of these?"

"Not a Walther," said Sarah.

"Shoot anyone?"

"A Russian, actually."

"Lucky girl. Where?"

"In the hip and the shoulder."

"I meant—"

"It happened in a bank in Zurich."

Keller racked the Walther's slide, chambering the first round. Then he thumbed the safety into place and handed the gun to Sarah. "It's now fully loaded. Seven rounds only. When you want to fire it, just disengage the safety and pull the trigger."

"What about you?"

"I'll manage."

Sarah practiced disengaging and engaging the safety. "The perfect wedding gift for the woman who has everything."

Keller raised his champagne glass. "Your first wedding, is it?"

"I'm afraid so."

"Mine, too." He walked to the window and stared at the granite sea. "Let's hope we defy the odds."

"Yes," agreed Sarah as she slipped the Walther into her purse. "Let's."

56

10 Downing Street

At eight fifteen that evening, as Keller and Sarah were dining well in the Bedford's grill room not twenty feet from their Russian quarry, a Jaguar limousine bearing Gabriel Allon and Graham Seymour passed through a heavily guarded gate off Horse Guards Road and parked outside the five-story redbrick building that stood at 12 Downing Street. Formerly the official residence of the chief whip, it now housed the prime minister's press and communications staff. The chancellor of the Exchequer resided next door at Number 11, and the prime minister himself, of course, at Number 10. The famous black door opened automatically as Gabriel and Seymour approached. Watched by a fierce-looking brown-and-white tabby cat, they went quickly inside.

Geoffrey Sloane, the prime minister's chief of staff

402 · DANIEL SILVA

and the most powerful unelected official in Britain, was waiting in the entrance hall. He thrust a hand in Gabriel's direction. "I was here the morning you killed that ISIS dirty bomber at the security gate. In fact, I could hear the gunshots from my office." Sloane released Gabriel's hand and looked at Seymour. "I'm afraid the PM hasn't much time."

"This won't take long."

"I'd like to sit in."

"Sorry, Geoffrey, but that's not possible."

Jonathan Lancaster was waiting upstairs in the Terracotta Room. Earlier that afternoon he had narrowly survived a vote of no confidence in the House of Commons. Even so, the Westminster press corps were at that very moment writing his political obituary. Thanks to the folly of Brexit, which Lancaster had opposed, his career was effectively over. Were it not for Gabriel and Graham Seymour, whom he greeted warmly, it might have ended much sooner.

The prime minister glanced at his wristwatch. "I have dinner guests."

"I'm sorry," said Seymour, "but I'm afraid we have a rather serious situation regarding the Russians."

"Not again."

Seymour nodded gravely.

"And the nature of this situation?"

"A known SVR assassin has entered the country."

"Where is he now?"

"A small hotel in Essex. The Bedford House."

"I remember it fondly from my youth," said Lancaster. "I take it the Russian is under surveillance."

"Total," answered Seymour. "Four MI6 watchers have checked into the hotel next door, the East Anglia Inn, along with two highly experienced Israeli field officers. Tech-Ops have planted transmitters in the Russian's room, audio and video. They've also hacked into the Bedford's internal network of security cameras. We're watching his every move."

"Do we have anyone inside the Bedford?"

"Christopher Keller. He's the one who—"

"I know who he is," interjected Lancaster. Then he asked, "Do we know the Russian's target?"

"We can't say for certain, Prime Minister, but we believe the Russians are planning to assassinate Crown Prince Abdullah during his visit to London."

Lancaster absorbed the news with admirable calm. "Why would the Russians want to kill the future king of Saudi Arabia?"

"Because the future king is a Russian agent. And if he ever reaches the throne, he will tilt Saudi Arabia toward the Kremlin and do irreparable harm to British and American interests in the Gulf."

Lancaster stared at Seymour, bewildered. "If that's the case, why on earth would the Russians want to eliminate him?"

"Because they're probably under the impression Abdullah is working for us."

"Us?"

"The Secret Intelligence Service."

"And just how did they come to *that* conclusion?"

"We told them."

"How?"

Seymour smiled coldly. "Rebecca Manning."

Lancaster reached for the phone. "I'm afraid we're going to be a while, Geoffrey. Please extend my apologies to our guests." He replaced the receiver and looked at Seymour. "You have my full attention. Keep talking."

But it was Gabriel, not the director-general of the Secret Intelligence Service, who explained to the prime minister why it appeared the Russians intended to assassinate the future king of Saudi Arabia while he was on British soil. The briefing was identical to the one Gabriel had given to Graham Seymour several weeks earlier in the safe house in St. Luke's Mews, though now it contained details of the deception operation targeted at Rebecca Manning, the former MI6 officer and daughter of Kim Philby. Lancaster listened in silence, his jaw clenched.

Before Russia's intervention in America's politics, they had meddled in Great Britain's, and Lancaster was the victim. There was also ample evidence to suggest the Kremlin had covertly supported Brexit, which had thrown Britain into turmoil and left his career in ruins. If there was anyone who wanted to punish the Russians as much as Gabriel, it was Prime Minister Jonathan Lancaster.

"And you're sure this man Bennett is working for the Russians?"

Gabriel deferred to Seymour, who explained that Bennett had twice been observed meeting with his SVR handler, Yevgeny Teplov, in Epping Forest.

"Another spy scandal," said Lancaster. "Just what the country needs."

"We always knew there would be others, Prime Minister. Rebecca was in the perfect position to spot officers who might be vulnerable to a Russian approach."

"How did Bennett escape detection until now?"

"He went dormant after Rebecca's capture. We took a hard look at him but—"

"You failed to notice another Russian spy staring you in the face."

"No, Prime Minister. I left a suspected Russian spy in place so I might use him later to destroy the woman who destroyed my service."

"Rebecca Manning."

Seymour nodded.

"Explain."

"If we arrest the members of an SVR hit team on the eve of your meeting with Abdullah, the Russians will suffer enormous international damage, and Rebecca will come under suspicion as the source of the leak."

"The Russians will think she's a triple agent—is that what you're suggesting?"

"Indeed."

The prime minister made a show of thought. "You said *if* we arrest the Russian hit team. What other option do we have?"

"We can allow the plot to go forward."

"If we do that, the Russians—"

"Will kill their own asset, Crown Prince Abdullah, the future king of Saudi Arabia. And with a bit of luck," added Seymour, "they might kill Rebecca, too."

Lancaster looked at Gabriel. "Surely, this is your idea."

"Which answer would you prefer?"

Lancaster frowned. "What happens if Abdullah is . . ."

"Removed from the line of succession?"

"Yes."

"Khalid's father will likely see that his son is reinstalled as crown prince, especially when he finds out that Abdullah conspired with the Russians to kidnap and murder Khalid's daughter."

"Is that what we want? A precocious man-child with impulse-control problems running Saudi Arabia?"

"He'll be different this time. He'll be the KBM we all hoped he would be."

Lancaster's smile was condescending. "You never struck me as the naive type." He looked at Seymour. "I don't suppose you've spoken to Amanda."

Amanda Wallace was Seymour's counterpart at MI5. With his expression, Seymour indicated she was in pitch darkness.

"There's no way she'll agree to this," said Lancaster.

"All the more reason why she must never know."

"Who does?"

"A small number of Israeli and MI6 officers working in a safe house in Harrow."

"Are any of them spying for the Russians?" Lancaster turned to Gabriel. "Do you know what will happen if a de facto head of state is assassinated on British soil? Our reputation will be destroyed."

"Not if the Russians are to blame."

"The Russians," replied Lancaster pointedly, "will deny it or blame us."

"They won't be able to."

Lancaster was clearly dubious. "How do they plan to kill him?"

"We don't know."

"Where will it happen?"

"We don't—"

"Have a clue," said Lancaster.

Gabriel waited for the heat of the exchange to dissipate. "We have one of the Russian operatives under surveillance. Once he contacts another member of the team—"

"What if he doesn't?"

Gabriel allowed a moment to pass. "Today is Tuesday."

"I don't need a spy to tell me what day it is. That's what I have Geoffrey for."

"Your meeting with Abdullah isn't until Thursday. Let us watch and listen for thirty-six hours."

"Thirty-six hours is out of the question." Lancaster pondered his wristwatch. "But I can give you twenty-four. We'll reconvene tomorrow evening." He rose abruptly. "Now if you don't mind, gentlemen, I'd like to finish my dinner."

57

Ouddorp, the Netherlands

The holiday bungalow stood in a cleft in the dunes outside the village of Ouddorp. It was white as a wedding cake, with a red tile roof. Plexiglass barriers shielded the small terrace from the wind, which blew without relent from the North Sea. Unheated, lightly insulated, it was scarcely habitable in winter. Occasionally, a brave soul in search of solitude might rent it in May, but typically it sat unoccupied until at least the middle of June.

Therefore, Isabel Hartman, a local estate agent who managed the property, was surprised by the e-mail inquiry she received in mid-March. It seemed a certain Madame Bonnard from Aix-en-Provence wished to rent the cottage for a period of two weeks, begin-

ning the first of April. She made the advance payment via wire transfer. No, she said in a subsequent
e-mail, she did not require a tour of the property when
she arrived; a printed brochure would suffice. Isabel
left it on the kitchen counter. The key she hid under a
flowerpot on the terrace. It was not her usual practice,
but she saw no harm in it. The bungalow contained
nothing of value other than a television. Isabel had recently installed a wireless Internet connection in a bid
to entice more foreign visitors—like Madame Valerie
Bonnard of Aix-en-Provence. Isabel could only wonder why she was coming to dreary Ouddorp. Even the
name sounded like something that had to be surgically
removed. If Isabel were fortunate enough to reside in
Aix, she would never leave.

Owing to the bungalow's isolation, Isabel was not
able to determine exactly when the Frenchwoman
arrived. She reckoned it was a day later than anticipated, for that was when Isabel spotted the car, a Volvo
sedan, dark in color, Dutch registration, parked in the
bungalow's unpaved drive. Isabel saw the car again
later that afternoon in the village. She saw the woman,
too. She was coming out of the Jumbo supermarket
with a couple of bags of groceries. Isabel considered
introducing herself, but decided against it. There was
something in the woman's demeanor and the guarded

look in her unusually blue eyes that made her entirely unapproachable.

There was also something unbearably sad about her. She had experienced a recent trauma, Isabel was certain of it. A child had died, a marriage had collapsed, she had been betrayed. She was preoccupied, that much was clear. Isabel couldn't decide whether the woman was grieving or plotting an act of vengeance.

Isabel saw the woman in the village the next day, when she had a coffee at the New Harvest Inn—and the day after that, when she lunched alone at Aker-shoek. Two days passed before the next sighting, which occurred once again at the Jumbo supermarket. This time, the woman's cart was filled nearly to capacity, suggesting to Isabelle she was expecting visitors. They arrived the following morning in a second car, a Mer-cedes E-Class. Isabel was surprised by the fact that all three were men.

She saw the woman only one more time, at two o'clock the next afternoon, at the foot of the old West Head Lighthouse. She was wearing a pair of Wellington boots and a dark green oilskin jacket, and was staring across the North Sea toward England. Isabel thought she had never seen a woman so sad—or so determined. She was plotting an act of vengeance. Of that, Isabel Hartman was certain.

The woman standing in the shadow of the lighthouse was aware she was being watched. She was not alarmed; it was only the busybody estate agent. She waited until the Dutchwoman had gone before setting out for the bungalow. It was a walk of ten minutes along the beach. One of her bodyguards was outside on the terrace. The other was inside the cottage, along with the communications officer. On the table in the dining room was an open laptop computer. The woman checked the status of British Airways Flight 579 from Venice to Heathrow. Then she ignited an L&B cigarette with an old silver lighter and poured herself three fingers of Scotch whisky. It was only the weather, she assured herself. The melancholia would pass once summer arrived.

58

Heathrow Airport, London

The flight from Venice was slow in disgorging its passengers. Therefore, Anna had to spend an additional five minutes pressed against the window in the twenty-second row of economy class to avoid the damp, fleshy arm of Henry, her space-invading seatmate. Her carry-on suitcase was stowed in the overhead. Her handbag was beneath the seat in front of her. In it was a German passport that identified her place of birth as Berlin. That much, at least, was accurate.

She was born in the eastern half of the city in 1983, the unwanted by-product of a secret relationship between two intelligence officers. Her mother, Johanna Hoffmann, had worked for the department of the Stasi that provided logistical support to Western European and Palestinian terrorist groups. Her father, Vadim

Yurasov, was a colonel in the KGB, based in the back-water of Dresden. They fled East Germany a few days after the fall of the Berlin Wall and settled in Moscow. After the wedding, which was approved by the KGB, Anna took the name Yurasova. She attended a special school reserved for the children of KGB officers, and after graduating from the prestigious Moscow State University, she entered the SVR's training academy. One of her classmates was a tall, handsome aspiring actor named Nikolai Azarov. They had worked together on numerous operations, and like Anna's parents they were secretly lovers.

Inside the terminal, Anna followed the procession to passport control and joined the queue for citizens of the European Union. The uniformed man on the dais scarcely looked at her passport.

"The purpose of your visit?"

"Tourism," Anna answered in her mother's German accent.

"Any special plans?"

"As much theater as possible."

The passport was returned. Anna made her way to the arrivals hall and then to the platform for the Heath-row Express. Upon arrival at Paddington she walked north along Warwick Avenue to Formosa Street and turned left. No one followed her.

She made another left into Bristol Gardens. A Renault Clio, silver-blue, was parked outside an exercise studio. The doors were unlocked. She tossed her suitcase into the rear compartment and slid behind the wheel. The keys were in the center console. She started the engine and eased away from the curb.

She had studied the route carefully so as not to be distracted by a navigation device. She headed north along the Finchley Road to the A1, then east on the M25 Orbital Motorway to the A12. Diligently, she scanned the road behind her for signs of surveillance, but when darkness fell her mind began to drift.

She thought about the night she and her parents had fled East Berlin. They had made the journey aboard a stinking Soviet transport plane. One of the other passengers was a little man with sunken cheeks and dark circles under his eyes. He worked with Anna's father at the KGB's Dresden bureau. He was a nobody who spent his days posing as a translator and clipping articles from German newspapers.

Somehow the little nobody was now the most powerful man in the world. In the span of a few years he had wreaked havoc on the postwar global economic and political order. The European Union was in shambles, NATO was hanging by a thread. After meddling in the politics of Britain and America, he had meddled in

Saudi Arabia's. Anna and Nikolai had helped him alter the line of succession in the House of Saud. Now, for reasons that had not been made fully clear to them, they were about to alter it again.

Anna never questioned orders from Moscow Center—especially when they concerned "active measures" near and dear to the president's heart—but the assignment unnerved her. She did not like taking orders from someone like Rebecca Philby, a former MI6 officer who scarcely spoke Russian. She was also worried about a piece of unfinished business from her last assignment.

Gabriel Allon . . .

Anna should have killed the Israeli in the café in Carcassonne when she'd had the chance, but Moscow Center's orders had been specific. They wanted him to die with the Saudi prince and the child. Anna was not ashamed to admit she feared Allon's vengeance. He was not the sort of man to make empty threats.

You're dead! Dead, dead, dead . . .

The Israeli receded from Anna's thoughts as she approached the market town of Colchester. The only route into Frinton-on-Sea was the level crossing at Connaught Avenue. Nikolai was staying at a hotel on the Esplanade. Anna left the car with the valet but carried her suitcase into the lobby.

A couple were sharing a bottle of Dom Perignon in

the lounge bar—a good-looking man of perhaps fifty, blond and tanned, and a woman with black hair. They paid Anna no heed as she walked over to reception to collect the room key that had been left under her cover name. The door it opened was on the fourth floor, and the room Anna entered without knocking was in darkness. She stripped off her clothing and, watched by the cameras of MI6, moved slowly toward the bed.

59

10 Downing Street

For the second consecutive evening, a Jaguar limousine passed through the security gate on Horse Guards Road at eight fifteen. The brown-and-white tabby cat beat a hasty retreat as Gabriel and Graham Seymour hurried along Downing Street through a pouring rain. Geoffrey Sloane wordlessly ushered them into the Cabinet Room, where the prime minister was seated in his usual chair at the center of the long table. Before him was a copy of the final schedule for Crown Prince Abdullah's visit to London.

When Sloane had gone and the doors were closed, Graham Seymour delivered the promised update. Earlier that evening a second Russian operative, a woman, had arrived by motorcar at the Bedford House Hotel in Frinton-on-Sea. After engaging in sexual activity with her colleague, she had taken possession of a Stechkin 9mm pistol, two magazines, a sound suppressor, and a small object that Tech-Ops was still attempting to identify.

"Best guess?" asked Lancaster.

"I wouldn't want to speculate."

"Where is she now?"

"Still in the room."

"Do we know how she got into the country?"

"We're still trying to determine that."

"Are there others?"

"We don't know what we don't know, Prime Minister."

"Spare me the clichés, Graham. Just tell me what they're going to do next."

"We can't, Prime Minister. Not yet."

Lancaster swore softly. "What if her car contains a bomb like the one that went off on the Brompton Road a few years ago?" He looked at Gabriel. "You remember that one, don't you, Director Allon?"

"We've already had a look at her car. Her boyfriend's, too. They're clean. Besides," said Gabriel, "there's no way they'll be able to get a bomb anywhere near Abdullah tomorrow. London will be locked down tight."

"What about his motorcade?"

"Assassinating a head of state in a moving car is nearly impossible."

"Tell that to Archduke Ferdinand. Or President Kennedy."

"Abdullah won't be in an open-top car, and the streets will be entirely cleared of traffic and parked cars."

"So where will they make their attempt?"

Gabriel looked down at the schedule. "May I?"

Lancaster pushed it across the tabletop. It was of the one-page variety, bullet points only. Arrival at Heathrow at nine a.m. Meeting between the British and Saudi delegations at Downing Street from ten thirty to one p.m., followed by a working lunch. The crown prince was scheduled to leave Number 10 at half past three and travel by motorcade to his private residence in Belgravia for several hours of rest. He was scheduled to return to Downing Street at eight p.m. for dinner. Departure for Heathrow was tentatively set for ten.

"If I had to guess," said Gabriel, pointing toward one of the entries, "it will happen here."

The prime minister pointed to an entry of his own. "What if it happens here?" His fingertip moved down the page. "Or here?" There was a silence. Then Lancaster said, "I'd rather not be a collateral casualty, if you understand my meaning."

THE NEW GIRL · 421

"I do," answered Gabriel.

"Perhaps we should increase security at Downing Street even more than we'd planned."

"Perhaps you should."

"I don't suppose you're available."

"I'd be honored, Prime Minister. But I'm afraid the Saudi delegation would find my presence curious, to say the least."

"What about Keller?"

"A much better choice."

Lancaster's gaze moved slowly around the room. "Of all the momentous decisions that have been made within these walls . . ." He looked at Graham Seymour. "I reserve the right to order the arrest of those two Russians at any moment tomorrow."

"Of course, Prime Minister."

"If anything goes wrong, you will be blamed, not me. I did not order, condone, or play any role in this whatsoever. Is that clear?"

Seymour nodded once.

"Good." Lancaster closed his eyes. "And may God have mercy on us all."

60

Walton-on-the-Naze, Essex

Christopher Keller remained at the Bedford House Hotel until three a.m., when he slipped from the rear service entrance and hiked north along the promenade to Walton-on-the-Naze. The car was waiting outside Terry's Antiques & Secondhand in Station Street. Keller walked past it twice before dropping into the passenger seat. The driver was a field support agent who went by the name Tony. As he eased away from the curb, Keller reclined his seat and closed his eyes. He had spent the last two nights in a hotel room with a beautiful American woman of whom he had grown quite fond. He needed a couple hours of sleep.

He woke to a vision of robed men moving along a street in semidarkness. It was only the Edgware Road. Tony followed it to Marble Arch. He crossed the park on West Carriage Drive and then made his way through the still-slumbering streets of Kensington to Keller's exclusive address in Queen's Gate Terrace.

"Nice," remarked Tony enviously.

"Nine o'clock okay?"

"I'd feel better about half past eight. The traffic is going to be a nightmare."

Keller climbed out, crossed the pavement, and descended the steps to the lower entrance of his maisonette. Inside, he loaded the automatic with Volvic and Carte Noire and watched *BBC Breakfast* while the coffee brewed. Crown Prince Abdullah's visit to Downing Street had managed to displace Brexit as the lead story. The analysts were expecting a warm meeting and many Saudi promises of future arms purchases. London's Metropolitan Police Service, however, was braced for a difficult day, with thousands of demonstrators expected to gather in Trafalgar Square to protest Saudi Arabia's imprisonment of pro-democracy activists and the murder of the dissident journalist Omar Nawwaf. All in all, said one senior MPS official, it was best to avoid the center of London if possible.

"No chance of that," murmured Keller.

He drank a first cup of coffee while watching the coverage and a second while shaving. In the shower he found himself unexpectedly daydreaming about the beautiful American woman he had left behind in a hotel in Frinton. He took more care than usual with his grooming and his dress, choosing a dark gray suit of moderate cut and cloth, a white shirt, and a solid navy-blue necktie. Examining his appearance in the mirror, he concluded he had achieved the desired effect. He looked very much like an officer of the Royalty and Specialist Protection, or RaSP. A branch of the Met's Protection Command, RaSP was responsible for safeguarding the royal family, the prime minister, and visiting foreign dignitaries. Keller and the rest of the RaSP had a long day ahead of them.

He went downstairs to the kitchen and watched *BBC Breakfast* to its conclusion at eight thirty. Then he pulled on a respectable mackintosh coat and climbed the steps to the street, where Tony was waiting behind the wheel of the MI6 car. As they headed eastward across London, Keller's thoughts once again drifted to the woman. This time, he removed his MI6 BlackBerry and dialed.

"Where are you?" he asked.

"Just leaving the dining room."

"Anyone interesting at breakfast?"

"A couple of birdwatchers and a Russian agent."

"Just one?"

"His girlfriend left a few minutes ago."

"Do Gabriel and Graham know?"

"What do you think?"

"Where's she headed?"

"Your way."

"Who's tailing her?"

"Mikhail and Eli."

Keller heard the ping of the Bedford's lift and the rattle of the doors. "Where are you going?"

"I was planning to curl up with a book and a gun and wait for my husband to come back."

"Do you remember how to use it?"

"Release the safety and pull the trigger."

Keller killed the connection and stared gloomily out the window. Tony was right, the traffic was a nightmare.

The protesters had already descended on Trafalgar Square. They were stretched from the steps of the National Gallery to Nelson's Column, a banner-waving, slogan-chanting multitude, some robed and veiled, some fleeced and flanneled, all outraged that the de facto ruler of Saudi Arabia was about to be fêted by a British head of government.

Whitehall was closed to vehicular traffic. Keller climbed out of the car and, after showing his MI6 identification card to a Met officer with a clipboard, was allowed to proceed on foot. Sarah Bancroft finally left his thoughts, only to be replaced by memories of the morning he and Gabriel had stopped ISIS's attempt to set off a dirty bomb in the heart of London. It was Gabriel who had killed the terrorist with several shots to the back of his head. But Keller was the one who prevented the device's dead-man detonator switch from automatically setting off the explosive charge and dispersing a cloud of deadly cesium chloride throughout the seat of British power. He had been forced to hold the bomber's lifeless thumb to the trigger for three hours while an EOD team worked feverishly to disarm the device. They were, without question, the longest three hours of his life.

Keller sidestepped the spot where he and the dead terrorist had lain together, and presented himself at the security gate of Downing Street. Once again, after displaying his MI6 identification, he was allowed to pass. Ken Ramsey, the leader of Downing Street operations, was waiting in the entrance hall of Number 10.

Ramsey handed Keller a radio set and a Glock 17. "Your boss is upstairs in the White Room. He'd like a word."

Keller hurried up the Grand Staircase, which was lined with portraits of prime ministers past. Geoffrey Sloane was waiting in the corridor outside the White

Room. Opening the door, he nodded for Keller to enter. Graham Seymour was seated in one of the wing chairs. In the other was Prime Minister Jonathan Lancaster. His expression was grave and tense.

"Keller," he said absently.

"Prime Minister." Keller looked at Seymour. "Where is she?"

"The A12 bound for London."

"What about Abdullah?"

"You tell me."

Keller inserted his earpiece and listened to the chatter on the RaSP's secure frequency. "Bang on target for a ten fifteen arrival."

"Then perhaps," said Lancaster, "you should be downstairs with your colleagues."

"Does this mean—"

"That we're proceeding with the summit meeting as planned?" Lancaster rose and buttoned his suit jacket. "Why in heaven's name wouldn't we?"

61

Notting Hill, London

At 10:13 a.m., as a motorcade of Mercedes limousines flowed through Downing Street's open gate, a single car, a dowdy Opel hatchback, drew up outside 7 St. Luke's Mews in Notting Hill. The man in the backseat, Prince Khalid bin Mohammed Abdulaziz Al Saud, was in a foul mood. Like his uncle, he had arrived that morning at Heathrow Airport—not by private jet, his usual mode of travel, but on a commercial flight from Cairo, an experience he would not soon forget. The car was the final straw.

Khalid caught the driver's eye in the rearview. "Aren't you going to open my door?"

"Just pull the latch, luv. Works every time."

Khalid stepped into the wet street. As he approached

the door of Number 7, it remained tightly closed. He glanced over his shoulder. The driver, with a movement of his hand, indicated that Khalid should make his presence known by knocking on the door. Another calculated insult, he thought. Never in his life had he knocked on a door.

A boyish-looking man with a benevolent face admitted him. The house was very small and sparsely furnished. The sitting room contained a couple of cheap-looking chairs and a television tuned to the BBC. Before it stood Gabriel Allon, a hand to his chin, his head tilted slightly to one side.

Khalid joined him and watched his uncle, in traditional Saudi dress, emerge from the back of a limousine as cameras flashed like lightning. Prime Minister Jonathan Lancaster was standing just outside the door of Number 10, a smile frozen on his face.

"I should be the one arriving at Downing Street," said Khalid. "Not him."

"Be glad you're not."

Khalid surveyed the room with disapproval. "I don't suppose there's any refreshment."

Gabriel pointed toward a doorway. "Help yourself."

Khalid went into the kitchen, another first. Bewildered, he called out, "How does the teakettle work?"

"Add water and push the power button," answered Gabriel. "That should do the trick."

Like his tempestuous young nephew, Crown Prince Abdullah was not impressed by the house he entered that morning. Though he had lived in London for many years and moved in lofty social circles, it was his first visit to Downing Street. He had been assured that beyond the rather staid entrance hall lay a house of extraordinary elegance and unexpected size. At first glance, however, it seemed hard to imagine. Abdullah much preferred his new billion-dollar palace in Riyadh—or the Grand Presidential Palace at the Kremlin, where he had met secretly on several occasions with the man to whom he now owed an enormous debt. Today he would make his first payment.

The prime minister insisted on showing Abdullah a scuffed, modular-looking leather chair beloved by Winston Churchill. Abdullah made appropriate noises of admiration. Inwardly, however, he was thinking that the chair, like Jonathan Lancaster, needed to be put out of its misery.

At last, Abdullah and his aides were shown into the Cabinet Room. *Cabinet* was definitely the right word for it. He took his assigned seat, and Lancaster sat down opposite. Before each of them was the agreed-upon agenda for the first session of the summit. Lancaster, however, after much throat clearing and shuffling of papers, suggested they get "some unpleasantness" out of the way first.

"Unpleasantness?"

"It has come to our attention that a dozen or more female activists are being held without charge in a Saudi prison and subjected to various forms of torture, including electric shock, waterboarding, and threats of rape. It is imperative these women be released at once. Otherwise, we cannot proceed with our relationship as normal."

Abdullah managed to conceal his astonishment. He had been assured by his foreign minister and his ambassador to London that the meeting would be amicable.

"Those women," he said calmly, "were arrested by my nephew."

"Be that as it may," Lancaster shot back, "*you* are responsible for their current confinement. They must be released at once."

Abdullah's gaze was level and cool. "The Kingdom of Saudi Arabia does not interfere in the internal matters of Great Britain. We expect to be shown the same courtesy."

"The Kingdom of Saudi Arabia has directly and indirectly helped to turn this country into the world's preeminent center for Salafist-jihadist ideology. This, too, must end."

Abdullah hesitated, then said, "Perhaps we should move on to the next item on the agenda."

"We just did."

Beyond the government zones of Whitehall and Westminster, London's midday traffic was its typical tangled mess. In fact, it took Anna Yurasova nearly two hours to drive from Tower Hamlets to the Q-Park garage on Kinnerton Street in Belgravia, much longer than she had expected.

The London *rezidentura* had clandestinely reserved a space at the garage. Anna concealed the Stechkin 9mm beneath the Renault's passenger seat before surrendering the car to the attendant. Then she walked up the ramp, handbag dangling from one shoulder, and made her way to Motcomb Street, a narrow pedestrian lane lined with some of London's most exclusive shops and restaurants. In her dark skirt and stockings and short leather coat, her heels clattering loudly over the paving stones, she drew admiring and envious glances. She was confident, however, that no one was following her.

At Lowndes Street she turned left and headed toward Eaton Square. The northwestern section was closed to vehicular and pedestrian traffic. Anna approached a Metropolitan Police officer and explained that she was employed at one of the houses on the square.

"Which one, please?"

"Number Seventy."

"I need to have a look inside your bag."

Anna removed it from her shoulder and held it open. The officer examined it thoroughly before allowing her to pass. The terrace of houses along the western flank of the square were some of the grandest in London: three bay windows, five stories, a basement, and a handsome portico supported by two columns, each bearing the house's address. Anna climbed the four steps of Number 70 and placed her index finger atop the bell push. The door opened and she went inside.

Though Anna Yurasova did not know it, the team at Hatch End was monitoring her every move with the help of the CCTV cameras. Eli Lavon, who was following her on foot, was a mere insurance policy. After watching her enter the house at 70 Eaton Square, he walked west to Cadogan Place and lowered himself into the passenger seat of a Ford Fiesta. Mikhail Abramov was behind the wheel.

"Looks like Gabriel was right about where the Russians plan to do it."

"You sound surprised," replied Lavon.

"Not at all. The question is, how are they going to get to him?"

Mikhail drummed his fingers nervously on the center console. It was, thought Lavon, a wholly unbecoming habit for a man of the secret world.

"Is there any way you can stop that?"

"Stop what?"

Lavon exhaled slowly and switched on the car radio. It was one p.m. At Downing Street, said the newsreader on the BBC's Radio 4, the prime minister and the crown prince were just sitting down to lunch.

62

Eaton Square, Belgravia

It was Konstantin Dragunov, friend and business associate of Russia's president, who admitted Anna Yurasova into the grand house in Eaton Square. He wore an oligarch's dark suit and a white dress shirt open to his breastbone. His sparse gray hair and beard were uniform in length. His prominent lower lip shone like the skin of a freshly polished apple. Anna recoiled at the thought of a traditional Russian kiss of greeting. Defensively, she offered her hand instead.

"Mr. Dragunov," she said in English.

"Please call me Konstantin," he replied in the same language. Then in Russian he said, "Don't worry, a team from the *rezidentura* gave the house a thorough sweep late last night. It's clean."

He helped Anna off with her coat. The look in his

eye suggested he wanted to help her off with her dress and her undergarments as well. Konstantin Dragunov was regarded as one of the worst lechers in Russia, a noteworthy achievement given the stiff level of competition.

Anna glanced around the graceful entrance hall. Before leaving Moscow she had familiarized herself with the interior of the house by studying photographs and floor plans. They had not done it justice. It was remarkably beautiful.

She reclaimed her coat. "Perhaps you should show me around."

"It would be my pleasure."

Dragunov led her down a hallway to a pair of double doors, each with a round window, like portholes on a ship. Beyond them lay a professional kitchen that was much larger than Anna's flat in Moscow. It was obvious from Dragunov's indifferent demeanor that he did not often venture into this room of his Belgravia mansion.

"I gave the rest of the staff the day off, just like the Englishwoman instructed. I doubt Abdullah will eat anything, but before the police cordon went up I took delivery of a couple trays of canapés from his favorite caterer. They're in the refrigerator."

There were two, actually, side by side. Both were Sub-Zeros.

"What will he drink?"

"That depends on his mood. Champagne, white wine, a whisky if he's had a hard day. The wines are in the cooler under the counter. The distilled drinks are kept in the bar." Dragunov pushed through the double doors like a headwaiter in a hurry. The bar was in an alcove to the right. "Abdullah prefers Johnnie Walker Black Label. I keep a bottle just for him."

"How does he drink it?"

"Lots of ice. There's an automatic maker under the sink."

"What time are you expecting him?"

"Between four thirty and five. For obvious reasons he can't stay long."

"Where will you entertain him?"

"The drawing room."

It was up a flight of stairs, on the first floor of the mansion. Like the rest of the house, there was nothing Russian about it. Anna imagined the scene that would take place there in a few hours' time.

"It is essential you behave normally," she said. "Just ask him what he wants to drink, and I'll take care of the rest. Can you manage that, Konstantin?"

"I think so." He took her by the arm. "There's one other thing you should see."

"What is it?"

"A surprise."

He guided Anna into a small wood-paneled lift and pressed the call button for the uppermost floor. Dragunov's enormous bedroom—the chamber of horrors—overlooked Eaton Square.

"Don't worry, I brought you here only for the view."

"Of what?"

He nudged her toward one of the three bay windows and pointed toward the southern side of the square. "Do you know who lives right over there at Number Fifty-Six?"

"Mick Jagger?"

"The chief of the Secret Intelligence Service. And you're going to kill his prized asset right under his nose."

"That's great, Konstantin. But if you don't take your hand off my ass, I'm going to kill you, too."

The topic they reserved for the working lunch at Downing Street was Saudi Arabia's war against the Iranian-backed Houthi rebels in Yemen. Jonathan Lancaster demanded Abdullah end indiscriminate air strikes on innocent civilians, especially air strikes carried out with British combat aircraft. Abdullah countered that it was his nephew's war, not his, though he made it clear he shared KBM's view that the Iranians could not be allowed to spread their malign influence throughout the Middle East.

"We're also concerned," said Lancaster, "about the growing regional influence of the Russians."

"Moscow's influence is on the rise because the Russian president did not allow his ally in Syria to be swept away by the madness of the Arab Spring. The rest of the Arab world, including Saudi Arabia, couldn't help but notice."

"May I offer you a piece of advice, Prince Abdullah? Don't fall for Russian promises. It won't end well."

It was three fifteen when the two leaders emerged from the doorway of Number 10. The trade and investment deal the prime minister outlined for the assembled press corps was substantial but fell a few billion short of presummit expectations. So, too, did Abdullah's commitment to purchase British arms in the future. Yes, said Lancaster, they had discussed thorny issues involving human rights. No, he was not satisfied with all of the crown prince's answers, including those regarding the brutal murder of the dissident Saudi journalist Omar Nawwaf. "It was," said Lancaster in conclusion, "an honest and fruitful exchange between two old friends."

With that, he shook Abdullah's hand and gestured

toward the waiting Mercedes limousine. As the motorcade departed Downing Street, Christopher Keller ducked into the back of a black Protection Command van. Under normal circumstances, the drive to Abdullah's private residence at 71 Eaton Square might have taken twenty minutes or more. But on empty streets with a Metropolitan Police escort, they arrived in less than five.

The square's CCTV cameras recorded that Crown Prince Abdullah entered his home at 3:42 p.m., accompanied by a dozen robed aides and several Saudi security men in dark business suits. Six RaSP officers immediately took up positions outside the house along the pavement. One member of the detail, however, remained in the back of the Protection Command van, invisible to the woman standing in the third-floor window of the house next door.

It took the same amount of time, five minutes, for Prime Minister Jonathan Lancaster to separate himself from his aides and make his way upstairs to the White Room. Entering, he removed a slip of official Number 10 notepaper from his breast pocket. The pad from which it had been torn was lying on the coffee table in front of Graham Seymour, beneath the MI6 chief's Parker pen.

"I suspect no British prime minister in history has ever been handed a note such as this in the middle of a state visit." Lancaster dropped it on the coffee table. "I told Abdullah it concerned Brexit. I'm not sure he believed me."

"I thought you should know her whereabouts."

Jonathan Lancaster looked down at the note. "Do me a favor, Graham. Burn that damn thing. The rest of the notepad, too."

"Prime Minister?"

"You left an impression on the pad when you wrote it." Lancaster shook his head reproachfully. "Didn't they teach you anything at spy school?"

63

Eaton Square, Belgravia

The recriminations began the instant the door closed. The meeting at Downing Street had been an unmitigated disaster. There was no other word for it. *A disaster!* How could they have not known that Lancaster intended to ambush His Royal Highness on the issue of human rights and the jailed women? Why were they not told he was going to raise the topic of Saudi financial support for Islamic institutions in Britain? Why were they blindsided? Obaid, the foreign minister, blamed it all on Qahtani, the ambassador to London, who saw conspiracies everywhere. Al-Omari, the chief of royal court, was so enraged he suggested canceling dinner and returning to Riyadh at once. It was Abdullah, suddenly the statesman, who overruled him. Backing out of the dinner, he said, would only offend the British and weaken him at home. Better to end the visit on a high note, even if it was a false one.

In the meantime, an aggressive media response was in order. Obaid hurried over to the BBC, Qahtani to CNN. In the sudden silence, Abdullah slumped in his chair, his eyes closed, a hand pressed to his forehead. The performance was for the benefit of al-Omari, the courtier. No task was too small, too demeaning, for al-Omari. He hovered over Abdullah night and day. Therefore, he would have to be handled carefully.

"Are you feeling unwell, Your Royal Highness?"

"Just a little tired, that's all."

"Perhaps you should go upstairs for a rest."

"I think I'll have a swim first."

"Shall I switch on the steam room?"

"There are some things I can still do for myself." Abdullah rose slowly. "Short of a palace coup or an Iranian attack on Saudi Arabia, I wish not to be disturbed until seven thirty. Can you manage that, Ahmed?"

Abdullah went downstairs to the pool room. A watery blue light played upon an arched ceiling painted with corpulent swirling nudes in the manner of Rubens and Michelangelo. How shocked the pious men of the ulema would be, he thought, if they could see him now. He had renewed the old covenant between the Wahhabis and the House of Saud to win clerical support for his coup against Khalid. Yet privately he loathed the bearded ones as much as the reformers did. Despite the unexpectedly contentious meeting at Downing Street, Abdullah had enjoyed his brief respite from religiously stifling Riyadh. He realized how much he had missed the sight of female flesh, even if it was only a bare lower leg, pale with winter, viewed through the tinted window of a speeding limousine.

He went into the changing room, switched on the steam bath, and shed his vestments. Disrobed, he contemplated his reflection in the full-length mirror. The sight depressed him. Whatever muscle he had acquired after puberty had long ago run to fat. His pectorals dangled like an old woman's breasts over his colossal abdomen. His legs, spindly and hairless, seemed to strain under the burden. Only his hair saved him from incontestable hideousness. It was rich and thick and only slightly gray.

He eased into the pool and, manatee-like, swam several lengths. Afterward, standing before the mirror once more, he thought he detected a slight improvement in his muscle tone. In his wardrobe was a change of clothing: woolen trousers, a blazer, a striped dress shirt, undergarments, loafers, a belt. After deodorizing his armpits and running a comb through his hair, he dressed.

The heavy glass door of the steam bath was now opaque with condensation. No one, not even the cloying al-Omari, would dare look inside. Abdullah locked the outer door of the dressing room before opening what was once a storage closet for robes and pool towels. It was now a vestibule of sorts. Inside was another door. On the wall was a keypad. Abdullah entered the four-digit code. The lock snapped open with a gentle thud.

64

Eaton Square, Belgravia

The communicating door on the other side of the common wall was already open. In the half-light of the passageway stood Konstantin Dragunov. He regarded Abdullah at length. There was nothing deferential in his direct gaze. Abdullah supposed the Russian was entitled to his insolence. Were it not for Dragunov and his friend in the Kremlin, Khalid would still be next in line to the throne, and Abdullah would be just another middle-aged, bankrupt prince from the wrong branch of the family tree.

At last, Dragunov bowed his head slightly. There was nothing genuine in the gesture. "Your Royal Highness."

"Konstantin. So good to see you again."

Abdullah accepted the outstretched hand. It had

been several months since their last meeting. On that occasion Abdullah had informed the Russian that his nephew Khalid had retained the services of one Gabriel Allon, the chief of Israeli intelligence, to find his kidnapped daughter.

The Russian released Abdullah's hand. "I saw the joint news conference with Lancaster. I have to say, it looked rather tense."

"It was. So was the meeting that preceded it."

"I'm surprised." Dragunov glanced at his big gold wristwatch. "How long can you stay?"

"A half hour. Not a minute more."

"Shall we go upstairs?"

"What about the reporters and the photographers in the square?"

"The shades and drapes are drawn."

"And your staff?"

"Just one girl." Dragunov smiled wolfishly. "Wait until you see her."

They climbed two flights of stairs to the large double drawing room. It was furnished like a Pall Mall gentlemen's club and hung with paintings of equines, canines, and men with white wigs. A maid in a short black dress was placing trays of canapés on a low table. She was about thirty-five, quite pretty. Abdullah wondered where Dragunov found them.

"Something to drink?" asked the Russian. "Juice? Mineral water? Tea?"

"Juice," answered Abdullah.

"What kind?"

"The kind that's made from French grapes and emits bubbles when poured into a tall slender glass."

"I believe I have a bottle of Louis Roederer Cristal in the cooler."

Abdullah smiled. "I suppose it will have to do."

The woman nodded and withdrew.

Abdullah sat down and waved away Dragunov's offer of food. "They stuffed me like a goose at Downing Street. Round two begins at eight o'clock."

"Perhaps it will be better than the first."

"I rather doubt it."

"You anticipated a warmer welcome?"

"I was told to expect one."

"By whom?"

Abdullah felt as though he were being interrogated. "The usual channels, Konstantin. What difference does it make?"

A moment passed. Then Dragunov said quietly, "There would have been no lectures if you had come to Moscow instead of London."

"If my first trip abroad as crown prince had been to

Moscow, it would have sent a dangerous signal to the Americans and to my rivals inside the House of Saud. It's better to wait until I'm king. That way, no one will be able to challenge me."

"Be that as it may, our mutual friend in the Kremlin would like a clear signal of your intentions."

And so it begins, thought Abdullah. The pressure to live up to his end of the deal. Cautiously, he asked, "What sort of signal?"

"One that makes it abundantly clear that you don't plan to go your own way once you become the leader of a family worth more than a trillion dollars." Dragunov's smile was forced. "With wealth like that, you might be tempted to forget those who helped you when no one else would go near you. Remember, Abdullah, my president invested a great deal in you. He expects a handsome return."

"And he'll get one," said Abdullah. "*After* I become king."

"He'd like a gesture of goodwill in the meantime."

"What did he have in mind?"

"An agreement to invest one hundred billion dollars from Saudi Arabia's sovereign wealth fund in several Russian projects that are of paramount importance to the Kremlin."

"And to you, too, I suspect." Receiving no reply, Abdullah said, "This sounds like a shakedown to me."

"Does it?"

Abdullah feigned deliberation. "Tell your president I'll dispatch a delegation to Moscow next week."

Dragunov brought his hands together in a show of unity. "Wonderful news."

Abdullah suddenly craved alcohol. He glanced over his shoulder. *Where the hell was that girl?* When he turned around again, Dragunov was devouring a caviar treat. A single black egg had lodged itself like a tick on his prominent lower lip.

Abdullah averted his gaze and abruptly changed the subject. "Why didn't you tell me you were going to try to kill him?"

"Who?"

"Allon."

The Russian dragged the back of his hand across his mouth, dislodging the speck of caviar. "The decision was made by the Kremlin and the SVR. I had nothing to do with it."

"You should have killed Khalid and the child the way we agreed and left Allon out of it."

"He needed to be dealt with."

"But you didn't *deal* with him, Konstantin. Allon survived that night."

Dragunov waved his hand dismissively. "What are you so afraid of?"

"Gabriel Allon."

"You have nothing to fear."

"Really?"

"We were the ones who tried to kill him, not you."

"I doubt he'll see the distinction."

"You're the crown prince of Saudi Arabia, Abdullah. Soon you'll be the king. No one, not even Gabriel Allon, can touch you now."

Abdullah glanced over his shoulder. *Where the hell was that girl?*

The SVR had trained Anna Yurasova in all manner of weaponry—firearms, knives, explosives—but never once had she rehearsed opening a bottle of Louis Roederer champagne under conditions of operational stress.

When the cork finally shot from the bottle with a loud pop, several costly ounces of frothy liquid spilled onto the counter. Ignoring the mess, Anna reached into the pocket of her maid's apron and removed a Pasteur pipette dropper and a slender glass vial. The clear liquid inside was one of the most dangerous substances on earth. Moscow Center had assured Anna it was harmless as long as it was in its container. Once she removed the cap, however, the liquid would instantly emit an invisible fountain of lethal alpha radiation. Anna was to work quickly but with extreme care. She was not to ingest the substance, inhale its fumes, or touch it.

On the counter was a serving tray with two crystal champagne flutes. Anna's hands trembled as she unscrewed the metal cap from the vial. With the Pasteur pipette she drew a few milliliters of the liquid and squirted it into one of the glasses. There was no scent at all. Moscow Center had promised it was tasteless as well.

Anna screwed the cap onto the vial and shoved it into the pocket of her apron, along with the pipette. Then she filled the two glasses with the champagne and with her left hand picked up the tray. The contaminated glass was on the right. She could almost feel the radiation rising with the escaping effervescence.

She pushed open one of the swinging double doors and snared a few linen cocktail napkins from the bar. As she approached the drawing room she heard the Saudi speak a name that made her heart give a sideways lurch. She placed a cocktail napkin before him and atop the napkin the contaminated glass. Dragunov she served directly, from her right hand to his.

The oligarch raised the glass formally. "To the future," he said, and drank.

The Saudi hesitated. "You know," he said after a moment, "I haven't touched a drop of alcohol since the night I returned to Saudi Arabia to become crown prince."

"She can get you something else if you prefer."

"Are you mad?" The Saudi swallowed the entire glass of champagne in a single draught. "Is there more? I don't think I can get through dinner at Downing Street without it."

Anna reclaimed the contaminated glass and returned to the kitchen. The Saudi had just consumed enough of the radioactive toxin to kill everyone in Greater London. There was no medication, no emergency treatment, that could forestall the inevitable destruction of his cells and organs. He was already dying.

Nevertheless, Anna decided to give him another dose.

This time, she did not bother with the pipette. Instead, she poured the remaining liquid toxin directly into the glass and added the champagne. Bubbles danced above the rim. Anna pictured a Vesuvius of radiation.

In the drawing room she served the drink to the Saudi and with a smile went hastily out. Returning to the kitchen, she removed her apron and placed it in the rubbish bin, along with the empty vial and the pipette.

The Englishwoman had ordered Anna to leave no contaminated items behind when making her escape. It was an order she had no intention of obeying.

Surrounded by an invisible fogbank of radiation, she checked the time on her phone. It was 4:42 p.m. Upstairs in the drawing room, His Royal Highness Prince Abdullah bin Abdulaziz Al Saud was already dying. Anna, her hand shaking, lit a cigarette and waited for him to leave.

65

Eaton Square, Belgravia

Konstantin Dragunov departed his home at 5:22 p.m. Because the northwest corner of Eaton Square was closed, he was compelled to walk a short distance to Cliveden Place, where his Mercedes May-bach limousine was waiting. Clutching an attaché case, an overcoat draped over his arm, he lowered himself into the backseat. The limousine sped east, followed by an Office watcher on a BMW motorcycle.

The woman emerged seven minutes later. At the base of the steps she turned left and walked past the home where His Royal Highness Prince Abdullah bin Abdulaziz Al Saud was said to be resting before an eight o'clock dinner at Downing Street. The six Protection Command officers standing outside the residence observed her carefully as she passed. So did Christopher

Keller, who was still sheltering in the back of the van, though Keller's interest in the woman was of a far different nature.

She slipped through the police cordon and, followed by Eli Lavon, walked directly to the Q-Park garage in Kinnerton Street. There she endured a wait of nearly ten minutes for the Renault Clio. When it finally arrived she headed north, into the London evening rush. A few minutes after six p.m., she passed the entrance of the Swiss Cottage Underground station on the Finchley Road. Lavon and Mikhail Abramov were behind her in the Ford Fiesta. The Anglo-Israeli team at Hatch End was tracking her with the CCTV cameras.

The team's two leaders remained in separate locations. Graham Seymour was at Downing Street; Gabriel, at the Notting Hill safe house. They were connected by an open secure phone line. The call had been initiated by Gabriel at 3:42 p.m., the moment Crown Prince Abdullah arrived at his home in Eaton Square. They had not seen him since. Nor had they seen any evidence to suggest Konstantin Dragunov or the female SVR operative had been in Abdullah's presence.

"So why are they making a run for it?" asked Gabriel.

"It appears they've decided to abort."

"Why would they do that?"

"Perhaps they noticed our surveillance," suggested Seymour. "Or perhaps Abdullah stood them up."

"Or perhaps Abdullah is already dead," said Gabriel, "and the two people who killed him are running for the exits."

There was silence on the line. Finally, Seymour said, "If Abdullah doesn't walk out the door as scheduled at seven forty-five, I'll ring the commissioner of the Metropolitan Police and arrange for the arrest of Dragunov and the woman."

"Seven forty-five is too late. We need to know whether Abdullah is still alive."

"I can't very well have the prime minister call him. I've involved him too much as it is."

"Then I suppose we'll have to send someone else into the house to check on him."

"Who?"

Gabriel hung up the phone.

66

Eaton Square, Belgravia

Nigel Whitcombe made the drive from Notting Hill to Belgravia in eight minutes flat. He and Gabriel remained in the car while Khalid approached the security cordon at Eaton Square. It was Christopher Keller who walked him to the front door of the house at Number 71.

The bell push summoned Marwan al-Omari, the chief courtier. He was clad in traditional Saudi dress. He fixed Khalid with a withering stare. "What are you doing here?"

"I've come to see my uncle."

"I can assure you, your uncle has no wish to see you."

Al-Omari tried to close the door, but Khalid stopped him. "Listen to me, Marwan. I am an Al Saud, and you are nothing more than a glorified butler. Now take me to my uncle before I—"

"Before you what?" Al-Omari managed a smile. "Still making threats, Khalid? One would have thought you'd have learned your lesson by now."

"I'm still the son of a king. And you, Marwan, are camel dung. Now move out of my way."

Al-Omari's smile vanished. "Your uncle left strict instructions not to be disturbed until half past seven."

"I wouldn't be here if it wasn't an emergency."

Al-Omari stood his ground a moment longer before finally stepping to one side. Khalid rushed into the entrance hall, but the courtier seized Keller's arm when he attempted to follow.

"Not him."

Keller went wordlessly into the square while Khalid, pursued by al-Omari, hurried up the stairs to Abdullah's bedroom suite. The outer door was locked. Al-Omari's anemic knock was scarcely audible.

"Your Royal Highness?"

When there was no answer, Khalid pushed the courtier aside and hammered on the door with the palm of his hand. "Abdullah? Abdullah? Are you there?" Greeted by silence, Khalid grabbed the latch and gave it a shake. The heavy door was solid as a ship.

He looked at al-Omari. "Get out of the way."

"What are you going to do?"

Khalid raised his right leg and drove the sole of his shoe against the door. There was the sound of splintering wood, but it held. The second blow loosened the latch from its fitting, and the third shattered the doorframe. It also broke several bones in Khalid's foot, he was sure of it.

Limping painfully, he stumbled into the magnificent suite. The sitting room was unoccupied, as was the bedchamber. Khalid shouted Abdullah's name, but there was still no answer.

"He must be bathing," fretted al-Omari. "We can't possibly disturb him."

The door to the master bathroom suite was closed as well, but the latch yielded to Khalid's touch. Abdullah was not in the bath or the shower. Nor was he grooming himself at the sink.

There was one final door. The door to the commode. Khalid didn't bother knocking.

"Dear God," whispered al-Omari.

67

10 Downing Street

Graham Seymour rang Stella McEwan, commissioner of the Metropolitan Police Service, at 6:24 p.m. Later, during the inevitable inquiry, much would be made of the short duration of the call, which was five minutes. At no point during the conversation did Seymour mention that he was in the White Room at 10 Downing Street, or that the prime minister was sitting anxiously next to him.

"An SVR hit team?" asked McEwan.

"Another one," lamented Seymour.

"Who's the target?"

"We can't say for certain. We assume it's someone who's run afoul of the Kremlin—or perhaps a former Russian intelligence officer living under an assumed identity here in Britain. I'm afraid I can't go into details."

"What about the hit team?"

"We've identified three suspects. One is a woman in her mid-thirties. She's currently headed east on the M25 in a Renault Clio." Seymour recited the car's registration number. "She should be considered armed and extremely dangerous. Make sure you have firearms officers on hand."

"Number two?"

"He's waiting for the woman at the Bedford House Hotel in Frinton. We assume they're planning to leave Britain tonight."

"Harwich is just up the road."

"And the last ferry," added Seymour, "departs at eleven."

"Frinton is in Essex, which means the Essex Police are responsible."

"This is a national security matter, Stella. Assert your authority. And handle him with care. We think he's even more dangerous than the woman."

"It's going to take us some time to get our assets into place. If you're watching him—"

"We are."

Stella McEwan asked about the third suspect.

"He's about to board a private jet at London City Airport," answered Seymour.

"Bound for Moscow?"

"That is our belief."

"Do you know his name?"

Seymour recited it.

"The oligarch?"

"Konstantin Dragunov is no ordinary oligarch, if there even is such a thing."

"I can't detain a friend of the Russian president without a warrant."

"Test him for chemical agents and radiation, Stella. I'm sure you'll have more than enough evidence to hold him. But do it quickly. Konstantin Dragunov must not be allowed to board that plane."

"I have a feeling you're not telling me everything, Graham."

"I'm the director-general of the Secret Intelligence Service. Why on earth would you think otherwise?" Seymour severed the connection and looked at Jonathan Lancaster. "I'm afraid things are about to get even more interesting."

"More?" There was a knock at the door. It was Geoffrey Sloane. He appeared more ashen than usual. "Something wrong, Geoffrey?"

"It seems the crown prince has taken ill."

"Does he need to be admitted to hospital?"

"His Royal Highness wishes to return to Riyadh at once. He and his delegation are leaving the Eaton Place residence now."

Lancaster placed a hand thoughtfully to his chin. "Have the Press Office draft a statement. Make sure the tone is light. Speedy recovery, look forward to seeing him at the next G20—that sort of thing."

"I'll see to it, Prime Minister." Sloane went out.

Lancaster looked at Seymour. "His decision to leave immediately is a stroke of good fortune."

"Fortune had nothing to do with it."

"How did you arrange it?"

"Khalid advised his uncle to return home for treatment. He plans to accompany him."

"Nice touch," said Lancaster.

Seymour's BlackBerry purred.

"What is it now?"

Seymour showed him the screen. The call was from Amanda Wallace, the director-general of MI5.

"Good luck," said Jonathan Lancaster before slipping quietly from the room.

68

London City Airport

Konstantin Dragunov heard the first sirens while stuck in rush-hour traffic on East India Dock Road. He instructed Vadim, his driver, to turn on the radio. The newsreader on Radio 4 sounded bored.

Crown Prince Abdullah of Saudi Arabia has taken ill and will not be attending dinner this evening at Downing Street as scheduled. Prime Minister Jonathan Lancaster has wished him a speedy recovery . . .

"That's enough, Vadim."

The driver switched off the radio and made a right turn into Lower Lea Crossing. It bore them past the old East India Dock Basin and the sparkling new office towers of the Leamouth Peninsula. London City Airport was three miles farther to the east, along North Woolrich Road. To enter the airport required navigating a pair of roundabouts. Traffic flowed normally through the first, but police had blocked the second.

An officer in a lime-green jacket approached the Maybach—cautiously, it seemed to Dragunov—and tapped on Vadim's window. The driver lowered it.

"Sorry for the delay," said the officer, "but I'm afraid we have a security situation."

"What kind of situation?" asked Dragunov from the backseat.

"A bomb threat. It's probably a hoax, but we're not letting any passengers into the terminal at this time. Only those flying privately are allowed to enter."

"Do I look like I'm traveling commercially to you?"

"Name, please?"

"Dragunov. Konstantin Dragunov."

The officer directed Vadim into the second traffic circle. He immediately turned to the left, into the car park of the London Jet Centre, the airport's fixed-base operator.

Dragunov swore softly.

The car park was jammed with vehicles and personnel from the Met, including several tactical officers from SCO19, the Specialist Firearms Command. Four officers immediately surrounded the Maybach, weapons drawn. A fifth banged his fist against Dragunov's window and ordered him to get out.

"What is the meaning of this?" demanded the Russian.

The SCO19 officer leveled his Heckler & Koch G36 directly at Dragunov's head. "Now!"

Dragunov unlocked the door. The SCO19 officer instantly flung it open and dragged Dragunov from the backseat.

"I am a citizen of the Russian Federation and a personal friend of the Russian president."

"I'm sorry to hear that."

"You have no right to arrest me."

"I'm not."

A strange-looking tent had been erected outside the Jet Centre. The SCO19 officer relieved Dragunov of his phone before shoving him through the entrance. Inside were four technicians clad in bulky hazmat suits. One examined Dragunov with a small scanner, running it over his torso and up and down his limbs. When the technician passed the instrument over Dragunov's right hand, he took a step back in alarm.

"What's wrong?" asked the SCO19 officer.

"Full-scale deflection."

"What does that mean?"

"It means he's off-the-charts radioactive." The technician ran the scanner over the officer. "And so are you."

At that same moment, Anna Yurasova was already beginning to feel the effect of the titanic amount of radiation to which she had been exposed inside Konstantin Dragunov's home in Belgravia. Her head ached, she was shivering, she was intensely nauseated. Twice she had nearly pulled to the side of the M25 to vomit, but the urge to empty the contents of her stomach had subsided. Now, as she approached the exit for a town called Potters Bar, it was rising again. For that reason alone, she was relieved to see what appeared to be a traffic accident ahead of her.

The three right lanes were blocked, and an officer with a red-tipped torch was directing all traffic into the left. As Anna passed him, their eyes met in the darkness.

The traffic halted. Another wave of nausea washed over her. She touched her forehead. It was dripping with sweat.

Again, the wave receded. Anna was suddenly freezing cold. She switched on the heater and then reached into her handbag, which was lying on the passenger seat. It took her a moment of fumbling to find her phone and another moment to dial Nikolai's number.

He picked up instantly. "Where are you?"

She told him.

"Have you been listening to the news?"

She hadn't. She'd been too busy trying not to be sick.

"Abdullah's canceled dinner. Apparently, he's a bit under the weather."

"So am I."

"What are you talking about?"

"I must have exposed myself."

"Did you drink any?"

"Don't be ridiculous."

"Then it will pass," said Nikolai. "Like the flu."

Another wave crested. This time, Anna flung open the door and was violently ill. The convulsion was so powerful it blurred her vision. When it finally cleared, she saw several men in tactical gear surrounding the car, weapons drawn.

She laid the phone on her thigh and put the call on SPEAKER.

"Nikolai?"

"Don't call me that."

"It doesn't matter anymore, Nikolai."

She reached beneath the passenger seat and wrapped her hand around the butt of the Stechkin. She managed to fire only a single shot before the car's windows exploded in a hurricane of incoming rounds.

You're dead, she thought. *Dead, dead, dead . . .*

The gunfire lasted two or three seconds at most. When it was over, Mikhail Abramov threw open the door of the Ford Fiesta and sprinted along the verge of the motorway toward the shattered Renault. The woman was hanging out the open driver's-side door, suspended by the safety belt, a gun in her hand. Police radios were crackling, passengers in the surrounding cars were screaming in terror. And somewhere, thought Mikhail, a man was shouting in Russian.

Are you there, Anna? What's happening? Can you hear me, Anna?

Suddenly, two of the SCO19 officers pivoted and leveled their HK G36 assault rifles at Mikhail. Hands raised, he backpedaled slowly and returned to the Ford.

"Is she dead?" asked Eli Lavon.

"As a doornail. And her friend at the hotel in Frinton knows it."

"How?"

"She was on the phone with him when it happened."

Lavon tapped out a message to Gabriel. The reply was instant.

"What does it say?" asked Mikhail.

"He just ordered Sarah to leave the hotel immediately. He wants us to get out to Essex as quickly as possible."

"Does he really?" Behind them, a chorus of car horns arose in the night. The traffic was at a standstill. "You'd better tell him we're going to be here awhile."

69

Frinton-on-Sea, Essex

Nikolai Azarov had allowed the connection to Anna's phone to remain active longer than he should have—five minutes and twelve seconds, according to the call timer on his own device. He had heard the burst of automatic gunfire, the sound of shattering glass, Anna's screams of agony. What came next were effectively the first chaotic moments of a highly unusual crime-scene investigation. There was a declaration of death, followed a moment later by a shouted warning of something called a full-scale deflection, a term with which Nikolai was not familiar. The same voice instructed officers to move away from the vehicle until it could be made secure. One officer, however, remained close enough to spot Anna's phone lying on the floorboard. He had also noticed there was a call in progress.

He had requested permission from a superior to retrieve the device, but the superior had refused. "If she touched the phone," he shouted, "the bloody thing is positively heaving with radiation."

It was then, five minutes after Anna's death, that Nikolai ended the call. No, he thought angrily. Not Anna's death, her assassination. Nikolai was well versed in the rules and tactics of the Metropolitan Police and the various county and regional forces. Ordinary officers did not carry guns, only AFOs, authorized firearms officers, or SFOs, the highly trained specialist firearms officers of SCO19. AFOs did not typically carry the type of automatic assault rifle Nikolai had heard over the phone. Only SCO19 officers were armed with such weapons. Their presence on the M25 suggested they had been lying in wait for Anna. So, too, did the presence of a hazardous materials team with a radiation-detection device. But how had the Metropolitan Police known that Anna would be contaminated? Obviously, surmised Nikolai, the British had been watching her.

But if that were the case, why had they not tried to arrest him? At present, he was drinking tea at his usual table in the lounge bar. He had checked out of his room earlier that afternoon. His car was waiting curbside in the Esplanade. His small overnight bag was in the custody of the porter. The bag contained nothing of operational value. Nikolai's Makarov 9mm was resting comfortably against the small of his back. In the right front pocket of his trousers was the spare vial of radioactive toxin that Moscow Center had insisted he carry into Britain. They had assured him the radiation could not escape the container. After hearing the voice of the hazmat technician, he was no longer certain that was the case.

A full-scale deflection . . .

He glanced at the television above the bar. It was tuned to Sky News. It seemed Khalid bin Mohammed had paid a visit to his uncle's house in Eaton Square shortly before Downing Street announced the cancellation of tonight's dinner. The event was noteworthy for another reason; it was the first public sighting of KBM since his abdication. Sky News had somehow obtained a video of his arrival. In Western clothing, his head bare, Khalid was scarcely recognizable. Nikolai's eye, however, was drawn to the British security agent walking next to him. Nikolai had seen him somewhere before, he was certain of it.

He picked up his phone. Sky News had posted the story on its Web site, along with the video. Nikolai watched it three times. He was not mistaken.

They're newlyweds. Apparently, it was all very spur of the moment . . .

He powered off his phone and removed the SIM card. Then he went onto the terrace overlooking the Esplanade. It was dark, the wind had died. He could see no sign of surveillance, but he knew they were watching him. His car, too. It was parked outside the hotel's entrance. Suddenly, another car drew up behind it. An open-top Jaguar F-Type. Bright red.

Nikolai smiled.

Upstairs, Sarah shoved the Walther PPK into her handbag and went into the corridor. Her phone rang as she was waiting for the lift.

"Where are you?" asked Keller anxiously.

She explained.

"How long does it take to leave a hotel?"

"I'm trying."

"Try harder, Sarah. And faster."

The lift arrived. She wheeled her suitcase into the carriage.

"Still there?" she asked.

"Still here."

"Any plans for tonight?"

"I was thinking about a late dinner."

"Anywhere special?"

"My place."

"Want some company?"

"Love some."

The carriage slowed to a stop and the doors opened with a wheeze. Passing reception, Sarah noisily bade farewell to Margaret, the head of guest services, and Evans, the concierge. In the lounge bar she glimpsed Keller walking across the screen of the television with Khalid at his side. Rising to his feet, as though in a hurry to be on his way, was the Russian assassin.

Sarah considered turning around and retracing her steps to the lift. Instead, she quickened her pace. It was no more than twenty steps to the entrance, but the Russian drew alongside her effortlessly and pressed something hard against the base of her spine. There was no mistaking it for anything other than a gun.

With his left hand he took hold of her arm and smiled. "Unless you want to spend the rest of your life in a wheelchair," he said quietly, "I suggest you keep walking."

Sarah squeezed the phone tightly. "Still there?"

"Don't worry," said Keller. "Still here."

70

Frinton-on-Sea, Essex

Outside, the Russian took the phone from Sarah's grasp and killed the connection. The two cars waited in the street, watched over by the valet. He was clearly confounded by the scene he was witnessing. Forty-eight hours earlier, Sarah had arrived at the hotel as a newlywed. Now she was abruptly leaving with another man.

The valet relieved Sarah of her suitcase. "Which car?" he asked.

"Mrs. Edgerton's," replied the Russian in a crisp British accent.

Sarah managed to conceal her astonishment. Clearly, the Russian had been aware of her presence at the hotel for some time. He accepted the car keys from the valet and instructed him to place "Mrs. Edgerton's" suitcase in the Jaguar's boot. Sarah tried to keep her handbag, but the Russian plucked it from her shoulder and tossed it into the boot as well. It landed with an unusually heavy thud.

The Russian's overcoat was draped over his right arm. With his left he closed the boot and then opened the passenger door. Sarah's eyes scanned the Esplanade as she climbed inside. Somewhere nearby were four MI6 watchers, none of whom were armed. It was imperative they not lose track of her.

The Russian closed her door and walked around the back of the car to the driver's side, where the valet was awaiting his gratuity. The Russian handed him a ten-pound note before dropping behind the wheel and starting the engine. The gun was now in his left hand, and it was pointed at Sarah's right hip. As they pulled away from the curb, she glanced over her shoulder and saw the valet running after them.

The Russian had forgotten his suitcase.

He turned onto Connaught Avenue and pressed the throttle to the floorboard. A parade of shops flashed past Sarah's window: Café 19, Allsorts Cookware, Caxton Books & Gallery. The Russian was pressing the barrel of his gun into her hip. With his right hand he was gripping the wheel tightly. His eyes were locked on the rearview mirror.

"You might want to look where you're going," said Sarah.

"Who are they?"

"They're innocent British subjects who are trying to enjoy a pleasant evening in a seaside community."

The Russian ground the gun into Sarah's hip. "The two people in the van behind us." His British accent was gone. "Essex Police? MI5? MI6?"

"I don't know what you're talking about."

He placed the barrel of the gun against the side of her head.

"I'm telling you, I don't know who they are."

"What about your husband?"

"He works in the City."

"Where is he now?"

"Back at the hotel, wondering where I am."

"I saw him on television a few minutes ago."

"That's not possible."

"He escorted Khalid into his uncle's house in Eaton Square."

"Khalid who?"

Sarah never saw the blow coming—the butt of the gun, an inch above her right ear. The pain was otherworldly. "You just made the second biggest mistake of your life."

"What was the first?"

"Strapping a bomb to Khalid's daughter."

"I'm glad we cleared that up." He swerved to avoid a pedestrian crossing the road. "Who does your *husband* work for?"

"MI6."

"And you?"

"CIA." It was an untruth, but only a small one. And it would make the Russian think twice about killing her.

"And the two people who are following me?" he asked.

"SCO19."

"You're lying, Mrs. Edgerton."

"If you say so."

"If they were SCO19, they would have killed me at the hotel." He turned off Connaught Avenue and drove dangerously fast through a quiet residential area. After a moment he checked his rearview mirror. "Too bad."

"Did you lose them?"

He smiled coldly. "No."

He sped along Upper Fourth Avenue to the car park of the Frinton rail station. It was an old redbrick building, with a steeply pitched white portico over the entrance. Sarah would always remember the flowers—the two pots of red-and-white geraniums hanging from hooks along the facade.

A train must have just arrived because a few passengers were filing into the pleasant evening. One or two glanced at the tall man who stepped from a flashy Jaguar F-Type, but most ignored him.

Swiftly, he walked over to the white Ford van that had followed him into the confined space of the car park. Sarah screamed a warning, but it was no use. The Russian fired four shots through the driver's-side window and three more through the windscreen.

"In case you were wondering," he said when he was behind the wheel again, "I saved one bullet for you."

From the rail station, he sped north on Elm Tree Avenue. It seemed to Sarah he knew exactly where he was going. He made a right at Walton Road and another at Coles Lane. A hedgerowed track, it bore them into a marshland. The first sign of human habitation was a blue, cube-like security office at the entrance of a marina. Inside was a single guard. Despite Sarah's pleas, the Russian shot him with the last round in his gun. Then he reloaded and shot him three more times.

Calmly, he returned to the Jaguar and drove along the access road to the marina. A part of Sarah was relieved to find it deserted. The Russian had just killed three people in less than five minutes. Once they were at sea, there would be no one left to kill but her.

71

Essex–London City Airport

Units of the Essex Police responded to reports of gunfire at the Frinton-on-Sea rail station at 7:26 p.m. There they discovered two victims. One had been shot four times; the other, three. A pair of distraught-looking men were desperately trying to resuscitate them. Traumatized witnesses described the gunman as a tall, well-dressed man driving a bright red Jaguar sports car. There had been a woman in the passenger seat. She had screamed throughout the entire incident.

In the United States, where firearms are plentiful and gun violence epidemic, police might have initially attributed the killings to road rage. The authorities in Essex, however, made no such assumption. With the help of the Metropolitan Police—and the two distraught-looking men—they established that the gunman was an operative of Russian intelligence. The woman was not his accomplice but his hostage. The Essex Police were told nothing about her professional provenance, only that she was an American.

Despite a frantic search for the Russian and the woman, more than ninety minutes would elapse before two constables called on the marina located at the end of Coles Lane. The guard at the gate was dead, shot four times at close range, and the bright red Jaguar was parked haphazardly outside the marina's office, which had been broken into and ransacked. With the help of the marina's video system, police determined that the Russian had stolen a Bavaria 27 Sport motor yacht owned by a local businessman. The vessel was fitted with twin Volvo-Penta engines and a 147-gallon fuel tank, which the Russian had filled before leaving the marina. Just twenty-nine feet in length, the Bavaria was designed for harbor and coastal cruising. But with a skilled seaman at the helm, the vessel was more than capable of reaching the European mainland in a matter of hours.

Though the two constables did not know it, the dead guard and missing motor yacht were but a small part of a rapidly unfolding diplomatic and national security crisis. The elements of this crisis included a dead Russian operative on the M25 motorway and a Russian oligarch who was being held in a hazmat tent at London City Airport because he was too radioactive to be moved.

At eight p.m., Prime Minister Lancaster convened COBRA, Britain's senior crisis management group. They gathered, as usual, in Cabinet Office Briefing Room A, from which the group derived its name. It was a contentious meeting from the start. Amanda Wallace, the director-general of MI5, was outraged she had not been told of the presence of a Russian hit team on British soil. Graham Seymour, who had just lost two officers, was in no mood for an internecine squabble. MI6 had learned about the Russian operatives, he said, as part of a counterintelligence operation directed against the SVR. Seymour had informed the prime minister and the Metropolitan Police about the Russians after confirming they had indeed arrived in Britain. In short, he had played it by the book.

Curiously, the official record of the meeting contained not a single reference to Crown Prince Abdullah—or the possibility there might be a connection between his sudden illness and the Russian hit team. Graham Seymour, for his part, did not lead the horse to water. And neither, for that matter, did the prime minister.

At nine o'clock, however, he once again went before the cameras outside Number 10, this time to brief the British public on the extraordinary events taking place in Greater London and in the Essex resort town of Frinton-on-Sea. Little of what he said was true, but he steered clear of outright falsehoods. Most were lies of omission. He said nothing, for example, of a dead security guard at a marina along the river Twizzle, a stolen Bavaria 27 motor yacht, or a captive American woman who had once worked for the CIA.

Nor did Lancaster find reason to mention that he had granted Gabriel Allon, the chief of Israeli intelligence, broad latitude to find the missing woman. At nine fifteen, he arrived at London City Airport, accompanied by two of his most trusted operatives and an MI6 officer named Christopher Keller. A Gulfstream G550 waited on the tarmac. As yet, it had no destination.

72

London City Airport

A Metropolitan Police officer was standing watch outside the entrance of the London Jet Centre. He tugged at the sleeve of his bulky hazmat suit as Gabriel approached.

"You sure you don't want one of these?" he asked through the clear protective mask.

Gabriel shook his head. "It might ruin my image."

"Better than the alternative."

"How bad is he?"

"A little south of Hiroshima, but not much."

"How long is it safe to be in his presence?"

"Ten minutes won't kill you. Twenty might."

Gabriel went inside. The staff had been evacuated. In the departure lounge a gray-haired man in a business suit was seated at one end of a rectangular table. He might have looked like a typical user of private aircraft were it not for the four heavily armed SCO19 officers in hazmat suits standing around him in a semicircle. Gabriel sat down at the opposite end of the table, as far away from the man as possible, and marked the time on his wristwatch. It was 9:22 p.m.

Ten minutes won't kill you. Twenty might . . .

The man was pondering his hands, which were folded on the table before him. At length, he looked up. For an instant he appeared relieved that someone had dared to enter his presence in normal clothing. Then, suddenly, his expression changed. It was the same look Gabriel had seen on Hanifa Khoury's face in the safe flat in Berlin.

"Hello, Konstantin. Don't take this the wrong way, but you look like shit."

Gabriel glanced at the SCO19 officers and with a movement of his eyes instructed them to leave the room. A moment passed. Then all four filed out.

Konstantin Dragunov watched the display of Gabriel's authority with evident dread. "I suppose you're the reason I'm here."

"You're here because you're a Roman candle of radiation." Gabriel paused, then added, "And so is the woman."

"Where is she?"

"In a situation not unlike yours. You, however, are in much more serious trouble."

"I did nothing."

"Then why are you dripping with radiation? And why is your fancy house in Belgravia a nuclear disaster zone? The hazmat teams are working fifteen-minute shifts to avoid overexposure. One technician refused to go back in, it was so bad. Your drawing room is a nightmare, but the kitchen is even worse. The counter where she poured the champagne is like Fukushima, and the rubbish bin where she tossed the vial and the pipette dropper nearly broke their scanners. The same was true of Abdullah's empty champagne glass, but yours was no picnic, either." Gabriel adopted a confiding tone. "It does make one wonder."

"About what?"

"Whether your good friend the Tsar was trying to kill you, too."

"Why would he do that?"

"Because he entrusted you with several billion dollars to turn Abdullah into a puppet of the Kremlin. And all the Tsar got for his money was an MI6 asset." Gabriel smiled. "Or so he thought."

"He isn't a British agent?"

"Abdullah?" Gabriel shook his head. "Don't be silly."

Dragunov's face was aflame with rage. "You bastard."

"Flattery will get you nowhere, Konnie."

"What did I ever do to you?"

"You told the Tsar that Khalid asked me to find his daughter, and the Tsar used the opportunity to try to kill me. If I hadn't spotted the bomb beneath Reema's coat that night, I'd be dead."

"Perhaps you should have tried to save her. Your conscience might be clearer."

Gabriel rose slowly, walked to the opposite end of the table, and with every ounce of strength he could summon drove his fist into Konstantin Dragunov's face. The Russian toppled sideways and came to rest on the floor of the lounge. Gabriel was surprised to see his head still attached to his shoulders.

"Who planned it, Konstantin?"

For a moment, Dragunov was incapable of speech. Finally, he groaned, "Planned what?"

"Abdullah's murder."

The Russian gave no answer.

"Do I need to remind you of your current situation, Konstantin? You're going to spend the rest of your life in a British prison. I think you'll find it much less luxurious than Eaton Square."

"The president will never allow it."

"He won't be in any position to help you. In fact, if I had to guess, the British government is going to issue a warrant for his arrest."

"And if I give you the name of the SVR officer who ran the operation? How will that change anything?"

"Your cooperation will not be forgotten."

"Since when do you speak for the British government?"

"I speak for Reema. And if you don't tell me what I want to know, I'm going to hit you again."

Gabriel gave his watch another check. *9:26 . . .* According to the Essex Police, Sarah and the Russian assassin had set sail from the marina north of Frinton at 7:49. By now, they were several miles out to sea. Her Majesty's Coastguard was searching for the vessel, as yet without success.

"You were saying, Konnie?"

Dragunov was still lying on the floor. "It was the Englishwoman."

"Rebecca Manning?"

"She uses her father's name now."

"You saw her?"

"I had a couple of meetings with her."

"Where?"

"A little dacha in Yasenevo. It had a sign outside. I can't recall what it said."

"The Inner-Baltic Research Committee?"

"Yes, that was it. How did you know?"

Gabriel didn't answer. "Under normal circumstances, I'd help you to your feet. But you'll understand if I don't."

The Russian hauled himself onto the chair. The left side of his face was already badly swollen, and his eye was beginning to close. All in all, thought Gabriel, it was a slight improvement.

"Keep talking, Konnie."

"It wasn't much of an operation, really. All we had to do was ask Abdullah to set aside a few minutes of time while he was in London."

"That was your job?"

Dragunov nodded. "That's the way these things work. It's always a friend."

"He came through the passageway in the basement?"

"He didn't come through the front door, did he?"

"What did you give him besides a glass of Louis Roederer?"

"He drank two glasses, actually."

"Both were contaminated?"

Dragunov nodded.

"What was the substance?"

"I wasn't told."

"Maybe you should have asked."

Dragunov said nothing.

"Why didn't the woman come to the airport with you?"

"Why don't you ask *her*?"

"Because I killed her, Konstantin. And I'm going to kill you unless you keep talking."

"Bullshit."

Gabriel awakened his BlackBerry and laid it on the table in front of Dragunov. On the screen was a photograph of a blood-spattered woman hanging out the front door of a Renault Clio.

"Jesus."

Gabriel returned the BlackBerry to his jacket pocket. "Go on, Konnie."

"The Englishwoman wanted us to leave Britain separately. Anna was supposed to leave tonight on the Harwich–to–Hoek van Holland ferry. The eleven o'clock."

"Anna?"

"Yurasova. The president has known her since she was a kid."

"The operative at the hotel was supposed to leave with her?"

Dragunov nodded. "His name is Nikolai."

"Where were they planning to go when they got to Holland?"

"If it was safe for them to get on a plane, they were going to head straight for Schiphol."

"And if it wasn't?"

"There's a safe house."

"Where?"

"I don't know." When Gabriel rose angrily from his chair, Dragunov covered his face with his hands. "Please, Allon, not again. I'm telling you the truth. The safe house is in South Holland, somewhere near the coast. But that's all I know."

"Is anyone there now?"

"A couple of gorillas and someone to handle secure communications with Yasenevo."

"Why do they need a secure link to Moscow Center?"

"It isn't just a crash pad, Allon. It's a forward command post."

"Who else is there, Konstantin?"

Dragunov hesitated, then said, "The English-woman."

"Rebecca Manning?"

"Philby," said the Russian. "She uses her father's name now."

73

The North Sea

Nikolai Azarov was by no means a skilled seaman, but his father had been a high-ranking officer in the old Soviet Navy and he knew a thing or two about boats. Leaving the marina, he had guided the Bavaria 27 through the shallow tidewaters of Walton Channel and into the North Sea. Once clear of the headland, he turned due east and increased his speed to twenty-five knots. It was comfortably below the vessel's top cruising speed. Even so, the onboard Garmin navigation system anticipated a 1:15 a.m. arrival.

It was a straight line to his destination. After establishing his heading, Nikolai switched off the Garmin so it could not be used by the British to locate his position. His phone—the phone Anna had called a few moments before she was killed—was on the bottom of

Walton Channel. So was the phone he had taken from the woman outside the hotel. Nikolai was not, however, without means of communication. The Bavaria had an Inmarsat phone and wireless network. He had switched off the system soon after leaving the marina. The handheld receiver was in his pocket, safely beyond the reach of the woman.

Her suitcase was still in the boot of the Jaguar, but Nikolai had taken her handbag. In it he had found a few cosmetics, a bottle of antidepressants, six hundred pounds in cash, and an old Walther PPK, an interesting choice of weapon. There was no passport or driver's license, and no credit or bank cards.

The sea before the Bavaria was empty. Nikolai ejected the magazine from the Walther and removed the round from the chamber. Then he engaged the autopilot and carried the gun and the bottle of antidepressants down the companionway. Entering the salon, Nikolai saw the woman glaring at him from the table. An angry red welt had risen on her cheek where Nikolai had struck her when she refused to board the boat.

The BBC was playing on the radio. The signal was weak, in and out. The prime minister had just addressed reporters outside Number 10. The radioactive corpse of a dead Russian agent had shut down the M25. A radioactive Russian oligarch had closed London City

Airport. A third Russian had killed two people at the Frinton-on-Sea rail station. Police were said to be desperately searching for him.

Nikolai switched off the radio. "They didn't mention the guard at the marina."

"They probably haven't found him yet."

"I rather doubt that."

Nikolai sat down opposite the woman. Despite the welt, she was quite attractive. She would have been prettier were it not for the ridiculous dark wig.

He placed the bottle of pills before her. "Why are you depressed?"

"I spend too much time with people like you."

He glanced at the bottle. "Perhaps you should take one. You'll feel better."

She stared at him without expression.

"How about this?" He placed the vial of clear liquid on the table.

"What is it?"

"It's the same radioactive chemical element that Anna gave to Abdullah when he visited Konstantin Dragunov's mansion in Belgravia. And for some reason," said Nikolai, "you and your friends allowed it to happen."

She looked down at the bottle. "Maybe you should get rid of that."

"How? Should I pour it into the North Sea?" He made a face of mock revulsion. "Think of the environmental damage."

"What about the damage it's doing to us right now?"

"It's totally safe unless it's ingested."

"Did Moscow Center tell you that?"

Nikolai returned the vial to the pocket of his trousers.

"That's the perfect place for it."

Nikolai smiled in spite of himself. He had to admit, he admired the woman's nerve.

"How long have you been carrying it around?" she asked.

"A week."

"That would explain your peculiar greenish glow. You're probably hotter than Chernobyl."

"And now you are, too." He examined the welt on her cheek. "Does it hurt?"

"Not as much as my head."

"Take your wig off. I'll have a look at it."

"Thank you, but you've done enough already."

"Perhaps you didn't hear me." Nikolai lowered his voice. "I said take it off."

When she hesitated, he reached across the table and ripped the wig from her head. Her blond hair was in disarray and matted with dried blood above her right ear. Still, Nikolai realized he had seen the woman before. It was the night he had given a briefcase bomb to the halfwit head of security from the Geneva International School. The woman had been at a table under the awning, next to the tall Russian-looking man who had followed Nikolai from the café. A car had followed him, too. Nikolai had not recognized the man behind the wheel, the man with gray temples. But by the following evening, Moscow Center had managed to confirm his identity.

Gabriel Allon . . .

Nikolai tossed aside the wig. Without it, the woman was even more beautiful. He could only imagine the sort of jobs she had done for them. The Israelis used honey traps almost as much as the SVR.

"I thought you said you're an American."

"I am."

"Jewish?"

"Episcopalian, actually."

"You made aliyah?"

"To England?"

Nikolai hit her a third time. Hard enough for blood to flow from her nose. Hard enough to shut her up.

"I'm Nikolai," he said after a moment. "Who are you?"

She hesitated, then said, "Allison."

"Allison what?"

"Douglas."

"Come now, Allison, you can do better than that."

She didn't look quite so brave any longer. "What are you going to do with me?" she asked.

"I was planning to kill you and throw your body overboard." Nikolai touched her swollen cheek. "Unfortunately for you, I've changed my mind."

74

Rotterdam

Prime Minister Jonathan Lancaster granted permission for a single aircraft to depart London City Airport that evening. A Gulfstream G550, it touched down in Rotterdam at 12:25 a.m. King Saul Boulevard had arranged for a pair of Audi sedans to be waiting outside the terminal. Keller and Mikhail headed straight for the town of Hellevoetsluis, home of one of South Holland's largest marinas. Gabriel asked Eli Lavon, who avoided boats whenever possible, to choose a second location.

"Do you know how long the Dutch coast is?"

"Four hundred and forty-one kilometers."

Lavon looked up from his phone. "How do you possibly know that?"

"I checked while we were on the plane."

Lavon looked down again and contemplated the map. "If I was at the helm . . ."

"Yes, Eli?"

"I wouldn't try to get into a darkened marina."

"What would you do?"

"I'd dump it on a beach somewhere."

"Where?"

Lavon studied the phone as though it were the Torah.

"Where, Eli?" asked Gabriel, exasperated.

"Right here." Lavon tapped the screen. "In Renesse."

After making a single brief call with the Inmarsat phone, Nikolai had increased his speed to thirty knots. As a result, he reached the Dutch coast fifteen minutes earlier than the Garmin had originally forecast. His running lights were doused. He switched them on and instantly saw the flash of a torch on land.

Nikolai doused the running lights again, increased his speed to full, and waited for the bite of the sandy bottom. When it came, the boat lurched violently to a stop, with a pronounced starboard list. He killed the engine and poked his head down the companionway.

The woman was struggling to gain footing on the sloped teak floor of the galley.

"You might have warned me," she said.

"Let's go."

She clambered awkwardly up the companionway. Nikolai pulled her into the cockpit and shoved her toward the stern.

"In you go," he said.

"Do you know how cold that water is?"

He aimed the Makarov at her head. "Get in."

After first removing her shoes, she slid from the swim step and found her footing on the bottom. The water was level with her breasts.

"Walk," commanded Nikolai.

"Where?"

He pointed toward the two men now standing at the tideline. "Don't worry, they're the least of your problems."

Shivering, she started toward shore. Nikolai entered the water soundlessly and, holding the Makarov aloft, followed after her. The car, a Swedish-made sedan with Dutch registration, was parked in the public lot behind the dunes. Nikolai sat with her in the backseat, the gun against her ribs. As they passed through the sleeping seaside town, a single car approached from the opposite direction and flashed past them in a blur.

The car park had been abandoned to the gulls. Gabriel hurried up the footpath to the beach and saw a darkened Bavaria 27 Sport motor yacht about thirty meters from shore. He rushed down to the sea and with his phone illuminated the hard, flat sand along the tideline. There were footprints everywhere. Three men in street shoes, a woman whose feet were bare. The impressions were recent. They had just missed her.

He ran back to the car park and climbed into the Audi.

"Anything?" asked Lavon.

Gabriel told him.

"They couldn't have arrived more than a few minutes ago."

"They didn't."

"You don't think she was in that car, do you?"

"Yeah," said Gabriel as he slammed the Audi into reverse. "I think she was."

They crossed a narrow land bridge, with a great inland bay on the right and the sea to the left. The juxtaposition told Sarah they were headed north. Eventually, a road sign appeared in the darkness. The name of the town, Ouddorp, meant nothing to her.

The car rounded a traffic circle and then sped across

an expanse of tabletop-flat farmland. The narrow track into which they finally turned was unmarked. It led to a collection of clapboard holiday bungalows hidden away in a range of grass-covered dunes. One was surrounded by tall hedges and had a separate garage with old-fashioned swinging doors. Nikolai locked the Volvo inside before leading Sarah to the bungalow.

It was white as a wedding cake, with a red tile roof. Plexiglass barriers shielded the veranda from the wind. A woman waited there alone, like a specimen in a jar. She wore an oilskin coat and stretch jeans. Her eyes were unusually blue—and tired-looking, thought Sarah. The night had been unkind to the woman's appearance.

A stray forelock had fallen over one of her eyes. The woman pushed it aside and studied Sarah carefully. Something about the gesture was familiar. The face was familiar, too. All at once Sarah realized where she had seen it before.

A news conference at the Grand Presidential Palace in Moscow . . .

The woman on the veranda was Rebecca Manning.

75

Rotterdam

The car had been a Volvo, late model, dark in color. On that point, Gabriel and Eli Lavon were in complete agreement. Both had caught a clear glimpse of the front grille and had noted the circular ornament and distinctive diagonal line sloping left to right. Gabriel was certain it had been a sedan. Lavon, however, was convinced it was an estate car.

There was no dispute over the direction it had been heading, which was north. Gabriel and Lavon concentrated on the little villages along the coast while Mikhail and Keller worked the larger towns inland. Between them, they spotted one hundred and twelve Volvos. In none did they find Sarah.

Admittedly, it was an impossible task—"a needle in a Dutch haystack," as Lavon put it—but they kept at it

506 · DANIEL SILVA

until seven fifteen, when they all four gathered at a coffee shop in an industrial quarter of south Rotterdam. They were the first customers of the morning. There was a petrol station next door and a couple of car dealerships across the road. One, of course, sold Volvos.

An environmentally friendly Dutch police cruiser rolled past in the street, slowly.

"What's his problem?" asked Mikhail.

It was Lavon who answered. "Maybe he's looking for the idiots who've been racing around the countryside all night. Or the genius who ran a Bavaria 27 aground near Renesse."

"Think they've found it?"

"The yacht?" Lavon nodded. "It's rather hard to miss, especially now that it's light."

"What happens next?"

"The Dutch police find out who owns the boat and where it came from. And before long, every officer in Holland will be looking for a Russian assassin and a pretty American woman named Sarah Bancroft."

"Maybe that's a good thing," said Mikhail.

"Unless Rebecca and her friend Nikolai decide to cut their losses and kill her."

"Maybe they already have." Mikhail looked at Gabriel. "You're sure they were a woman's footprints?"

"I'm sure, Mikhail."

"Why bother to bring her ashore? Why not lighten their load and make a run for Moscow?"

"I suppose they want to ask her a few questions first. Wouldn't you if you were in their position?"

"You think they're going to get rough with her?"

"That depends."

"On what?"

"Who's asking the questions." Gabriel noticed that Keller was suddenly working the keyboard of his Black-Berry. "What's going on?"

"Apparently, Konstantin Dragunov isn't feeling well."

"Imagine that."

"He just admitted to the Metropolitan Police that he and the woman poisoned the crown prince last night. Lancaster's making the announcement at Downing Street at ten."

"Do me a favor, Christopher."

"What's that?"

"Tell Graham and Lancaster to announce it now."

76

10 Downing Street

Graham Seymour was waiting in the entrance hall of Number 10 when Jonathan Lancaster came down the Grand Staircase with Geoffrey Sloane at his side. Sloane was nervously adjusting his necktie, as though he were the one who was about to face the battery of cameras arrayed outside in Downing Street. Lancaster was clutching a few light blue notecards. He led Seymour into the Cabinet Room and solemnly closed the door.

"It worked to perfection. Just like you and Gabriel said it would."

"With one problem, Prime Minister."

"The best-laid plans of mice and men . . ." Lancaster held up the notecards. "Do you think this will be enough to keep the Russians from killing her?"

"Gabriel seems to think it will."

"Did he really punch Konstantin Dragunov?"

"I'm afraid so."

"Was it a good one?" asked Lancaster mischievously.

"Quite."

"I hope Konstantin wasn't too seriously injured."

"At this point I doubt he even remembers it."

"He's ill, is he?"

"The sooner we get him on a plane, the better."

Lancaster looked down at the first notecard and, lips moving, rehearsed the opening line of his prepared remarks. It was true, thought Seymour. It *had* worked to perfection. He and Gabriel had beaten the Russians at their own game. The Tsar had killed before, recklessly, with weapons of mass destruction. But this time he had been caught in the act. The consequences would be severe—sanctions, expulsions, perhaps even excommunication from the Group of Eight—and the damage was likely to be permanent.

"She has some nerve," said Lancaster suddenly.

"Sarah Bancroft?"

"Rebecca Manning." The prime minister was still looking down at his remarks. "One would have thought she would have remained safely in Moscow." He lowered his voice. "Like her father."

"We've made it clear we want nothing to do with

her. Therefore, it's safe for her to travel outside Russia."

"Perhaps we should reevaluate our position vis-à-vis Ms. Philby. After this, she deserves to be brought back to Britain in chains. In fact," said Lancaster, waving the notecards, "I'm thinking about making a small revision to my prepared remarks."

"I would advise against that."

The door opened and Geoffrey Sloane leaned into the room. "It's time, Prime Minister."

Lancaster, the consummate political actor, squared his shoulders before striding out the world's most famous door, into the glare of the lights. Seymour followed Sloane into his office to watch the announcement on television. The prime minister seemed entirely alone in the world. His voice was calm but knife-edged with anger.

This monstrous and depraved act carried out by the intelligence services of the Russian Federation, on the direct order of the Russian president, will not go unpunished . . .

It had worked to perfection, thought Seymour. With one problem.

77

Ouddorp, the Netherlands

It became apparent within minutes of Sarah's arrival at the safe house that they were not prepared for a hostage. Nikolai cut a bedsheet to ribbons, bound her hands and feet, and tied a gag tightly around her mouth. The bungalow's cellar was a small, stone-lined chamber. Sarah sat with her back to a damp wall and her knees beneath her chin. Soaked to the skin from her walk to shore, she was soon shivering uncontrollably. She thought of Reema and the many nights she had spent in captivity before her brutal murder. If a child of twelve could bear up under the pressure, Sarah could, too.

There was a door at the top of the stone steps. Beyond it, Sarah could hear two voices conversing in Russian. One belonged to Nikolai, the other to Rebecca Manning. Judging by their tone, they were attempting to piece together the series of events that led to the arrest of the Russian president's close friend and the death of a female SVR operative. By now, they had no doubt determined that their operation had been compromised from the beginning—and that Gabriel Allon, the man who had unmasked Rebecca Manning as a Russian mole, was somehow involved. Rebecca was now fighting for her career, perhaps even her life. Eventually, she would come for Sarah.

She willed herself into restless sleep, if only to stop the convulsive trembling of her body. In her dreams she was lying on a Caribbean beach with Nadia al-Bakari, but she woke to find Nikolai and the two goons staring down at her. They lifted her from the cold, damp floor as though she were made of tissue paper and carried her up the steps. A table of pale unfinished wood had been placed in the center of the sitting room. They forced her into a chair and removed only the gag, leaving her hands and feet bound. Nikolai clamped a hand over her mouth and said he would kill her if she screamed or tried to call for help. There was nothing in his demeanor to suggest the threat was hollow.

Rebecca Manning seemed unaware of Sarah's presence. Arms folded, she was staring at the television, which was tuned to the BBC. Prime Minister Jonathan

Lancaster had just accused Russia of attempting to assassinate the crown prince of Saudi Arabia during his state visit to Britain.

This monstrous and depraved act . . .

Rebecca listened to Lancaster's announcement a moment longer before aiming a remote at the screen and muting the sound. Then she turned and glared at Sarah.

At length, she asked, "Who are you?"

"Allison Douglas."

"Who do you work for?"

"The CIA."

Rebecca glanced at Nikolai. The blow was open-handed but vicious. Sarah, fearful of Nikolai's warning, smothered a scream.

Rebecca Manning took a step closer and placed the vial of clear liquid on the table. "One drop," she said, "and not even your friend the archangel will be able to save you."

Sarah stared at the vial in silence.

"I thought that would refresh your memory. Now tell me your name."

Sarah waited until Nikolai drew back his hand before finally answering.

"Is it a work name?" asked Rebecca.

"No, it's real."

"Sarah is a Jewish name."

"So is Rebecca."

"Who do you work for, Sarah Bancroft?"

"The Museum of Modern Art in New York."

"Is it a cover job?"

"No."

"And before that?"

"The CIA."

"What is your connection to Gabriel Allon?"

"I worked with him on a couple of operations."

"Name one."

"Ivan Kharkov."

"Did Allon know about the plot to kill Abdullah?"

"Of course."

"How?"

"It was his idea."

Rebecca absorbed Sarah's words like a blow to the abdomen. She was silent for a moment. Then she asked, "Was Abdullah *ever* an MI6 asset?"

"No," said Sarah. "He was a Russian asset. And you, Rebecca Manning, just killed him."

It was half past eight when Gabriel's BlackBerry shivered with an incoming call. He did not recognize the number. Ordinarily, he terminated such calls without a second thought. But not that call. Not the call that arrived on his phone at half past eight in Rotterdam.

He tapped ANSWER, lifted the BlackBerry to his ear, and murmured a greeting.

"I was afraid you wouldn't pick up."

"Who is this?"

"You don't recognize my voice?"

It was female and slightly hoarse with fatigue and tobacco. The accent was British with a trace of French. And, yes, Gabriel recognized it.

It was the voice of Rebecca Manning.

78

Ouddorp, the Netherlands

The beach pavilion was called Natural High. In summer it was one of the busiest spots on the Dutch coast. But at half past ten on an April morning, it had the air of an abandoned colonial outpost. The weather was fitful, blinding sun one minute, blinding rain the next. Gabriel watched it from the shelter of the café. *So fair and foul a day I have not seen . . .* Suddenly, he thought of a seaside café atop the cliffs of Lizard Point in West Cornwall. He used to hike there along the coastal path, have a pot of tea and a scone with thick clotted cream, and then hike back to his cottage in Gunwalloe Cove. It seemed a lifetime ago. Perhaps one day, when his term was over, he would go back again. Or maybe he would take Chiara and the children to Venice. They would live in a grand apartment in Cannaregio, he would restore paintings for Francesco Tiepolo. The world and its many problems would pass him by. He would spend his nights with his family and his days with his old friends Bellini, Titian, Tintoretto, and Veronese. He would be anonymous again, a man with a brush and a palette atop a work platform, hidden behind a shroud.

For now, however, he was very much in plain sight. He was sitting alone at a table against the window. On the table before him was his BlackBerry. He had nearly run the battery dry putting in place the pieces of the deal. Rebecca had quibbled over one or two details regarding the timing, but after one final call to London, it was done. Downing Street, it seemed, wanted to make the exchange as badly as Gabriel.

Just then, the BlackBerry flashed. It was Eli Lavon. He was outside in the car park. "She just arrived."

"Alone?"

"Looks like it."

"What does that mean?"

"It means," said Lavon, "there is no one else visible in the car."

"What kind is it?"

"A Volvo."

"Sedan or an estate car?"

The call went dead. It was a sedan, thought Gabriel.

He glanced over his shoulder at Mikhail and Keller. They were sitting at a table in the back corner of the room. At another were two SVR hoods in leather jackets. The Russians watched Rebecca Manning carefully as she entered the café and sat down opposite Gabriel. She looked very English in her dark green Barbour jacket. She placed her phone on the table, along with a packet of L&B cigarettes and an old silver lighter.

"May I?" asked Gabriel.

She nodded.

He picked up the lighter. The inscription was scarcely visible. *For a lifetime of service to the motherland . . .*

"Couldn't they have bought you a new one?"

"It belonged to my father."

Gabriel glanced at her wristwatch. "And that?"

"It was gathering dust in the SVR's private museum. I took it to a jeweler and replaced the timepiece. It works quite well, actually."

"Then why are you ten minutes late?" Gabriel placed the lighter atop her packet of cigarettes. "You should probably put those away."

"Even at a beach café?" She returned the cigarettes and the lighter to her handbag. "Things are a bit more relaxed in Russia."

"And your life expectancy rates reflect that."

"I believe we've fallen below North Korea on the latest list." Her smile was genuine. Unlike their last meeting, which had taken place in a secret MI6 detention center in the north of Scotland, it was all very cordial. "My mother was asking about you the other day," she said suddenly.

"Is she still in Spain?"

Rebecca nodded. "I was hoping she might settle with me in Moscow."

"But?"

"She didn't care for it much when she visited."

"It's an acquired taste."

The waitress was hovering.

"You should order something," said Gabriel.

"I wasn't planning to stay long."

"What's the rush?"

She ordered a *koffie verkeerd*. Then, when the waitress was gone, she unlocked her phone and pushed it toward Gabriel. On the screen was a still image of Sarah Bancroft. One side of her face was red and swollen.

"Who did that to her?"

Rebecca ignored his question. "Play it."

Gabriel tapped the PLAY icon and listened for as long as he could stomach it. Then he tapped PAUSE and glared at Rebecca over the tabletop. "I would advise you never to make that recording public."

"We would be justified."

"It would be a grave mistake."

"Would it?"

"Sarah's an American, not Israeli. The CIA will retaliate if they find out you roughed her up like that."

"She was working for you when you spoon-fed us that disinformation about Abdullah being an MI6 asset." Rebecca reclaimed the phone. "Don't worry, the recording is for my personal use only."

"Do you think it will be enough?"

"For what?"

"To save your career at the SVR."

Rebecca fell silent while the waitress placed a glass of milky Dutch coffee before her. "Is that what this was about? Destroying me?"

"No. It was about destroying *him*."

"Our president? You're tilting at windmills, Don Quixote."

"Wait a few hours for the news to sink in that the Kremlin ordered the assassination of the future king of Saudi Arabia. Russia will be the pariah of pariahs."

"It was your assassination, not ours."

"Good luck with that."

"By the time the trolls from the Internet Research Agency are finished, no one in the world will believe we had anything do with it." Rebecca added sugar to her coffee and stirred it thoughtfully. "And who's going to enforce this so-called pariah status of yours? You? Great Britain? The United States?" She shook her head slowly. "Perhaps you haven't noticed, but the long-cherished institutions of the West are in tatters. We're the only game in town. Russia, China, the Iranians . . ."

"You left out Saudi Arabia."

"Once the American withdrawal from the Middle East is complete, the Saudis will realize they have nowhere else to turn to for protection but us, with or without Abdullah on the throne."

"Not if Khalid is king."

She raised an eyebrow. "Is that your plan?"

"The Allegiance Council will choose the next king, not the State of Israel. But my money is on the man who stayed by his beloved uncle's side while he was suffering the terrible effects of a radioactive Russian poison."

"You mean this?" She placed a small glass vial on the table.

Gabriel leaned away. "What is it?"

"It doesn't have a name yet. I'm sure the Internet Research Agency will think of something catchy." She smiled. "Something very Israeli-sounding."

"Is there any chance Abdullah will survive?"

"None whatsoever."

"And what about you, Rebecca?"

She returned the vial to her handbag.

"They'll never trust you again," said Gabriel. "Not after this. Who knows? They might even assume you've been working for MI6 since the moment you set foot in Moscow Center. Either way, you'd be a fool to go back. The best you can hope for is that they'll lock you away in some desolate little village, the kind of place that has a number instead of a name. You'll end up like your father, a broken-down old drunk, alone in the world."

"You've no right to speak of my father like that."

Gabriel accepted her rebuke in silence.

"And where would I go? Back to England?" Rebecca frowned. "I appreciate the heartfelt advice, but I think I'll take my chances in Russia." She reached for her phone. "Shall we finish this?"

Gabriel picked up his phone, typed a brief message, and hit SEND. The reply arrived ten seconds later. "Dragunov's plane has just been cleared for departure. He'll be out of British airspace in about forty-five minutes."

Rebecca dialed a number. She spoke a few words in Russian, then severed the connection. "There's a large square in the middle of Renesse with a church in the center. Very busy, lots of people. We'll drop her outside the pizzeria exactly one hour from now." She glanced at her father's old wristwatch, as if marking the time. Then she dropped the phone into her bag and looked toward the table where Mikhail and Keller were sitting. "The very pale one looks familiar to me. Was he in that Starbucks in Washington where you trapped me into betraying myself?"

Gabriel hesitated, then nodded.

"And the other one?"

"He's the one you shot on that little street in Georgetown."

"What a pity. I was sure I'd killed him." Rebecca Manning rose abruptly. "To be continued," she said, and went out.

79

Renesse, the Netherlands

The church was brick, austere, and ringed by a cobbled traffic circle. Gabriel and Eli Lavon were parked in front of a small hotel. Mikhail and Keller had found a spot outside a seafood restaurant called Vischmarkt Renesse. Behind them was the pizzeria where Rebecca Manning had promised to drop Sarah at 11:43 a.m. exactly.

It was 11:39. Mikhail was watching the pizzeria in the rearview mirror; Keller, in the side-view. He was chain-smoking Marlboros. Mikhail lowered his window a few inches and scanned the square.

"You realize we're sitting ducks." Mikhail paused, then added, "And so is the director-general of my service."

"We have a deal."

"So did Khalid." Mikhail watched as Keller crushed out his cigarette and immediately lit another. "You really need to stop that, you know."

"Why?"

"Because Sarah hates it."

Keller smoked in silence, eyes on the mirror.

"Don't you think we should talk about it?"

"About what?"

"Your obvious feelings for Sarah."

Keller gave Mikhail a sidelong glance. "What is it with you people?"

"You people?"

"You and Gabriel. Have you nothing better to do than meddle in the personal lives of others?"

"Like it or not, you're one of us now, Christopher. And that means we reserve the right to poke our noses into your love life whenever we feel like it." After a brief silence, Mikhail added quietly, "Especially when it involves my ex-fiancé."

"Nothing happened in that hotel, if that's what you're suggesting."

"I'm not."

"And I'm not in love with her."

"If you say so." Mikhail checked the time. It was 11:41. "I don't want it to be awkward, that's all."

"What's that?"

"Our relationship."

"I didn't realize we were having one."

Mikhail smiled in spite of himself. "We've done a lot of good work together, you and I. And I suspect we're going to be working together again in the future. I wouldn't want Sarah to complicate things."

"Why would she?"

"Do me a favor, Christopher. Treat her better than I did. She deserves it." Mikhail lifted his eyes to the mirror. "Especially now."

A moment passed. Then another. The dashboard clock read 11:44. So did the clock on Keller's phone. He swore beneath his breath as he crushed out his cigarette.

"You really didn't think Rebecca was going to be on time, did you? Thanks to Gabriel, she's going home to a rather uncertain future."

Keller absently rubbed his clavicle. "Couldn't happen to a nicer person."

"Look," said Mikhail suddenly. "There's the car."

It had drawn to a stop outside the pizzeria, a Volvo sedan, dark in color, two men in front, two women in back. One was the daughter of Kim Philby. The other was Sarah Bancroft. In one final act of rebellion, she left her door open after climbing out. Rebecca leaned across the backseat and closed it. Then the car shot forward, passing a few inches from Mikhail's window.

Sarah stood for a moment in the bright sunlight, looking dazed. But when she spotted Keller running toward her, her face broke into a wide smile.

"Sorry about standing you up for dinner last night, but I'm afraid it couldn't be helped."

Keller touched her bruised cheek.

"Our friend from the hotel did that. His name is Nikolai, by the way. Perhaps one day you can return the favor."

Keller helped her into the backseat of the car. She watched a row of pretty little cottages flow past her window as Mikhail followed Gabriel and Eli Lavon from the town.

"I used to like Holland. Now I can't get out of here fast enough."

"We have a plane in Rotterdam."

"Where's it taking us?"

"Home," said Keller.

Sarah leaned her head against his shoulder and closed her eyes. "I am home."

PART FIVE

Vengeance

80

London–Jerusalem

It began in a room at the InterContinental Hotel in Budapest. From there, it hopscotched its way from the back of a taxi, to Seat 14A of a Boeing 737 operated by Ryanair, to the lounge of an Irish ferry called *Ulysses*, to a Toyota Corolla, and to the Bedford House Hotel in the Essex resort town of Frinton-on-Sea. High levels of radiation were also found in the ransacked office of a marina on the river Twizzle, in an abandoned Jaguar F-Type motorcar, and in the salon of a Bavaria 27 Sport that had run aground off the Dutch beach community of Renesse. Later, Dutch authorities would also find contamination in a holiday bungalow in the dunes near Ouddorp.

Ground zero, however, was a pair of neighboring houses in Eaton Square. There the story of what had transpired was written indelibly in a trail of radiation stretching from a bathroom on the uppermost floor of Number 71 to the drawing room and kitchen of Number 70. In the rubbish bin, the Metropolitan Police found the murder weapons—an empty glass vial, a Pasteur pipette dropper, a crystal champagne flute, a maid's apron. All registered readings of thirty thousand counts per second. Too dangerous to store in the Met's evidence rooms, they were sent for safekeeping to the Atomic Weapons Establishment at Aldermaston, the British government's nuclear facility.

The woman who wielded the weapons had been the first to die. Her corpse was so radioactive it had been stored in a nuclear-safe casket—and the driver's seat of her car, a Renault Clio, was so saturated with radiation it was sent to Aldermaston. So, too, was a lounge chair from the London Jet Centre. The source of the chair's contamination, one Konstantin Dragunov, had been allowed to leave Britain aboard his private jet after suffering symptoms of acute radiation sickness. The Russian government, in its first official statement, attributed Dragunov's ill health on the night of the incident to a simple case of food poisoning. As for the contamination inside Dragunov's home, the Kremlin said it had been planted by the British Secret Intelligence Service in a bid to discredit Russia and harm its standing in the Arab world.

The Russian line of defense collapsed the next day when Commissioner Stella McEwan of the Metropolitan Police took the unusual step of releasing a portion of the videotaped statement Dragunov made before boarding his plane. The Kremlin dismissed the recording as a fraud, as did Dragunov himself. He was said to be recovering at his mansion in the Moscow district of Rublyovka. In truth, he was under heavy guard at the Central Clinical Hospital in Kuntsevo, the facility reserved for senior government officials and Russian business elites. The doctors struggling to save his life did so in vain. There was no medication, no emergency treatment, that could forestall the inevitable destruction of Dragunov's cells and organs. For all intents and purposes, he was already dead.

He would linger, however, for three dreadful weeks, as Moscow's standing in the world plunged to depths not seen since the downing of Korea Air Lines Flight 007 in 1983. Anti-Russia demonstrations swept the Arab and Muslim world. A bomb exploded outside the Russian Embassy in Cairo. Protesters stormed the embassy in Pakistan.

In the West the response was peaceful, but devas-

534 • DANIEL SILVA

tating to Russia's diplomatic and financial interests. Meetings were canceled, bank accounts were frozen, ambassadors were recalled, known operatives of the SVR were sent packing. London was selective in its expulsions, for it wished to send a message. Only Dmitri Mentov and Yevgeny Teplov, two SVR officers operating under diplomatic cover, were declared persona non grata and ordered to leave. That same evening a senior MI6 officer named Charles Bennett was quietly taken into custody while attempting to board a Paris-bound Eurostar at St. Pancras. The British public would never be informed of the arrest.

Much else was kept from them, all in the name of national security. They were not told, for example, precisely how or when the intelligence services learned a Russian hit team was on British soil. Nor were they given a satisfactory explanation as to why Konstantin Dragunov had been allowed to leave the country after admitting his role in the operation.

Under the relentless glare of the media, cracks soon appeared in the official account. Eventually, Downing Street acknowledged that the order came directly from the prime minister himself, though it said little regarding the PM's motives. A respected investigative reporter from the *Guardian* suggested that Dragunov had been released in exchange for a hostage after first being subjected to a harsh interrogation. Stella McEwan's cautious statement, that no officer of the Metropolitan Police Service had mistreated the oligarch, left open the possibility that someone else had.

Nearly forgotten amid the swirl of controversy was Crown Prince Abdullah bin Abdulaziz Al Saud. According to Al Arabiya, the Saudi state broadcaster, he died nine days after his return from London, at 4:37 in the morning. Among those at his bedside was his beloved nephew, Prince Khalid bin Mohammed.

But why had the Russians poisoned the crown prince in the first place? Was the Kremlin not actively courting new friends in the Arab world? Was Russia not in the process of replacing the retreating Americans as the region's dominant power? From Riyadh, there was only silence. From Moscow, denials and misdirection. The rented television experts speculated. The investigative reporters burrowed and sifted. None strayed remotely close to the truth.

There were clues everywhere, however—in a consulate in Istanbul, at a private school in Geneva, and in a field in southwest France. But like the trail of radiation, the evidence was invisible to the naked eye. One journalist knew much more than most, but for reasons she did not share with her colleagues, she chose to remain silent.

On the evening the Kremlin belatedly announced the death of Konstantin Dragunov, she emerged from her office in Berlin and, as was her custom, scanned the street in both directions before making her way to a café on Friedrichstrasse near the old Checkpoint Charlie. They were following her, she was certain of it. One day they would come for her. And she would be ready.

There was one final trail of radiation, the existence of which would never be revealed. It stretched from London City Airport, to a beach café in the Netherlands, to an apartment in Jerusalem, and to the top floor of an anonymous office block in Tel Aviv. It was, declared Uzi Navot, yet another milestone in Gabriel's already-distinguished tenure as chief. He was the only director-general to have killed in the field, and the only one to have been injured in a bombing. Now he had earned the dubious distinction of being the first to have been contaminated by radiation, Russian or otherwise. Navot jokingly bemoaned his rival's good fortune. "Perhaps," he told Gabriel upon his return to King Saul Boulevard, "you should quit while you're ahead."

"I've tried. Several times, in fact."

Someone had plastered a yellow sign on the door of his office that read CAUTION RADIATION AREA, and at the first meeting of his senior staff, Yossi Gavish presented him with a ceremonial Geiger counter and a hazmat suit stitched with his name. It was the extent of their celebration. By any objective measure, the operation had been an overwhelming success. Gabriel had brilliantly baited his rival into a colossal blunder. In doing so, he had managed to simultaneously check Russia's rising influence in the Middle East and eliminate the Kremlin's puppet in Riyadh. The Saudi throne was once again within Khalid's grasp. All he had to do was convince his father and the Allegiance Council to grant him a second chance. If Khalid were successful, his debt to Gabriel would be enormous. Together they could change the Middle East. The possibilities for Israel—and for Gabriel and the Office—were endless.

His first priority, however, was Iran. That evening he spent several hours at Kaplan Street briefing the prime minister on the contents of the secret Iranian nuclear archives. And the evening after that he was standing just off camera when the prime minister disclosed those findings in a prime-time news conference broadcast live around the world. Three days later he instructed Uzi Navot to give a sanitized briefing about the Iran operation to the reporters from *Haaretz* and the *New York Times*. The message of the stories was unmistakable. Gabriel had reached into the heart of Tehran and stolen the regime's most precious secrets.

And if the Iranians ever dared to restart their nuclear weapons program, he would be back.

And yet for all his successes, Reema rarely left his thoughts. During the heat of the operation against the Russians, he had been granted a brief respite. But now that he had returned to King Saul Boulevard, Reema gave him no peace. In dreams she appeared in her misshapen toggle coat and her patent leather shoes. Sometimes she bore an uncanny resemblance to Nadia al-Bakari, but in one terrible dream she appeared as Gabriel's son Daniel. The setting was not a remote field in France, but a snowy square in Vienna. The child in the toggle coat and patent leather shoes, the girl with a young boy's face, was trying to start the engine of a Mercedes. "Isn't it beautiful?" the child remarked as the bomb exploded. Then, as the flames consumed her, she looked at Gabriel and said, "One last kiss . . ."

The next evening, over a quiet dinner of fettuccine and mushrooms at the little café-style table in the kitchen, he described for Chiara precisely what had transpired in the field in southwest France. The Russian woman's voice on the phone, the gunshot through the car's rear window, Khalid gathering up Reema's limbs by the harsh white light of the headlamps. The bomb, said Gabriel, had been meant for him. He had punished the men responsible, beaten them in a great game of deception that would change the course of history in the Middle East. And yet Reema was gone forever. What's more, her abduction and brutal murder had not yet been made public. It was almost as if she had never existed.

"Then perhaps," said Chiara, "you should do something about that."

"How?"

She laid her hand on Gabriel's.

"I don't have time," he protested.

"I've seen how fast you can work when you set your mind to it."

Gabriel considered the idea. "I suppose I could ask Ephraim to let me use the restoration lab at the museum."

"No," said Chiara. "You'll work here in the apartment."

"With the children?"

"Of course." She smiled. "It's time for them to see the real Gabriel Allon."

As always, he prepared his own canvas—180 by 120 centimeters, oak stretcher, Italian linen. For his ground he used the formula he first learned in Venice from the master restorer Umberto Conti. His palette was Veronese's, with a touch of Titian.

He had seen Reema only once, under conditions that, try as he might, he could not forget. He had also seen the photograph the Russians had taken of her while she was in captivity in the Basque Country in Spain. It, too, was engraved in Gabriel's memory. She had been tired and thin, her hair had been a mess. But the photo showed her regal bone structure and, more important, her character. For better or worse, Reema bint Khalid was her father's daughter.

He established his makeshift studio in the sitting room, near the terrace. As was his habit, he was protective of his workspace. The children were given strict instructions not to touch his supplies. As a precaution, however, he always left one of his Winsor & Newton Series 7 brushes at a precise angle on his trolley so he could tell if there had been an intruder, which was invariably the case. For the most part, there were no mishaps, though on one occasion he returned from King Saul Boulevard to find several fingerprints in the lower left corner of the canvas. Forensic analysis determined they were Irene's.

He worked when he could, an hour or so in the morning, a few minutes in the evening after dinner. The children rarely left his side. He made no preparatory sketches or underdrawing. Nevertheless, his draftsmanship was flawless. He posed Reema as he had posed Nadia, on a couch of white against a background of Caravaggesque black. The arrangement of her limbs was childlike, but Gabriel aged her slightly—sixteen or seventeen instead of twelve—so Khalid might have her a little longer.

Gradually, as she came to life on the canvas, she took leave of Gabriel's dreams. During her last appearance she handed him a letter for her father. Gabriel added it to the painting. Afterward, he stood for a long time before the canvas, right hand to his chin, left hand supporting his right elbow, head tilted slightly down, so lost in thought he was unaware that Chiara was standing at his side.

"Is it finished, Signor Delvecchio?"

"No," he said, wiping the paint from his brush. "Not quite."

81

Langley—New York

CIA director Morris Payne called Gabriel on the dedicated secure line that afternoon and asked him to come to Washington. It wasn't quite a summons, but it wasn't an open-ended invitation, either. After pretending to consult his calendar, Gabriel said he could come the following Tuesday at the earliest.

"I have a better idea. How about tomorrow?"

In truth, Gabriel was anxious to make the trip. He owed Payne a full accounting of the operation to remove Abdullah from the line of succession. Furthermore, he needed Payne and his boss at the White House to sign off on Khalid's ascension to the throne. The Allegiance Council had yet to name a new crown prince. Once again, Saudi Arabia was being ruled by an ailing octogenarian with no ordained successor.

Gabriel caught an overnight flight to Washington and met with Payne the following day in his seventh-floor office at Langley. As it turned out, it wasn't necessary for Gabriel to confess his role in Abdullah's demise. The American knew everything.

"How?"

"A source inside the SVR. It seems you've turned the place inside out."

"Any word about Rebecca Manning?"

"You mean Philby?" Payne shook his head bitterly. "When were you going to tell me?"

"It wasn't my place, Morris."

"Apparently, she's hanging on by a thread."

"I told her not to go back."

"You've *seen* her?"

"In the Netherlands," said Gabriel. "We had to arrange an exchange of prisoners."

"Dragunov for the girl?" Payne rubbed his lantern jaw thoughtfully. "Do you remember our recent dinner?"

"With considerable fondness."

"When I suggested you might want to think about moving aside Abdullah for the good of the region, you looked at me as though I'd just told you to bump off Mother Teresa."

Gabriel said nothing.

"Why didn't you include us?"

"Too many cooks."

"Saudi Arabia is *our* ally."

"And thanks to me, that's still the case. All you have to do now is send a signal to Riyadh that Washington would look favorably on Khalid's reappointment as crown prince."

"From what we hear, he won't be crown prince for long."

"Probably not."

"Is he ready?"

"He'll be different, Morris."

Payne didn't seem so sure. He abruptly tacked, a conversational habit of his. "I hear the Russians gave her a pretty good going-over."

"Sarah?"

Payne nodded.

"Under the circumstances," said Gabriel, "it could have been worse."

"How did she hold up in the field?"

"She's a natural, Morris."

"So why is she working in a museum in New York?"

"Read her file."

"I just did." There was a copy on Payne's desk. "Any chance you could convince her to come back to the Agency?"

"I doubt it."

"Why not?"

"I could be wrong," said Gabriel, "but I believe she's already spoken for."

Gabriel left Langley in time to make the three o'clock train to New York. A car from the Israeli consulate met him at Penn Station and took him through the warm spring evening to the corner of Second Avenue and East Sixty-Fourth Street. The restaurant he entered was Italian, old-fashioned, and very noisy. He squeezed past the crowd at the bar and made his way to the table where Sarah, in a dark business suit, was sipping a three-olive martini. As Gabriel approached, she smiled and lifted her face to be kissed. It bore no trace of her night journey across the North Sea with the Russian assassin named Nikolai. In fact, thought Gabriel as he took his seat, Sarah looked more radiant than ever.

"Have one of these," she said, clicking a polished nail on the edge of the glass. "I promise it will take care of that pain in your back."

Gabriel ordered Italian sauvignon blanc and promptly took delivery of the largest glass of wine he had ever seen.

Sarah raised her martini a fraction of an inch. "To

the secret world." She looked around the crowded room. "No little friends?"

"I couldn't get them a reservation."

"You mean I have you all to myself? Let's do something positively scandalous." Sarah smiled wickedly and sipped her drink. She had a voice and manner from a different age. As always, Gabriel felt as though he were conversing with a character from a Fitzgerald novel. "How was Langley?" she asked.

"Morris couldn't stop talking about you."

"Do they miss me?"

Gabriel smiled. "The whole town is desolate. Morris would do anything to have you back."

"What's done cannot be undone." She lowered her voice to a confiding murmur. "Except where Khalid is concerned. You prevented our tragic hero from destroying himself." She smiled. "He's restored."

"Literally," said Gabriel.

"Morris green-lit Khalid's return?"

Gabriel nodded. "So did the White House. Season two of the Khalid show is about to begin production."

"Let's hope it's a little less exciting than season one."

A waiter appeared. Sarah ordered *insalata Caprese* and sautéed veal. Gabriel had the same.

"How's work?" he asked.

"It seems the Nadia al-Bakari Collection did not fall

from the walls of the Museum of Modern Art while I was away. In fact, my staff barely noticed my absence."

"What are your plans?"

"A change of scenery, I think."

This time it was Gabriel who surveyed the room. "It's rather nice here, Sarah."

"The Upper East Side? It has its charms, but I've always preferred London. Kensington, especially."

"Sarah . . ."

"I know, I know."

"Have you been back to London to see him?"

"Last weekend. It was almost as good as this martini. I must say, his maisonette is divine, even without furniture."

"Did he tell you where he got the money to buy it?"

"He mentioned something about a certain Don Orsati from the island of Corsica. He has a home there, too, you know."

"And a Monet." Gabriel fixed Sarah with a reproachful stare. "He's too old for you."

"He's the youngest man I've been on a date with in a long time. Besides, have you ever seen him without his clothes on?"

"Have *you*?"

Sarah looked away.

"Is there nothing I can do to talk you out of this?"

"Why would you try?"

"Because it's probably unwise for you to get involved with a man who used to kill people for a living."

"If you can overlook Christopher's past, why can't I?"

"Because I've never considered moving to London to live with him." Gabriel exhaled slowly. "What do you intend to do for work?"

"This might come as a shock to you, darling, but money isn't exactly an issue. My father left me quite well off. That said, I would like something to do."

"What did you have in mind?"

"A gallery, perhaps."

Gabriel smiled. "There's a nice one in Mason's Yard in St. James's. It specializes in Italian Old Masters. The owner's been talking about retiring for a couple of years. He's looking for someone to take over the business."

"How are his finances?" asked Sarah with justified concern.

"Thanks to his association with a certain Russian businessman, they're quite good."

"Christopher told me all about the operation."

"Did he?" asked Gabriel, annoyed. "And did he tell you about Olivia Watson, too?"

Sarah nodded. "And about Morocco. I'm only sorry I wasn't invited."

"Olivia's gallery is in Bury Street," warned Gabriel. "It's possible you might bump into her."

"And Christopher will bump into Mikhail the next time we . . ." Sarah left the thought unfinished.

"It could get a bit incestuous."

"It could, but we'll manage somehow." Sarah smiled with a sudden sadness. "We always do, don't we, Gabriel?"

Just then, his BlackBerry vibrated. The distinctive pulse told him it was an urgent message from King Saul Boulevard.

"Anything serious?" asked Sarah.

"The Allegiance Council just appointed Khalid the new crown prince."

"That was fast." Suddenly, Sarah's iPhone was vibrating, too. She smiled as she read the message.

"If that's Keller, tell him I want a word."

"It isn't Keller, it's Khalid."

"What does he want?"

She handed Gabriel the phone. "You."

82

Tiberias

In his first official act after regaining the post of crown prince, Khalid bin Mohammed severed ties with the Russian Federation and expelled all Russian citizens from the Kingdom of Saudi Arabia. The regional analysts applauded his restraint. The old Khalid, they said, might have acted rashly. But the new Khalid had displayed the acumen and prudence of an experienced statesman. Clearly, they speculated, a wiser voice was whispering in his ear.

At home, he moved quickly to undo the damage of his uncle's brief reign—and some of his own damage as well. He released the jailed women's rights activists and supporters of democratic reform. He even freed a popular blogger who, like Omar Nawwaf, had criticized him personally. As the dreaded Mutaween withdrew from Riyadh's streets, life returned. A new cinema opened its doors. Young Saudis filled cafés late into the night.

But for the most part, Khalid's actions were characterized by a newfound caution. His royal court, while filled with loyalists prepared to do his bidding, contained several old-guard traditionalists, suggesting to Middle East observers he intended to return to the Al Saud practice of ruling by consensus. Where the old Khalid had been a man in a hurry, the new Khalid seemed to favor incrementalism over haste. "Shwaya, shwaya" became something of an official mantra. Still, he was not a ruler to be trifled with, as a prominent reformer discovered after heckling Khalid during a public appearance. The one-year prison sentence made it clear there were limits to KBM's tolerance for dissent. Khalid was an enlightened despot, said the observers, but he was a despot nonetheless.

His personal conduct changed as well. He sold his superyacht and his palace in France, and returned several billion dollars to the men he had imprisoned at the Ritz-Carlton Hotel. He also parted company with much of his art collection. He entrusted the sale of *Salvator Mundi* to Isherwood Fine Arts of Mason's Yard in London. Sarah Bancroft, formerly of the Museum of Modern Art in New York, was listed as the dealer of record.

His wife, Asma, appeared at his side in public, but Princess Reema, his daughter, was nowhere to be seen. A rumor circulated that she was enrolled at an exclusive school in Switzerland. It was soon put to rest, however, by an explosive exposé in the German newsmagazine *Der Spiegel*. Based in part on the reporting of Omar Nawwaf, it detailed the series of events that had led to KBM's dramatic fall from grace and his eventual restoration. Khalid, after several days of silence, offered a tearful confirmation of the report's authenticity.

Which prompted, mainly in the West, yet another great reassessment. Perhaps the Russians, for all their recklessness, had actually done them a favor. Perhaps it was time to forgive the youthful prince and welcome him back into the fold. From Washington to Wall Street, and from Hollywood to Silicon Valley, there arose a great clamor as all those who had shunned him suddenly pleaded with him to return. One man, however, had stood by him when no one else would. And it was this man's invitation, on a sultry summer's evening in June, that Khalid accepted.

The new KBM, like the old, was forever running late. Gabriel expected him at five p.m. but it was approaching half past six when his Gulfstream finally landed at the IAF base in Ramat David. He emerged from the cabin alone, in a trim-fitting blazer and stylish avia-tor sunglasses that glinted with the earlyevening sun. Gabriel offered Khalid his hand, but once again he received a warm embrace instead.

Leaving the airbase, they passed through the town of Gabriel's birth. His parents, he explained to Khalid, were Holocaust survivors from Germany. Like every-one else in Ramat David, the Allon family had lived in a little breeze-block bungalow. Theirs was filled with photographs of loved ones lost to the fires of the Shoah. To escape the grief of his family home, Gabriel had wandered the Valley of Jezreel, the land given by Joshua to the tribe of Zebulun, one of the twelve tribes of ancient Israel. He had spent most of his adult life living abroad or in Jerusalem. But the valley, he told Khalid, would always be his home.

As they headed east on Highway 77, Khalid's phone pinged and vibrated without cease. The messages were from the White House. Khalid explained that he and the president were planning to meet briefly in New York during the annual meeting of the UN General As-sembly in September. If all went well, he would return to America later in the autumn for a formal summit in Washington.

"It seems all is forgiven." He looked at Gabriel. "I don't suppose you had anything to do with this?"

"The Americans didn't need any encouragement from me. They're eager to normalize relations."

"But you're the one who made me palatable again." He paused. "You and Omar Nawwaf. That article in *Der Spiegel* lifted the cloud over me once and for all."

Khalid finally switched off the phone. For the next thirty minutes, as they crossed the Upper Galilee, he gave Gabriel a most remarkable briefing—a secret guided tour of the Middle East led by none other than the de facto ruler of Saudi Arabia. The Saudi GID was hearing naughty things about the head of Iran's Revolutionary Guard Corps, something about a financial indiscretion. Raw intelligence would soon be heading King Saul Boulevard's way. Khalid and the GID were anxious to play a role in Syria now that the Americans were heading for the exits. Perhaps the GID and the Office could undertake a covert program to make life a little less comfortable in Syria for the Iranians and their allies, Hezbollah. Gabriel asked Khalid to intervene with Hamas to stop the rockets and missiles from Gaza. Khalid said he would do what he could.

"But don't expect much. Those crazies from Hamas hate me almost as much as they hate you."

"What do you hear about the administration's Middle East peace plan?"

"Not much."

"Maybe we should come up with our own peace plan, you and I."

"Shwaya, shwaya, my friend."

In time, they came upon the parched plain where, on a scalding afternoon in July 1187, Saladin defeated the thirst-crazed armies of the Crusaders in a climactic battle that would eventually leave Jerusalem once again in Muslim hands. A moment later they glimpsed the Sea of Galilee. They headed north along the shoreline until they came to a fortress-like villa perched atop a rocky escarpment. Several cars and SUVs lined the steeply sloped drive.

"Where are we?" asked Khalid.

Gabriel opened his door and climbed out. "Come with me," he said. "I'll show you."

Ari Shamron waited in the entrance hall. He appraised Khalid warily for a moment before finally extending a liver-spotted hand.

"I never thought this day would come."

"It hasn't," replied Khalid conspiratorially. "Not officially, at least."

Shamron gestured toward the sitting room, where most of the senior staff of the Office were gathered—Eli Lavon, Yaakov Rossman, Dina Sarid, Rimona Stern, Mikhail Abramov and Natalie Mizrahi, Uzi and Bella

Navot. Chiara and the children stood next to an oaken easel. Upon it was a painting covered in black baize cloth.

Khalid looked at Gabriel, perplexed. "What is it?"

"Something to replace that Leonardo of yours."

Gabriel nodded toward Raphael and Irene. With Chiara's help, they removed the black shroud. Khalid swayed slightly and placed a hand over his heart.

"My God," he whispered.

"Forgive me, I should have warned you."

"She looks . . ." Khalid's voice trailed off. He stretched a hand toward Reema's face, then toward the letter. "What is it?"

"A message for her father."

"What does it say?"

"That's between the two of you."

Khalid studied the bottom right corner of the canvas. "There's no signature."

"The artist wished to remain anonymous so as not to overshadow his subject."

Khalid looked up. "He's famous, the artist?"

Gabriel smiled sadly. "In certain circles."

They ate outside on the terrace, watched over by Reema's portrait. The meal was a sumptuous affair of

Israeli and Arab cuisine, including Gilah Shamron's famous chicken with Moroccan spices, which Khalid decreed the finest dish he had ever tasted. Discreetly, he declined Gabriel's offer of wine. He would soon be the custodian of the two holy mosques of Mecca and Medina, he explained. His days of even moderate alcohol consumption were over.

Surrounded by Gabriel and his division chiefs, Khalid spoke not of the past but the future. The road ahead, he cautioned, would be difficult. For all its riches, his country was traditional, backward, and in many ways barbaric. What's more, another Arab Spring was stirring. He made it clear he would never tolerate an open rebellion against his rule. He asked them to be patient, to maintain realistic expectations, and to make life bearable for the Palestinians. Somehow, someday, the occupation of Arab land had to end.

Shortly before eleven o'clock, sirens sounded along the lakeshore. A moment later a Hezbollah rocket arced over the Golan, and from an Iron Dome battery in the Galilee a missile rose to meet it. Afterward, Gabriel and Khalid stood alone along the balustrade of the terrace, watching a single craft beating up the lake, its stern aglow with a green running light.

"It's rather small," said Khalid.

"The lake?"

"No, the boat."

"It probably doesn't have a discotheque."

"Or a snow room."

Gabriel laughed quietly. "Do you miss it?"

Khalid shook his head. "I only miss my daughter."

"I hope the portrait helps."

"It's the most beautiful painting I've ever seen. But you have to let me pay for it."

Gabriel waved his hand dismissively.

"Then allow me to give you this." Khalid held up a flash drive.

"What is it?"

"A bank account in Switzerland with one hundred million dollars in it."

"I have a better idea. Use the money to establish the Omar Nawwaf School of Journalism in Riyadh. Train the next generation of Arab reporters, editors, and photographers. Then give them the freedom to write and publish whatever they want, regardless of whether it hurts your feelings."

"Is that really all you want?"

"No," said Gabriel. "But it's a good place to start."

"Actually, I was planning to start somewhere else." Khalid returned the flash drive to the pocket of his blazer. "There's something I must do before I become king. I was hoping you might be willing to play the role of intermediary."

"What did you have in mind?"

Khalid explained.

"She's not terribly hard to find," said Gabriel. "Just send her an e-mail."

"I have. Several, in fact. She doesn't respond. She doesn't answer my calls, either."

"I can't imagine why."

"Perhaps you can approach her on my behalf."

"Why me?"

"You seem to have something of a rapport with her."

"I wouldn't go that far."

"Can you arrange it?"

"A meeting?" Gabriel shook his head. "Bad idea, Khalid."

"My specialty."

"She's too angry. Let a little more time pass. Or better yet, let me handle it for you."

"You don't know much about Arabs, do you?"

"I'm learning more every day."

"It is an essential part of our culture," said Khalid. "I must personally make restitution."

"Blood money?"

"An unfortunate turn of phrase. But, yes, blood money."

"What you need to do," said Gabriel, "is accept full responsibility for what happened in Istanbul and see that it never happens again."

"It won't."

"Tell that to her, not me."

"I intend to."

"In that case," said Gabriel, "I'll do it. But let it be on your head if anything goes wrong."

"Is that a Jewish proverb?" Khalid glanced at his watch. "It's late, my friend. Perhaps it's time for me to be leaving."

83

Berlin

Gabriel rang her the next morning and left a message on her voice mail. A week passed before she bothered to call him back, hardly a promising beginning. Yes, she said after hearing his proposal, she would be willing to hear Khalid out. But the last thing he should expect from her was a grant of absolution. She wasn't interested in his blood money, either. When Gabriel told her about his idea, she was skeptical. "The Palestinians will have an independent state," she said, "before Khalid opens a journalism school in Riyadh with Omar's name on it."

She insisted the meeting take place in Berlin. The embassy, of course, was out of the question, and she wasn't comfortable with the idea of going to the ambassador's residence or even a hotel. It was Khalid who suggested the apartment she had once shared with Omar in the old East Berlin neighborhood of Mitte. His agents had been regular visitors and knew it well. Even so, a thorough search—a ransacking, actually—would be required before his arrival. There would be no recording of the encounter, and no public statements afterward. And, no, he would not be taking refreshment of any kind. He was worried the Russians were plotting to kill him the same way they had killed his uncle. His fears, thought Gabriel, were entirely justified.

And so it was that on a warm and windless Berlin afternoon in early July, with the leaves hanging limply on the linden trees and the clouds low and dark, a line of black Mercedes motorcars arrived like a funeral procession in the street beneath Hanifa Khoury's window. Frowning, she checked the time. It was half past three. He was an hour and a half late.

KBM time . . .

Several car doors opened. From one emerged Khalid. As he crossed the pavement to the entrance of the building, he was trailed by a single bodyguard. He wasn't afraid, thought Hanifa. He trusted her, the way she had trusted him that afternoon in Istanbul. The afternoon she had seen Omar for the last time.

She stepped away from the window and surveyed the sitting room of the apartment. There were photographs of Omar everywhere. Omar in Baghdad. Omar in Cairo. Omar with Khalid.

Omar in Istanbul . . .

That morning, a team from the Saudi Embassy had torn the apartment to pieces, looking for what, they did not say. They had neglected to check the large clay flowerpot on the terrace overlooking the internal courtyard. Oh, they had brutalized Hanifa's geraniums, but they had failed to probe the damp soil beneath.

The object she had hidden there, wrapped in an oily cloth, zipped into a waterproof plastic bag, was now in the palm of her hand. She had acquired it from Tariq, a troubled kid from the Palestinian community, a petty criminal, a failed rapper, a thug. She had told Tariq it was for a story she was working on for ZDF. He hadn't believed her.

Her building was old and the lift was fickle. Two or three minutes passed before she finally heard heavy male footfalls in the corridor. A male voice, too. The voice of the devil. It sounded as though he was on his phone. She only hoped he was talking to the Israeli. Such perfect poetry, she thought. Darwish himself could not have written it any better.

As she moved into the entrance hall, she saw Omar walking into the consulate at 1:14 p.m. She could only imagine what had happened next. Had they feigned a brief moment of cordiality, or had they set upon him instantly like wild beasts? Did they wait until he was dead before taking him apart, or was he still alive and conscious when the blade carved into his flesh? Such an act could not be forgiven, only avenged. Khalid knew this better than anyone. He was an Arab, after all. A son of the desert. And yet he was walking toward her with only a single bodyguard to protect him. Perhaps he was still the same reckless KBM after all.

At last, the knock. Hanifa reached for the latch. The bodyguard lunged, the devil shielded his face. *Omar,* thought Hanifa as she raised the gun and fired. *The password is Omar . . .*

Author's Note

The New Girl is a work of entertainment and should be read as nothing more. The names, characters, places, and incidents portrayed in the story are the product of the author's imagination or have been used fictitiously.

The International School of Geneva portrayed in *The New Girl* does not exist and should in no way be confused with Ecole Internationale Genève, the institution founded in 1924 with the help of the League of Nations. Visitors to the Museum of Modern Art in New York will see countless extraordinary works of art, including Van Gogh's *Starry Night*, but nothing called the Nadia al-Bakari Collection. The stories of Zizi and Nadia al-Bakari are told in *The Messenger*, published in 2006, and its 2011 sequel, *Portrait of a Spy*, both of which feature Sarah Bancroft. Sarah also appears in *The Secret Servant, Moscow Rules*, and *The Defector*. I enjoyed her return to the secret world as much as she did.

I have manipulated airline and rail schedules to suit the needs of my story, along with the timing of certain real-world events. *The New Girl*'s depiction of the Mossad's astonishing theft of the Iranian nuclear archives is entirely speculative and not based on any information I received from Israeli or American sources. I am certain the Mossad did not plan or oversee the real operation from an anonymous building located on King Saul Boulevard in Tel Aviv, as it is the headquarters only of my fictitious "Office." Chapter 7 of *The New Girl* contains a not-so-veiled reference to the true location of Mossad headquarters, which, like Gabriel Allon's address on Narkiss Street, is one of the worst-kept secrets in Israel.

There is no French counterterrorism unit known as the Alpha Group, at least not one that I know of. A fine establishment called Brasserie Saint-Maurice occupies the ground floor of an old house in medieval Annecy, and the popular Café Remor overlooks the Place du Cirque in Geneva. Both are typically free of intelligence operatives and assassins, as is the charming Plein Sud on the avenue du Général Leclerc in Carcassonne.

Natural High is the name of the beach pavilion in the lovely Dutch resort town of Renesse. To the best of my knowledge, neither Gabriel Allon nor Rebecca Philby have ever set foot there.

One should not attempt to book a room at the Bedford House Hotel or the East Anglia Inn in Frinton-on-Sea, for they do not exist. There is indeed a marina on the banks of the river Twizzle in Essex, but Nikolai Azarov's brutal murder of the security guard might well have been witnessed by customers of the Harbour Lights restaurant. Shortly before entering the Dorchester Hotel in London, Christopher Keller borrowed a line from the film version of *Dr. No* to describe the stopping power of a Walther PPK pistol. Devotees of F. Scott Fitzgerald surely noticed that Gabriel and Sarah Bancroft exchanged two lines from *The Great Gatsby* while dining in an Italian restaurant near the corner of Second Avenue and East Sixty-Fourth Street in Manhattan. Rumor has it the restaurant was Primola, my favorite on the Upper East Side.

It is true that visitors to 10 Downing Street often spot a brown-and-white tabby cat lurking near the famous black door. His name is Larry, and he has been granted the title Chief Mouser to the Cabinet Office. Apologies to the owner of 7 St. Luke's Mews in Notting Hill for turning the dwelling into an MI6 safe house, and to the occupants of 70 and 71 Eaton Square for using the exclusive properties as the setting for a Russian assassination. I am confident no British prime minister or MI6 chief, had they known of such a plot, would have allowed it to go forward, even if the end result was a strategic and public-relations disaster for the Russian president and his intelligence services.

I chose not to identify the radioactive poison wielded by my fictitious Russian assassins. Its deadly properties, however, were clearly similar to polonium-210, the highly radioactive chemical element used in the November 2006 murder of Alexander Litvinenko, a dissident former Russian intelligence officer living in London. Britain's feeble response to the use of a weapon of mass destruction on its soil undoubtedly emboldened the Kremlin to target a second Russian living in Britain, Sergei Skripal, in March 2018. A former GRU officer and double agent, Skripal survived after being exposed to the Soviet-era nerve agent Novichok. But Dawn Sturgess, a forty-four-year-old mother of three who lived near Skripal in the cathedral city of Salisbury, died four months after the initial attack, a collateral casualty in Russian president Vladimir Putin's war on dissent. Not surprisingly, Putin ignored a request by the woman's son to allow British authorities to question the two suspected Russian assassins.

There is no such thing as the Royal Data Center in Riyadh, but there is something very much like it: the ridiculously named Center for Studies and Media Affairs. Run by Saud al-Qahtani, a courtier and close confidant of Crown Prince Mohammed bin Salman, the center obtained its initial arsenal of sophisticated cyberweapons from an Italian firm called Hacking Team. It then acquired software and expertise from the Emirates-based DarkMatter and from NSO Group, an Israeli company that reportedly employs veterans of Intelligence Unit 8200, Israel's signals intelligence service. According to the *New York Times*, DarkMatter has also hired graduates of Unit 8200, along with several Americans once employed by the Central Intelligence Agency and the National Security Agency. Indeed, one of DarkMatter's top executives reportedly worked on some of the NSA's most advanced cyberoperations.

Saud al-Qahtani oversaw more than the Center for Studies and Media Affairs. He also led the Saudi Rapid Intervention Group, the clandestine unit responsible for the brutal murder and dismemberment of Jamal Khashoggi, a dissident Saudi journalist and columnist for the *Washington Post*. Eleven Saudis face criminal charges in the killing, which was carried out inside the Saudi consulate in Istanbul in October 2018. Saudi officials have claimed, among other things, that the operatives acted unilaterally. The CIA, however, concluded that the murder was ordered by none other than Crown Prince Mohammed bin Salman.

Not for the first time, President Donald Trump disagreed with the findings of his intelligence community. In a written statement, he repeated Saudi claims that Khashoggi was an "enemy of the state" and a member of the Muslim Brotherhood before seeming to absolve MBS of complicity in the journalist's death. "It could very well be that the crown prince had knowledge of this tragic event—maybe he did and maybe he didn't." The president went on to say: "In any case, our relationship is with the Kingdom of Saudi Arabia."

But Saudi Arabia is not a democracy with entrenched institutions. It is one of the world's last absolute monarchies. And unless there is another change to the line of succession, it will be ruled, perhaps for decades, by the provenly reckless Mohammed bin Salman. My fictitious Saudi crown prince—the Western-educated, English-speaking KBM—ultimately was a redeemable figure. But I'm afraid Mohammed bin Salman is probably beyond restoration. Yes, he has delivered modest reforms, including granting women the right to drive, long forbidden in the backward-looking Kingdom. But he has also imposed an iron-fisted crackdown on dissent unparalleled in recent Saudi history. MBS promised change. Instead, he has delivered instability to the region and repression at home.

For now, the U.S.-Saudi relationship appears frozen, and MBS is trotting the globe in search of friends. China's Xi Jinping entertained him in Beijing in early 2019. And at a G20 summit in Buenos Aires, MBS exchanged an unseemly high five with Vladimir Putin. A source close to the crown prince told me the exuberant greeting was a message to MBS's critics in the U.S. Congress. Saudi Arabia, he was saying, no longer had to depend only on the Americans for protection. Putin's Russia was waiting in the wings, no questions asked.

A decade ago, such an implicit warning would have been toothless. But no more. Putin's intervention in Syria has once again made Russia a power to be reckoned with in the Middle East, and America's traditional friends have taken notice. MBS's father, King Salman, has made a single overseas trip. It was to Moscow. The emir of Qatar embarrassed the Trump administration by stopping in Moscow on the eve of a visit to Washington. Egypt's al-Sisi has visited Moscow four times. So, too, has Benjamin Netanyahu. Even Israel, America's closest ally in the Middle East, is hedging its regional bets. Putin's Russia is too powerful to be ignored.

But would a Saudi leader ever break the historic bond with America and tilt toward Russia? A version of the tilt has already begun, and it is Mohammed bin Salman who is leaning Moscow's way. The U.S. relationship with Saudi Arabia was never based on shared values, only on oil. MBS knows full well that the United States, now a major energy producer, no longer needs Saudi Arabian petroleum the way it once did. In Putin's Russia, however, he has found a partner to help manage the global supply of oil and its all-important price. He has also found, if need be, a source of weapons and a valuable conduit to the Shiite Iranians. And perhaps most important, MBS can rest assured his new friend will never criticize him for killing a meddlesome journalist. After all, the Russians are rather good at that, too.

Acknowledgments

I am eternally grateful to my wife, Jamie Gangel, who listened patiently while I worked out the plot and larger themes of *The New Girl* and then expertly edited my first draft—all while covering the extraordinary events in Washington as special correspondent for CNN. I would not have completed the manuscript before my deadline were it not for her support and attention to detail. My debt to her is immeasurable, as is my love.

I spoke to several American and Israeli intelligence officers, policy makers, and politicians about the rapidly unfolding events in Saudi Arabia. I also received invaluable guidance from several sources close to Crown Prince Mohammed bin Salman. I thank them now in anonymity, which is how they would prefer it.

I am forever indebted to David Bull for his advice on all matters related to art and restoration. Bob Woodward helped me to better understand the tangled relationship between the Trump White House and Saudi Arabia's capricious crown prince. Andrew Neil was an indispensable source on Britain's broken politics and emerging trends in the Middle East. Tim Collins explained the economic challenges facing Saudi Arabia in language even I could comprehend.

I consulted hundreds of newspaper and magazine articles while writing *The New Girl*, far too many to cite here. I owe a special debt to the brave reporters and editors of the *Washington Post*, who had the unenviable task of covering the brutal murder of a beloved colleague. They did so with extraordinary professionalism, proving once again why quality journalism is essential to a properly functioning democracy.

Louis Toscano, my dear friend and longtime editor, made countless improvements to the novel. Kathy Crosby, my eagle-eyed personal copy editor, made certain the text was free of typographical and grammatical errors. Any mistakes that slipped through their formidable gauntlet are mine, not theirs.

We are blessed with family and friends who fill our lives with love and laughter at critical times during the writing year, especially Jeff Zucker, Phil Griffin, Andrew Lack, Elsa Walsh, Michael Gendler, Ron Meyer, Jane and Burt Bacharach, Stacey and Henry Winkler, Maurice Tempelsman and Kitty Pilgrim, Nancy Dubuc and Michael Kizilbash, Susanna Aaron and Gary Ginsburg, and Cindi and Mitchell Berger. My children, Lily and Nicholas, were a constant source of inspiration and support. To better understand what it is like to live with a novelist on deadline, I recommend the breakfast table scene in the film *Phantom Thread*.

Finally, heartfelt thanks to the remarkable team at HarperCollins, especially Brian Murray, Jonathan Burnham, Jennifer Barth, Doug Jones, Leah Wasielewski, Mark Ferguson, Leslie Cohen, Robin Bilardello, Milan Bozic, David Koral, Leah Carlson-Stanisic, William Ruoto, Carolyn Robson, Chantal Restivo-Alessi, Frank Albanese, Josh Marwell, Sarah Ried, and Amy Baker.

About the Author

Daniel Silva is the award-winning, #1 *New York Times* bestselling author of *The Unlikely Spy*, *The Mark of the Assassin*, *The Marching Season*, *The Kill Artist*, *The English Assassin*, *The Confessor*, *A Death in Vienna*, *Prince of Fire*, *The Messenger*, *The Secret Servant*, *Moscow Rules*, *The Defector*, *The Rembrandt Affair*, *Portrait of a Spy*, *The Fallen Angel*, *The English Girl*, *The Heist*, *The English Spy*, *The Black Widow*, *House of Spies*, *The Other Woman*, and *The New Girl* (2019). He is best known for his long-running thriller series starring spy and art restorer Gabriel Allon. Silva's books are critically acclaimed bestsellers around the world and have been translated into more than thirty languages. He resides in Florida with his wife, television journalist Jamie Gangel, and their twins, Lily and Nicholas. For more information, visit www.danielsilvabooks.com.

HARPER LUXE

THE NEW LUXURY IN READING

We hope you enjoyed reading
our new, comfortable print size and found it
an experience you would like to repeat.

Well – you're in luck!

HarperLuxe offers the finest in fiction and
nonfiction books in this same larger print size and
paperback format. Light and easy to read, HarperLuxe
paperbacks are for book lovers who want to see
what they are reading without the strain.

For a full listing of titles and
new releases to come, please visit our website:

www.HarperLuxe.com

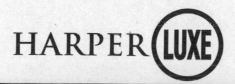